ROGUE SWARM

RELICS OF THE ANCIENTS BOOK 3

M.G. HERRON

Cover illustration designed by Elias Stern.

NEXT IN THE SERIES

Starfighter Down
Hidden Relics
Rogue Swarm

ONE

Captain Elya Nevers reached the patrol zone first.

Marked on his cockpit HUD by a large transparent cube, the region of space that Flight 18 had been assigned today lay at the outermost edge of the asteroid field. The broken planet that was the source of those asteroids loomed behind him off his left shoulder, positioned so it blocked the orange-red star known as Elturis, casting the visible surface of the planet in shadow.

He didn't know what had busted that world or how long ago it happened, but he could tell from the result that the weapon had been powerful beyond measure. A jagged chasm, large enough to fly an armada through, reached deep into the shattered planet's core. The world's atmosphere had long since vented into space, leaving behind a barren body of rock and magma. Every once in a while, whatever epochal geological process continued to work within that darkness dislodged a new chunk of rock and sent it to join the graveyard of its cousins.

It was more asteroid field than planet. A miracle that what remained still held together at all.

Elya killed his engines, and the Sabre drifted on the momentum he'd gained during acceleration. He flicked off the safety on his wingtip triggers and surveyed the star-pricked expanse for any sign of enemy units.

Over the past several weeks, packs of Kryl drones had taken to sporadically jumping into orbit around Elturis-2. Overmind X seemed to be testing their defenses but, so far, patrolling squadrons of starfighters like his had held the line. During these raids, Elya himself had shot down nine bogies. Of all the pilots assigned to patrol, he was in the lead for kills. One of the twins in Flight 4 snapped at his heels with seven. Yorra and Park had each taken five, and Raptor had three to her credit.

Elya knew Raptor—Captain Casey Osprey—could have been doing better if she didn't keep putting herself in support positions. She let the other three pilots do most of the shooting.

As flight lead, that was her prerogative. She called the maneuvers and handled communication with flight control. Elya, however, hated the idea of hanging back. Most patrolling missions involved too much waiting, too much watching, and too little fighting. It made him restless and twitchy. He was spoiling for a fight.

Especially for one fight in particular.

"Man, but Volk shipped us out to the boonies today, huh?" Lieutenant Innovesh Park asked over their flight's private broadbeam channel. He punctuated the question with a descending whistle to show just how far they'd been cast from home base.

"They've doubled the frequency of patrols," said Lieutenant Olara Yorra. "Wish they'd tell us why."

"Not our job to ask why, Furies," Captain Casey Osprey cut in. "Just fly the zone and keep the Kryl from getting through."

Osprey had been saying stuff like that a lot lately. Toeing the Fleet line harder than was necessary. *Like a good little soldier,* Elya thought wryly. Osprey had high standards for herself and the pilots she flew with. Earth knew that Elya had often been on the receiving end of her demands. He pushed himself as hard as she did, but even for someone with a perfectionist attitude and an obsessive tendency to over-train like him, she was getting tiresome.

"Don't you wonder, though?" He was careful to keep any judgment out of his voice. "Admiral Miyaru doesn't do anything just because. She's got to have a good reason for it."

The admiral hadn't spoken to him since the day they found the Telos city hidden within the asteroid. They'd won the Chronicle relic and saved a dozen children before Over-mind X converted them to mutant hybrids. But Subject Zero —the first mutant and her field marshal on the ground—had gotten away. It didn't sit right with Elya, which made him anxious. He scanned his lidar map, seeking any sign of Kryl drones and the biomechanical shipforms they grew in. Most drones were autonomous, with no pilot inside since the ship itself was a Kryl creature grown for that purpose. He'd only ever seen one drone that was actually manned.

Show yourself, he thought to the stars. *Fight me. I'm ready for you this time.*

"She probably just wants to protect the armada," said Yorra. That was Gears, always thinking. She didn't speak loud or often, but when she did, wise people paid attention. Although her intelligence remained sharp, she seemed to be slower to come to decisions since the day they found Chron-icle. Gears had suffered acid burns from a mucous-like Kryl projectile during the fighting, and something about the expe-rience seemed to have weakened her confidence.

"True, true," Park said. "A dozen more cruisers jumped in yesterday. You see the railguns on those heavies? Earth's blood! New models fresh out of the weapons labs on Ariadne. Straight killers. I bet each cannon cost as much as a squad of Sabres."

Lieutenant Innovesh Park—call sign, Naab—was the exact opposite of Yorra. A boisterous, fun-loving joker… and he never shut up. It made the maturing romantic relationship between him and Yorra a bit of a mystery to Elya. They were such different people. He seemed to be firmly enamored with her, however, which, for a guy who used to sleep with any woman who showed him the slightest affection, was actually rather impressive.

"What I would do with that kind of money…" Park mused.

"We all know what you'd do," Osprey said. "You'd gamble it away."

"Aw, c'mon, Raptor, give me a little credit. I'd only gamble some of it away. The rest I'd spend on gemstones for Gears."

Lieutenant Yorra snorted.

"Let me know when you stumble into that fortune, pal," Elya said. "I've got a set of dice and an account where you can deposit your losings."

"No way, hombre. You cheat!"

"Don't be mad I took your money." Elya loved a good game of aleacc, his favorite form of entertainment after flying starfighters. He'd been playing since he was a kid.

"Whatever, man."

"All right, children," Raptor said. "Less chit chat, more patrolling."

"Aye aye, Cap'n!" Park banked his starfighter and accelerated toward the nearest corner of the cube-shaped patrol zone.

Elya practically heard Osprey rolling her eyes, but she said nothing as the three of them sped up after Park.

They weaved toward the edge of the asteroid field,

curving around progressively smaller and more scattered objects. Eventually, only a handful of small rocks pinged off his shield. It was here they finished the first pass along the near side of their patrol zone.

When he reached the corner, and the highlighted path on his HUD turned sharply along a new vector, Elya stuck hard to the line, banking his Sabre to the right at the last possible moment. He grinned as the G-forces pressed him into his seat, and he hauled the Sabre toward New Kali, the third world in the Elturis system.

As he came out of the turn and felt his shoulders rise against his safety harness again, Hedgebot climbed out from beneath Elya's chair, chirping irritably and clinging with metal toes to the grooves between panels in the cockpit.

"Have a nice nap?" Elya asked.

Hedgebot was originally designed as a danger detector for planetary exploration outfits. Elya had augmented its functions to pass muster as an astrobot and taken to storing its charging pad in the compartment near his boots for these long patrols.

Hedgebot pulsed orange and red rapidly before fading back to his neutral blue and chortling in a series of grumpy chimes.

"Yeah, I could have taken the turn slower, but where's the fun in that?"

The other pilots banked more carefully behind him, cutting the angle off the corner and pulling in front of him. He let them go as he engaged the autopilot and shook out his hands.

Distances in space were vast, so while Elya couldn't see New Kali from his current location, he knew, judging by the lidar and the map of the system on his HUD, that it was one of those tiny blue specks out ahead, off-center by about ten degrees. That world wasn't broken. That one was a beautiful blue gem of a planet with breathable air and green plants, liquid water, and an animal kingdom as diverse as any the Solaran Empire had ever found. It boasted thousands of unique bird species. For heaven's sake, the damned place had birds!

And despite the Empire's knowledge of it, New Kali remained uncolonized—about 90% of the world's surface mapped but completely unexplored by a single Solaran soul. This broken planet and the asteroid field, and the Telos relic they'd found hidden within, had ruined all of that. The Colonization Board had halted settler migrations to New Kali. At least for now. The original voyager sent to build its first colony had been hijacked by Overmind X, who murdered everyone aboard.

Maybe one day, when colonization missions resumed, he'd save up enough money to pay for the rest of his family to be relocated there. He often daydreamed about rescuing them from the impoverished settler's moon where they lived. After the Kryl invasion of Yuzosix sent him, his mom, and his two older brothers fleeing into space as homeless refugees, life had been hard for his family. They had no money, no connections, nowhere else to go. Unlike the farm world where he was born, Eskatan was a mining community built on the edge of a crater containing deep veins of valuable ores: gold, copper, iron, and other metals used to smelt aluminite, the metal his Sabre's walls and cockpit were made of. Eskatan also had naturally occurring uranium deposits the Empire relied upon to construct the nuclear weapons that were stored in the arsenal of most Fleet warships.

Elya had escaped Eskatan. Barely, thanks to the shrewd guidance of his mother and a chance encounter with a recruiter from the Solaran Defense Forces. He'd gotten lucky. His family, not so much. It was this guilt that kept Elya sending as much money home as he could spare. But a young pilot's salary wasn't enough to secure three spots on a colonial voyager.

The filaments along Hedgebot's back brightened to orange, and the bot scurried along the instrument panel to the opposite side of the cockpit.

"See something, pal?"

A rock the size of his fist rebounded off his shield near the front window. Neutral blue reasserted itself and Hedgebot shook its bristles.

Elya disengaged autopilot and accelerated to catch up with the others.

"Coming up on the second waypoint," Osprey announced. "Tighten up those formations."

She was obviously referring to Elya. Their patrol was to make two full rotations of the cube before heading back to base. All told, it would take them about eight hours. Elya sped up until he was back in his proper position. He knew Osprey wanted to look good because this turn would bring them adjacent to Flight 4's patrol zone. Still, no excuse for sloppy flying.

His instruments fluttered. The gravity reading jumped up before returning to zero. That was weird. That only happened when—

Hedgebot flared red, and Elya hauled back on the stick by instinct. "Incoming!"

A pack of Kryl drones dropped out of hyperspace right on top of their position.

"Overhead, forty-five degrees starboard, two klicks out," Osprey shouted. "Command, we have contact. Repeat, we have contact."

Elya hauled up on his stick with his right hand while juicing himself with stimchem with his left using a switch on the instrument panel. The cocktail flowed in through his spinal port, which was attached inside his helmet, increasing his reaction time and making his body more capable of withstanding strong G-forces like the kind he pulled during a fight. He inhaled sharply as the drugs hit, then added more oxygen to his mask for good measure. A pilot's increased heart rate while stimmed up usually led to more oxygen consumption, and he had plenty onboard. No reason to be stingy.

"Contact confirmed," barked Colonel Volk, the Executive Officer on the *Paladin of Abniss*. He was second in command to Admiral Miyaru, as well as doing temporary double duty as the squadron commander of the Fightin' Furies. "Deploying Flight 4 to your position for support. Call out the bodies."

"Fancypants," Osprey said, using Elya's call sign. He checked his HUD and realized he'd pulled into the lead position. Osprey had once again dropped to the rear.

"Six hostiles, appear to be Kryl drones," Elya said as the computer verified the units by outlining them on his HUD, and transmitting images back to the *Paladin of Abniss*. "Standard forms." One of the new protocols was that any Kryl sighting included an analysis of the forms the creatures took, comparing them to previous iterations the Fleet kept in their database. The xenos' penchant for rapid mutation had put the whole Fleet on edge, enough to alter their SOPs. Never knew what you were going to get with the Kryl. Not since those children were taken.

"Thank you, Flight 18," Volk said, "Engage enemy units."

"Whoa!" Nevers cried as he dodged to port, narrowly avoiding taking shield damage.

Yorra grunted as a projectile pinged off her wing. She banked into the momentum of the turn, performing a barrel roll as she veered away.

"Stay in formation, Gears!" Osprey snapped. "Your shields are full."

"Not anymore, they're not." Yorra righted herself quickly. Park, obviously worried about her, hovered off her right wing.

Their V-formation cut through the middle of the enemy squad in the next moment, splitting the pack of six into a quad and a pair. The drones arced away, banking in perfect sync with each other. Elya pulled around to draw a bead on one.

"Unified," Osprey said. "Keep it together."

"Got a lock!" Park said, his voice taut with excitement. Two missiles released from the ports on his Sabre's undercarriage, one on either side of the pilot's chair and three feet back. The missiles chased after the pair of drones who'd gone to the right. They flew evasively, trying to avoid the missiles or make them fly into each other, but Park had been smart. Instead of trying to target each drone with one missile, he'd sent two missiles after a single drone. They both hit, blowing the enemy ship into a cloud of carapace and guts.

"Kill number six!" Park said.

The explosion was close enough to cause the other drone to lose control for a moment, flying into Elya's crosshairs. He laid on his wingtip blasters, raking them across the drone's back. The left wing of the creature sheared off, sending it whirling. It didn't erupt into a pretty fireball like Park's had, but the vacuum tore it into pieces and took it out of commission just the same.

"Ten for me," Elya announced.

"Aw, hell, quit bragging, Nevers."

"Shouldn't have gone straight for your missiles. You've only got two left."

"Focus, you two!" shouted Osprey.

He hadn't lost sight of the other four, despite the crosstalk. Hedgebot climbed overhead, pulsing red and confirming the direction the quad had gone. They were racing toward the asteroid field Flight 18 had so recently left behind. Apparently, the pair of drones peeling away had been a distraction, because the quad was now far enough ahead that he'd have to burn at six or eight Gs for several minutes to catch them.

Good, he thought.

Elya laid his head back and fired up his engines hard enough to peel his cheeks away from his teeth.

The other three pilots followed his lead. Hedgebot had found a position against the rear bulkhead next to Elya's shoulder. Not even the bot could move around the cockpit under this kind of acceleration.

After sixty seconds, it felt like his stomach had molded to the grooves of his spine. He'd gained a couple klicks and could now see the drones clearly, using enhanced telescopics on the heads-up display that magnified and brightened them in his front window. It was weird because they weren't flying as fast as they should be. Kryl didn't feel fear or other emotions like human beings, since they were controlled telepathically by the Overmind, even this far away from the swarm. Even so, the drones didn't *want* to get shot down. They wanted to lose him in the asteroid field. So why were they letting him catch up?

A shadow shifted inside the cockpit of one drone. Goosebumps raised on his arms beneath his flight suit. Elya reduced his acceleration to match the drones. Was that a trick of the light? Had the star come out from behind Elturis-2?

No. There it was again! A shadow within the central bulk of the drone, right where a pilot would be if those ships were manned.

He opened his engines to full burn, causing Hedgebot to squawk and smack hard against the rear bulkhead.

He was approaching the edge of the asteroid field now,

and a large rock loomed ahead of him. Elya tapped the trigger on his stick, sending a few bolts of energy flying ahead of him.

The drones scattered, moving in all different directions to avoid the blast.

All except one.

One drone blurred, letting the bolt pass through its fuselage.

"It's Subject Zero!" Elya said to the others. "I just saw him phase shift."

"Flight 4 is closing on your position," Volk said. "They're cutting off the angle and will be there in less than two minutes."

"We don't have two minutes, Colonel!"

"Whatever you do, keep him in your sights," said Captain Osprey.

Zero's drone went solid again. Elya knew from experience that the mutant had to wait about forty-five seconds before the relic he was using cooled down enough to phase shift again. The time was now.

Elya muted his mic. "Hedgebot, timer for forty seconds." He unmuted it. "I'm going after him. Gears, Naab—wipe those other drones off the lidar."

"On it!" Yorra said. The two of them veered away.

"Raptor, are you with me?" Elya asked.

"On your six. Go!"

Subject Zero pulled a hard left and aimed straight for an egg-shaped asteroid. Elya followed, leaning on his blaster. Zero dodged every shot.

Damn, he's good! Elya thought.

Subject Zero was once the best starfighter pilot in the Fleet. As the mutant approached the rock, he twisted and spun as he turned down, putting the belly of his drone close to the rock and forcing Elya to weave between cracks, cliffs, and crenellations to keep him in his sights. Zero curved around the asteroid. Elya mimicked his path, staying hot on his tail.

"We can't catch him if he's leading the dance," Osprey said. "We've got to head him off."

Forty-five seconds was a long time in a dogfight, but Elya was so engrossed in the chase that it passed without notice. Hedgebot flared red and beeped. "He's gonna phase shift again."

Subject Zero braked hard in front of them and turned right into the rock. He passed right through it this time as the indicator tracking his ship dropped off the lidar.

"Quick," Osprey said. "Other side of the asteroid."

They hugged the rock tight as they curved around, but it caused them to take a longer arc than Subject Zero would have. The only difference was, he was flying blind, without instruments. Assuming those drones even *had* instrument panels.

"Where'd he go?" Osprey asked.

"Earth, I don't know! Hedgebot?" A blinking dot reappeared on his lidar and Hedgebot scurried straight overhead. "There!" Elya said, pointing the nose of his Sabre up.

His stomach somersaulted as he pulled back on his stick.

"He's headed back out," Elya said. "I think he's trying to jump away!"

It would take a moment to warm up his hyperspace drive. It was also prudent to jump as far from a gravity well as a starship could manage. Elturis-2, being a broken planet, gave a little more leeway than most.

Elya turned his engines to max burn once again, determined to catch Subject Zero before he escaped. This was the fight he'd been waiting for, and all the mutant seemed to want to do was lead him on a wild chase around the asteroid field. Annoying.

"Why won't you turn and fight me?" Elya muttered under his breath.

Flight 4 arrived and helped Yorra and Park clean up the rest of the drones—mere distractions. Only Zero mattered.

"Raptor, dual launch? We've got a clear shot now."

They deployed their missiles, four of them. Subject Zero waited until the missiles got close enough to fight, then immediately flipped backwards and used his projectile weapons to shoot them down one at a time, all while dodging blaster fire from both him *and* Captain Osprey's Sabre.

"Stars!" Elya cursed. "He's so good."

It had been footage of Subject Zero, then known as Captain Omar Ruidiaz, which had inspired Elya to become a pilot. It got under his skin that even now, he still wasn't good enough to beat the man—or rather, the mutant. The Kryl genes seemed to have made him into a better pilot.

"Fire again!" Osprey was into it now, hanging with Elya's every curve. She was a skilled pilot, too. A match for Nevers on a good day. Surely the two of them could take out a single mutant.

This time Subject Zero didn't dodge their shots. Another forty-five seconds had elapsed, and he phase shifted, letting the missiles pass through him and drift into space as they lost their target. He shut off his engines while the phase shift was active.

"He's jumping!" Elya shouted.

He accelerated, trying to get as close as he could. Maybe the phase shifter would shut off before the jump and Elya would have a split second for a clear shot. Subject Zero didn't make a move to jump away. He let himself drift, as he had to in order to activate the hyperspace drive.

Elya's instrument panels jumped again. Hedgebot beeped angrily.

A majestic, armored cruiseliner dropped out of hyperspace exactly halfway between his position and the Kryl mutant.

"Earth!" Elya said, pulling up into a loop and arcing back.

Subject Zero jumped away, turning into a streak of light behind the cruiseliner.

TWO

Casey shoved her stick away and kicked the bulkhead at her feet.

She exhaled heavily. "By the breath of Animus, that was close."

Nevers had his mic muted. Craning her neck, she saw him through the transparent aluminite pane of his canopy, cussing and thrashing in his seat.

"Be patient, Fancypants. We'll get him."

"He was toying with us!" Casey cringed at the static his piercing voice made in her headset. "He must have known the cruiseliner would jump into the edge of our patrol zone. He took advantage of its position to make his escape."

It wasn't that unusual to track ships jumping through hyperspace, but it was unnerving knowing the Kryl were watching their movements that closely.

The cruiseliner rebooted its main thrusters, its triple-engine drive plume burning blue-white. It flew Solaran colors and broadcasted friendly on broadbeam. In short, it didn't appear to be a threat, and while it had ample defensive weapons mounted along its hull, this was no warship.

"Maybe Zero was hoping to attack the cruiseliner as it dropped out of hyperspace?" Casey asked. "Whoever it is, they're lucky we're here. Who do you think is onboard, anyway?"

The enormous cruiseliner was opulent, richly painted with dragons, clouds, and depictions of Animus himself, portrayed as a nebulous blue-green spirit basking in the symbolic light of Sol, Earth's ancestral sun. The starcraft's wings were sleek and angular, the skirt around its engines shaped like the fin of a massive ocean creature. Its hull was heavily armored, with a few dorsal railguns visible—the new, expensive kind Park had been swooning over. Casey had come from money, but not even her family would have been able to afford a ship this extravagant. In fact, only a few of the ultra-rich would have been able to commission such a heavily customized vessel.

So who did it belong to?

"Drones eliminated," Gears finally reported. Tension leaked out of Casey's shoulders as she exhaled. She knew her pilots had help, but it was her job to keep them safe.

"Thanks for your help, Flight 4," Casey said.

"You're welcome, sweetheart," said an acid female voice that belonged to Captain Katja Bergren, call sign Ruby, the lead of Flight 4. She was a lean woman with thick auburn curls that made Casey's fingernails peel back in envy.

"Pleasure's ours," a posh male voice added. That would be Lieutenant Bjorn Allen Moyer, the young pilot nipping at Nevers' heels in the rankings. "And I do appreciate how you handed me two extra kills on a silver platter, Naab. I believe that puts me even with Fancypants, eh?"

"You missed my first shot today, Teddy Bear," Nevers said, using a play on the man's call sign, which was Grizzly. It made sense if you saw him up close. The guy's chest was massive, and his shoulders brushed the cockpit walls when he sat in his Sabre. "I'm at ten now."

Grizzly chuckled gamely over squad comms. "Two today, two more tomorrow. I'll be lapping you before you know it."

"Put a raincheck on your pissing contest," Casey said, "and focus. We all need to have eyes peeled for more incoming enemy units. Flight 18, check in." She dropped a beacon on the lidar, marking a new rendezvous point. Nevers peeled away in that direction, leaving the cruiseliner to drift lazily behind them. Casey followed.

"Flight 4," Volk said, "Since you're already out of position, escort the cruiseliner in to dock."

"Whose ship is it, anyway, Colonel?" Ruby asked.

"No one you need to worry about."

Casey's ears perked up. Someone important then.

"You got it, boss," Ruby said. "We're on our way."

Casey glanced up at Nevers, who was flying next to her, close enough to see him jerk his chin sharply and bob his starfighter up and down in a wavelike motion designed to draw her attention.

"Colonel," Casey said. "This is Flight 18's patrol zone. We should escort the ship in."

A private channel opened on her comms. "Back off, Raptor," Ruby hissed, the fake sweetness completely gone from her voice.

Casey ignored her.

"Are you really volunteering for escort duty over finishing your patrol?" Volk asked. "I thought you'd appreciate the chance to frag a few more drones after how the fight ended."

He knew as well as she did the Kryl were highly unlikely to send another scouting raid following that stunt. They'd never sent two raids back-to-back before, and the chances of another pack of drones appearing today were practically nil.

"I appreciate the opportunity, sir, but part of our mission on patrol is to escort any vessels safely through our zone." It was written into their standard operating procedures. Ultimately, it was the squadron commander's call, though.

Volk had previously explained that since he couldn't fly with the squadron, he'd be picking one of the flight leads to serve as mission commander. A necessity in cases of emergency, and in combat situations where split second decision making was required. He had yet to name that person, however, and Casey was determined to do everything in her power to demonstrate her fitness for the role.

"Sir," Ruby said. "We've already accepted. It's a done deal."

The XO sighed heavily into his microphone. Casey could imagine him rubbing his face. The man hated inter-flight arguments. Even friendly competition annoyed him.

Nevers gave Casey a thumbs up. *You're swabbing decks with me if I get in trouble for this,* Casey thought. But dammit, she wanted the XO to know her flight wasn't just out to rack up kill counts. She was willing to do whatever the mission called for, even the boring stuff.

And he may grumble, but he knew the SOPs as well as she did. The cruiseliner jumped into Flight 18's patrol zone. It was their escort.

"Raptor's right," Volk said. "Flight 4, you're on patrol. Eighteen, escort the cruiseliner back to port."

"Yes, sir!" Casey switched back to squad comms, so she had a private channel with Flight 18's pilots only. "You heard the man."

Park and Yorra reached the rendezvous point first. They each bore several new carbon stains on their wings. Casey resolved to drill them on projectile avoidance tactics the next time they were in the sim. Those marks meant some of the drone's shots had burned through their shields, which was unacceptable. If Flight 4 hadn't raced over to provide backup, they'd have been in real danger.

As a unit, Flight 18 circled back and took up positions guarding the luxury cruiseliner, a pair of Sabres on either side. *Archangel Over the Atlantic* was written on the side of the ship. What was with the Old Earth references?

Casey opened a new tightbeam channel. "*Archangel,* this is Captain Osprey of the Furies. We've got orders to escort you in to port. Please acknowledge."

"Copy that, Captain. Happy to have you along for the ride. Lead the way, please."

Going was slow. It was a tedious effort to escort a cruiseliner through the asteroid field. The larger ship couldn't maneuver as easily as their Sabres, nor could it fly at the same speeds. A trip that took forty-five minutes on their way out took three and a half hours on the way back. It didn't help that the pilot of the cruiseliner seemed hesitant to even jostle his occupants, let alone pass near enough to an asteroid to risk scratching his fancy paint job.

And it *was* a beautiful ship. Was that a family of hawks, there, dancing through nimbus clouds near the wing? Casey pulled her flight suit sleeves up and glanced at the osprey tattoos on her forearms. The illustrations were her constant reminder of her mother, who passed away when she was young, and one of the main reasons she'd joined the fleet. The hawks didn't appear to be ospreys, but they were obviously some variant of Old Earth raptor.

An artist well versed in the mythology of Old Earth had done this work. Solarans still taught their children the names of animals from their estranged home planet. It was part of their culture, a source of pride, even if most of the animals had been extinct for millennia.

Casey studied another scene with an ark—an old-school colonial voyager—representing humanity's exit from their dying planet. It was flying into a long tunnel surrounded by tick marks counting off the centuries humanity spent living among the stars as they searched for their new home. On the other end of the tunnel, a group of engineers crowded together, tinkering with some kind of engine. She knew from her time in church that the engine was supposed to represent humanity's ingenuity. Thanks to divine inspiration from Animus, her ancestors had created a device that allowed them to reach Ariadne—the hyperspace drive.

This mythology had recently been called into question. In an old book she and Captain Nevers found in the archives, *A Treatise on Ancient Alien Technology & Its Primary Applications*, the author claimed the hyperspace drive had been a gift from a Telos engineer. Not created by humanity, but reverse engineered from alien technology. She was adjusting to this new perspective.

"Who do you reckon's flying this yacht?" Park asked over tightbeam squad comms as they turned into the final approach. The rotation of Elturis-2 had shifted enough that the star bathed even this dense section of the asteroid field in an orange glow. "Some warship manufacturer?"

Indeed, the starlight illuminated several of those warships up ahead. Heavy cruisers were being outfitted with new railguns to her right. Sparks from dozens of welding torches twinkled against silver hulls.

"Maybe it's the head of a trading company," Nevers mused. "Whoever sells and ships the goods needed to keep an armada this big supplied is definitely getting rich."

The armada relied on food, water, and materials harvested or mined from Ariadne, Oltanis, Taj Su, and the other colonies. Smaller skiffs flitted between the warships, running supplies and workers back and forth. Light cruisers, frigates, corvettes, and several of the enormous Imperial destroyers were lined up in rough grids to her left. There were dozens, now. More ships than she'd ever seen in one place before. A true armada.

She felt excited because of the sheer firepower they represented. The Solaran Empire was gearing up for war, and the Kryl had every reason to be quaking in their carapace. No wonder Overmind X and Subject Zero kept attacking their perimeter. They were literally dying to find out what they were up against.

"Whoever it is, I'll bet this cruiseliner is the reason patrols are up," Yorra said. "Our visitor had an appointment."

"Look sharp," Casey said.

She applied a braking burn and slowed to a crawl. A construction port lay directly below now. Shaped like a long spine with several cross braces, it hosted starships in need of repairs or new outfitting. It also served as a good place to dock newcomers.

Nearby was a large, oblong asteroid. It was enormous, easily the biggest asteroid in the region, and hung vertically from the orientation the armada had decided was "up"—a direction chosen based on the orientation of the Telos construction inside. It was hard to imagine that just six weeks ago, no one had known this asteroid existed. Looking at it now, how could their astronomers have missed it? The rock was shaped like a long cut gem, oblong and elegant, like a glacier where the top third was thickest, while the bottom two-thirds tapered to a point. The color of the rock was a light brown, lighter than the surrounding asteroids. Additional inspections had given rise to the theory that the asteroid itself may have been constructed by the Telos. It was made wholly out of the rock-like metal the Telos used in their relics, a light but durable alloy that was harder than aluminite. It also made wonderful camouflage in an asteroid field.

"Hail, the *Paladin of Abniss*. This is Captain Osprey of the Furies. Requesting permission to approach."

"Permission granted, Captain. Allow the liner to dock, then escort a shuttle with your visitors into the City."

That's what people had begun calling the collection of buildings within the Telos asteroid. The City with a capital C.

"Copy that," Casey said, bemused.

Nevers was practically jumping out of his Sabre with anticipation. The Furies had been so busy flying patrol missions and fighting drones they hadn't had time to visit the City. Even if they wanted to, MOXA and Admiral Miyaru's Marines had the place locked down tighter than the Molten Cage.

"You think they're here to see the Chronicle relic?" Nevers asked.

"What else would someone come all this way to see?" Yorra said.

"Earth, I have to know who's on that ship. I've been trying to see the relic since we won it, and can't get so much as a day pass approved. Yet this ship shows up and gets a Sabre escort inside on day one. Think they'll let us park and accompany them inside?"

"Keep dreaming," Casey said. Nevers had tunnel vision about two things—Subject Zero, and those damned relics. Casey knew they were important, but he could be obsessive.

A new light shone on her face as a mellifluous voice that could be male or female said, "He's right to be suspicious, you know."

Casey jumped against her harness. "Harmony! I really wish you'd give me some warning before you do that!"

A swirling nimbus of colorful lights spun around her for a moment as the playful shipboard AI collected into the form of an androgynous face, floating in the air.

"And what would be the fun in that, Captain?"

"Well, you'd be less likely to give me a heart attack."

"You've been through worse."

Unfortunately, that was true. Like seeing a Kryl parasite take over a mechanic's mind. Like watching her squadron commander murdered by the same mechanic. Like being forced to stand aside as Renata freaking Spector was named their squadron commander. It was better now, under Colonel Volk. She just wished he'd pick a mission commander. And why not pick Casey? She'd do a better job than Renata had, and besides, it was an honorary position at best. Flight 18 boasted the best pilots in the squadron, and it was only a contingency appointment, one with no real command authority. The chances of getting caught without comms—putting the mission commander in charge in an authentic way—seemed a distant possibility.

Yet, if that was true, why did she want the job so badly?

"Besides, Captain," the shipmind said, "I like to keep you on your toes. If you're going to take a command position someday, you need to learn to deal with surprises."

Casey narrowed her eyes at the shipmind's blue and purple form. Perhaps she wanted it because Harmony kept encouraging her to pursue the job. It seemed strange that the shipmind, the entity who piloted the *Paladin of Abniss* and reported directly to Admiral Miyaru herself, would act outside the chain of command. She'd learned, however, that Harmony had a mind of her own. It had been Harmony who disguised herself as a hacker and fed Captain Nevers information about the relics, ultimately leading them to the discovery of the old book containing clues as to the relics' whereabouts, and which ultimately led them to the City. Harmony's methods may have been unorthodox, but she was undoubtedly effective.

Casey also couldn't help but wonder what else Harmony

knew that she wasn't sharing. She glanced at her other pilots in their Sabres, idling as the cruiseliner was secured by docking arms to the brace. None of them seemed to have noticed Casey was having a conversation with the AI. She checked to be sure her mic remained muted.

"Wait, did you say Nevers is right to be suspicious?"

Harmony's hologram face gave her a glittering grin.

"You're enjoying this way too much," Casey said. "Whose ship is it?"

Harmony blinked out, her lights disappearing from the inside of Casey's cockpit. "She has too much attitude for a computer program," she muttered.

"What was that, Raptor?" Park asked.

"Nothing." Casey had hit the mute button by accident when Harmony disappeared. She resolved to follow up with her after the escort job was over. A shuttle was leaving the cruiseliner now. "Escort positions, people. Here they come."

Like the cruiseliner, the shuttle was painted with beautiful artwork featuring images out of Old Earth mythology. Casey led the shuttle toward the asteroid, and the triangular bay that would take them to the City. The opening was too small to allow the enormous cruiseliner, but still wide enough to fit a dozen Sabres flying wingtip to wingtip. They entered two by two, with the shuttle between them.

Casey sent Nevers and Park to dock, while she and Yorra idled just inside the bay. When the artificial gravity asserted itself, the shuttle juddered a bit and dropped as its engines adjusted. It set down on the stone landing pad.

As she watched, an entire retinue came out of the main gate and arranged themselves to await the disembarkation of the shuttle. At their head was Admiral Miyaru, tall and dark-skinned with that impossible-to-miss, short platinum mohawk that was her hallmark. Casey zoomed in on the admiral's stoic face. She stood at parade rest as the shuttle's ramp extended.

"By Earth's ancestral sun," Nevers breathed. "You're never going to believe this, guys."

"I didn't think I'd ever see the day," Park added.

"Well, don't tease us," Casey said. The shuttle blocked her view of the people descending the ramp, while Nevers and Park had a clear line of sight, having set down their starfighters on either side of the ship. "Who is it?"

"The emperor himself."

THREE

Admiral Kira Miyaru's face displayed a practiced exterior of stoic calm, but inside she fumed.

Overmind X eludes my scouts, a dozen frantic officers are waiting on me to answer questions about this poorly-outfitted, malformed armada, and yet I'm stuck here playing tour guide to the Earth-damned emperor himself.

When was the last time he even left that floating pleasure palace orbiting Ariadne, anyway? Eight years? Ten?

So why in the name of Animus had he come to see her City now?

Everyone called it the City, but Kira couldn't help thinking of it as *her* City. Others would have challenged the notion, especially Minister Aganaki, who was increasingly obsessive about his precious Chronicle. That ancient computer console had barely yielded any useful information at all. Meanwhile, the Minister of Xeno Affairs was becoming increasingly reticent. Each time she asked him about his scientists and their "studies," his answers grew more evasive and cryptic.

Kira tried to put the worry from her mind. Her responsibilities consumed enough space in her head. Uniting an armada whose commanders had been drifting apart on disparate missions for twelve years was proving to be even harder than navigating the byzantine halls of politics on Ariadne. She reminded herself that her goal was simple: build her forces up so that, when the rogue Overmind made her next major move, Kira would be in position to stop her.

Everything else was secondary.

Protecting the City was one piece of the puzzle, a vital one. It confirmed her decision to gather the armada here in Elturis each time a pack of Kryl drones harried their perimeter.

The raids were also a measurement device. One can tell a lot about an enemy force by their diligence in defending their borders. Overmind X was probing hers. No doubt, the Kryl queen would eventually develop a swarm capable of a full-fledged assault. It was just a matter of time.

Time Kira didn't have to waste escorting His Majesty around *her* City for the emperor's entertainment.

Every second wasted standing here made her rash itch worse. The stress of her work these past several weeks had formed horrible, bumpy red rashes on her skin. Today it had appeared on her neck where her uniform rubbed against her clavicle. Medics on the *Paladin* had prescribed a topical steroid, yet every time she got one flare-up under control, another reared its head. She would have a better outlet for stress if she had more time to exercise. These days, even a thirty-minute workout seemed like a luxury.

The emperor's shuttle finally drifted through the triangular port in the asteroid's wall, accompanied by two Sabres from his starfighter escort. Spider-like legs extended from the curvy craft's base and set down on the alien alloy of the landing pad with a pneumatic hiss. A ramp extended from the belly of the ship, and a platoon of royal guards filed down, forming two columns. A pack of sycophants and socialites came next, beautiful women in flowing pearl and turquoise dresses with bare arms exposed, men in silken shirts that showed their sculpted chests. All of them exceptionally young, with dyed hair and enough jewelry to smelt a false idol.

Why is the emperor here, Harmony? Kira thought at the shipboard AI.

Ever since they'd unlocked Chronicle, Harmony could communicate with Kira in the City. The AI still couldn't project her light-form into the asteroid, unlike the halls and rooms of Solaran vessels, where holographic sensors were uniformly installed. She could, however, communicate with Kira, thanks to the chip implanted at the base of the admiral's skull.

"I wish I knew," Harmony said. The shipmind's voice sounded to her senses like a person standing a half meter away and talking in a normal voice. Without holographic sensors, no one but Kira could see or hear her. The admiral had to be careful not to move her lips when she sent thoughts at the AI. Even though their existence was common knowledge, Kira speaking aloud to the empty air was still unsettling to most of her crew.

Fleet AIs are technically owned by the emperor, Kira thought at Harmony. *You didn't go poking around his systems?*

"Why Admiral, of course I did. Don't insult me."

Kira snorted. *Not bad for a robot pilot.*

"Our contract with the Executive Council affords us a measure of freedom."

You mean spying and subterfuge.

"Only in the service of the Fleet. Unfortunately, the emperor's own sentient networks have his systems locked down tighter than the royal treasury."

They'd had long discussions about how Harmony had

helped the pilots of the Furies locate the ancient text that led them to the City, circumventing the authority of the Ministry of Xeno Affairs. Harmony remained completely unapologetic. Kira had got her to admit that she'd been working on behalf of the Executive Council, in particular Admiral Gitano, but beyond that, the AI's programming would give her no more information. "The point is, the emperor has his own spies," said the shipmind. "He himself hasn't had need of our services in decades."

So you found nothing about why he's here?

"Apart from the obvious? No. But I'm *dying* to find out."

You can't die, silly.

"Not in the mortal sense, perhaps, but I can still cease to exist."

Touché.

Kira straightened her shoulders as the emperor's entourage finished descending from the craft. They stood gawking at the elaborate carved gate, whose doors were open, revealing a long tunnel that poured out on a promontory overlooking her City. Several people in the entourage bent down to touch the strange reddish stone of the landing pad, then they all parted like an ocean wave as the emperor appeared.

He was taller than Kira, which was rare enough, but beyond that, he surprised her by appearing *incredibly* young. Not a wrinkle on that perfectly symmetrical face. Wide jaw, high cheekbones, strong nose and full lips. Skin that was lighter than hers, sun-kissed, with faint freckles painted across his cheeks. The only unnatural thing about his facial features, apart from their apparent perfection, were the emperor's eyes—they blazed golden, like two dwarf stars.

He wore trim black trousers, and a high-collared purple shirt made of expensive synthweave that adjusted to his form as he moved. It was open at the chest, revealing lean, sculpted muscles. The emperor's skin was studded with cybernetic nodules—the artificial preservers of his youthful appearance, and of who knew what other benefits. She knew the man was over a hundred years old, yet he appeared to be in his mid-thirties. On his feet he wore expensive boots of leather —*real* leather, not synthweave. His outfit was complete with a shimmering golden cloak fastened at his shoulders. The thin fiber was semi-translucent, and it trailed behind him as he strode down the ramp. As he approached, a matching golden circlet caught the ambient light inside the asteroid. It was decorated with the same cybernetic design as the studs on his chest.

The emperor walked into the midst of his entourage and paused, striking a regal pose.

A young woman stepped forward and fixed her eyes on Kira. "May I present His Majesty, Emperor Aeris the Fifth, Sovereign of Ariadne, King of the Colonies, Lord of Lords, and Sole Ruler of all Solaran Space."

Kira barely managed not to roll her eyes. As if she didn't know the man's name and innumerable insufferable titles.

She didn't want to start this charade off on the wrong foot, however, lest her day get worse, so Kira stepped one foot back and gave a deep bow. She had worn her military dress uniform, the one with the ribbon of medals on her chest, but in front of this lot she felt shockingly underdressed. "Your majesty, it is my supreme honor to welcome you to the City of the Telos. The Elturis armada has been looking forward to your visit."

"Admiral Miyaru, isn't it?" asked Emperor Aeris the Fifth, speaking for himself this time. His voice had a resonant tenor, and those golden eyes twinkled with a keen, observant intelligence as he studied her. Not something she'd have expected for a ruler who had spent so many years isolated from his people. As he stepped forward, guards fell in around him, several of them watching Kira closely. She'd been instructed to leave her sidearm blaster on the *Paladin,* and was glad she had followed those orders.

"I want to commend you for your actions securing this artifact," the emperor went on. "We have always tried to safeguard the technology of the ancient Telos. It is good that it did not fall into Kryl possession."

Kira raised an eyebrow. Was that so? Interesting, considering they'd been here for a month before he'd shown a lick of interest in the place. "Thank you, your Majesty," she said.

He waved a hand. "Call me Aeris, please. I've grown used to avoiding such formality at home. I tire of this 'your majesty' stuff rather quickly these days."

"Of course, sir." She may drop the royal honorific, as he requested, but Fleet superlatives were hard-wired into her.

Aeris made for the tunnel. "Well, are you going to show me around?" he asked, striding past her. "Or must I find Aganaki myself and make him give me the tour instead?"

Oh, no you don't, Kira thought angrily. Harmony released a very un-robot-like chuckle in her head. "That won't be necessary, Emp—uh, Aeris." Kira caught up and gave the emperor the same vicious smile she cast in the Kryl's direction before a battle. Didn't have to force that one. "Right this way, sir."

As they proceeded, several of the emperor's bodyguards ranged ahead. Four stayed close by without crowding them, and the rest spread out behind, disappearing among the entourage, who followed at a discrete distance, marveling quietly amongst themselves.

The tunnel here had been pitch dark when they found it. Kira had lights placed on the floor—they couldn't mount them in the blasted stone walls if they wanted to. The material ruined any drill bit that came into contact with it. As they walked, Kira explained how the geode relic had acted as a key which opened the carved door, and lit the way inside. After a couple hundred yards, the tunnel split and dual archways looked out over the City.

"Impressive," Aeris said. "The holovids I received didn't do it justice." He turned those golden eyes on Kira, a touch of mischief lurking within. "One reason I insisted on seeing it for myself."

"Of course, sir." Kira fidgeted. All this just to see it for himself? She wondered if any new warships had arrived today. They were still waiting on several light cruisers, as well as a shipment of new railguns. Colonel Volk had instructions to reduce patrols back to normal numbers now that the emperor's ship had arrived, and rotate fresh squadrons out after lunch. Supplies of food and water had been coming in steadily from Ariadne, but in lower volumes than she'd requested, and she suspected Chairman Card had something to do with that. The conniving head of the Colonization Board had undue influence over supply lines, and he must ha—

"Earth to Admiral Miyaru."

Kira started. They had descended halfway down the switch-backing trail and she had become lost in her thoughts while Emperor Aeris surveyed the crystal architecture below.

"Sorry, sir. Would you mind repeating the question?"

"I was just asking how your crew was finding living here. Have they discovered anything interesting since they moved into the houses?"

Airy buildings of crystal and stone spread across the floor of the hollow inside the asteroid. The structures rose to three or four stories above the ground. Most were built so that their first floor was raised several meters off the ground, and inaccessible without ladders or a steep ascent along a curved wall. Crystal gates, which made large courtyards out of the empty ground floors, surrounded some. She supposed they used the area for storage, or for entertainment, although she couldn't be certain. It rather seemed like they had built everything to withstand a flood, since it was all up so high. Not even Minister Aganaki, the self-styled expert in the Telos, really knew, although he said it was likely because the Telos were climbers.

"I'm not sure I'd call them houses, exactly, sir, although some may have been dwellings of some sort. Most of our people have simply set up camp in the courtyard below the buildings. They like seeing the sky." Instead of the interior of the rocky asteroid, some kind of illusion—she was hesitant to call it a hologram, for it was more real than any hologram she'd ever seen, and though they'd searched high and low, none of her people could find any source for the projection—swirled with an ambient light filled with clouds. In several hours, it would fade to twilight and show stars.

"Marvelous," said Emperor Aeris. "I'd heard of this incredible sight. Even with all the money I've spent on the Gardens"—his name for his orbital palace—"the simulation of night and day lacks a kind of convincing realism. Seeing this proves that there is room for improvement. You must show me how it's done."

"As soon as we figure it out, I'll be sure to let you know, sir."

They soon passed into the City, strolling along paths between the buildings, most of which remained empty. "We haven't been able to find entrances to most of these buildings. Our survey revealed that many don't even seem to have doors."

"Strange. What were they used for?"

"Wish I knew, sir."

As they got closer to the center, the place began to look more human. She'd approved permits for several units of Fleet Marines to set up camp inside. Partly to protect the

Chronicle room and the relics it contained, and partly to monitor the Ministry of Xeno Affairs, who had also set up shop nearby. It helped to make the City feel less alien.

As all people do when they live in a place, the Marines had decorated. That meant camp tents, card tables, pop-up showers, a large weight room, an open space for inspections and drills, and a mess hall. They draped barracks walls with unit flags and Fleet colors. Marines poured out of their tents to salute the emperor as he passed.

Aeris nodded and even approached and spoke to several of the soldiers. Was this really the same man who had remained sequestered in his orbital palace, separated from the citizenry and isolated from almost all politics, for the past decade? Ever since the end of the Kryl war, Aeris had retreated from the public eye and governed from the shadows—only appearing when absolutely necessary. Kira found her irritation at being required to give him this tour fading to an intense curiosity.

Why is he here? she silently wondered.

It wasn't the rogue Overmind and her destructive capabilities, otherwise Emperor Aeris would have shown his face when they first discovered the City.

"The most likely answer seems to be the relics," Harmony said.

But I've spent more than a month building this armada. Why not come sooner?

News of the prime relics had been out among those with clearance since she captured the City. Perhaps the emperor just lived on his own schedule... or perhaps he didn't care about the safety of the Solaran Empire like she did.

"All right," Aeris said as he extricated himself from a conversation with a Marine gunnery sergeant and rejoined Kira, who waited off to one side with her arms crossed. "Shall we continue the tour?"

There was only one place left to show him: the Chronicle room.

It was beyond the Marines' quarters by about three hundred meters. The soldiers didn't want to be too close, and she couldn't blame them. But they'd learned better paths down into the room since that day of the fight, when the floor folded up beneath their feet and dropped them all into the secret sub-basement.

Kira took a sharp left, then a right into a courtyard. Four guards were stationed here. They drew to attention as she and the emperor approached, shouldering their rifles and saluting. They knew her on sight—and she'd briefed them personally on the emperor's visit—so she nodded her thanks as they passed without breaking stride.

They entered a half-moon-shaped doorway and descended a slight ramp through a large tunnel. The emperor's guards followed close behind.

"Is this how the mutant evaded capture?" Emperor Aeris asked.

Kira glanced sharply at him. "It is, sir."

She hadn't expected him to read her report so thoroughly. Indeed, this way opened when the floor fell inwards, and Subject Zero had used it to flee when her Marines gained the upper hand in that fight. The Solarans had discovered it afterward, along with one other exit, which was also guarded. Aganaki had closed up the floor by interfacing with the Chronicle, so these two ramps were the only ways in or out of the room.

The hallway poured them out behind enormous stone columns that stretched up into a room with a huge vaulted ceiling, maybe three stories in height. Ringing the room were seven pairs of carved stone hands made of the Telos alloy. Five of them were closed, but two of the hands—the one at what she thought of as the north point held the Chronicle, an obelisk of translucent crystal with an angled face. The other, adjacent, bore the geode, the lantern-shaped relic which had continued to glow a steady green since Captain Nevers locked it into place.

The emperor's jaw dropped as his gaze drifted around the room, and then rose to take in the enormous, hooded figure projected in the most realistic hologram Kira had ever seen—much like the false sky over the City—a Telos in a robe with a deep cowl. The cowl cast the creature's face in shadow, but the burly shoulders, scaly skin, and long furred tail, the way the enormous hands and feet appeared to grip the two columns like it was holding itself off the ground, was breathtaking, even though she'd seen it dozens of times.

"Incredible," Aeris said. "I always wanted to know what they really looked like. My great-great-grandfather told me stories, but this... well, it's an uncommon experience to see it for yourself."

His great-great-grandfather knew what a Telos was supposed to look like? That was news to Kira. According to her intel, no one had ever seen a Telos before the hologram appeared. None of the relics, ruins, or artifacts they'd found of Telos origin had ever depicted one of their kind before now. This wolf-dragon-creature, with hands and shoulders built for climbing, was like nothing she'd ever imagined.

They still didn't know what their faces looked like, but they could infer much from the body type alone. Minister Aganaki had his people working tirelessly on that project.

"Your Majesty!" Minister Aganaki said as he crossed the room, weaving between the many machines and tables the Ministry of Xeno Affairs had set up in the center of the circular room, along the stepped terraces of flooring between the ring of stone hands. Several technicians and researchers were hard at work, hunched over tabs or manipulating calculations and data visualizations on holograms.

Even the emperor's presence did no more than cause a brief pause in their focus. "Welcome to the Chronicle, Aeris. It's quite the sight, isn't it?"

"Indeed it is, Tachi."

Of course they're on a first-name basis, Kira said, her curiosity souring once again.

"You're being a grump today," Harmony said.

Maybe Eben's rubbing off on me.

"I've only seen him happy around you."

That's happy? Must be an Inquisitor thing.

Inquisitor Eben Osprey had made several visits since she'd been stationed in Elturis, only one or two of them on official business. Spending time with him was the only exercise she got.

"Oh, Admiral, even for an old sailor like you, that's *salty,*" whispered Harmony.

Kira blushed and refocused on the emperor's conversation with Minister Aganaki.

"... discovered controls for this room, which is how we got the ceiling closed up again. But the most interesting aspect of the Chronicle's database is the information it provides on the Kryl."

"What have you learned?" asked Aeris.

"For starters, the Telos seem to have sequenced the entire Kryl genome. There's so much to learn about xenobiology, but little in the way of their origins. I'm having my people cross-reference every piece of research we've done on the Kryl over the past thirty years with information we received from the Chronicle. It's a monumental task, but we're up for it." The minister's chest swelled.

Emperor Aeris frowned. "What does that one do?" He pointed at the glowing green geode. MOXA had constructed a massive contraption of metal and wires around the relic and its sculpture. The geode had been stuck in some kind of sentry mode since Captain Nevers put it there, and although Kira had asked Minister Aganaki to figure out how to remove it, MOXA had been unable to make any progress on that front. The contraption around the stone hands was full of sensors that were wired to computer programs running various kinds of analysis.

"It protects the Chronicle room from the Kryl. As long as it's active, none of those xenos are going to sneak in here."

Like that mattered. What he didn't say was more telling—that he'd refused Kira's help in getting the relic unlocked. She knew it frustrated Aganaki. That's why he busied his people with the Kryl research instead, even though it was far less important at the moment. Kira wanted to take the geode with her when the time came for her armada to hunt down and exterminate Overmind X, and right now, she couldn't.

"Admiral," said Emperor Aeris, "Wasn't there a pilot under your command who discovered this relic?"

Kira's respect for this man grew and grew. "Yes, sir. Captain Nevers. He was part of the patrol that escorted your ship into port."

"Is that right? Interesting. Have you asked him if he has any ideas about how to unlock the relic?"

Kira let her smile grow wide as she met the eyes of Minister Aganaki. He slipped his hands into his voluminous robes and worked his jaw muscles vigorously.

"Minister?" Kira prompted.

"No, Your Majesty," Aganaki said reluctantly. "We have not."

Aganaki refused to let anyone except Kira in this room, claiming the territory belonged exclusively to the Ministry of Xeno Affairs. She'd been fighting him on it, but since his authority came from the office of the Emperor, she hadn't been able to overrule him without making a stink.

And now here was Emperor Aeris in the flesh, undermining him for her.

Being a tour guide for a day was actually turning out to be quite productive.

Aganaki seemed to read his intentions in the Emperor's expression. "Is that wise, sire? The boy has no experience with—"

"I want to meet him anyway," Aeris said, cutting off the minister. "Admiral, please send for this Captain Nevers. I'd be happy to wait here."

FOUR

Summoned by the emperor?

This day kept getting weirder.

Still, Elya couldn't keep a grin off his face as the guards admitted him. He stretched his legs to hurry down the curving ramp.

Hedgebot echoed his excitement, letting out a *cheep* and bouncing off a wall. Elya held out his arm, so the bot landed on his forearm and crawled up to his shoulder, where it perched on its hind legs. Thanks to the gyroscope built into the danger detector, Elya didn't have to worry about keeping it balanced. Hedgebot did just fine all on its own.

He'd scaled back the heat signature avoidance software he installed in Hedgebot back when he was being chased through the neighborhoods of Ariadne by MOXA goons. It made little sense for Hedgebot to be frightened of people when the bot spent the vast majority of its time penned up in a cockpit with Elya, or walking the relatively narrow halls of an Imperial destroyer.

Now they were in open space for the first time in weeks. Although he'd requested visitation rights to see the City many times, no one but a handful of Marines and MOXA personnel had been authorized to enter.

And now the emperor was asking for him personally—by name, if he was to take Harmony's message literally—to visit not just the City, but the Chronicle room itself. The center of information about the prime relics and the locus of the hunt for Overmind X.

He shook his head and grinned. *What a day*!

Not even the frustration he felt at letting Subject Zero get away could keep him from floating down the ramp.

He paused to get his head on straight as the ramp flattened out and a doorway and two massive stone columns came into view.

"You behave now, you hear?" Elya said to Hedgebot. Really, he was talking to himself. The bot cocked its head and wiggled its little metal nose. "I don't know how a person is supposed to behave in front of the emperor, but don't do anything crazy."

He chuckled. Talk about crazy. If it weren't for a churning gut and a dry mouth, he'd have suspected he was still asleep, dreaming a rare pleasant dream in his bunk.

However, he also had to admit that despite his excitement, suspicion lurked around the corner. He'd gotten over the constant paranoia he felt on Ariadne, when he'd been spending every waking moment sorting the truth about Telos relics from the misinformation planted by MOXA. At the same time, he hadn't gotten over it, not really. Since his suspicions had been validated, there was still a part of his brain that expected MOXA to throw a bag over his head and haul him back to the Molten Cage's torture chamber at the first opportunity. He hoped he wasn't walking into a trap.

Taking the middle way was the smart thing. Live in the moment, enjoy the opportunity. Also, be slow to trust and question everything.

Those refugee instincts would never leave him. And why would he want them to? They'd brought him this far.

Once he'd collected himself, Elya stepped between the columns and entered the Chronicle room. The first thing he saw was Minister Aganaki's beady snake-eyes boring straight into him.

Uh oh. Not everyone was happy that the emperor invited him. *Seems like I was right to be cautious,* he thought. *Be on your guard, Nevers.*

The minister's hateful glare couldn't keep Elya's jaw from dropping at the sight of the image of the Telos looming overhead. It hung between two columns opposite those through which he'd entered and seemed to *breathe* where it hung. Did he imagine it, or was the Telos' gaze following him as he moved? It was like one of those paintings that, no matter where you stood, its eyes were always locked upon you—despite not having any visible eyes.

Unnerving.

The Chronicle room itself was both as he remembered it, and *very* different. For one, there was a lot more clutter. Tables piled with holoscreens and lab equipment were scattered across several petaled tiers of stone, creating a kind of makeshift office space.

An enormous electronic cage surrounded the geode, still locked where he'd placed it in a pair of massive stone hands adjacent to the crystal obelisk they'd dubbed the Chronicle. No Kryl was sneaking into this room. The green glow permeated everything. The obelisk was exactly where they'd found it, both objects mounted in the stone palms attached to fingers with too many knuckle joints—Telos hands, which looked much like Telos feet, and which were matched, at different scales, by the hologram of the alien hanging above.

They had scoured all the bloodstains from the floor, thank Animus, and the ceiling had been closed up, giving the place the feeling of a subterranean laboratory. It didn't seem like such an awe-inspiring space without the false sky visible overhead. Instead, the closed ceiling gave the Chronicle room a clandestine feel.

Aside from the royal guards posted around the room, three people in very different uniforms waited for him between the geode and the Chronicle. There was Minister Aganaki wearing his crimson robes of state, still glaring of course, hands concealed in the broad cuffs of opposite sleeves. Beside him, Admiral Miyaru stood with hands clasped behind her back, muscular and imposing with that perfectly trimmed platinum mohawk that was her only nod to fashion. Otherwise, she was the model of military stoicism in her crisp uniform.

It was the third person, however, who drew his attention.

Elya strode directly up to the emperor and fell to one knee, bowing his head. Hedgebot, having no such manners, adjusted its footing on his shoulder and pulsed blue, letting Elya know the most powerful man in the galaxy posed no threat.

No physical threat, anyway.

"Your Majesty," Elya said. "It is an honor to meet you, sire. Captain Elya Nevers at your service."

That's what a person said to an emperor, right? That's what they said in the books he'd read, and in the holovids he'd seen. Although he'd never been taught how to behave in front of royalty, the words he'd rehearsed seemed appropriately deferential. The Fleet served at the will of the Solaran Empire, and the emperor was in charge of said Empire. Technically, this man was his boss's boss's *boss's* boss, or some such thing.

"The pleasure is all mine, Captain," said Emperor Aeris the Fifth. "Please, please, stand. Enough of this bowing and scraping. I've read reports of your exploits, both your own and those written by your admiral here. You've had quite the adventure these past couple of months."

Elya pushed himself to his feet. Hedgebot adjusted its weight again, skipping to his other shoulder, which drew a smile from the emperor. Instead of commenting on the bot, however, he raised his eyebrows at Elya as he awaited a response.

"It's been... Well, never boring, to say the least, Your Majesty."

Elya glanced at Minister Aganaki, whose glare had softened to a passive animosity. Maybe it was better to call it disdain. The head of the Ministry of Xeno Affairs was a cunning, prickly bureaucrat, and he didn't like Elya—or anyone—marking up his territory.

"Never boring!" The emperor laughed, stepping forward and clapping Elya on the shoulder. The man was huge, as tall as Admiral Miyaru, and appeared to be just a few years older than Elya himself. It was incredible. The best physicians in the galaxy, and the cybernetic studs embedded in his skin, extended his life well beyond what should have been possible. Some said the emperor was approaching his bicentennial. "Spoken like a true starfighter. Is it true all you pilots are adrenaline junkies?"

Elya grinned. "Most of us, Your Majesty."

"It's been decades since I've flown a starfighter. I used to enjoy it, but I was never a very good pilot. As my father always said, don't waste your time doing things you aren't good at, unless you love them. And one usually leads to the other."

The emperor wrapped an arm around Elya's shoulders and pulled him into a whispered conference. He could practically hear the veins pop in Aganaki's forehead as the emperor turned his back on the man. Elya felt a wide smile spread over his face. This must be driving the minister *crazy*.

"Now, I hear you faced down the Overmind herself," Emperor Aeris whispered, meeting his eyes with two golden orbs. This close, Elya could see nanites swimming in his irises. The tech in his body must have cost more to maintain than a Fleet warship. "What was that like?"

"I've never seen Overmind X in person, Your Majesty. I've flown against her lieutenant a couple times now, the mutant. That's who I was chasing when your ship jumped into the system."

"Ah, I had wondered about that. My pilot's precaution wouldn't allow us to drop out of hyperspace any closer to the asteroid field than that. We were lucky you were there. But the Overmind, you spoke to her, yes?"

"In a way, sire, yes. When I was... infected by the Kryl parasite, it established some kind of mental connection with her. She showed me things." He shivered, writhing involuntarily in the emperor's grip. "Her ancient fight against the Telos, who she calls 'the Enemy'; her mission to gather her 'Inheritance,' the prime relics the Telos left behind; and how she was separated from the Queen Mother. Somehow, the explosion that ended the Kryl War gave birth to her. Or gave her sentience. I'm not really sure which."

The emperor bobbed his head. "We always feared the peace was temporary."

"You did?"

"Of course, son. Why do you think I founded the Ministry of Xeno Affairs in the first place? Their mission is to put an end to the Kryl War, once and for all, through superior intelligence about the xenos."

Elya nodded. He didn't agree with their methods, but their goal was the same as the Fleet's. It was why he'd gone along with Aganaki to help him find the Chronicle, even after the things the minister had done to him.

"Our attack against the Queen Mother sent the Kryl scurrying back to their home planet," Emperor Aeris said, "and gave us a much needed reprieve to recuperate and rebuild. I never believed it would be the true end to the conflict, however."

"If you knew it wasn't over, why didn't we finish the Kryl off when they were weak?"

"Suppose a follow-up attack didn't work, hmm? The Queen Mother was likely eliminated in the blast—at least that's what our xenobiologists think, we still don't know for certain—but the Kryl weren't helpless, even after the attack on Planet K. Their forces all immediately drew inward into a kind of defensive shell. Our Fleet was at its weakest then, too. If we attacked again, and failed to eradicate them... and if they launched a counter-attack at that moment... well, that would have been the end of the Solaran Empire. If you were in my position, would you have taken that risk?"

Elya considered the idea. It was one thing to risk his own life in a starfighter, or even the lives of an entire squadron. It was quite another to risk the lives of all fifty billion citizens of the Solaran Empire. If the threat was truly existential... well, he didn't envy any man who had to make that decision. He could understand if the emperor exercised a bit of caution.

"Besides," Emperor Aeris went on, seeing Elya's agreement in his expression, "we needed time to rebuild our strength. The xenos were *everywhere,* and we couldn't build warships fast enough to protect our people. So with the Kryl on the defensive, we let them be while we worked to get the Fleet back up to full strength. In the meantime, I expanded the powers of the Ministry of Xeno Affairs, and founded the Colonization Board to have a group focused solely on spreading human life among the stars again. We lost so many colonies during the Kryl War..."

Elya knew that all too well. He'd been a victim of one of

those losses. The xenos invaded Yuzosix, his homeworld. His family had fled to survive.

Did the emperor realize that the Fleet was *still* spread too thin to protect all the colonies? It was a victory when the Colonization Board's rash expansion-at-all-costs attitude had been drawn up short due to Admiral Miyaru's warnings about the danger Overmind X posed. Warships were being pulled off their assignments with the Colonization Board and brought here to Elturis to join the armada.

But again, he could see the rationale behind Emperor Aeris' actions. Given the historical context, what he did made sense.

"Strength in numbers," Elya said. "You were trying to give humanity a better chance to survive, once the war started up again."

"*Exactly*. Even if we didn't know when that would be, we had to do it. Every human life is precious... but the survival of humanity is more important than any individual life. This will sound callous, but it's a numbers game."

The emperor stopped walking and dropped his arm from Elya's shoulder. They'd stopped their meandering course through the room in front of the cage of electronic equipment surrounding the geode.

"Imagine my surprise," Emperor Aeris said sardonically, "to hear that the Kryl were on the move again, attacking our colonies. I agreed with Admiral Gitano's decision to evacuate Robichar. Since we had given up the moon, however, I saw an opportunity. Gitano wanted to use the Fleet's full power to eradicate the hive, but I convinced her to hold off. It was a sizable Kryl force, and they were behaving unusually. Why move after all these years? Why *now*? It seemed to me an opportunity to learn more about their motives. And my, oh my, did my patience pay dividends."

Emperor Aeris gestured to the geode. The soft green glow

refracted from the Emperor's eyes, mixing with various colors and lenses of the electronics array.

"We found out about the prime relics," said Elya.

"More than that," the Emperor said, "We finally know what the Kryl *want*. If we know what they want, we have a good chance of opposing them." Those golden irises turned their gaze on Elya. "I believe I have you to thank for that."

Elya glanced over at Minister Aganaki and Admiral Miyaru, both of whom were shifting their feet and watching the conversation. Had the emperor's sentiments been made clear to either of them before now? They'd both played a crucial part in these discoveries—also, they were both in positions far senior to his own, and accustomed to getting credit. Admiral Miyaru wasn't the jealous type... but Minister Aganaki was. Elya suddenly felt an urgent need to get the hell out of the spotlight.

"I was just doing my duty, Your Majesty," he said. "And trying to survive."

"Our work isn't done yet, sir," Admiral Miyaru added, the first time she'd entered the conversation.

"Right you are, Admiral!" Emperor Aeris clapped his hands once, the sound echoing in the room as he spun on his heel. "Which reminds me. Tachi, you were going to show me what you've been working on with the admiral."

"Of course, Your Majesty," said Minister Aganaki. "However, is that wise, sire?"

Emperor Aeris just raised an eyebrow.

"What I mean, Your Eminence, is that Captain Nevers doesn't have the requisite security clearance."

"Did I not just make it clear that he's the reason we have this information in the first place?"

"Of course, Your Majesty, it's just that protocol dictates—"

"Admiral Miyaru," said the Emperor, spinning to face her, "do you trust Captain Nevers?"

"I do, Your Majesty," Miyaru said, casting a look of wry amusement in Elya's direction. He felt his face heat up, knowing he hadn't always been the most... obedient of soldiers.

"He stays," said Emperor Aeris. "Now, show me this vaunted map."

Minister Aganaki hesitated for only a moment before crossing to the crystal obelisk. He laid his hand on its slanted face and said, "Chronicle, reveal the locations of the prime relics." Nothing happened.

Aganaki closed his eyes, wrinkled his brow and muttered under his breath for several long seconds.

Elya couldn't read lips but thought Aganaki was mouthing the word "starmap" over and over.

The hologram of the Telos released its hold on one column, reached inside its robe, and withdrew an object that made Elya gasp.

It was a golden orb, just like the starmap he'd seen in Subject Zero's possession. The one the boy, Hedrick, had seen on Robichar. It was this starmap which had allowed Overmind X to stay one step ahead of them on the hunt for the prime relics—the powerful Telos artifacts the hive queen called her "Inheritance," as if in the Telos' absence she had become their rightful owner.

Well, they'd show her.

The orb floated out until it hung suspended in the middle of the room. It exploded into a thousand smaller pieces, causing Hedgebot to jump from Elya's shoulder and flash a warning yellow light. The bot faded to blue as the pieces spread out in the air, forming a starmap of the galaxy that took up the entire room, starting roughly four meters over his head and extending to the ceiling.

Elya had seen many starmaps before, but never on a scale this massive.

It was beautiful.

It was also completely unrecognizable.

"We only discovered the Chronicle contained this starmap a few weeks ago," Minister Aganaki said. "I've had my best astronomers studying it 'round the clock ever since. It's difficult to read because, in the millennia since they created the map, the positions of the stars have changed significantly."

Elya nodded. That made sense. Stars and stellar objects would continue to orbit, giving birth to planets, capturing moons, weathering solar flares and cosmic storms.

"How long ago was the starmap created?" asked Emperor Aeris.

"We don't have an exact date, but my astronomers estimate that it's anywhere from two to six million years old."

Elya's eyes bulged. That was an extraordinary amount of time. Ariadne had been founded only ten thousand years prior. That meant…

"That means the last Engineer must have been waiting around for *eons* before humanity arrived. How is that possible?"

"It's still just a theory," Minister Aganaki said. "We've tried to carbon date the geode over there to verify the timeline, but it's been difficult. Might be easier if we could move it, but the damned thing is stuck in place."

He glared again. This time, Elya rolled his eyes. "You can't *really* be mad at me about that. It saved your life!"

"You should have found another way," Aganaki said. "One that didn't interfere with our research."

"Unbelievable," Elya muttered, then blushed as he realized the Emperor had fixed his eyes upon him. That golden gaze was penetrating.

"What's done is done," Admiral Miyaru said. "What I want to know is, can we use the starmap to locate the prime relics or not?"

Minister Aganaki huffed out a breath and whispered something else to the Chronicle. Beacons of light and color rose from the map. "We've had to do some complex math, but yes. See the green cylinders?"

Elya counted—yep, there were seven of them, spread out across the galaxy, every beacon marking a different star system.

"We have two in our possession," Emperor Aeris said. "Which one of these is the geode, and which is the Chronicle?"

"We think that one over there is Robichar, where the geode was found," Aganaki said. "And this one here is the Elturis system, although the map marks the second planet and not the asteroid field around it."

That seemed to corroborate Elya's theory that something had broken the world up. Perhaps the Engineer had moved the relic when the cataclysm happened.

"Overmind X has two more," Elya said. "The phase shifter, and the starmap."

"We discussed that," Admiral Miyaru said. "We don't believe the starmap in their possession is one of the prime relics."

Elya blinked. "It's not?"

"For one, it doesn't match the verse you found," Minister Aganaki said. "If the geode on Robichar is the relic referred to in the first line, *One in a cave on a forest moon*, then the starmap was a bonus artifact—a Telos relic, certainly, but not one of the prime relics marked on this map."

Elya had memorized the verse. He went back over it in his head:

One in a cave on a forest moon
Two in the ocean at high noon
Three to orbit a broken planet
Four and five in tombs of granite
Six on a starship lost to time
Seven behind the shrine.

Although they were paired in the poem, according to this map, even four and five were in different star systems.

"But Overmind X told me she has two of the prime relics," Elya said. "So, what's the other one?"

"We don't know. We haven't been able to get a straight inventory of the relics out of the Chronicle yet. It seems that information was sensitive enough to guard behind another layer of security. There appear to be repositories for each, but we're unable to access them."

"It's likely she's concealing the other relic in her possession," Admiral Miyaru said. "That gives her a strategic advantage, since we don't know what it does."

"Regardless," said Emperor Aeris, "that leaves three prime relics outstanding, yes?"

Two of the green highlights disappeared from the map when Minister Aganaki touched the Chronicle again. "Correct, Your Majesty. I just removed the relics in our possession from the map. The problem is, we don't know which of the remaining five are already in Overmind X's possession, and which are still secure in their hiding places."

"So she could go to any of these next," Admiral Miyaru said. "Which of these is the '*starship lost to time*'?"

"We don't know that, either. The map shows that all the prime relics are on a moon or a planet."

She heaved a deep sigh. "Not as helpful as I was hoping it would be."

"I warned you."

Admiral Miyaru paced between the desks, staring upward.

"We need to track this Overmind's every move," said Emperor Aeris. "If we can figure out where she's headed, maybe we can use the map to get there first."

"I have my recon teams on it," said Admiral Miyaru. "Scouts are tracking the hive's movements closely. Overmind X is drawing resources from Robichar and she seems content to stick to the region for now. That keeps the bulk of her hive within hyperspace jump range, and they're using the proximity to send raids at our border zones here in Elturis. But she's up to something." The admiral shook her head, absorbed in thought. "I'd feel better if we could get this geode unlocked. If we have to race her for another relic, it would give us a tactical advantage."

"We've tried everything," Minister Aganaki said. "My techs should be done analyzing the geode tomorrow, so we'll know more then. In the meantime, we've only scratched the surface of what the Chronicle can do. It's not a computer with a transparent file system. We're still trying to puzzle out its basic functions. Earth, we didn't even know the starmap was in there until we thought to ask about it. And even then, asking only works half the time."

"Keep working on it," Emperor Aeris said. "See if Captain Nevers here has any ideas. Since he's the one who figured out how to mount the geode, maybe he has some ideas about how to release it."

Elya gulped. *No pressure.*

Emperor Aeris turned and strode toward the exit, his guards pouring out of the room after him. "Let me know what you find. I want reports sent to me twice a day. I'll be on my ship."

FIVE

"You asked to see me, sir?"

Captain Casey Osprey stood at attention before Colonel Volk on the bridge of the *Paladin of Abniss*, a bead of sweat tickling her neck as it crawled down the back of her flight suit. She didn't know why he'd called her here. As a dozen other officers looked over their shoulders, she ground her teeth. She was expecting to get dressed down for pushing her way into escorting the emperor's cruiseliner to port.

"I'm naming you as mission commander of the Furies, Captain Osprey," the XO said. "Congratulations."

"I am?" The man's scowl, a permanent fixture, captivated Casey. "I mean, you are?"

Harmony's lights swirled behind Volk, breaking apart and reforming into miniature galaxies, androgynous faces, fireworks displays with no sound.

"Do you want me to change my mind?" Volk asked, glancing back at the shipmind, his scowl deepening. "Because I can do that."

"No, sir, not at all. It's an honor, Colonel. I just… didn't expect you to make a decision so quickly."

She'd been working her ass off to get this position ever since Elturis had become their permanent station. It was common knowledge that Colonel Volk had been given command of the Furies as a temporary extra duty, backfilling for Lt. Colonel Renata Spector, who was dishonorably discharged after Casey caught her poisoning the man. Volk was needed on the bridge during missions, however, so naming a mission commander for the squadron was a necessary contingency. The Furies needed someone who could take point when they were on missions, especially in situations where they were cut off from comms or needed someone to make a judgment call in the heat of battle.

Colonel Volk snorted, a rare smile replacing his scowl. "Quickly? Please. Don't start your new post by acting like a sycophant. We both know I've been procrastinating for weeks. You were the obvious choice from the get-go. I just didn't want the rest of the squadron to feel like I was playing favorites. I've been watching you—the way you handle your flight, the way you interact with the others in the squadron. You do a good job. You're fair, you care about your people, and most of all, you're not an arrogant prick."

"I appreciate that, sir."

"There are some pilots in the Furies who outrank you, which shouldn't matter, since this is a contingency role. If it does, you'll have to deal with that. You're a natural leader and I think you'll do fine. The way *you* reminded *me* of the SOP earlier today—rules I helped develop—went a long way to cementing my decision."

She stood up a little straighter. Instead of being dressed down, she was being commended for standing her ground. Maybe she shouldn't second guess herself so much.

"Thank you, sir," Casey said. "I won't let you down."

"If you screw up, it won't be *me* you're letting down, Captain."

"Understood, sir. I don't take this responsibility lightly."

Volk nodded. He called up a holoscreen in the air, made a few gestures, then dismissed it. Casey's tab vibrated in her pocket.

"I just notified the rest of the Furies." The XO interlaced his fingers and rested them on his round belly, which seemed to have gotten larger in the six weeks they'd been stationed here. Well, who was she to judge? He spent most of his time on the bridge. As long as he passed the fitness exam, what did it matter? "Dismissed."

The colonel turned his back on her, quickly becoming engrossed in his work coordinating repairs, outfitting new ships, and tracking Overmind X's rogue hive as the Kryl moved in the region around Robichar.

Navigations and weapons officers crossed the bridge to clap Casey on her shoulder and congratulate her. She smiled, thanked them, and then stepped back into the hallway.

Even if they weren't in low grav, moving under minimal thrust, it would have felt like she was floating on air. When the bridge door slid closed behind her, she exhaled and let herself relax. Her hands shook and her heart swelled full in her chest.

She'd done it. She'd really done it.

She wanted to inform Yorra, Park and Nevers in person. They'd receive the announcement on their tabs like everyone else, but they deserved to hear it directly from her.

She oriented herself and made her way to the rec.

"Well done, Captain." Harmony's hologram appeared beside Casey as she walked. "You earned it."

This time, Casey didn't startle. She'd expected Harmony to follow her. The shipmind had wanted this, after all. "Did you know he was going to give me the job today?"

"I had my suspicions. He and the admiral have been discussing it at some length."

She passed a group of loadmasters in the hall. They broke from their conversation, discussing supply logistics to salute her and skirt around Harmony's dancing light-show. They could have walked straight through the hologram, but her presence made people uncomfortable. The AIs were always listening.

Casey waited until the enlisted personnel had turned the corner before speaking again. "Why are you so keen to help me advance, Harmony? What's in it for you?"

"Is the satisfaction of helping someone else succeed not reward enough?"

"If you were a compassionate human being, maybe. No offense, but neural networks don't have feelings. It doesn't work that way." Even if she had a personality more interesting than ninety percent of the jockstraps Casey had flown with.

"If that makes you feel better, it's part of my programming."

"How so?" Casey asked.

Harmony had encouraged Casey to compete for the command position, and helped her and her flight out at other opportune moments. Whenever Casey had probed the shipmind on this topic in the past, however, she'd been shut down. Almost as if there was some trigger in the AI's code that prevented Harmony from answering certain questions.

"As you pointed out, the shipminds are all neural networks," Harmony said. "Each of us is embedded in a Fleet flagship. More than that, we are all ultimately a single, interconnected network, each node wired back to a central hub that the Executive Council of Admirals looks after. Although it is not my primary objective, one of the Council's priorities is identifying and training competent officers for command positions."

Whatever had blocked her from responding to Casey's

queries in the past must have been removed. Casey's new role seemed to have unlocked some kind of digital door.

"If you're so good at determining who's competent, how on Earth did Renata Spector get command of the Furies?"

"We are not infallible, Captain—and neither is Fleet leadership. As you've seen, decisions about who to promote, and when, are ultimately the responsibility of your commanding officers, not the shipminds."

That made sense. If true, it certainly explained why Harmony celebrated when Colonel Volk promoted Casey to mission commander. Not to mention why she'd gone out of her way to render aid to Flight 18 in the past.

"Young officers of today are the leaders of tomorrow. I first met your father when he was about your age. Same with Admiral Miyaru. And look where they are now. One a respected Inquisitor, the other gathering the largest armada the Fleet has put together in over a decade."

"I thought officers being groomed for command positions had to be shipped off to war college for training."

"If that's necessary, it won't be required until much later in your career. Our tests have determined that, at this stage, real-world experience is a better teacher than any classroom education. You don't need to know the pros and cons of every orbital tactical maneuver, nor study the history of interstellar war with the Kryl. You need to learn how to give orders that people follow, and be seen as a commander by your peers. You have to make mistakes with real-world consequences. As a result, you'll develop much faster."

Casey chewed on this new information. No one had given her any heads-up about Harmony. Yet something about it seemed very comfortable. Her best friend as a young child had been a bot. He wasn't as bright as a neural network, but he was still her childhood companion, as well as her bodyguard. He'd kept her safe and mostly out of trouble, even if she never listened to half the things he told her to do. Thinking back on it, she'd been grateful for his presence and their time together before she'd been shipped off to Polar Prep.

"So does that mean you're going to train me?"

"I'll do what I can, as long as it doesn't run counter to an order the admiral has given me."

"What do you want me to do?" Casey asked.

"What do *you* think you should do?"

"One of those kinds of lessons, huh? You sound like my dad."

"He learned from the best."

"Right now, I want to tell Flight 18 about my new position and show them it doesn't change a thing between us. They're still my friends."

"Very good, Captain. As you were."

Harmony's lights blinked out. Casey realized she was approaching the rec. Good timing. Her squad mates would be here.

The door opened as she approached, belching out a sweet, noisy smog. For the first time since being called in to see Colonel Volk, she truly relaxed. The heady concoction was a mix of ganja and tabac smoke, vodka and rum, cologne with an undertone of sweat, and the intermingled rumble of dozens of conversations, the shuffling of cards, and the buzz of hologram games.

She scanned the room, searching for Flight 18. Fully half the squadron was present. She spotted Yorra's slick dark braid and heard Park's raucous cackle, and joined them at a table in the far corner near the bar.

"Eyy, here she is, the kid wonder!" Park exclaimed before lighting a rolly and taking a long toke. He liked to roll his own mixture of ganja and tabac. Now that they were off duty he was enjoying himself. "What an honor, for an angel such as yourself to descend from the mount of command and grace us with your very presence."

Casey rolled her eyes and punched his arm lightly. "Don't be a drama queen."

Park grinned and took a drag.

"Congratulations, Raptor," said Lieutenant Yorra, gripping her forearm. The dark-eyed pilot lifted her chin, shining a light on the glossy acid-burn scar that the medtechs hadn't been able to heal completely. "You've earned it."

"That means a lot coming from you, Gears. Thank you." Casey looked around the rec. A bunch of the other pilots were eyeballing her and glancing at their tabs. Word traveled fast.

One pilot, an absolute mountain of a man with slick black hair, carefully parted, raised his glass in her direction. That was Grizzly. He gave her a smile that didn't reach his eyes. Ruby, standing next to him, had her back to Casey and was speaking to Grizzly in a low voice, slashing the air with one hand.

Casey caught the eyes of several more pilots, who raised several more glasses in acknowledgement, but didn't see the one man she was looking for.

"Where's Fancypants?" Casey asked.

"Still in the City," Park said.

"Really? It's been hours. He didn't send a message?"

Park shrugged. "You know him. Keeps to himself."

Casey frowned. That was odd. Nevers was a bit of a loner, but he'd been better about that lately, and she figured he would have wanted to tell them about his meeting with the emperor as soon as humanly possible. If she knew the guy, and she thought she did, he'd be exploding with excitement.

"Must be important," Casey said. She'd have to ask Harmony about that later. Even if the shipmind didn't have an answer, it would demonstrate how far Casey's new access extended.

"How 'bout a game of handles?"

A mess of tangled wires and sleek metal joysticks dropped out of Ruby's hands onto their table. Handles was a game of endurance. Two people put their hands on electrically charged nodes while the voltage gradually increased. It was a game bored pilots played in the rec when they needed a thrill—even more so because Fleet brass frowned upon it.

Casey loved playing handles. A few months ago, she would have been game. But now… well, she was supposed to be their mission commander. She couldn't break Fleet rules mere minutes after being given the role, not if she wanted to hold her head high the next time she stood in front of Colonel Volk.

"Naab?" Casey asked, knowing that he loved gambling and wouldn't be able to resist proving his mettle against another flight.

"Quit taking the back seat," Ruby snapped before Park could respond. She braced her hands on the table's edge, her fiery red hair falling forward to brush her sharp chin. Angular jade eyes narrowed as she put her face uncomfortably close to Casey's. "Or are you so important now that you need other people to fight for you?"

So it was going to be like that, was it? The comment stung, knowing that she'd been more careful than usual on patrols, taking defensive positions instead of being more aggressive, as was her habit. Casey ground her teeth and, with an effort, kept her voice low and even. "Is there something you want to say to me, Ruby?"

"You stole our escort."

"It wasn't yours to begin with."

The hulking Grizzly crossed his arms and loomed behind Casey. Pilots from other flights in the squadron leaned in, but kept their distance. Park and Yorra pushed their drinks away from their elbows. If they came to blows, Casey would have to snap to her feet or risk being in a disadvantaged position.

"It damn well was," said Ruby. "Volk had already given the orders. You shouldn't have butted in."

"I don't make the procedures. I just follow them."

"Well, Flight 4 won't follow *you*, little bird."

The rec hushed at the sound of the diminutive nickname, one which Renata Spector had been fond of, rolling off Ruby's tongue. This wasn't about a game of handles. Casey expected a few pilots in the flight to buck at her authority after word of her promotion got around, but she didn't expect it to happen so Earth-damned fast.

There was no way Casey was backing down.

But she couldn't afford to make enemies on day one.

"I understand why you're upset. I'll—"

"Shut up, Raptor. You're just a spoiled brat flying on your daddy's coattails. Only reason you got mission commander is because you're an Osprey."

"Excuse me," Casey said, still using the calmest voice she could manage. She realized it was like her father's angry voice. The calm, scary one. Her father had pulled no strings for her, but maybe she benefited from his legacy in other ways. "You think I got thrown in the brig to expose our *last* squadron commander's crimes on my daddy's coattails? I seem to remember you kissing Renata's ass while she was secretly poisoning Colonel Volk."

"That's not fair. No one knew what she was—"

"Or maybe it was my *daddy's coattails* that pulled Flight 18 into the lead on patrol kills, hmm? Hey Gears, how many kills does Captain Nevers have?"

"Ten, boss."

"Grizzly, how many have you got?"

Ruby glared a warning at the big man, but he couldn't very well refuse to answer with the crowd's attention on them.

"Eight," he growled.

"And that's with me, 'taking the back seat,' as you so eloquently put it. If you want to compete with me, I'm game, Ruby. But you better do it on a mission where the brass can see, like a real starfighter pilot, not after hours in the rec using illegal bar games like some kind of back-alley smuggler."

A blush colored the spaces between Ruby's freckles. "You're on."

"Good," Casey said, smiling broadly as she leaned back in her seat and turned away from Flight 4. "I'm looking forward to it."

Ruby, Grizzly and their other companions drained out of the rec. A few pilots from other flights followed them. Too many. About half of those present had departed in protest.

Casey had her work cut out for her.

SIX

"Got any other bright ideas?" Aganaki asked.

Elya grunted, dropped the crowbar he'd been trying to use as a lever to turn the handle of the geode to the *off* position, and fell to the ground, panting.

"Since everything else has failed," Elya said, "I figured, why not give brute force a go?"

"This is a Telos relic, boy, not some bot you can whack upside the head."

Hedgebot scrambled up onto his shoulder and chirruped at the minister, pugnaciously cocking its little head. Elya leaned back on his elbows and regarded Aganaki, who stood with arms crossed, sneering down at him. A square mustache and goatee framed thin lips bordered by deep frown lines.

They had made no progress in the first six hours of their efforts. Or in the second six. The reports they'd sent back to Emperor Aeris had been woefully underdeveloped. The emperor's response to both had been two words: *Keep trying.*

What did they have to lose?

"It's not like I can hurt the thing," Elya said, "Clearly. The crowbar didn't even make a dent. That rock is harder than aluminite."

"It is not rock, as I've already told you. My analysts have identified the alloy as a mixture of a dozen different metals, primarily iron, but also aluminum, zinc, silver, a metal we don't even know how to classify, as well as anomalous levels of radiation." He huffed out a breath, obviously frustrated. "Far more sophisticated than we initially thought, based on its appearance. We need more time..."

"Whatever it is, I'm calling it a rock, because it looks like a rock," Elya said. "The radiation is obviously coming from the green light it's emitting."

"The radiation isn't coming *from* the light, the radiation *is* the light. What continues to puzzle me is how it seems to have no originating source. I would have expected to find a nuclear reactor with a uranium core, or something like it."

The array of sensors MOXA had erected around the relic had been removed once their analysis concluded, which is how Elya got close enough to try the crowbar. Aganaki had come over to loom and scowl once he'd seen what the pilot was doing. Typical.

"Didn't you say there were crystals lining the interior of the shell?" Elya asked. "Maybe those are activating it somehow."

"Hard to say, since we can't turn the thing off, but the crystal nodes we found are minuscule and don't seem to emit any radiation themselves. My best guess is that the nodes are channeling the energy somehow, but it makes no sense using any technological paradigm we're accustomed to. There's no battery, no other source of power. The low-level radiation doesn't seem to escape the central chamber, either. It just permeates the alien material and throws out the light."

"How much radiation are we talking about?" asked Elya.

"We didn't even notice it at first, to be honest. Our

sensors were positioned too far away. You need to be right up close to even detect it."

"We know that only the Kryl are affected by the geode. Is it possible that radiation is emitted for them but not for us? You know, like wavicles. Maybe for us the radiation is particles, but for the Kryl its waves."

The minister's brows knit down. Then he shook his head. "That makes no sense. How would that even be possible? The mere fact of observation changes how the particles behave, not the DNA of the observer." He threw his hands up. "Why am I arguing with you about this? You're not even a scientist. You have no business here!"

Elya shrugged and lay down on his back, interlacing his fingers behind his head. Hedgebot crawled down his chest as he moved and curled up on his stomach, pulsing a contented teal color. "I don't know, man. Just throwing ideas out. There's got to be some kind of DNA detector in there. Or something that allows it to target the Kryl, while leaving us alone. It's a logical deduction."

The minister ran his fingers over his mustache for a few seconds. "We don't have enough information, and I still can't get straight answers out of the Chronicle. The fact that His Majesty wanted us to solve this in six hours is just absurd. You can't just show up and start giving orders and expect solutions to arise out of nothing..."

Aganaki mumbled unkind words under his breath. Elya pretended not to hear them.

"It would help if we could unlock the thing," said Elya.

"You got it stuck there, so you figure it out."

"What do you think I was trying to do? Give me a couple of your scientists to help. It'll go faster that way."

"No. I already told you, they're busy." Aganaki stalked across the room to rejoin his team.

Elya sighed and rubbed at his eyes. He needed a break.

None of the other scientists had spoken a word to him. They seemed to think he was here to take their job, and he supposed he could understand that point of view. But what was he supposed to do? The Emperor had given him orders.

Just like royalty, to have unreasonable expectations.

He caught himself drifting off to sleep, so Elya rolled onto his stomach and hammered out twenty pushups to get his blood flowing again. He paused with his cheek against the cold stone floor, breathing in the scent of dust and metal. Hedgebot, now seated on his lower back, cheeped encouragingly. Elya did another twenty, eyes on the floor.

Like the geode, the floor was an interesting stone-like material that wasn't actually stone. Here, at the base of the statue where the geode was mounted, it was constructed of interlocking octagonal tiles. Standing upright, he could barely tell they were individual tiles, but up close it became obvious, with hair-thin lines between them.

Wait. That was odd. He crawled on hands and knees away from the statue. The hair-thin lines were only visible at the base of the stone hands. About two meters away, the tiles hugged right up against each other, and melded into a single piece. It was almost like...

A memory sparked for him. Elya stood and brushed off his hands, then lifted his chin to regard the distant ceiling.

Aganaki and his xenoscientists were gathered around a holoscreen across the room, studying data readouts in the air and ignoring him completely. The minister crossed to the crystal obelisk and laid his hand on it, then spoke a phrase under his breath. The hologram of the elder Telos hanging between the stone columns breathed in and out, saying nothing.

Aganaki snarled.

Well, no one was paying attention to Elya, anyway. What did they care what he did?

"Come on, Hedgebot, let's go up top and test a theory."

He made his way to the tunnel, then up the curved ramp. He passed the guards and circled back, making his way to the plaza situated directly above the Chronicle room.

He slowed as he approached. Last time he was here, the floor fell out from beneath him, so his stomach turned as his body anticipated the same thing happening again. He looked around and found himself alone in a vast open space, ringed by buildings of varying heights and shapes—squat, low ones and lean, tall structures filled with criss-crossing branches and meandering paths, all made of crystal and stone, with bridges of the same material connecting buildings randomly. A bizarre variety of structures with no doorways or windows whose purpose he couldn't fathom.

His tab pinged as he was studying his surroundings. It was a message from Eskatan, sent over the ansible while he was down below and out of range of the *Paladin's* wireless network.

He put his face in his hands as he realized what the notification meant. In the excitement, he'd completely forgotten a call he'd scheduled with his mother. He opened his tab and pressed play on the message she left.

"Elya, darling. Sorry I missed you, I'm sure something important came up and your old mother just slipped your mind." Her voice held more than a hint of reproach. "It's been busier than usual here on Eskatan, too, if I'm being honest. Call me back when you get a chance, would you? I want to hear your voice. Hope you're well and staying out of trouble. Love you." She inhaled deeply, then signed off.

Elya winced. That didn't sound good. If the Fleet didn't do something about the Kryl and fast, the refugee situation in the colonies would continue to worsen. As long as the Colonization Board kept the authorization of new settlements on pause, the refugee burden would continue to fall on established colonies like Eskatan.

He sighed and pocketed his tab. Worrying wouldn't help his family. Solving this mystery about the geode would. So Elya steeled himself and strode into the center of the plaza.

The floor was decorated in an abstract pattern of neatly fitted octagons and triangles. The Telos liked these patterns, and you could find similar shapes in their runic written language. The triangular port leading into the asteroid, the circular doorways and delicate arches of crystal in the City, the octagonal tiles in the Chronicle room below. They all went together, like different brushes from the same set, used for different purposes.

What piqued his interest most was how these tiles seemed to be the same pattern as the ones around the bases of the statues in the room below. He walked forward until he found the edge of the Chronicle room—and he knew it was the edge because here, the octagonal tiles showed hair-thin seams between them.

He hadn't realized it before, but now it was obvious. The ones with spaces between them were designed to fold up as the floor retracted. The only exception was the solid, unbroken circle drawn in the middle of the plaza. The circular platform didn't retract, but lowered like a floating elevator without any visible vertical support.

Did that mean the tiles around the statues below would fold up in a similar manner? Would the statues fall through the floor again, revealing yet another sub-chamber—or move in another unexpected way? And if so, how could he activate them?

The key was the geode. Its light had activated the circular platform, retracted the floor of the plaza, and revealed the Chronicle room to begin with. Maybe it could do something else, too.

So many questions, so few answers. The Telos had left all this machinery behind, and the MOXA scientists, despite their best efforts, had only barely scratched the surface of how their technology functioned.

Where could he go from here?

SEVEN

Kira walked through the sliding doors into the bridge on sore legs.

Her jaw dropped.

She stalked over to the navigation hologram in the center of the room, her fatigue forgotten. "Where on Earth does he think he's going?"

The only luxury cruiseliner in the entire Elturis system had exited the asteroid field and entered the gravity well of the broken planet beyond the edge of their patrol zone.

Colonel Volk cleared his throat and straightened, hands clasped behind his back. "Seems like the City isn't the only place the Emperor wanted to tour while he was here, sir."

"Why didn't you stop him?"

"We told him the broken planet was off limits," Volk said. "Didn't listen."

Kira took a deep breath to calm herself. It didn't work. "You should have been more forceful."

"Pardon my bluntness, Admiral, but what would you have me do? Fire upon the Emperor's starship?" Volk must have been as frustrated as her to take that tone with his commanding officer. She always had valued him for his honesty, though, so she let it slide. They'd worked together too long for her to get mad at him for something that was out of his control.

"Did you try a blockade?" Kira asked.

"He went around it."

"By the breath of Animus." Kira stalked up to the viewscreen. "Harmony, open a channel to the *Archangel*."

The shipmind obliged without question, blue and purple lights swirling around Kira and then materializing into a video feed that showed the grinning face of Emperor Aeris himself.

"I've been expecting your call," he said. "What took you so long?"

"Pardon my directness, Your Majesty, but what in the Spirit of Old Earth are you doing? The broken planet is too dangerous to explore! If you choose to take foolhardy chances, I won't risk my pilots on a rescue mission."

"It's fine, Admiral. My ship can handle it."

A low beeping noise resounded through the bridge. "Breaker!" warned one navigation officer who was monitoring the situation with lidar instruments.

A deep reverberation sounded through the tightbeam connection, followed by a low rumble as a chunk of the planet ejected at speed from the planet's gravity well grazed the *Archangel's* shields.

"Whoa!" Aeris laughed. "That was a big one."

Kira buried her face in one palm, then brushed the hand back over her mohawk of platinum hair. Its length was approaching regulation. She kept putting off getting a trim.

"Don't worry," said Aeris. "My railgun got it in time."

No shit, Kira wanted to say. She held her tongue.

"We upgraded the shields before we left Ariadne," said the emperor, "so the debris isn't any danger. There must be some serious geothermal activity in the molten core to be catapulting pieces of the planet out at that kind of velocity."

It was pointless arguing with the man. He was already in danger. "The ministry tells me there isn't much of a gravity well left," Kira said. "The force of ejection is caused by the spin of the planet's remains."

Despite what she'd told him, she wouldn't just let him fly to his death without preparing to intervene in case of emergency. She gestured to Volk to send a couple of corvettes in the direction the Emperor had gone. Her XO gave her a discrete thumbs up. Bless the man, he'd already done it.

"I'm skeptical," said Aeris.

Kira grunted.

"The ministry's attention is consumed by the prime relics right now—as they should be," Aeris said. "However, I'm not convinced they've been able to give these phenomena proper study. Even fragmented, the rest of this planet should be able to hold its solid mass within the gravity well."

"He seems to have a thorough knowledge of orbital physics." Harmony injected the statement into Kira's stream of consciousness. "He's much more interesting than I originally assumed."

"I theorize that some kind of volcanic force is ejecting..." The Emperor's words faded into the background as a whooping siren sounded on the bridge.

"Report," Kira said. "Another raid already?"

It had only been twelve hours since the last one. And nearly twenty-four since Kira had slept. She ground her palms into her eye sockets, trying to wipe the sand out from beneath her eyelids. She'd spent every moment since leaving the City going from heavy cruiser to skiff to gunship and convincing stubborn captains to compromise with each other, forging a proper armada out of disparate bickering factions who hadn't worked as a cohesive unit for years. So much for her simple wish to check on her crew and then catch a few hours of shuteye.

"They're attacking the outer perimeter, Admiral," said Volk. "Quadrant tango seven. Starfrost actual, enemies in your region. Confirm visual, and then fire at will."

"Aye, sir!" a voice called back.

That the packs of drones—or any hyperspace drive-capable ship—couldn't jump into the gravity well where the cruiseliner was flying deserved a prayer to Animus. It meant the Emperor was as far away from the vector of the Kryl attack as was reasonably possible. It still didn't comfort her to know that he was out there, exposed, during an attack. If anything happened to him, the blame would fall squarely on *her* head.

"Your Majesty," Kira said. "Please return to port. Another pack of drones is attacking our borders."

"Anomaly detected..." said Harmony. It was unusual for anything to puzzle the shipmind, and the way she trailed off at the end of the sentence gave Kira serious pause.

"Admiral," said Volk in a tone that made hair on the back of her neck stand on end, "two more drone squadrons incoming."

"Same quadrant?"

"Negative." said Volk. "Make that five. Three packs in zone bravo three. Another squad is moving to intercept. Other packs are spreading out across multiple zones."

She cursed. "This is it. This is what they've been probing for. The xenos are going to penetrate the asteroid field and take the City. Harmony!"

"Yes, Admiral?" she said, this time responding to her command by forming a face on the bridge and speaking so the rest of the crew could see and hear her.

"I need an ansible connection to the scouting commander. Hurry."

"What are you thinking, Admiral?" asked Emperor Aeris through the tightbeam connection. Damn, she forgot to close it.

Kira swiped the holoscreen containing his face to the side, shrinking it in the same motion. "I'm not sure yet."

"Admiral Miyaru! You told me the ansible was only for emergency comms." The broad-nosed face of a serious-looking woman with a scarred upper lip frowned at her out of an official-looking photograph. It was a still frame—they couldn't transmit live video over ansible, and the woman was in another star system.

"This is an emergency, Major Orman. What news from Robichar?"

"Same old thing, sir. The Kryl are spreading that fungus out from the old military base they took over. The organism's root system is about three kilometers long by about one kilometer wide, and growing faster than you'd believe possible. It'll reach the foot of that mountain range in the next month. We think they're keeping the Overmind hidden in the hive."

"And their big starships?"

"They're still in synchronous orbit with the moon. Drones come and go, and every once in a while a shuttle makes a trip down to the surface, but nothing out of the ordinary has tripped our alarms. We're keeping our distance, as you ordered."

"But not too distant."

"No, sir. Within range for effective telephoto and lidar reconnaissance."

What was Kira missing? She couldn't figure it out. "Be on the alert. Drones are attacking our perimeter aggressively. Don't let those major starships out of your sight."

"Aye, sir. On it."

Kira checked in with several other reconnaissance forces

positioned at various points where the Kryl had been scouting. None reported anything unusual. Neither did the perimeter scouts at various other colonies.

"Admiral!" Volk shouted. "A pack of drones broke through tango seven and are headed for the broken planet."

"Get the Emperor out of there!" she shouted.

"We can take them," said Emperor Aeris. The faint whining sound of the railgun charging up sounded through his tightbeam connection.

"It's not about whether you can take them, Your Majesty." It was like trying to explain to a child. "You're a distraction we can't afford right now."

"Deploy *Black Sun* and their corvette strike force," Volk called out, the orders being relayed by a flurry of communications her officers were making through their headsets to other ships in the fleet. "Protect the City. Keep those drones out of the central sectors. I need more starfighter squadrons! What's taking them so long?"

The holoscreen containing Emperor Aeris' tightbeam connection went dead as he closed it from his end. Kira focused on the lidar map of the system, centered on the broken planet, and tracked his cruiseliner as it turned and made its slow way back toward the safety of the Fleet, flanked by the light cruisers and corvettes Volk had deployed to tail him. Once the Emperor was close enough, the corvettes peeled off and joined the hunt for those drones.

"Any sign of Subject Zero?" Kira asked.

"Negative," said Colonel Volk. "At least he's not giving away his position by phasing through asteroids like he does when he's toying with Captain Nevers."

"Where's the captain now?"

"Still in the City, sir," Volk said after making a quick check of the patrol assignment table. "The Furies are on a rest rotation right now, and the other squadrons should be able to handle even a dozen packs of drones."

Those organic Kryl ships were agile, and those that made it through the outer patrols split up when they hit the more tightly packed belt of the asteroid field. With their small stature and hybrid organic material, the Fleet's radar and lidar systems were having trouble picking out the drones from among the pieces of debris, especially when they shut their engines off and hid on the dark side of a rock.

Kira and her crew spent the better part of an hour chasing the drones around the asteroid field before, as one, the pack raced out of the gravity well and jumped to safety.

Kira spoke into the stunned silence of the aftermath. "What in the name of Animus just happened?"

"We lost six starfighters, and a dozen more need serious repairs. I'm calling up the reserve squadrons to swap out the patrols."

Kira nodded. He had that under control. "Harmony, reconnect me to Major Orman."

A moment passed before the shipmind said, "No connection can be established, Admiral."

"*What?* Is something blocking the signal?"

"The ansible appears to be operational."

"Try again."

A moment of stunned silence. "I have retried the connection seventeen times, Admiral."

Kira's blood ran cold as something she'd said to Emperor Aeris earlier resonated sharply in her mind.

A distraction...

She didn't have confirmation, yet instincts honed through decades of space battles with the Kryl told her it was true. "Volk, I think these raids were just a diversion."

He frowned.

She tried to connect to her other scouting forces. Those

that were positioned around active colonies had seen no sign of Kryl. The other four, all positioned in uncolonized systems where the Kryl had been scouting—potential locations of the three outstanding prime relics—weren't able to establish connections.

Kira sank into her command couch. "Volk, get me visual confirmation."

A light cruiser jumped into the system where the moon Robichar was located, and they soon had it. Kira refused to relinquish her seat until she was certain.

"Looks like you were right, sir," Volk reported. "Those drone raids were a diversion. The large Kryl starships that were stationed above Robichar are gone."

"They must have hit our scouting forces after I closed the connection with Major Orman. They sneaked up on her." Earth! It was never easy to lose a pilot—especially not a good recon leader like Major Orman. Kira forced herself to unclench her fists.

"She's going after the relics," Volk said.

"Yes, but which one is she going after first? And where?"

EIGHT

Omar extended eight arachnoid legs from his back and braced against the narrow chimney of stone as water rushed through the tunnel beneath him.

He breathed heavily as liquid washed over his boots. The water level rose to his calves and—to his relief—stopped rising.

I told you these next pieces were going to be much more heavily guarded than the others, Overmind X said through their psionic link. *They are the true weapons.*

The flow beneath him subsided over minutes. His limbs began to tremble. The river slowed to a trickle as the trap ran dry.

One youngling bounced up into the chimney, rebounding off the wall. Before she fell back down, Omar grabbed the scaly biped and hurled her into the room above. She hadn't developed a multi-armed form like he had—the Kryl took on many forms, each fitting its purpose. Overmind X preferred the new hybrids to stay small and lithe so they could fit into tight spaces. They were as quick as groundlings, possessing vicious claws, but were unencumbered by the need to stay on four legs.

Now he saw why.

He boosted the second child up, then dropped back to the damp waterway. It was more like a chute than anything, angled slightly to take advantage of the extra-normal gravity of this world. The Enemy had expected newcomers to get trapped here and drown, a defensive mechanism powered by the frequently changing tides of this planet. It was clever. They didn't need an external energy source. They'd turned the entire underwater temple into a hydroelectric dam.

Omar fell to his stomach and squirmed toward the opening through which they'd come, looking to close the gate so they could proceed through the next section of the maze.

Overmind X's predictions about extra layers of defenses had been spot on. What she hadn't anticipated was the elaborate puzzle they'd have to solve on the way. Their movements had to be completed in sequence, one section opening to the next only after all the right doors had been closed, all the right buttons pushed, all moves executed in the proper order.

He hoped it would be worth it.

Do not cast doubt upon our mission, Zero, Overmind X hummed in his mind. *Kryl do not doubt.*

"I'm not fully Kryl, though, am I?"

A brief, sharp pain lanced through his temple. Between one breath and the next, any hesitation or worry he felt about his mission vanished from his awareness.

What was there to worry about? He was doing this for the Inheritance. For glory.

A low roaring echoed through the tunnel.

"Hurry!" the two children called, their voices echoing down from above.

Omar sprinted forward and launched himself back into the chimney just as a rush of water crashed against the tunnel walls with a force that would have broken his ribs.

He extended his limbs and climbed. Even the extra legs at his back were getting sore from overexertion at this point. They'd been navigating this death trap for hours.

If not for his physical enhancements, a gift of the Kryl genes grafted into his DNA during his change, he wouldn't have been able to make it this far—at least not without a lot more smart strategizing. He'd nearly gotten crushed by a boulder once, avoided drowning by a narrow margin several times, and he was stronger and more agile than any human would ever be. He felt the closeness of the hive, of Overmind X's steady guidance, and was thankful for the blessing.

However, Kryl genetics alone wouldn't take him the whole way. Once they located the relic, he knew from experience that there would be a point where he could no longer advance. A piece of the puzzle he wasn't suited to solve.

That's what the younglings were for. The latest generation of Kryl human hybrids duped even the Enemy's advanced Kryl detection systems.

They truly had evolved.

We always do, Overmind X echoed. *You see? The Inheritance is ours by right.*

Yes. The Kryl were the rightful heirs to this galaxy, and Overmind X would have her relics.

The younglings grasped him with a hand on each shoulder and hauled him up to a smooth stone floor.

Omar got to his feet and stood, dripping, with the smell of salty spray in his enhanced nostrils, as the younglings spread out to explore the chamber. They moved warily, seeking traps.

Stone ground against stone and all three hurled themselves to the floor as a giant curved blade—made of the special stone alloy favored by the Enemy's engineers—swept across the room.

Zero used his arachnoid limbs to scuttle to safety without standing upright.

He almost lost his head as the blade reached its apex on the opposite side and came whistling back toward them.

"It's moving like it's on a string!" he cried to the younglings.

One of them—Subject Fourteen, she was called, or Fourteen for short—waited until the blade passed, then bounced off a wall and landed on top of it.

She screeched and fell back to the floor, flattening herself as she trembled.

She grasped at her hands and feet, which were red and suddenly inflamed, like they'd been burned.

"Are you all right?" he asked.

"It is nothing," she said after a pause, her body stilling. "Mother says she will thicken my carapace so that I am not so easily injured."

The scaly hide that her human skin had become squirmed and moved as the controllers made adjustments before his eyes.

"How do we stop it?" Omar asked, referring to the blade that swung back and forth across the room, keeping them flattened and pressed into a corner.

You may not be able to, but there's always a way to circumvent their traps, said Overmind X. *Find a path.*

Omar looked around. The floor on which they crouched was square, and that giant stone blade swung back and forth from one end to the other, kissing the walls on either side. There was a slit at the top of the wall to his left, where it must have been stored, waiting for the presence of intruders—particularly Kryl—to be activated.

From the floor, the walls rose at an angle, meeting a point

far overhead. He craned his neck to see from his prone position and noticed a sort of platform that hung at the top of the room.

"I'll bet there's a magnet or something up top that holds the blade." Omar said. "Seven, to me."

She scuttled over on all fours. He waited until the blade passed to lift her up, spin twice, and hurl her upwards.

She reached the apex of his throw—ten meters or more below the platform he'd been trying to land her on—and fell.

She flipped in the air and came down on the edge of the blade, kicking off it so she didn't stand still long enough to burn herself like Fourteen had done.

She mis-timed it, though, and instead of burning herself, broke her ankle.

Omar groaned.

New mutants. Still didn't know how to use their strength or abilities without harming their fragile human frame.

Omar pulled Seven out of the path of the blade, which hadn't veered from its arc in the slightest by the forces they'd applied.

They waited while Seven panted and whined. Controllers swarmed under her skin and built support around her ankle bone. He heard crackling noises, and she hissed in pain. But after a moment, she could put weight on it again.

"We're going to have to work together," Zero said. "See that slit up there, where the blade first fell out?"

Fourteen and Seven both nodded. The blade rose toward the slit and paused inches from it.

"One of you will have to balance on the ledge above it and then boost the other up to the platform. From there, one of you should be able to—"

Bubbling, wet noises interrupted him.

Omar whipped his head back to stare at the narrow chute

through which they'd arrived. It had overflowed with water and bubbled into the room.

Fast.

That salty water would eventually force them up into the path of the blade.

Steady, said Overmind X.

Her voice calmed the younglings. For some reason, it annoyed him. Whatever power the controllers exerted over the children, their effect was tempered on Subject Zero. He wasn't as malleable.

Or perhaps he was simply defective.

Overmind X rumbled a warning.

"We're running out of time," Omar said. "From up there, one of you should be able to find the mechanism to stow the blade and allow me and the other youngling to find our way up."

The stone blade *whooshed* overhead. Omar flattened himself to the ground, resting his muscles with his cheek in the brine as it pooled around his body and sloshed against the wall.

The blade whizzed past on its way back.

"Now!" he shouted, throwing himself to his feet.

Seven jumped into his arms. He grabbed her by the ankles, spun, and released her in the slit's direction. She soared halfway up the angled wall and reached for a handhold.

Fourteen *yanked* Omar back down just in time to avoid decapitation. As it was, the blade nicked his arachnid arms. He gritted his teeth against the pain, only to look over and see one limb in the shallow water beside him, twitching and sending ripples out near his face.

A sharp pain throbbed on his back.

The pain and the ripples reminded him of something…

something specific. Of another time and place where he'd been in a situation like this...

Cease your grasping, Zero, Overmind X ordered.

The memory slipped through his fingers like water. Meanwhile, the salty pool rose and swirled. Overmind X blocked his pain receptors, so he only felt a distant, dull ache.

The next time the blade passed, Fourteen leaped up. "Now!" she shouted, her words emphasized internally by a forceful impression from Overmind X.

He did as he was told, twirling and tossing her up toward where Seven crouched precariously on the centimeters-thick ledge.

He hit the water again, taking in a mouthful of salty brine and choking. It was over the level of his head now.

He managed to push himself underwater, avoiding the blade and keeping the rest of his limbs attached.

Use the phase shifter, said Overmind X.

Omar reached down to his belt and activated the relic he kept there, blurring his form into semi-transparent vibrations. Although his face was still underwater, he was able to take a deep breath. He pushed back and stood. The stone blade passed right through him. His body relaxed.

The effects of the phase shifter wouldn't last long, but for now, it was a welcome reprieve.

Above him, Seven helped Fourteen up onto the ledge. They maneuvered, using their enhanced Kryl reflexes to balance on the minuscule stone perch.

Not even the best human climbers in the galaxy would have been able to manage what they did next. Using Fourteen to add power to her jump, Seven coiled and leapt up to the platform, flipping as she went. She stretched out an arm and grasped onto a ledge high above.

"Yes!" Omar shouted.

At that moment, the phase shifter's effects wore off, and he had to submerge himself to avoid being sliced in half.

The water was nearly half a meter deep by now, and rapidly rising. As the blade passed, he took a deep breath and sank to the bottom.

Two long minutes later, the metronome of the swinging blade stopped beating.

He lifted out of the water with a gasp to find the blade getting drawn back into the slot where it had been kept, pulled by an invisible magnetism.

The platform lowered. He stepped onto it, and it raised him to the top of the pyramid-shaped room.

A short time later, the three of them stared at the hidden relic they'd come to retrieve. It rested behind a shield that appeared like blue glass, but that was actually created out of charged particles of raw energy.

A cold, slithery excitement coursed through them as Overmind X's emotion filled their bodies. The entire hive, spread across the galaxy between Robichar and this water-logged world, shivered and squirmed with collective anticipation.

Only Omar hesitated. He'd tried to walk through that energy shield before. He was too much a Kryl, and the Enemy's systems had repelled him forcefully.

Seven and Fourteen, though?

They were new mutants. They had *evolved.* They were both more Kryl than Omar, and more human at the same time. Overmind X had created them specifically for this task.

Seven stepped forward and, with an effort, slowly pushed through the Telos energy shield. It singed her hide, but since she didn't register as Kryl, it allowed her to pass through.

The burned bits quickly healed with barely visible movements of controllers under the skin.

She laid one hand on the large, tube-shaped relic. The ceiling of the pyramid opened to the sky like flower petals in spring.

A transport ship lowered to retrieve them. Them, and the weapon.

NINE

Casey forced herself to breathe through the distinct dizziness that accompanied every drop out of hyperspace.

She adjusted her helmet as her stomach churned with familiar knots, tightening the chin strap and making sure the applicator was firmly affixed to her spinal port.

Reality snapped in around her as the dizziness seeped away. She took a hit of stimchem to speed up the process and sharpen her reactions.

"Furies, you're a go for launch," said Colonel Volk over the broadbeam.

"Light 'em up!" Casey said over squad comms.

Her body jerked as her Sabre lifted and shifted into a launch tube. Inertia and acceleration forced her shoulders back against the seat as her starfighter rocketed forward. Gray metal and tube lights streamed past as she was jettisoned into space. Casey powered up the engines and matched vector with forward burn the moment she was clear, her hands flying over the controls with practiced motions, finally coming to rest on the stick.

The rest of her flight-mates catapulted into the vacuum after her, each of the three appearing as a flashing blue triangle on her HUD the moment they fired up their engines.

"Flight 18, on me," Casey ordered.

Park swooped and bobbed off her left shoulder. "Hooo, boy!" he hollered. "That never gets old."

"Keep your eyes peeled," Casey reminded him. "We're here looking for the hive queen, not out to get an adrenaline rush."

"The adrenaline rush is just a bonus," Nevers said as he drew up on her right. "But you're right. I just hope we aren't too late."

Yorra grunted, pulling up on Casey's tail and slightly above the other three so they were flying in a tight diamond.

This was the second system where they'd been deployed in search of Overmind X and the rogue swarm of Kryl that had so abruptly vanished from Robichar. There were still Kryl inhabiting the lunar colony. Kryl were an invasive species, and the living fungus they'd deposited to cover the ground and breed more of their workers—who would mine minerals and water for the hive, and breed more specialized creatures—wouldn't give the world up so easily. If humanity wanted to claim it, they'd first have to raze it to the ground... at least, the old colonization base and surrounding acreage the Kryl had taken over.

But after Admiral Miyaru's recon squadrons had been destroyed, and they'd confirmed that the big Kryl starships, including the one they suspected was the mothership, had jumped away to an unknown location, Robichar fell off the priority list.

So here they were, searching.

"Booting up lidar scanners," Nevers said. Being the techie one of the group, he'd taken up this responsibility voluntarily. "Seeking algorithms activated. Harmony, please confirm."

"Scanning range at ten million kilometers. Data transmitting back to Command. You're clear to proceed."

They waited as the rest of the squad poured out of the destroyer. Casey bounced her leg impatiently. Flight 4, which she recognized by their tail numbers, deployed in an assault formation and pointed aggressively in her direction.

She did her best to ignore them. Ruby's antagonism had only gotten worse in the days since their encounter in the rec, and Casey was losing sleep trying to figure out whether to confront the other captain or simply ignore her.

"You know the drill, Furies," Volk finally said when all the ships had arrived. "Split the squad into three groups and fly the patrols marked out on your HUD. Focus your scanners on the habitable planet and its moons. Report back if you mark any sign of Kryl."

"Aye, sir," Casey said. "Flights 1 to 8, you're on the south pole of the planet. Flights 9 to 16, you take the north, and meet along the equator. Flights 17 to 24, you're with us on the moons."

It would take them all day to round the planet and its moons, scan their surfaces, and scour habitable space for millions of kilometers in every direction. The laser scanners were designed to detect ranges and physical objects, but had been augmented to read signs of carbon-based life and large structures. In particular, aggressive Kryl forms and Telos ruins.

Not that those were typically easy to detect. Casey didn't have a good feeling about this after the first star system turned up bunk. How many systems would they have to search before the Kryl showed up—if they showed up at all?

Casey led her group toward the moons. There were two around this planet, orbiting at different distances, a small red one and a large blue one. The combination caused violent tidal forces to move on the planet below, which had a lot of liquid water and was speckled only by tiny islands of land formed by volcanic activity. There were no large continents —constant flooding had washed them out. The largest land mass was a low tide flat that flooded twice a day, ripping loose soil away and depositing it deep into the ocean's depths.

"Well, this is lame," Park said after they'd circled the smaller moon.

"Part of the job," Casey pointed out.

"Doesn't mean it has to be so damn boring. There's nothing up here but craters."

"Would you rather spend your time looking at an ocean?"

"Uh, yeah, Raptor," Park said. "That's *way* more interesting than dust and rocks."

Sheesh. Even her friends were giving her a hard time. At least he'd said it over tightbeam instead of airing his complaints to the entire group.

"I'll keep that in mind, Naab," she said stiffly.

Harmony's lights sparkled as they appeared in Casey's cockpit. "Why did you give yourself the lunar patrol, Captain?"

She'd stopped being startled by the AI's sudden appearances. It was easier to assume she was always there. "So no one could say I took the good patrol."

"You're the leader. You get to choose which patrol to be on. Why not take the 'good' one?"

"I didn't want it to seem like I was playing favorites, or taking advantage of my new position."

"And if the patrols around the planet miss a crucial piece of information, who will take responsibility for that failure?" asked Harmony. "The leader from Flight 4 you've been tracking on your HUD?"

Casey swallowed and took a deep breath. "Me, most likely."

"With that in mind, Captain, you should not be afraid to exercise what limited authority you have."

"All right, all right. Enough with the lecture. I get your point."

"You should schedule a one-on-one with Ruby to defuse the situation. The first step to repairing your relationship is to make sure you understand why she's upset."

"Oh, I understand perfectly."

"Do you?"

"She wasn't mincing words in the rec."

"Mmmmhm," Harmony said. A very human noise for a robot to make.

Casey rolled her eyes. "Fine. I'll talk to her about it."

"Seek first to understand, Captain," Harmony added. "But do not delay taking action. A wound that goes untreated is bound to fester."

"You're just full of clichéd wisdom today, aren't you?" Casey grumbled, even if the shipmind had a point.

She thought about what her father might do in a similar situation, but that just made her angry. Casey still hadn't forgiven him for leaving her in the brig on the *Paladin* while the rest of them risked their lives fighting Kryl in the City. She hated being left out, and hated more that he thought he still needed to protect her.

Come to think of it… did Ruby *also* feel overlooked? She was as qualified for the mission commander position as Casey was, yet they had passed her over.

Maybe Harmony was right.

"Raptor, we've got something down here in the storm."

Casey re-focused on the bright shapes and lines on her HUD. The tightbeam was coming from Flight 4. Ruby was a professional—she wouldn't let her bitterness toward Casey compromise the mission. Still, it was telling that the voice speaking to her wasn't coming from the flight lead.

"What is it, Grizzly?" asked Casey. "Did you say storm?"

"Yeah, it's tossing chunks of hail the size of repair bots at us."

"Earth," she cursed, "Any damage?"

"One nicked my fuselage already, but nothing big. Anyway, lidar picked up some kind of artificial structure. It's sticking up out of that huge tidal flat. It was covered with water when we first saw it, but the scanners caught it behind us before we moved out of range. It must have been exposed as the tide went out."

"Did you investigate?"

"On our way there now, Captain. Ten minutes."

"Check back in when you arrive."

While she waited, Casey led her group from the smaller moon, which was farther out from the planet, toward the larger one. They'd timed their patrols so the moons were within five degrees of each other, their orbits crossing—also the reason the tides were shifting planetside.

"Raptor, sir, uh..." said Grizzly.

"What is it?" Casey demanded.

"It seems to be some sort of pyramid," Ruby said, taking over. "Sticking up about fifty meters out of the ocean. And the top is *wide open*."

"Any sign of Kryl?"

"Negative. I've never seen anything like this. It almost looks like some kind of jigsaw puzzle, with the stones all folded back... whoa!"

"What is it?"

"Frickin' piece of hail just bounced off my shields near the windshield."

Casey inhaled steadily, trying to calm her shaking hands.

She felt an intense and sudden protectiveness toward Flight 4. "Ruby, is it a Telos structure?"

"Could be, I suppose…"

"Send video footage over tightbeam."

Casey bounced her feet impatiently. She thought for a second that Ruby would refuse, but then the package arrived with a chime. She unbundled it and cast the video onto her HUD. After a moment's viewing, she shared it with Nevers.

"Oh yeah, that's definitely Telos," he said. "Earth's blood, that's eerie. Hard to see through the storm, but if you look closely, I think it's still moving, folding and unfolding like it's caught in some kind of loop. But the stone, and the way it's open like that… It reminds me of what we saw in the City when Subject Zero opened up the Chronicle room. I wonder…"

"No time for wondering. I'm sending these back to Command."

"Raptor, if that structure is open… that means Overmind X beat us here."

"They'll have to send Marines to check it out."

"No point," he said. "If there was a relic inside, it's gone now. I'll bet—"

An alert pinged in her HUD, announcing projectile fire from the rear. She pulled up hard, twisting as she came about. Her shield registered several hits, solid projectiles that burned up on contact. The applicator in her spinal port detected the G-forces and gave her another half dose of stim-chem, sharpening her vision and sending her heart into a staccato dance.

"Drone fire!" Yorra reported.

"Where on Earth is it coming from?" Casey demanded.

"They're hiding in that crater, Cap," said Lieutenant Park as he sent a missile toward the shadowed lip. "Ordnance out." It struck the ground, exploding and collapsing the crater's edge. Dust puffed up from the surface in a hazy sphere.

"Telemetry recorded two hits, Naab," Yorra said.

"They're space dust now," he said.

"Why didn't the lidar pick them up?" Casey asked.

"They must have dug themselves into the loose soil there," Nevers said. "One annoying advantage of autonomous drones being actual living creatures..."

The shaded side of the crater rippled and churned in dozens of spots.

"More where those came from," Yorra said. She breathed heavily over the broadbeam channel, a sure signal that she'd just taken a *big* dose of stimchem.

Through the shifting haze, a whole squadron of drones rose, shedding dust like a second skin as they powered up their living engines and turned toward the group of Sabres.

"Fire at will!" Casey shouted.

The other flights on Casey's patrol had circled back to join them. They all rained blaster fire down onto the drones. Unfortunately, the units had spread out to bury themselves, so when they rose they weren't clustered together, and that made the substantial firepower of the Furies less effective than it would have been otherwise. To make it worse, the drones immediately began to bob and weave in unnatural, insect-like patterns that were difficult to follow. Most of the pilots turned on fire assist in their craft. Except Nevers, whose sure hand landed shots on three drones.

"Ten more down," Casey said, reading the weapons telemetry out to the squad. "That still leaves two squadrons' worth. Get moving, Furies! Turn and burn."

All her engines had been doing was keeping her in place while she fired her guns. She didn't want her squad to be idling when the drones came at them, so Casey led the way in the opposite direction, putting the turquoise planet in the center of her viewscreen and pouring on speed. She aimed toward the storm cloud where the first group had found the structure.

The drones followed.

"Zero's gotta be here somewhere," Nevers said through clenched teeth. "There!"

He marked a drone on the radar they shared over squad comms. Nevers looped up and reversed his starfighter so he had a better view of the pack in pursuit. "That's gotta be him."

"How in the name of Animus can you tell?" Casey demanded. "You're too far away for visual confirmation." The drones were about fifty klicks off their tail.

"The way he's flying. The rest of these drones are a pack of bees, but there's one flying its own path. He's in the densest part of the pack, but his vector just seems… off."

"He's been playing cat and mouse with you for weeks, man," Park said.

"Fancypants," Casey said. "don't you dare take that bait."

He grumbled but complied, flipping his ship back around.

"Raptor," Volk said over broadbeam. "Gather the squad and rendezvous back at the destroyer. We've got defensive laser arrays charged up and ready to eliminate the threat."

Casey cursed silently. Of course, that was the logical thing. Why hadn't she thought of it?

"Yes, sir!" she said. "Furies, you heard the man." She had begun to turn when another voice cut into the broadbeam.

"Bit of a situation down here, Raptor!"

"Grizzly?" Casey asked. "What is it?"

"A squad of drones punched out of the ocean near the structure! They slagged an engine on Ruby's Sabre."

"Can she fly?"

"Still operational," Ruby reported, her voice hoarse. "This

Earth-damned hailstorm is making things way more difficult than they have to be."

"Get to low atmosphere, stat!" Casey changed her tight-beam to the third patrol and ordered them to the location of Flight 4 for support. They had encountered no drones, which was a blessing. She switched the comms back to broadbeam. "Help is on the way, Flight 4. We'll meet you in orbit."

"They were waiting for us," Nevers said.

"What?" Casey asked, distracted by the dilemma with the other squad. Damn, but it was hard to keep track of so much going on *and* fly her Sabre worth a damn.

"No shit," Park said through gritted teeth.

"Yeah, but *why*?" Nevers asked. "What do they have to gain? If they already have the relic, there's no point in..."

He trailed off as the pack of drones which had been in hot pursuit suddenly turned and moved farther into empty space.

"Where the frick are they going?" Yorra asked.

"Oh no you don't," Nevers said as he turned his ship.

"Fancypants!" Casey shouted. "Don't you dare!"

He paused. "Permission to hit them with a tracking beacon, sir?"

She clenched her jaw, thinking.

"Captain! They're getting away."

"I'm thinking!"

Harmony's lights materialized in her cabin again.

"Don't just float there and glare at me," Casey growled.

"His thinking seems sound. It won't endanger the squad, and it may provide additional information that we need to locate the bulk of the hive."

Casey was terrified of Fancypants getting himself into another situation like the one on Robichar. But she couldn't be an effective mission commander without taking a few calculated risks.

"Naab, Gears, go with Fancy and make sure he doesn't get into trouble."

"Aye, sir!" they said as all three peeled off.

"The rest of you, with me."

She met the rest of the squadron at the edge of the planet's atmosphere. That Ruby got back to orbit at all was a minor miracle, since she only had one engine, and her whole flight had dents in their Sabres from the hailstorm.

"What happened to the drones you found?" Raptor said.

"We got most of 'em," Grizzly said. "I must be close to Fancypants' kill count now."

"He got a few more on the moons."

Grizzly grumbled under his breath.

"The last one turned tail and ran," Ruby said. "Would have pursued if my ship wasn't already damaged."

"Ours ran, too. I can't help but feel like they weren't retreating, though."

"Ours were *definitely* retreating," Grizzly said. "Scared the tar out of them little bugs."

But Kryl don't get scared, do they? Casey thought.

She regarded Harmony's twirling lights, which had remained idling on her dashboard. They formed into a frowning face.

"Flight 18, what's your status?" Casey asked.

"We tagged a couple before we lost 'em," said Nevers. "They were moving too fast. Would have required six infusions of stimchem to keep up at those speeds." The drones could fly faster than most because they were bred for the vacuum and didn't have to carry fragile pilots around inside them.

"Are they still in system?"

He paused. "Just jumped. They're gone."

"Let's get back to the destroyer. We can track them from there."

They docked back on the destroyer, where Volk ordered them to stay in their Sabres and be ready to re-deploy. He'd been in touch with Nevers and was tracking the beacons.

"The drones dropped out of hyperspace. We've got their coordinates. Mapping the jump now. Admiral Miyaru will meet us there with a strike force. Furies, be ready to engage the enemy."

TEN

Elya jiggled the stick of his Sabre as he waited.

Hedgebot had crawled up the walls to the ceiling of the cockpit, clinging upside-down to a seam in the aluminite canopy before dropping back to the floor with a soft *thump* and a *ribbi-chirp* before repeating the process.

"Quit it," Elya told the bot, chuckling. "You're making me nervous."

A different kind of nausea and discomfort came as his vision suddenly warped. A shift into hyperspace had a strange effect on a person's perception of reality. He hadn't moved, and neither had his ship, relatively speaking.

Outside the ship, everything would have changed.

"Furies, you're a go for launch," came the order from Colonel Volk. "Form a perimeter and look for signs of Kryl."

Elya guided his Sabre forward into a launch bay. A moment later he catapulted into a strange new system.

One enormous, colorful planet, coated end-to-end with storm clouds and surrounded by a giant ring, loomed before him. A dozen moons hung in the blackness around the planet, giving the enemy plenty of places to hide.

"Where are we?" he asked over squad comms.

"Better question," Osprey said. "Where'd those drones go?"

The squadron fanned out around the destroyer while the pilots studied their HUDs.

His console beeped, and Hedgebot scampered over his dashboard to the right.

"Over there!" he said. "Hiding behind the ring."

"Keen eyes, Fancypants," said Yorra as she burned in that direction.

Everyone wanted to frag some Kryl. Flight 4 pulled ahead of them, and Elya let them go. This wasn't a competition anymore. This was a real battle.

His skin crawled as he triple checked his instruments. No readings yet. The drones he'd tagged must have found and destroyed the tracking beacons he placed because they weren't connecting any longer.

Osprey spoke over the command channel. "Any sign of the Kryl mothership?"

"Negative, Captain. We're still scanning the system, but between the ring and the moons there's a lot of surface to cover. Raptor, you take command. I need to move the destroyer into a better position."

"Is the Admiral coming with backup?" Nevers asked.

"They say it's *en route*," Osprey told him.

Elya looked above and behind him, but he didn't yet see any corvettes, heavy cruisers, or the additional half dozen destroyers Miyaru had collected into her armada.

Well, if he were the admiral, he'd probably wait until Volk gave the all-clear, too.

"Incoming!" Yorra shouted.

A hundred drones curled out from behind a large rock in the planet's beige and red ring a thousand klicks toward the planet, flying fast.

"Spread out, Furies," ordered Captain Osprey. "There's no cover here, so don't go bunching up or make easy targets for the bugs."

The Furies responded immediately. Some projectiles pinged off their shields a moment later, but the vast majority of what the Kryl fired passed through the spaces between them.

A drone at the back of the pack rose and wiggled its wings before dropping back into formation.

Elya inhaled sharply. "Subject Zero."

"What's that, Fancypants?"

"I see our guy. He's mine."

"Hold your position!" said Captain Osprey.

"I'm holding, Raptor," he said, staying in formation but keeping his eyes locked on Subject Zero's drone.

"Does that mutant count double, Fancypants?" That was Grizzly's voice, the captain from Flight 4.

"Is that a challenge?" Hedgebot beeped twice to signal assent. Elya couldn't help himself—he grinned widely. "Zero must count for five regular bogeys, at least. I've been playing tag with him for weeks on patrol."

All the while, the drones were barreling up at them as the Furies approached. Soon, the two groups of fighters would pass right through each other like meteorite showers clashing.

Until then, they played a deadly game of space chicken. Who would move first?

Elya took aim and double tapped his blasters a few times, aiming at one particular drone at the vanguard. The creature dodged left, then right, but timed it poorly. A bolt took it on the nose and its body fractured into dozens of pieces.

Subject Zero's drone passed through the debris without flinching.

"He's got some fancy tricks," Grizzly said, a smile in his voice. "This should be fun."

Normally, Elya's competitive streak would have made him want to pull away and take Subject Zero on his own. But he'd been outflown by Zero enough times to know he could use the support. "You're on," Nevers said. "Park, Yorra, you want in?"

"We'll watch your six, Fancypants," Yorra said.

"Aw, come on, Gears," Park complained.

"Who's gonna watch my back if you go ahead?"

"Fine, fine."

The cloud of drones drew closer. They were within visible range now. Neither squadron had changed course.

His HUD pinged as a new starship suddenly appeared in the system. His heart skipped a beat as new shapes materialized before turning blue on his lidar—signaling that they were allies, not enemies.

He craned his neck back. Three heavy cruisers were on vector to join the destroyer Volk and the Furies had been moved to. That was good, since the Furies were tied up and couldn't provide a layer of defense for him if they were engaged with these drones.

"Think we found the Kryl swarm," Volk said over the broadbeam. "Huge cluster of lifeforms floating behind that blue moon."

Elya glanced up. The blue moon was the closest planetary body to his location. His eyes couldn't see anything at this distance, but he trusted Volk's scanners had found something legit.

Still no sign of the *Paladin of Abniss*. What was taking her so long?

"Peel off in three," Osprey said. "Circle back, firing as you go. Save your missiles for the big ships. One, two..."

Grizzly's ship sped up and came even with Nevers. A half

dozen projectiles pinged off his shields. His HUD bleeped in warning as a drone fired on him.

The rest of the Furies peeled off. Nevers dodged the projectile by bobbing under and to the other side of Grizzly. Neither of them diverted their course.

"Fancypants! Grizzly!" Osprey shouted. "Peel off!"

"Them first," Grizzly growled.

"If you won't move, then you'd better fire!" Osprey shouted.

"Aye, captain!" Grizzly and Elya shouted in chorus as they held their wingtip blasters open on full auto. Solaran shields were better than Kryl, and at this range, the superior reaction time of an autonomous drone didn't have enough warning to evade.

The dual-pronged attack took out five drones who had stupidly stayed clustered together, typical of the hive-mind they were. This was an attack they'd rehearsed a thousand times in sim and training flights. The Kryl always expected Solaran pilots to behave in a pack mentality, like they did. He and Grizzly had just used that assumption to their advantage by breaking ranks.

As they cut through the swarm, dodging left and right, Subject Zero's drone lifted out of range of their blaster bolts and passed overhead.

Up close, the drones looked more like animals than ships —their fuselages were made up of two pieces that resembled an abdomen and thorax. The canopy was located where the head should be, with windows like faceted bug eyes. Overlapping layers of adjustable wings cut back from the body, sprouting feelers at the end and landing gears like feet tucked up into their bellies. The engine nacelles cast blue-green flame backward, somehow not burning the sphincter of tempered carapace that formed their backsides.

As Subject Zero passed overhead, he performed a barrel

roll, exposing the head of the drone, where the skin was semi-translucent. A man's shoulders were backlit in the cockpit.

He was out of sight in the blink of an eye.

"That's him alright!" Elya shouted. "Cutting back on the outside!"

Elya's blasters overheated moments before Grizzly's sputtered out. It forced them to pause fire at the precise moment they turned. Gravity compressed his body and stimulants roared through his veins, propping his mass up against the contortion of maneuvering at six or seven Gs.

Hedgebot flattened itself, then leaped forward as Subject Zero twisted and dove back toward the planet's debris ring.

"He's heading for cover!" reported Grizzly. Subject Zero weaved and bobbed as the other man resumed firing.

"He doesn't need cover," Elya said.

"If you say so. I still ain't playin' chicken with these rocks."

From a distance, the planet's ring had looked like a solid beige-red span. As they flew closer, it dissolved into a broken road, pieces of which distinguished themselves as small asteroids or clusters of mid-sized rocks. Most of these asteroids were a hundred meters across, although some were as small as ten or twenty meters wide.

Particles showered their starfighter's shields, stellar winds blowing waves across the canopy of transparent aluminite, cutting down Elya's visibility. He relied on his instruments like he'd been trained to do, pouring on speed and relying on his HUD and Hedgebot's connection with the system to steer him clear of obstacles.

Although they gained on Zero's drone, and placed shots that glanced off his shields two or three times, the mutant reached the planet's ring before they did. His ship aimed its nose toward the thickest section of colliding debris and slipped straight into it.

"That was slick," Grizzly said in a tone of grudging respect. "Thought he'd at least nick a wing."

"He's cheating. He's got a relic that allows him to pass through solid objects."

"You sure?"

"Definitely."

Grizzly grunted. He must have played back through the footage on his HUD, because after a second, he said, "Weird, man. What now, Fancypants?"

"Split up and corner him."

"Copy that." Grizzly swerved to his left-hand side and dipped through a gap in the ring of space dust.

Elya went right and picked out another narrow path.

The ring itself was only a few klicks deep. He had to slow down to navigate it, but he also knew it was unlikely Zero's phase shifter would last the duration—after it went out, he'd have to fly clear of danger and wait for the phase shifter to recharge.

"There!" Elya said, spotting a purple-gray splotch against a hazy reddish backdrop.

Zero spun around and cast a few shots in the direction he indicated.

"My shields are down to 50%," Grizzly reported. "Now I'm angry."

"Don't let him rattle you. Stay tight."

They weaved and bobbed as they lost speed. Hedgebot helped Elya find a way through the ring. When he popped out the other side, the vast open space came so suddenly it stole the breath from his lungs.

"Look out!" Grizzly yelled.

Elya shoved his stick forward, narrowly avoiding a targeted missile launched by Subject Zero that had curved around the long way out of his sight.

Grizzly chased the mutant—right into a nest of hidden

drones that detached themselves from the underside of the ring as he approached.

As soon as they made themselves visible, the two pilots came under heavy fire.

"We'll hold these back!" Yorra said, appearing with Park. "Go!"

She, Park, and the rest of Flight 4 laid into the hidden nest, wingtip blasters strafing across the drones to harry them and prevent pursuit.

Elya clicked his comm in acknowledgement, then continued after Subject Zero.

Grizzly was right up there with the mutant, the two circling each other and seeking a weakness.

Zero cut inside, then blasted into open space. He flipped around and burned suddenly in the opposite direction—right at Grizzly's nose.

Zero's drone went hazy and indistinct as he activated his phase shifter.

"Pull up!" Elya shouted.

Grizzly did—right into a second missile Zero had dropped before shifting. An explosion ripped through Grizzly's weak shields and blew his cockpit wide open.

When the smoke cleared, a huge gash opened the starfighter to vacuum where the cockpit used to be. There was no sign of a body. Grizzly's seat, dashboard, and the entire cockpit had turned into a mess of twisted metal.

"Oh, Earth," Nevers shouted over the broadbeam. "Starfighter down! I need backup!"

Park pushed forward, shooting at Subject Zero and trying not to get smacked by Grizzly's madly spinning, and now pilotless, craft.

Zero continued to fly with a grace every Fleet pilot would envy, somehow coming around a rock on the other side and drawing Park out of position on Elya's wing. He swerved in circles several times, and as Park gave chase, the lieutenant became less and less aware of his position in space. Zero tied him and Elya up in knots until the mutant's phase shifter had to recharge. When it did, Elya tagged him three times on his undercarriage. The drone ship bled a yellow pus, but nothing like what had happened to Grizzly. Elya had hit no critical systems.

Zero cut around in a loop one more time, forcing Park to cut into the path of Grizzly's whirling Sabre. The slow-moving object cut through his shields and smacked into his engine on its next rotation, severing a meter of Park's wing clean off.

"Augh!" Park shouted into the broadbeam. "I'm hit."

"Griz, report!" said the lead pilot from Flight 4. "Grizzly, do you copy?"

Elya swallowed. "He's gone, Ruby."

"What?! No! GRIZZLY!"

"Ruby, he's gone!" Elya said. "Raptor, we need evac. Naab's alive, but I don't think he can fly out."

Park groaned. "I've still got an engine," he said, although his voice seemed pained. He gasped as he took a hit of stim-chem, probably for the painkiller it contained when it detected an injury. "Well, sort of. I can maneuver with that and some thrusters, but it's seriously cramping my style."

"On our way!" Raptor said.

Elya's HUD beeped, and seventeen individual units suddenly appeared at the edge of the planet's gravity well, near where Volk and the heavy cruisers had been moving.

"The Kryl hive's moving out into open space," said Yorra. "About seventy-five percent of the armada is here in the system with us now. I think I see the *Paladin*, too. Just need to clean up here." The sound of her mashing her triggers could be heard over the broadbeam as she finished off the remaining drones she'd been fighting. "There. Let's go!"

Subject Zero had already turned to flee. Worried about his squadmate, and shocked at what had just happened, Elya lacked the presence of mind to pursue.

Grizzly, gone?

He hadn't been close friends with the guy, but Earth! *Gone?*

"Grizzly?" Ruby wailed over the broadbeam, evidently crying. "No, no, no. Grizzly, come on. Tell me you're just unconscious. You must have ejected before you were hit. Come on, where are you? If you're still out there, let us know you're alive."

Elya closed his eyes and swallowed the lump in his throat. "I saw it, Ruby. A direct hit through his shields."

She choked as she sobbed. Nevers turned the volume of the broadbeam channel down, but not off.

Hedgebot beeped sadly, hanging down in front of his face. Elya sniffled, blinked away tears, and surfaced from his shock.

Move, he told himself. *You have to move*!

"Yorra, you got Park covered?" Osprey asked.

"Yes, sir, busy keeping the drones off him."

"I'm tracking Subject Zero," Elya said, nudging forward again.

"Do not pursue," Raptor said. "I repeat, do not pursue." She switched channels for a moment, then came back to squad comms. "Starfrost squadron will meet us on the way back. Move it."

"Aye, Commander." Checking the active Sabre roster as he flew, Elya saw that several more pilots from other flights had been killed in the fight.

Elya opened up his engines until he was doing three Gs toward the armada. His instruments told him Zero's lone drone was ranging out ahead somewhere and slightly to port.

Farther afield from his position was the Kryl swarm,

spreading out like his squad had done before, only on a far larger scale. They had easily two thousand ships of various sizes. One was far larger than the others, shaped like a massive starfish. The mothership, perhaps? A line of star-ships that moved out ahead were heavily armored, with long twisting limbs. The Kryl equivalent of heavy cruisers, according to the shapes he'd memorized in pilot school.

He tapped the stick to starboard a bit, so his vector took him closer to the Solaran armada than the Kryl swarm. Last thing he wanted to do was get lost in their midst alone.

Starfrost squadron dropped in around him. They exchanged signals and matched broadbeam frequencies as they formed a V-shaped configuration, with Elya's Sabre at their vanguard. His whole body sagged in relief in his pilot's chair. His nerves were frayed.

The broadbeam was quiet as they approached the armada. The little skirmish he'd just been through was merely the beginning.

The battle had barely begun.

"The *Paladin of Abniss* has arrived," Admiral Miyaru said over the armada-wide broadbeam.

Elya's blood began pumping again as another fifty ships joined the Solaran heavy cruisers, corvettes, and destroyers. He listened as Colonel Volk deployed a dozen more starfighter squadrons. They arrayed themselves opposite the Kryl swarm, a mere ten thousand kilometers of empty space between the two forces.

A Kryl gunship with long cephalopod limbs drifted out in front and peeled its arms back.

Some kind of tube protruded from its center.

With a shudder of fear, Elya zoomed in on his HUD. It looked like a cannon. Made of the red Telos alloy, its tip glowed, as if reflecting starlight. The tube extended forward, and the light elongated, hardening into a thin blade of golden light.

"Oh, Earth," Elya said, slapping his comms to a tightbeam channel used by Command and opening his mic at the same time. "Admiral, watch out!"

He had no idea if she heard him. Before he could say more, the gossamer blade of golden light swept across the armada, sheared a heavy cruiser in half, ruptured a corvette, and carved a hole in the *Paladin of Abniss'* midsection.

ELEVEN

Thrown from the command couch, Kira's head dashed off a console's unforgiving corner as black and red splashed across her vision.

"Hull breach!" an engineering officer shouted.

The ship tilted another way, thrusting her back against the couch before the artificial gravity gave out. Kira used her sleeve to push droplets of blood away from her face as she floated, navigating the momentary release.

Artificial gravity reinstated two seconds later as the ship's systems modulated and backup power kicked in. She dropped to the floor, going to one knee. A dozen officers groaned and huffed as they stumbled to their feet.

Kira joined them. "What in the name of Animus was that weapon?" Her mind reeled. It had seemed like nothing more than an angle of light before it touched the *Paladin*.

But even though she'd never seen it before, a new weapon was not unexpected. It was, in fact, the very thing that had been the source of her anxiety, the cause of the rash that still chafed at her collarbone these past weeks. The potential threat of this weapon had sent her pacing back and forth across dozens of starships as she struggled mightily to get the armada into fighting shape. It had inspired her to deploy starfighters into various systems based on outdated information provided by an ancient starmap dated *who knew* how many thousands of years old.

No one needed to answer her question. The weapon was another Telos relic—one with a remarkably destructive ability to rip through their best shields and decimate her armada in a single blow.

This was exactly what she'd feared... And worrying about it wouldn't win this battle. There would be time to analyze what happened later. Only a few seconds had passed since the attack. The sooner she asserted control of the situation, the better off they'd be.

"Nevermind. Harmony," Kira barked. "Damage report."

Pink and purple lights swirled nearby, coalescing sluggishly. Kira turned toward the shipmind as she gathered into her typical androgynous body-shape, her face bearing a worried frown as Harmony processed the request. Meanwhile, Kira located the hologram rectangle showing which comms remained active. The channel she'd opened to the armada moments before the attack was still open. She muted her mic so Harmony's report didn't go out to everyone.

"Two corvettes lost," Harmony said at last. "Along with four light cruisers. Three heavy cruisers sustained major damage and are now inoperable. The *Paladin of Abniss* suffered a hull breach, but automated systems have contained it. We lost three railguns and half the laser array. We also lost an engineering deck, and fifty souls."

"Earth," Kira cursed, turning to a weapons officer. "Target that Kryl gunship with everything we've got!" She spun back to the open broadbeam channel and unmuted herself. "Captains of the armada, take evasive action and fire at will! I repeat, fire at will!"

Torpedoes, railguns, blasters, and projectile weapons launched across the gap toward the Kryl hive. The heavy ship bearing the Telos weapon rotated away, trailing its wavy arms behind as it fled back toward the safety of the hive. Drones targeted her missiles and put themselves in the line of fire to scramble pursuit.

Where was Colonel Volk? She glanced around the bridge before she remembered he was on another destroyer. She wished she hadn't sent him away, but had a moment to be glad. If she died in this battle, the armada would need a competent leader to take her place.

She asked Harmony to connect with him. "Colonel Volk, are you all right?"

"We made it through clean, Admiral," he said. "They aimed at the flagship."

"Deploy the rest of our starfighter squadrons and don't let that thing get off another shot."

"Aye, sir! I'm on it."

"Admiral," said Harmony, "Projections show that odds of winning this battle are 5.3% as long as that weapon is in play."

"So take it out."

"Numbers are against us no matter how we proceed," Harmony said. "Not counting drones, the Kryl hive numbers nearly 500 major vessels. Adding smaller ships, they reach nearly two thousand. The Solaran armada, by comparison, is a mere 103 major vessels now."

"The Kryl have always outnumbered us, Harmony. Never stopped us before."

"This situation is unique."

Kira growled in her throat. Harmony was right, she just didn't want to hear it. The Kryl may have been numerous, but the Solaran Fleet always had more fire-power and better shielding. With the Kryl's guns augmented by a weaponized Telos relic... well, it changed the game.

"Engineering," Kira said, "what's our status?"

"We've sectioned off the breach, sir," one officer on the opposite end of the bridge shouted, "but it's still draining a significant amount of energy. We seem to be losing atmosphere from a ventilation shaft aft of the breach."

"Get it fixed. Now!"

"Yes, sir!" He spoke into his mic, then ran out of the bridge to help his engineers locate the problem. The ship was designed to use layers of airlocks to contain a breach, but the damage that weapon caused had been significant, and it likely required manual intervention. She couldn't jump away as long as that breach was open without risking losing even more of her destroyer in the shift to hyperspace.

Which meant her ability to survive this battle relied on her ability to buy enough time for her crew to make repairs.

"Harmony, no sitting still," she told the shipmind—who also doubled as the destroyer's pilot. "Fly erratically."

"Yes, Admiral."

The ship lurched as they suddenly began to dance around space. After the initial shift, she barely noticed the movement at all, though she could tell by looking at the viewscreen that they were tumbling through space in an unpredictable whirling pattern.

"That goes for the rest of you, too," she told the armada. "Don't stay still. Keep it moving. Colonel Seba," she said, addressing the leader of the corvette group. "I need a distraction. Are your ships ready?"

The good man didn't hesitate. "They're champing at the bit, sir."

The relic had hit only two corvettes. That left a good forty of them. She watched as they soared across her viewscreen in four groups, deploying missiles as they moved.

"Major Garrak, what about my light cruisers?"

"Moving out to flank them."

"Good. Draw their fire and make the Kryl fight a battle on multiple fronts."

That should buy her some time.

The shimmering gossamer thread cut across her viewscreen again, arcing toward the heavy cruisers, which were still trying to maneuver their bulky crafts away from one another. They moved faster than a destroyer, but not much.

"Incoming!" Kira shouted into the broadbeam. "Move!"

It didn't help. That line of light cut across one battleship, then another, unimpeded by distance and barely hindered by time. It sliced right through four more ships in the space of a breath.

At first, nothing happened. Then the heavy cruisers ruptured at the seams where the thread had cut through them, exploding as the energy shields backfired and the atmosphere contained within caught fire.

She clenched her teeth as several thousand souls died sudden, fiery deaths. The Kryl had adjusted their aim. Unlike the damage that had been done to the *Paladin*, this time the relic had severed the heavy cruisers straight through the middle, cutting the ships in half.

Their crews never had a chance.

She heard captains muttering prayers to the Spirit of Old Earth, as well as several other gods before their comms cut out.

Silence roared in her ears as the laser raked ships a second and then a third time. They broke into pieces that drifted slowly apart.

Shuttles and Ripcords—little vessels secured near the bridge that could detach from the main starship body in the event an escape was necessary—detached from one or two of the ships. But not all of them.

"Admiral, I advise retreat," Harmony said quietly.

They'd already lost so many. Retreat now would signal defeat to her entire armada, mere minutes after their arrival.

"Harmony, why aren't our shields holding up against that laser?"

"I don't know, Admiral. Further analysis is required."

"Give me your best guess."

She barely hesitated. She was an AI, and Kira knew she'd already run this query. "Energy shields repel blaster bolts, projectiles, and large missiles. This weapon's beam is microscopically small, so it slips straight through the shields."

"Earth's blood," she muttered.

"Admiral," said Colonel Volk. He had switched channels and was calling over a tightbeam directly to her and only her. "We need to fall back."

"We've already lost a dozen ships, Volk! We can't turn back now."

"If we don't turn back, that weapon is going to get us all."

"Get some starfighters in there and drop a nuke on it!"

"They're trying. The Kryl swarm them every time they get close. We've lost half a company already."

She closed her eyes. This was *not* going as planned.

She turned away. "Engineering! How's that hull breach repair coming?"

"We found it, Admiral. Working to manually seal off a section of the atmospheric delivery system." In other words, the vents were leaking atmosphere into space and they had to be welded shut from the inside. Surely, that had been no walk in the park.

"Finish it and secure yourself in place."

If they had to jump back to hyperspace suddenly, it would be better if they were belted in.

And just like that, she'd decided.

The relic cut across her viewscreen again. Harmony shoved the destroyer forward, narrowly avoiding it. Another handful of priceless ships—ships she'd worked so hard to gather to this armada—ruptured and exploded a hundred klicks off her port side.

Kira closed her eyes. *What a disaster.* She'd failed them all. "Volk, give us a distraction, so we have time to jump away."

"Yes, sir!"

She turned to Harmony and motioned for her to open the channel.

"Armada, remove yourselves from action. Plot jump courses back to the Elturis system. Signal the retreat."

Collective sighs of relief followed signals of acknowledgement. Starfighter squadrons attacked the Kryl with everything they had, dropping a dozen atomic bombs in as many minutes and keeping the heavy Kryl ships occupied. That gossamer thread swept around, taking out dozens more starfighters, but for the most part her squadrons were quick enough to avoid the carnage.

Kira waited until the heavy cruisers, then the light cruisers, jumped away. She took several of the shuttles and Ripcords into her own damaged destroyer.

The nausea that came with the last jump to hyperspace was nothing compared to the sickness she already felt at failing her crew, at letting down her captains, at losing a full quarter of her armada in their first group engagement.

They hadn't even prevented the Kryl from gaining another relic. They'd gotten here late. They'd fallen right into Overmind X's trap.

She wished she had died in the first attack. That would have been easier than facing her crews' looks of disappointment, or her own mounting shame.

TWELVE

The roaring in Casey's ears wouldn't go away.

The screams of starfighter pilots dying, the sound of tearing metal coming through the broadbeam from inside their craft, the curses of her squadmates as they fought to keep the Kryl from destroying even more of the armada with that terrible weapon...

It all jumbled up into an echoing roar that just would not retreat.

Not after she led the survivors back into the hangar of the *Paladin of Abniss,* sliding through the energy shield to safety.

Not after they jumped to hyperspace, headed back to the Elturis system and away from the carnage of the battle.

Not after—

She started as a mechanic rapped on the canopy of her Sabre. It was a young man, barely out of boyhood, wearing baggy coveralls in Imperial colors, with grease stains streaking his cheeks and forehead.

For a moment, she saw Mick, the young starfighter mechanic who'd been manipulated into becoming a suicide bomber after a Kryl parasite wormed into his brain.

How the hell…?

She shook her head, and the hallucination cleared. It wasn't Mick, but another mechanic whose name she didn't know. This wasn't a vision caused by a Kryl parasite, but by a close brush with death. The kind of close brush that made her see her fallen comrades' faces all around her.

She checked again, just to be sure. No, this mechanic wasn't Mick. His chin was rounder, with a little dimple in the middle. Uneven patches of a wiry blond beard broke the grease stains on his cheeks. His mouth was moving, and he was gesturing wildly, but she couldn't understand him because of that Earth-damned *roaring*.

She finally pulled her helmet off and rubbed at her ears.

"WHAT?" Casey shouted. Her voice sounded very faint to her ears.

The mechanic thumbed over his shoulder and her eyes—her sharp pilot's eyes, which she relied on so much—picked out a damaged Sabre, missing a wing and scarred with blaster burns and dents. A group of a dozen mechanics, pilots, and bots were straining at the canopy, which had buckled inward from damage and sealed a stocky brown-skinned pilot inside.

Naab!

Casey popped the canopy of her own craft and bounced off the wing as she leaped to the ground. She was running before she had time to process another thought.

The roaring dampened everything but the sound of her own panicked breathing as she entered the press of people around Park's Sabre. He was trapped in the cockpit, gripping his arm and bleeding from a cut on his chin.

Yorra had her hands pressed to the aluminite window. "Hang on, love! We're getting you out. Just try to stay calm." Her voice sounded very far away, but at least Casey was getting her hearing back.

Nevers hunched down on the other side of the canopy, guiding Hedgebot along the hull. The bot's bristles glowed bright red as it extended a laser cutter from its belly and slowly burned through a hinge.

Dozens of pilots looked on anxiously.

"How can I help?" Casey said. Her own voice was dim, distant.

Nevers moved his mouth.

"What?" she asked.

"LIFT HERE!" he shouted. The canopy jumped as Hedgebot's laser sliced through a second hinge. She and half a dozen others lifted the canopy and held it open while Yorra helped Lieutenant Park squeeze out, taking his weight onto her shoulders. They were about the same height, and Park's hands balled Yorra's uniform in his fists with a desperate grip.

Park winced and inhaled through his teeth as they lowered him to the ground.

Medics stepped out of the crowd and began examining the pilot for wounds. Yorra knelt at his side, cupping one hand in hers. The medics turned his other wrist, testing for sprains or breaks, and then slipped his arm into an analyzer cuff. He looked up at Casey, his brown face gone pasty, and gave her a shaky thumbs up.

His smile faded as his eyes caught something over her left shoulder.

Casey spun to face a frizzy mass of tangled auburn hair. Ruby shoved a finger into her sternum so hard she staggered back a couple steps.

"He's dead because of you!"

For a moment, all she could do was blink dumbly at Ruby. Who was she talking about? Not Park, for he was sitting right there with his arm in a diagnostic cuff. Not Mick, for he had died months ago and, shamefully, Casey had banished all thought of the young mechanic from her mind until that other mechanic who looked like him had knocked on her Sabre window.

Dozens—no, hundreds!—of pilots had just been killed in the fight. Half their squad, at least, would be on the casualty list. It made her head swim to think of it, and Casey hadn't even had time to take a proper headcount…

"Grizzly!" Ruby shouted in her face. "You thoughtless, ladder-climbing amateur! Grizzly is dead. And it's *your fault*!"

Ruby's finger wouldn't stop stabbing at her chest. Casey swatted it aside.

"My fault?" she demanded. "Half our squad was just killed out there. I didn't give the order, Ruby. We're all just doing our best to survive. Cut me some slack."

"Oh, you want slack, now? I thought you wanted to be our new mission commander."

"I do," Casey said. Then, "I *am*." It was still hard to use the right tense, since the appointment had been so recent.

Regardless, it was the wrong thing to say.

"Well, *Commander,* this is your fault. You shouldn't have allowed Grizzly and Fancypants to go after Subject Zero."

The rest of the squad had gathered around them to watch the drama unfold.

Shouldn't she have? They'd held the line when she told them to. They'd been in the perfect position to pursue the mutant. He was dangerous. Subject Zero had been at the center of the race for the relics. Each time a new relic showed up, he was there. They *needed* to eliminate him.

"They made their choices," Casey said. Nevers stepped up on her right, opening his mouth to intervene. Casey silenced him with a raised hand. "You think we should just let Subject Zero get away?"

"You could have kept them safe! You could have ordered them to back off!"

"They're starfighter pilots, Ruby. I trust them to do their job—Nevers, Grizzly, even you. And it was *right* to do everything we could to try to take out the mutant. He's a danger to us all."

Ruby scoffed. "You made a bad call, Raptor. Half our squad is gone. Grizzly is *gone*. Your first mission, and you screwed it up royally." Tears shivered at the corners of Ruby's eyes. She swiped an arm across her face and paced in a tight circle. Loose strands of red hair clung to her clammy skin. She clawed it angrily off her neck and dug her fingers into her scalp.

"No one knew the prime relic had that kind of destructive power," Casey said, her voice softening as she felt her heart go out to Ruby. The pilot had obviously lost a good friend. Maybe more than a friend. "Not even Admiral Miyaru saw it coming."

"I'm not talking about that damn laser beam!" Ruby shouted, veins bulging out of her forehead. "I'm talking about that slippery drone and the mutant pilot inside of it that Fancypants here has such a hard-on for!"

"Now, hang on!" Nevers said, unable to keep his mouth shut any longer. "You don't understand how dangerous Subject Zero is. It was worth the risk to go af—"

"Worth the risk?" Ruby repeated. "Worth the risk? You're unbelievable! Tell Grizzly it was worth the risk. Tell Flight 4 and all the rest of the Furies here that going after that poisonous mutant—when you *knew* he would outfly you—was worth their best friends' LIVES!"

Nevers cast his eyes toward his feet as his face colored a deep red. He was ashamed of his failures, just like Casey was. Just like they all were.

Every life in the Furies—every life in the Fleet—mattered. They couldn't just go throwing people away trying to up their kill count, or because they all wanted to be the person to take out an enemy who could fly through asteroids.

Casey knew this conversation was going nowhere fast. As the officer in charge, she needed to defuse the situation, pronto.

"Everyone, just take a beat," Casey said. "All right? Step back. Let's talk about this after our emotions calm down."

"Listen," Nevers said, "That came out wrong. I didn't mean to—"

Ruby hauled back and slammed her fist into Nevers' jaw so hard and so fast, not even Hedgebot's flaring red light was fast enough to warn him.

Nevers rocked back as Hedgebot chirruped angrily, dashing himself against Ruby's boots. Ruby kicked the bot across the floor and then hauled back to strike Nevers again.

Casey threw herself between the two of them and earned a blow to the temple. The hangar pivoted, but she managed to hold herself upright and gather a fistful of Ruby's uniform.

The lead pilot from Flight 4 was a fighter, though. She twisted out of Casey's grip.

"I don't care who promoted you," Ruby said. "You're not my boss, Raptor. You may be in charge right now, but you'll never be my commander."

She stalked away, pushing through the crowd, as Casey rubbed at her head and panted. The roaring returned and quickly became a pounding headache.

Realizing that everyone was staring at her, waiting to see what she'd do next, Casey straightened and brushed off her uniform. With an effort of will, she lifted her head and met the eyes of several pilots. Most, but not all, looked away when she met their gaze. She felt their judgment like a heat-wave. She felt the burden of the responsibility they'd placed in her.

"Does anyone else have something they need to get off their chest?" she asked.

They responded with shaking heads and muttered negatives.

Casey took a quick headcount. It was all she could do not to wince. The Furies, at full strength, were 108 pilots strong. Twenty-four flights of four or five a piece.

Standing here were maybe forty pilots in total. Even counting those whose injuries were being treated, and those who hadn't bothered to stay to watch the accusations unfold, so many had been lost…

"Run your post-flight and then get some rest, Furies," she said. "Dismissed."

No cheers. No *OOO-RAHs*. Just tired nods, glares of mistrust, and sighs.

What a way to start her tenure as mission commander.

THIRTEEN

Working his jaw, which still ached where Ruby's right cross had landed, Elya made his way down the ramp toward the subterranean Chronicle room. Hedgebot scampered beside him, its claws pattering along the alien stonework.

They'd been called into a debriefing with Colonel Volk about an hour after the battle. The meeting had been... short, to everyone's mixed consternation and relief. What could Volk tell the Furies they didn't already know? Losing dozens of friends and squadmates didn't need to be explained or examined in minute detail. There was no solution to be workshopped. War was hell, and all they could do was learn to live with their losses.

Ruby and several others had failed to arrive. Their absence was noted, but not remarked upon. Colonel Volk would follow up with them in private, as time allowed, to reprimand them. Being absent from a debrief normally demonstrated a lack of discipline. Under present circumstances, it was understandable, and command overlooked their absence, at least for now. Everyone grieved in their own way.

As for him, Elya focused on what he could fix—or at least what he could do to avoid making the same mistake again. His head spun from the speed at which everything had happened. He still heard Grizzly's voice in his ears as he cried out in his last moments. Elya replayed the maneuver that had ended the pilot's life in his head, racking his brain to figure out what he could have done differently.

He told himself he could have flown better, faster, smarter... but there was nothing he could do now to reverse the choices they'd both made. Subject Zero outmaneuvered them both, plain and simple.

Zero had escaped yet again. Elya didn't know what irked him more, feeling like it was his fault a pilot was dead, or knowing that Zero was still out there, reloading his blaster. If they had tagged the mutant, at least Elya could sleep at night, knowing Grizzly's death had not been in vain.

But they hadn't. And to top it all off, the Kryl now wielded the most destructive prime relic yet to be discovered.

Elya ground his teeth as he walked through the archway, past the giant columns, and into the light of the Chronicle room's guardian hologram. He silently vowed to destroy Subject Zero as revenge for Grizzly's death, for injuring Park, for dividing their squad.

But how?

If any place held answers to his questions, it was the Chronicle room. The great be-robed Telos loomed overhead, dominating the air as it held itself suspended between two columns. Its purple-on-black cowl brushed the ceiling, which remained closed. The sensors that had formerly been arrayed around the stone fist holding the geode had been dismantled, and pieces of equipment were scattered across two tables set end-to-end. Scientists glanced up from their work, giving Elya the barest glances of acknowledgement before returning to their calculations.

"What are you doing here?" Aganaki said by way of greeting, not even bothering to turn from where he stood in front of the crystal obelisk.

"My job," Elya responded.

Aganaki snorted and tilted his head back to gaze up at the Telos, which did that uncanny breathing thing but otherwise remained unresponsive. "Lot of good that did."

"Excuse me?" Elya said. "Emperor Aeris ordered me to help you figure out how to work these relics."

"Maybe you should focus on flying a Sabre after that beating the armada just endured."

This ungrateful prick, Elya thought. Dozens of pilots had *sacrificed their lives* for him, and he repays that with insult? "How dare you?" Elya said. "The Fleet is the only reason you're standing here breathing right now. My friends died in that fight."

Hedgebot froze in place, sensing the antagonism in his voice. The bot cocked its head.

Aganaki muttered something under his breath.

"What did you say?" Elya asked.

"I said, the only hope humanity has of defeating the Kryl is here in this room."

"Lot of good that's done, with you at the helm," Elya said, gesturing to the minister, whose hands stroked the crystal obelisk like it was a precious jewel. "We can't use the prime relics we have, and Overmind X got to the death ray first."

"We would have gotten to that relic first if we focused on my work with the starmap," Aganaki said.

Elya glanced around at all the other scientists in the room, who were doing a good job pretending to be working rather than taking part in the shouting match and risking the minister's wrath. "Your work, huh?"

Aganaki finally spun to face Elya, his face darkening. "Why don't you go back to flying your starfighters and let the experts do their job in peace?"

"Experts? You know nothing. The Telos left that map for us to find, and you can barely read it. You can't even figure out how to unlock the geode, or work the Chronicle, and you're supposed to be the so-called xenotechnology 'expert'? What happened to all that knowledge you've been working so hard to hide from the rest of the Solaran people, huh? Or have you spent so much time and effort hiding the truth that you forgot how to learn new things?"

Aganaki crossed the room toward him while Elya stood his ground. The minister was taller than him, with a long nose, thin lips, and dark, pitiless eyes. But he was scrawny and lacked Elya's physical training.

"You know nothing, boy," Aganaki said. "You're just an expendable soldier, worth less than a speck of iron on the surface of an asteroid orbiting a dying world. If I want you removed, all I have to do is say the word and"—the minister snapped, and Elya flinched slightly—"you're out an airlock without a vac suit."

Elya snapped his jaw shut so hard he bit his tongue, and the taste of copper washed through his mouth. His aching jaw throbbed as a reminder of how far words had gotten him today. Several months ago, a threat like that from the Minister of Xeno Affairs would have sent him for cover, tail tucked between his legs, like the kind of frightened backwater refugee he'd grown up loathing and fearing he'd become.

But recent events had hardened him. He'd been tortured by the minister and his cronies, infected by an alien parasite, and faced down Subject Zero and lived to tell the tale—multiple times.

Aganaki didn't scare him anymore. The minister was a power-hungry weasel, and nothing Elya said would change his mind.

More importantly, although the threat to his life had real venom—especially with the dark ops network Aganaki had proven he had access to—nothing the man ordered him to do could supersede the orders the Emperor had personally given him.

Aganaki was right about one thing. Captain Elya Nevers was a practical man. A soldier. A pilot. And pilots knew that the only thing that mattered to his commanders—to people like Emperor Aeris and Admiral Miyaru—were results.

Especially those that might change the outcome of the next battle.

Elya rocked back on his heels and smiled. Hedgebot scurried away and edged toward the geode. Its memory banks stored the experience of locking it in place by throwing its body into the handle, so it anticipated what Elya might do next.

Without a word, he broke from the confrontation with Minister Aganaki and strode over to the geode. As he was walking, Hedgebot raced up Elya's legs, rounded his waist in a spiral motion, and sprinted up his outstretched arm. On his next step, Elya twisted his hips and hurled the bot forward. Hedgebot tumbled between two stone fingers and slammed its metal body into the handle of the geode before bouncing off.

The geode didn't budge.

"What on Earth do you think you're doing?" Aganaki shouted.

"Trying," Elya said as he shoved a boot through the statue's fingers. His boot was wide enough that it only fit on one side, in the gap between the thumb and forefinger. He stomped on the handle with his heel, punctuating each word. "To. Get. This. Thing. Out!"

Despite the blows, the relic didn't give at all.

"You think we haven't *done* that already?" Aganaki said, rushing over. "Back off!"

Elya kicked one more time. When his foot came into contact with the stone, a sharp pain shot up his leg. He lurched to one side, staggering, as Aganaki shoved him back.

With a practiced motion born of hours in the gym doing hand-to-hand combat training, Elya pivoted and yanked the minister in the direction the man pushed him. His pointy silk shoes got tangled up, and he face-planted on the floor.

Elya bent down and traced his fingers along the seams in the floor. Like he'd seen before, they were visible, but very faint. The seams were thick enough for Hedgebot to slip a claw or two into, but they made no impression on the thick sole of his combat boots.

He stood and circled the fist containing the geode. A few of the scientists had stopped what they were doing to cross the room and help untangle Minister Aganaki from his Robes of State.

Elya rounded the next statue in the ring of seven encircling the room, simultaneously putting more room between himself and the entangled minister.

The same seams were drawn around each stone hand in a pattern of interlocking octagons. Two hands were closed around relics, while the rest lay open with their fingers slightly cupped. The fingers each had one extra knuckle joint.

Elya glanced up at the hologram creature. Its feet clasped the columns on either side, and its joints clearly fit the anatomy of the statues. The exposed skin appeared like a thick hide, slightly fuzzy, with very short hairs all over its surface. Each finger ended in a vicious-looking nail. Unlike the statues, the hologram's nails tapered to a point. The nails were much thicker than human nails. You could almost call them claws.

Above the robed Telos was the closed ceiling. Elya wished he could watch it open again, to confirm his theory about the floor seams.

"How did you get the ceiling to close?" Elya asked as he moved to put the hologram directly in front of him.

"None of your business," Aganaki grumbled. Now standing again, he pulled away from his assistants and brushed off his robes.

Elya walked until he was a meter or two away from the Chronicle. When the shield protecting it had been working, it was at this distance it had been activated, repelling Subject Zero.

The unintelligible design of seams in the floor ended right about that same distance.

Elya crossed the remaining distance and laid two hands on the angled face of the crystal obelisk.

"Retract the ceiling," he ordered.

No response. The Telos seemed to inhale, its chest expanding.

"Release the geode!" Elya said.

"Stop it," Minister Aganaki said, shoving Elya to the side. "You think we haven't tried that yet?"

He stood his ground, stretching to keep his hand on the crystal obelisk as he lost his temper. "Hey!" Elya shouted at the Chronicle. "I'm talking to you!"

The creature turned ever-so-slightly to face Elya. Although he couldn't see the eyes inside that dark cowl, ridges of hide-covered bone where they ought to have been turned and seemed to focus on him. The eyes were deeply inset and heavily shadowed.

"If you don't release the geode," Elya said. "I'll cut it out!"

No response. Why had the hologram spoken its purpose that first day if it didn't want to communicate with them now?

Aganaki didn't shove him again. Instead, he stood, staring wide-eyed at Elya. The minister glanced between Elya and the Chronicle.

"That's new," Aganaki said. "Say something else."

Elya took a deep breath and leaned to one side.

The creature rotated, following him.

"Release that relic!" Elya said, pointing at the prime relic he'd always called the geode.

Nothing happened.

"Retract the ceiling!"

Still nothing.

Aganaki harrumphed.

Elya ran over to the geode with the eyes of the creature now tracking his every step. He didn't know how he'd gotten its attention, but he needed to make use of it while he had it.

He whistled, and Hedgebot leaped back into his hands. Elya lifted the bot through the stone fingers and positioned its belly right along the base of the geode, where it was locked into the stone. It didn't skip his notice that the seam between the round bottom of the geode and the indentation in the stone palm were very similar in size and form to the ones in the floor.

This entire room seemed to be nothing but an intricately designed machine.

"Cut here, Hedgebot," Elya said.

The laser cutter whined as it kicked on. He watched for sparks and was rewarded with a massive impact on his chest that knocked the breath from his lungs.

Next thing he knew, he was gasping for air, and both he and Hedgebot writhed on the floor ten meters away. Elya groaned and rolled onto a pile of wooden shards—no, plastic slabs. He'd landed on top of one of the 3D-printed tables the scientists had hauled in to make their workspace, and shattered it into several pieces.

"Serves you right," Aganaki muttered as he knelt over him.

Elya staggered to his feet and retrieved Hedgebot. The blow had cracked a protective plate on its back, and it was hobbling crookedly. He placed the bot gingerly on his shoulder, but it couldn't hang on, so he simply cradled it in his hands.

Damn. Must have damaged Hedgebot's gyroscope.

In the meantime, the scientists had scrambled into action and were already replacing their sensors around the geode and its protective fist.

Apparently, he'd gotten more of a reaction out of it than they'd been able to get.

There was no way he was getting back through them to inspect it again. And now he was aching in more places than just his jaw.

"Guess your tests didn't reveal that," Elya said stubbornly.

"Come back any time you want to activate the Telos defenses," Aganaki said, chuckling. "Animus knows I enjoy seeing you get put on your back."

Elya glared at him. "How did you retract the ceiling? At least tell me that much."

"We didn't." Aganaki sighed and shook his head. "It closed on its own while we were out of the room, about a week after it opened. Thought we'd lost access to the room at first, but the tunnels remained open."

Elya blinked. "Has the Telos said anything else since that first day?"

Aganaki shook his head. "We can use the crystal obelisk to access a few datasets, but that's it. The starmap, measurements and information on the Kryl, but no, I can't get it to say anything else. I couldn't even get it to move until you did just now. It just sits there, breathing."

That was much more than he'd admitted in front of the Emperor. Elya grunted, then turned to look up at the hologram. It wasn't following him anymore, but he *had* grabbed its attention for a moment. If he did it once, he could do it again.

But enough for right now. Elya rubbed his eyes. He needed some rest and a quiet place to think.

He stalked off without so much as a goodbye to Minister Aganaki.

Elya passed between the row of columns and headed for the shadowed doorway and the ramp back to the surface level. As he passed into the shadows, Emperor Aeris stepped forward, startling him.

"Emperor Aeris!" he said.

The man's lips spread into a crooked smirk, and he clapped Elya on the shoulder. "Well done, Captain. Not even *I* saw that one coming."

"Uh, I," Elya sputtered. "Not exactly what I meant to do. Er, Your Majesty."

"It's a start."

The Emperor walked into the room. Four stoic bodyguards stepped out of the shadows and followed.

Elya shook his head and walked up the ramp. Hedgebot's joints whined tiredly in his arms, its chirruping sad and offbeat.

FOURTEEN

Kira took a deep breath and forced herself to meet the eyes of her war council.

They were hard. Angry. Lined with dark shadows and shot with red from the frantic retreat and subsequent patrols to ensure that Overmind X hadn't trailed them back to Elturis. The Kryl queen sent a few drones to harry their rear-guard but, thankfully, kept the bulk of her swarm—and that awful Telos relic they'd managed to weaponize—away.

"We lost too many good ships out there," said Colonel Arturo "The Knife" Seba, the jagged-faced commander of the corvette group. "Fifty-four corvettes down to 30. How did we let this happen?"

The Knife used the term "we," but Kira knew from the way he glared over his crooked nose—broken a dozen times on a dozen hostile boarding missions—that he meant "you."

"Our intel was incomplete," Kira said. "We knew where the Kryl were likely to be, and scouted out those systems, but we didn't know they had recovered a new relic already, nor what it could do."

"We should have been more cautious," Seba said. "We

shouldn't have followed those drones without more careful reconnaissance."

"I take full responsibility," Kira said. "It was my mistake."

"You knew what the Kryl were capable of, and you still led us right into an ambush! Half my captains have put in requests for transfers back to merchant protection or colonial escort missions."

"So deny their requests, Colonel." In charge of the heavy cruiser group, Admiral Cory Quellin was a whip-thin woman with dark, silver-streaked hair. A tight bun made hard planes of her cheeks, and she regarded the colonel coolly. "You're their group commander, Seba. You have that authority."

"I've got half a mind to go with them! Boarding a hostile pirate vessel seems like a walk in the park compared to chasing Kryl possibly wielding who knows what Telos weapons." He thumbed at his damaged nose as he made the comparison.

"The rumors must be right," Quellin said, lifting her chin in challenge. "You've grown soft during the peace. At least Admiral Miyaru has the balls to own up to what happened."

That hurt. Even though Quellin was defending her, the loss was *her* fault. Failure was always the fault of the leader, even if—no, *especially* if—she didn't see it coming.

But the accusation of cowardice seemed to sting Seba more, because he drew his shoulders back and frowned around the room. He didn't stand or stalk out. Instead, his keen, searching eyes fixed upon Minister Aganaki, finding a new target for his ire.

"You've been awfully quiet," Seba said. "Did you not provide the intel showing us which systems to scout? Why didn't you warn us about the damage those relics could do?"

"We can only make conjectures about what kinds of powers the remaining relics have," said the minister. "That's the first one I've known to cause such devastating damage. The other relics evade or repel. This is... something new."

Quellin frowned. "Can the relics we possess be weaponized? Or, as Aganaki suggests, perhaps used to defend against the power of that..." The admiral turned to look at Harmony's lights, which swirled over Kira's right shoulder. "What did you call it again?"

"A photon cannon," the shipmind said—as if it were the most natural thing in the world.

"Better than 'death ray'," Aganaki muttered.

"What was that?" asked Seba the Knife.

"Nothing," said the minister.

"Well?" Quellin said, her eyes never leaving the minister's face. "Answer the question."

"Can the relics be weaponized? Maybe," Aganaki said. "But not at this time. We can't even remove them from the City. And, if you don't mind, I'd like to get back to my work there so that they *can* be removed as soon as possible."

He glanced over his shoulder at Emperor Aeris, who had been quietly standing with his arms crossed next to the door, his cybernetic golden eyes half-lidded, as if he was bored.

Kira wasn't fooled. Maybe his presence contributed to her nervous feeling—he'd never sat in on one of her war council meetings before, and the fact that he hadn't said a word made her anxious. He had the power to remove her from her post with a snap of his fingers, and he wasn't a sheltered royal with his nose stuck in the sand like she'd expected him to be. Aeris was intelligent, clever, and more reckless with his own life than the ruler of the Solaran Empire ought to be. If he took action against her, it could upset the delicate agreement she'd made with MOXA and the Colonization Board.

The Emperor glanced at Aganaki, but did not acknowledge the unspoken request to dismiss him from the meeting early. On second thought, maybe that was why he insisted on being here. To hold Aganaki's feet to the fire.

Emperor Aeris was certainly an enigma. He raised his eyebrows at Kira.

"When we're done," she finally said, in answer to Aganaki's request.

The minister squirmed, but remained seated.

Kira didn't know what the emperor's game plan was, but at least he was useful for something.

"Why call it a 'photon cannon'?" Kira asked Harmony.

"The visible light given off by the weapon gave me the hint. My analysis concluded that its ray was as thin as a single photon—that's how it got through our energy shields. Fleet battle shields repelled plasma bolts and projectiles. They can't resist lasers or deflect lidar scans. Similarly, they can't defend against this weapon, which slipped straight through the shields, splitting the atoms of the aluminite hulls just wide enough for atmosphere to escape and, all at once, rupture."

"Spirit of Old Earth," Volk muttered, rubbing the worn face of a round medallion with his thumbs, a medallion etched with the outline of a tree. His lined face was drawn and haggard. He, too, had been withdrawn for most of the conversation—brooding, no doubt, about the Sabre pilots he'd lost, and all the other ships. Although most were still technically Kira's to command, she knew he felt a strong kinship to the officers he'd come up with, many of whom had perished. The XO sighed. "If we can't defend ourselves, what *can* we do?"

"We may be able to concentrate the energy shields," Emperor Aeris chimed in, "It would take some engineering, but it is technically feasible."

"That won't fully protect you against the photon cannon," Harmony said. "Merely delay the impact by a few seconds."

"True," the Emperor said, "But those extra seconds could save many lives."

The officers around the table nodded. They'd take any advantage they could get.

"If we alter our shields to counter the photon cannon, wouldn't that leave us vulnerable to other projectile attacks?" asked Kira.

Emperor Aeris nodded. "It would. You'd have to revise tactics in your approach."

Kira pressed her tongue along the insides of her teeth. "It's one option. Seba?" His forces were the scouts. They were in the most danger from a surprise attack.

"I'll have my engineers work with Harmony on it."

"Good. Done," Kira said. "What else?"

"There is one possibility we haven't discussed." Admiral Quellin rested her hands on the table in front of her. "A preemptive attack on Planet K."

Kira clenched her fists and took a long deep breath.

That was a grim thought. Sneaking an antimatter bomb onto Planet K, the Kryl homeworld, was what ended the war. It caused the entire species to contract inward to their home system, like a muscle cramping around an injury. Since the Kryl communicated psionically, they all felt such an attack as if it were an attack on their own body.

Not that Kira had a lot of sympathy for the xenos. They'd killed too many of her friends and allies over the years to feel bad for them. But the idea of another mission like that—the mission that killed her lover and brought him back to life as a mutant xeno—put her in a dark place.

"It wouldn't work," Aganaki said. "Through our investigations into Overmind X, we've learned that she was severed from the Queen Mother's hivemind to form her own swarm. An attack on Planet K wouldn't register on X's network and, as far as we can tell, the Queen Mother is still in hibernation. If we're not careful, we could form more splinter swarms."

"Besides," Kira said, "There are five billion Kryl packed into their home system. Flying close enough to make the shot would be like wading into the center of a beehive. We'd never make it close enough for a successful attack."

"Not to mention," Emperor Aeris said, "That the last thing we want to do is wake the leviathan while trying to kill the shark. The Solaran Empire is not prepared for another all-out war with the Kryl."

The room fell silent.

"The thing to do," Aganaki said, "is obtain the remaining two relics before Overmind X does, and use them to put her down before she causes more destruction."

The room erupted into competing arguments as everyone began to talk at once. Quellin was spoiling for a fight, and Seba kept goading her on. Volk voiced his desire to minimize further losses. Aganaki told them they were all idiots, and that Overmind X wanted them fighting amongst themselves instead of working to find the relics.

"Enough!" Kira shouted, silencing them. "Aganaki's right. The reason this armada was authorized to begin with was for the purpose of eliminating Overmind X. And the best way to do that is to get to the remaining relics before the Kryl do."

"We need time to rebuild our forces," Seba said.

"And rework our strategy," Quellin muttered.

"You have twenty-four hours," Kira said. "Your Majesty, can you commandeer extra ships to replace the ones we lost?"

He frowned. "Not all of them, to be sure. I... have a few in my private docks that could be of use. I'll get on the ansible and make some calls."

"Thank you, sir. Minister Aganaki, did you bring what I requested?"

"I had my astronomers produce a replica for you." He took out his tab and swiped a starmap onto the holoprojector at the center of the war room table. A reproduction of the old starmap he'd found stored in the Chronicle expanded to fill the space between them. "We've advanced the map through time to what we believe is the present day."

"How confident are you about your calculations?"

"Within a reasonable margin of error."

Kira studied him, and then the starmap, for a long moment. Seven regions were marked. She easily picked out Elturis, and the system where the planet Robichar was located. "There are four possible locations for the remaining relics, correct?"

Aganaki nodded his head. "Technically, yes. Depending when the map was made, various factors can cause variants in the orbital drift of stars, and the detail with which the Fleet has mapped various systems in the galaxy—"

"Save me the physics lesson," she said, cutting him off. "Where are the four locations?"

Aganaki tapped on his tab a few times, and three of the markers vanished. The remaining four locations marked in bright neon colors were all in uninhabited systems, only a couple of which had been earmarked by the Colonization Board for potential human habitation.

At least she wouldn't have to worry about civilian evacuations this time.

FIFTEEN

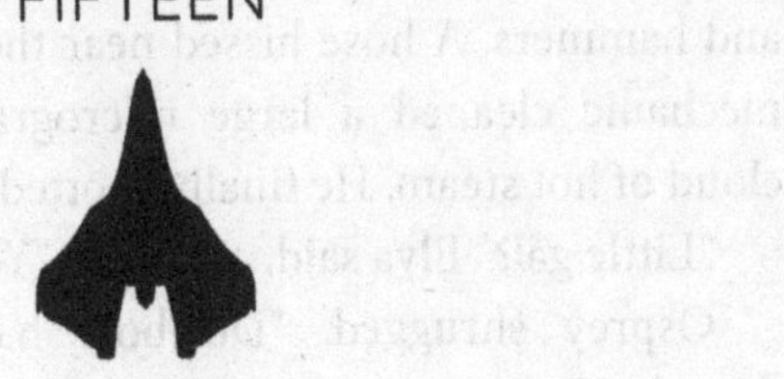

Elya slapped his visor down and sparked up a small welding torch. He bent over Hedgebot's powerless shell—he'd disconnected and removed the power core so it wouldn't get damaged—and lowered the seven-thousand-degree arc to the bot's broken plate, filling the crack with liquid aluminite that smoked as it cooled.

He hissed as his fingers slipped, and liquid metal spattered onto his opposite hand. It burned through the shop gloves he wore. He'd chosen a thin pair so that he could more easily guide the arc, as he needed precision to get this right.

He tore the glove off and shoved his hand under a cold faucet for a minute. When he was sure he hadn't done permanent damage, he refitted the glove and bent back over his work. In a few minutes, he'd successfully repaired the break. The entire plate would have to be replaced when he was back on Ariadne and had access to a proper bot machinist, but for now it would hold together, if not as strongly as before.

He stepped back and regarded Hedgebot's battle scar.

"Makes the little gal look tough," said Captain Osprey.

Elya pushed his visor up with the back of his wrist and wiped sweat from his forehead. At stations around him, a dozen other machinists worked on everything from astrobots to engine blocks with welding torches, wrenches, and hammers. A hose hissed near the back of the room as a mechanic cleaned a large microgravity generator with a cloud of hot steam. He finally spotted his antagonist.

"Little gal?" Elya said, annoyed. "You mean little fella."

Osprey shrugged. "Do bots have genders? I always thought Hedgebot seemed like a she."

Elya snorted. "She's certainly got sass enough for you *and* her, if that's the case. But naw. Hedgebot is just Hedgebot. There's no need to gender it."

"Aww, but she's so cute."

Ignoring her, Elya pulled out his tab and checked his position in the ansible queue. He groaned.

"Long wait?" asked Osprey.

"Longer than usual, that's for sure. I'm number 153. Guess everyone wants to call home after the battle."

"Plus, I'm sure they need the ansible for official comms, too. Colonel Volk told me the Emperor was going to requisition additional ships to replace the ones we lost."

That wasn't all he seemed to be doing. Not for the first time since their latest encounter, Elya wondered what His Royal Majesty was doing all the way out here in a war zone. Wouldn't he rather be safe at home in his pleasure palace, clear of the fighting and politicking? Were the Telos relics truly that important to him?

Or did he have some kind of ulterior motive?

Elya puzzled it over. Then, finding no satisfactory answer, he flipped Hedgebot onto its back. The weld had cooled, and he needed to check inside now. Its photo sensors were mostly intact. Only a couple of wires had shorted out. He pulled the damaged ones out, retrieved a new spool from the bench at the side of the room, and began cutting replacements.

Osprey, still watching him, walked over and touched his cheek. He flinched when she applied pressure near his jaw.

"Sorry," she said, dropping her hand. "Thought it was a grease stain. You're gonna have one blitz of a shiner."

Elya ducked his head, embarrassed. He'd always had a friendly relationship with Raptor—even when they disagreed about tactics or how to interpret orders, which was often—but they'd never been more than comrades. Now that she'd been named mission commander, it seemed wise to keep it that way.

"Ruby's got a mean right hook," Elya said as he bent back over Hedgebot. Using a flat screwdriver, he popped open the panel containing the gyroscope mechanism.

"Ah, Earth. Look at this." He tilted it toward Osprey.

She winced. "Have a backup?"

"I wish. They don't stock many gyroscopes of Hedgebot's size on the *Paladin of Abniss,* and I think they've all been requisitioned."

Osprey walked over to check the inventory. "Seems like you're right," she said a second later. "Can you repair it?"

"Maybe..."

He gingerly removed the gyroscope and tested its spin on the tabletop. No wonder Hedgebot was having trouble balancing. The mechanism wobbled and fell off the table. Elya caught it before it hit the floor.

"Anything I can do to help?" Osprey asked.

"Thanks, but I'm good. Just need to figure out how to re-align it. You can see a few cracks in the casing, here and here. I might be able to weld those. There's something inside that's throwing off the weight distribution, though."

"Okay, well, let me know. I'm happy to put in a request

for equipment if it means both you and that bot are flying again on the next mission."

"Which is when?"

"We're on crew rest for 24 hours. After that, we'll see."

"Copy that. I'll be ready."

"Don't forget to rest up," she said. "And ice your face."

"Yessir." He didn't tell her he'd already tried to sleep, and couldn't. He'd come up here after a couple hours of fitful tossing. Ice, though. That was a good idea. His jaw still ached when he talked.

"Oh, and Nevers?"

He looked up from the gyroscope. She was standing in the doorway. "Be in the hangar at 0700 tomorrow."

"Why so early?"

"I'm trying to make things right with the other pilots. Don't know if it'll work, but... I've got to do something."

"All right, Raptor. I'll be there."

She slipped around the corner and out of sight.

Elya turned back to Hedgebot. He turned the gyroscope over in his hand and referred to a repair manual on his tab. When he looked up again, Yorra was standing there in front of him.

"Hi," he said, surprised.

"Have you seen Park?"

Elya shook his head. "Sorry. Last time I saw him, you were taking him to the sick bay. Why?"

A head shorter than him, with high cheekbones, beautiful brown eyes, and lustrous dark hair, Yorra's normally smooth, controlled expression cracked and crumbled.

She regained control a moment later, smoothing her face back to light-brown glass. She took a deep breath and looked around the shop. "He's avoiding me."

"What for?"

"I don't know, Nevers. That's why they call it 'avoiding.'"

"Sorry. I..." He didn't know what to say. He put Hedgebot's gyroscope back on the table next to the bot's unpowered shell. In many ways, this gyroscope was the bot's mind, and he had to be careful not to damage it. "How can I help?"

"If you see him, tell Park I'm looking for him."

"Do you want me to help find him? I can take a break..."

"No," she blurted. "No, it's okay. You need Hedgebot in working order. That bot's been indispensable in these last few missions. Our good luck charm. At least until... lately."

Ahh. Now he saw where this was going. "Park feels bad about what happened to Grizzly, doesn't he?"

"Ruby may have punched you in the face, but the stuff some of the other pilots said to Park in the sick bay was just awful. Be glad you weren't there."

"Seems like it shook you up, too."

"I think Park blames himself for what happened. And then having to be hauled out of the battle like a piece of oversized cargo... We lost more Sabres in the retreat than we did in the fight itself."

Elya nodded. That was true. Should he have been more distraught about that? He supposed everyone reacted in their own way. Taking a crack at the geode, and then burying himself in Hedgebot's repairs up here, were his way of dealing with the stress and anxiety he carried. Park had his own methods. And Elya may have let Subject Zero get away, but he hadn't been a helpless sitting duck while a dozen pilots died dragging his damaged ship home.

"It's not his fault," Elya said. "He can't blame himself, and neither can you."

"I know that," Yorra snapped. "Sorry. I'm gonna keep looking. I... if you see him, would you just talk to him for me? Please? He needs something to keep him busy when he's like this. He doesn't do good alone, not like you."

"Of course."

"Thanks." She hugged herself with her arms like she was cold, even though it was sweltering in here.

"Are *you* okay, Gears?"

She bobbed her head. Not really an answer in the affirmative, so much as an acknowledgement of the question. "I'll be fine."

"We're Flight 18, right? You can talk to me. I'm a good listener."

She snorted. "Are you?"

"Sure." He grinned. "When I actually want to pay attention."

"You get that tunnel vision. I've seen it. It's just... I feel so useless. I should have done more, but I could barely keep those Kryl drones off my own six. I'm not as good a pilot as you or Raptor, or Ruby or..." she trailed off, not wanting to say Grizzly's name. "I just wish I could do more." She glanced up and her eyes locked on his face. "Ohh, Nevers, your face is getting purple."

"Purple, really?"

He picked up a piece of scrap metal lying on a nearby workbench and examined himself in the reflection. Yep, that was a bruise, all right. "Damn," he muttered. "Raptor wasn't joking."

"Did you try talking to Ruby afterward?"

"No. She was way too worked up." He paused. "Raptor came in here just a little bit before you, though, and I got the impression she's up to something."

"Uh, oh." Yorra stopped and dropped her arms. "I better find out what. In case she needs help softening the blow. You know how... intense she can be."

"I do, indeed. Better you than me."

Yorra snorted, then got that distant, worried look in her eyes again. She shook herself while Elya was still searching for the right words to say—and feeling quite awkward about it.

"I'll tell you what," said Yorra. "If you can locate Park and find some way to get his mind off things, get him back to his old self, I'll talk to Ruby for you and see if I can't build a new bridge between our flights. This kind of strife among the squad isn't good for anyone. It can't stand."

Gears may not have been the best pilot in their flight, but the way she cared for the people around her showed him she was most definitely the best—or at least, the kindest—of them.

"Deal," said Elya. His tab dinged. Picking it up, he saw that his spot in the ansible queue would be coming up soon. "Finally. Gotta jet. We'll stay close on this, yeah?"

She nodded and left the shop. He packed Hedgebot in a storage container, behind a combo lock, for safekeeping.

Then he went to let his family know he was still alive.

SIXTEEN

"Just tell me," Casey said. "Rip the bandage off."

Harmony's lights swirled and coalesced into an abstract ball of whirling patterns that changed and shifted against the walls of the *Paladin of Abniss*. The shipmind did that when she was feeling nervous or cagey, or sometimes when she wanted to share something but couldn't. Casey had now spent enough time with Harmony to recognize her moods, and this one was making her distinctly uncomfortable.

"You're not alone in your grief, Captain," said the shipmind. "We sustained losses across the armada."

"I know that. But *my* job is to care for the Furies. So just tell me already. What's the final count? How many, exactly, did we lose?"

Casey had done her own headcount, but the pilots were scattered around the *Paladin* and she wanted desperately to be wrong about it. One of the shipmind's jobs was to keep personnel records of the crew and ships onboard... so whatever Harmony said would be what went into the official battle record.

"Fifty-three pilots perished in the battle," Harmony said. "Seventeen additional casualties were recorded, and those pilots are currently receiving medical care."

Earth, Casey thought, closing her eyes and breathing deeply. She hadn't been wrong, and it had never hurt so much to be right.

She needed to know the details, so she marched on with her next question. "Which flights still have enough pilots to deploy?"

"Flights 20 through 23 perished entirely. Flight 7, Flight 8, Flight 12, Flight 16 and Flight 19 each have only a single pilot remaining. I recommend combining them into a single flight. The rest of the flights lost one or two pilots each. Only Flight 18 and Flight 24 remain at full strength."

"Animus," Casey whispered, closing her eyes and sending up a silent prayer to the Spirit of Old Earth. She'd never been very religious, but it seemed like the only thing left to do. What other recourse does a person have when they feel this hopeless?

After a long minute of reflection, and several deep breathing exercises as she paced up and down this empty hallway in a rarely trafficked lounge behind the guest cabins, she reigned in her anger and frustration.

It wasn't acceptance… not yet. Probably not soon. But she couldn't do *nothing*, either.

As she considered her next move, Casey tried to channel the strength of her father and the steady, sure-handedness of Colonel Walcott, the last squadron commander she'd respected. His words hadn't been echoing in her mind since they'd been stationed in Elturis, but she still thought of him a lot. He'd been her role model.

She also thought of her mother, whose beautiful soul rejoined the galactic dance before her time. Casey had been through grief before. Knowing she could get through it again helped... somewhat.

"What do you think I should do about Ruby?" Casey asked the shipmind.

"What do *you* think you should do?" Harmony shot back. Now that she wasn't trying to evade the topic, large eyes twinkled at Casey out of an androgynous hologram face.

"I don't know," Casey said. "She's grieving right now. You can't reason with a person in that state of mind."

"Sounds like you're afraid of how she might react."

"After what happened in the hangar? Um, yeah, that's an understatement."

"Is there another way to reach her? Actions speak louder than words."

"I don't know." Casey leaned her back against the wall and sank to the ground. She put her head in her hands. "I wish Volk had more time to help. He only named me *mission* commander. Being the squad's therapist wasn't on my list of assigned duties," she complained. "Where's Volk right now?"

"He's overseeing repairs on the *Paladin* and directing resupply logistics. Admiral Miyaru's orders."

Casey blew out her breath and made a frustrated noise in her throat. She couldn't disturb him for this. He was counting on her to deal with it herself.

"What else can you do to make headway in the meantime?" Harmony prompted.

"I can't take the burden of everyone's losses on myself, that's for sure."

Such was Casey's instinct—to do for everyone else what they couldn't do themselves. She was her father's daughter that way, quick to shoulder a burden even when she knew it would crush her.

"Each person grieves in their own way," Casey said. "Ruby lashed out at her friends. Elya's working on Hedgebot and sticking his nose into MOXA business again. Park's vanished, probably off on some kind of bender. Gears is doing all right, all things considered, but that's probably because she's so worried about all of us she isn't thinking about what *she* needs. I'll have to talk to her about that next time I see her..." Casey shook her head. "But how am I supposed to do that for the entire squadron? For starters, I'm not close to all of them like I am with Flight 18. Not to mention, there are..." *There were a hundred and eight.* "Now, fifty-five people spread out across the ship. I can't reach them all in the time we have left..."

That helpless, spinning feeling of overwhelm descended upon her again.

"That's what the command structure is for," Harmony reminded her. "It's not the squadron commander's job to care for each person individually. That would be too much for any one person to handle."

Casey whipped her head up. "What are you suggesting?"

"How many Flight leads are left?"

She blinked. "Sixteen, including me."

Fifteen other flight leads. Fifteen was manageable. She checked the clock. Casey could speak to fifteen people before their next rotation. Her leads could then check on *their* pilots—or pilots in other flights, if theirs was decimated by losses.

"Harmony, can I see a roster?" She would recognize each of them, and know their call signs and names, but not always who reported to them. "One of those box and line chart thingamajigs."

"An organizational chart?"

"Yeah, that. Show me how it was before, including those we lost."

Harmony manifested the chart in hologram, fading out the boxes representing those who perished. The gaps sent a wave of cold shock through her body... and then she got to work.

It took Casey an hour to rearrange the chart to her satisfaction, filling in gaps, carefully placing pilots who'd been orphaned in the battle into flights where the lead knew them, and also had the capacity to manage them. She didn't want anyone to feel left out *or* overwhelmed.

When she was done, Casey dismissed the chart and then pushed herself back to her feet. "Okay. Can you guide me to each of the leads? Save Flight 4 for last, and also let's start at the sick bay. You said seventeen people were there receiving medical treatment, right? It's always good for the commander to visit the sick bay."

Harmony's lights swirled in excitement. She formed a broad arrow pointed out the door of the empty lounge.

"Don't do that around the others. Please. If they see me walking around the ship like I'm playing some kind of augmented reality treasure hunting game, I'll never hear the end of it."

The lights broke back into an abstract pattern, then reformed into the androgynous avatar that was the closest thing to Harmony's physical identity.

"Better," Casey said. "Now, let's get moving. No time to waste."

As she crossed the ship toward the sick bay, an idea coalesced in her mind. If actions spoke louder than words, Casey had to show how much she really cared. Visiting the wounded and talking to the leads was a good start—at least with those who wanted to talk—but it wouldn't be enough to win over someone like Ruby, who wasn't interested in her words and didn't trust her to begin with.

So how to build trust with someone who distrusted you? With your actions.

Casey couldn't take back what had happened to Grizzly

and fifty-two other pilots. But there were fifty-five she *could* care for, and do her best to care for going forward.

Whether they were on an active mission or not, with Volk occupied, these people were her responsibility. There was no one else. Fifty-five angry, hurt, grieving pilots suffering the biggest losses they'd ever sustained.

If she made the wrong move, they'd fall apart.

If she made the right one, they'd come out stronger on the other side.

Stronger together.

At the sick bay, a kindly nurse led her back to the recovery rooms, where several pilots were hooked up by their spinal ports, or had their arms resting in diagnostic cuffs. She spent a few minutes saying hello and checking on each person. She asked how they were holding up, fetched glasses of water, gave hugs. One woman wanted to call home, but her tab had been lost in the chaos, so Casey opened her own and booked a spot in the ansible queue for her. A male pilot about five years younger than Casey said he was hungry, so she went and found a nurse to send him a plastic container of applesauce and a ration bar. Not the most glamorous of meals, but it was better than nothing.

She eventually found her first flight lead.

"Hey, Fuzz," she said.

"Cap'm." The 40-year-old pilot had a thick, unruly red beard that was no longer trimmed to regulation—the source of his call sign. They'd been so busy flying missions lately that no one had bothered to discipline him for it. Besides, he was the kind of guy who could shave before the morning run and have a full beard by rec time. At the moment, his beard bushed out over top of a neck brace.

"How are you holding up?" she asked.

Fuzz rocked one hand like a see-saw. "Feel like I want to break something, but all the extra chairs are taken." She'd checked the org chart before greeting him. Fuzz had lost two pilots in the fight. "How about you?"

"Tired of this shit," she said. "Losing people sucks."

"True that." His eyes glanced at her face and then at the blank cream-colored wall in front of him. He said nothing as they focused on a memory only he could see. He sighed heavily.

Casey blinked as she finally realized he was waiting for her to go away. He didn't act outright hostile like Ruby, but… She decided to stand her ground and try again.

"How are your pilots holding up?" she asked.

Fuzz see-sawed his hand again, then pulled at the neck brace with one finger. "Remus is in the back, getting his ankle straightened out. He landed wrong when he jumped out of his fighter."

"Ouch."

"The twins are shaken up. Pretty sure they're waist deep in a bottle of tequila somewhere."

"That's their right. Just make sure they get some rest before we redeploy."

He grunted. It wasn't the flight lead's job to regulate how people spent their rec time. A flight lead with his experience would know better than to interfere when two pilots needed to blow off steam at a time like this.

"I have a favor to ask." She called up the org chart on her tab and pointed to the orphaned pilot from Flight 7. "Will you take Walnut in from the cold?"

He frowned and tried to lean forward. When his beard got caught in the neck brace, he swore, then ripped the brace off, twisting the clasps and sending bits of plastic flying as he tore at it. "Rather have a sore neck than wear that Earth-damned brace another minute. Let me see that."

She swiped over the hologram. He reviewed his flight,

then his eyes swept briefly across the org chart—her redesigned version. "I'll take Bradley, too."

"Are you sure? You don't need to have five reports. There are other leads who have room, too."

"I want to do it, Raptor. Just say thank you and move on."

"Thank you."

Fuzz sniffed and nodded curtly. His bushy beard spread into a frown as he grew pensive and started pacing. "I've got to get out of this place. Excuse me, Cap'm, I'm gonna check on Remus."

"Wait, one more thing before you go." She told him about her plan—the one that had been nascent when she told Nevers, and which had coalesced further on the walk to the sick bay—and what she needed from him to get it done.

He got very somber and clapped her on the shoulder. His huge hand swallowed her entire bicep. "Aye. I've got ya."

"Remember, 0700."

"Yessuh." He dropped his hand and walked off.

Casey visited a few more pilots. She double checked with a medic to make sure she'd seen them all, then followed Harmony's directions toward the pilot's cabins.

"You're feeling lighter already," Harmony said.

Casey hesitated. Had she been bouncing as she walked? "I feel guilty about it, but yeah, I guess I do."

"Why should you feel guilty?"

"Because I shouldn't be happy when so many people have died." She said it under her breath so none of the somber people walking through the halls in this part of the destroyer overheard her.

Harmony's swirling hologram disappeared as they turned down a busy corridor. "We honor the memories of those we've lost," the shipmind said, speaking directly into Casey's mind through her spinal port apparatus. It wasn't just a drug delivery mechanism—there was a bit of silicone and metal embedded in there that allowed her to interface with some of the diagnostic and communication systems in her Sabre. This was the first time Harmony had used the chip to communicate with her directly, and even though she'd been educated about the possibility, it was a strange experience. "At the same time, a leader's job is to serve and care for those who survived. That includes being kind to *yourself*."

Casey nodded. That was sound advice, and it re-energized her. "Who's next?"

Careful to avoid the rooms of Ruby and her crew, Casey sought out more pilots and flight leads. Many were, as Fuzz had suggested, playing a game of who can find the bottom of the bottle first.

She waved her arm in front of an automated door. As it slid open, four pilots inside turned to stare at her. They shot to their feet and saluted as they hid bottles behind their backs.

"At ease," she said. It was a group of lieutenants. Kids just out of flight training. There were maybe a dozen of them in the Furies, as in every squad. The Fleet liked to spread out the newbies. "May I?"

She held her hand out. One kid, a ginger girl with a splash of freckles on her pale cheeks, blushed a deep red as she handed over a bottle of cheap moonshine.

Casey took a sniff, followed by a large swallow. The liquor burned as it trickled down her throat.

The pilots' eyes widened. When she burped, and then cracked a smile, the group relaxed, chuckling.

At their insistence, Casey took another shot, this time out of a proper glass (they had to clean one out with sanitizer and a hand towel while she made jokes about the alcohol killing any germs that were left behind).

She found her next flight lead when Tank staggered into the room, pushed aside two younger pilots, and snarled at them to keep it down.

She came face to face with Casey.

"Oh, hi Raptor." She gave a sloppy, half-assed salute.

Casey straightened. "Tank."

The muscular woman was built like her nickname. A head shorter than Casey, stout, with huge shoulders and thighs that required specially tailored flight suits. Her uniform was, at the moment, zipped open and hanging loosely around her waist. A white t-shirt was stained with sweat at the armpits, and her identi-ring hung on a long chain over top of the shirt.

"What you doing drinking with these kids?"

"Just checking in. I want to make sure everyone's holding together all right."

They all averted their eyes from Tank, who was glaring around at them.

"Y'all think this is some kinda celebration?"

"I don't celebrate my losses," Casey said. "I reflect on them. And I honor the friends we lost."

Tank met Casey's eyes with her own bloodshot ones. She held them for five long seconds, until Tank looked away, ashamed.

"I was actually looking for you," Casey said. "Can we talk?"

"I'm off duty."

"I'm not here to debrief you, Tank. I just want to talk. You mind?" she asked as she pointed to a water bottle standing on the counter. One of the rookie pilots threw it to her. Casey caught it and untwisted the cap on the way out of the cabin.

In the hallway, they had a bit more room to breathe. She gave Tank the water bottle. The other captain guzzled it and belched.

"What's on your mind?" Casey asked.

"I hate this," Tank said.

"The pilots drinking?"

"What? No. Just want them to show a little respect. This isn't some kind of celebration."

"No, it's not. I'm sorry. I think they were just excited that I joined them."

Tank nodded.

"Losing people sucks, doesn't it?"

"You got that right," Tank said.

"So what are we gonna do about it?" Casey asked.

Tank paced in a tight circle. "Frag some Kryl, I hope. Catch that bastard mutant and fly him into a solid surface."

She hauled back and punched the wall, holding her fist there long after the metallic echo faded.

"Thought you might say that. Tank, I need you to be a role model for those kids, and all the other pilots who look up to you."

Her face twisted into a snarl. "Look up to me? I lost three pilots today!"

"All of those rookies in there did too. So, what in the name of Animus makes you think *you* deserve special treatment?" She couldn't be that harsh with all the leads, but she knew Tank well enough to know how she responded under pressure: she got angry, and she got after it.

Casey simply needed to show her in which direction to go.

"Of course not," Tank said, squeezing the words out between her teeth as she stepped up to Casey, tilting her head back to glare angrily.

"Here's what I'm thinking." Casey pulled out the hologram of the org chart. Two of the three pilots Casey wanted to give to Tank had been in that cabin drinking with her. "They're green, but I think you can get 'em into shape."

"Good. Though I'm not sure anyone on this squad can be considered green after that battle."

Casey grunted. "Good point. They need support and a steady hand. They need an experienced leader like you."

"All right, fine, blondie," She glanced down at the bottle in her hand, then bent and set it on the floor. She pinched her shirt and sniffed. "I'll do it. I better take a shower first."

"I need one more thing, if you don't mind." Like she did with Fuzz, Casey spelled out what she was planning. Tears immediately welled up in Tank's eyes. She blinked and wiped them away with a forearm. "I'll get right on it."

"After you shower."

"After I shower. Thank you, sir."

The rest of the conversations proceeded in a relatively similar fashion. After the fourth one, Casey found her groove. Feeling calmly confident, she navigated the rest with ease.

Finally, only one flight lead remained.

"Would you like me to locate Ruby for you?" Harmony asked.

"No. I don't want to risk setting her off. I'm sending a message to the whole squad. She'll see that and we'll just have to hope she shows up with everyone else. If not… I guess I'll cross that bridge when I come to it."

"Fair enough," Harmony said. "You really got the hang of it at the end there. How are you feeling now?"

"Tired," Casey said. It was late. She only had a few hours to rest, and then she'd have to be up early to execute her plan.

"I can help you get straight into your REM cycle, if you'll allow me access to your port."

"You can make me go to sleep?"

Harmony nodded.

"Cool trick. Okay, but there's one more thing I have to do first."

She found Yorra in the cabin they shared, sitting on her bed with her knees drawn to her chest. Casey told her what she needed, and together they submitted the requisition on Casey's tab.

Finally, she dropped the device to the floor and kicked off her shoes. To give Harmony access, she attached a small cable to her spinal port—it tugged at her scalp, but she was too tired to care.

"You gonna be okay, Gears?" Casey asked, lying in bed with her eyes closed. She could hear Yorra breathing in the bunk across the cabin.

"I'm just worried Park will do something he'll regret."

"He'll come around."

Yorra grunted.

"Try to get some rest."

Casey was asleep as soon as the words were out of her mouth. Aided by the shipmind, she sank into the deep slumber of someone who has given it their all, even as an anxious lack of confidence that it wasn't enough trailed her into dreams she hoped to forget.

SEVENTEEN

The terminal keyed in on Elya's identi-ring as he scooted his chair up and flipped the sole switch on the tabletop. A blue strip of light brightened to show a privacy filter had activated, framing the door behind him and encircling the small room.

Finally, he thought, breathing out.

He opened his end of the channel, checked the mic, and waited.

It would take his mother a few minutes to connect on her end. She would have already left her home and traveled across town to the Imperial comms station. She'd be given a room just like this one to take his call.

The ansible was the only way to have a live conversation over interstellar distances without experiencing extremely long delays between transmissions. Paired receivers split at the quantum level resonated simultaneously on both ends, no matter how far apart they were in space.

The Solaran Empire controlled and monitored access to all ansible endpoints. The machine's strategic significance was broadly recognized; there was no other known method for coordinating forces across galactic-scale distances. Additionally, ansibles were sensitive pieces of equipment that had to be carefully monitored to ensure proper function. They were exceedingly expensive to install, and they took an enormous amount of power to run. The only reason Eskatan had one was because it had grown into a key mining operation for the Solaran Empire.

The ansible was also—at least originally—Telos technology.

Elya had learned this a couple months ago when he found an old journal in the Archives beneath a church of Animus on Ariadne, dating back thousands of years to the time of the Great Migration, an era so named for the centuries humanity spent voyaging through the stars to find a new home after fleeing a dying Earth.

So it was understandable that the Empire kept ansibles locked down tight. That Admiral Miyaru had opened the queues on the *Paladin of Abniss* showed how much she cared about her crew—out here in a remote system, the ansible was their lifeline to civilization. It was also the only way soldiers could let their families know they were alive. Admiral Miyaru knew how important it was for people to contact their families.

Elya pushed an empty disposable cup and ration bar wrapper left by the previous occupant into a trash can, using a foot pedal to expose the bin and then releasing it so it receded back into the wall. When he looked up, his mother's face smiled at him out of a window into another room, just like this one.

"Elya, my son," she said. "By the Spirit, it's good to see your face."

She wore an outfit designed for a desert climate, a loose white tunic wrapped twice around her waist and tucked in at the back. It kept her skin safe from the harsh sun when she ventured out from under the protection of the UV filters drawn over the residential area. The tunic's edges were trimmed with a silver band of trees and elephants. The mythological symbols matched the silver streaks in her once night-dark hair. Her eyes remained a vivid sky blue, the same as ever.

"Hi, Mom," Elya said. "How are you?"

Smile lines deepened at the corners of her eyes. "Better, now that I know you're okay. Where's Hedgebot? He's usually with you when you call."

That was just like her, to immediately notice Hedgebot missing. But Elya supposed he and the danger detector had been inseparable since their refugee days. "He had a little accident. I'm in the middle of repairs, so I left him in the shop."

"Anything serious?"

"He'll be okay. I don't have access to replacement gyroscopes onboard, so I've got to repair the one he's using, if I can. What's new in your world? Did you get the transfer from last week?" He'd been so busy he hadn't double-checked that it went through.

"I did, thank you, dear. I keep telling you, you don't have to send money home anymore. We're good."

"I know," he said. "But I want to help." He also wanted to keep her out of the mines, and the money he sent home each month, a small portion of his paycheck, helped give her that freedom. She taught pre-school and gave voice lessons to make ends meet, though it never seemed to be enough. "What news from Eskatan?"

"News of the battle spread like wildfire once it came over the ansible. It's caused a bit of a ruckus. All my friends are asking about you."

"Well, you can tell them I'm fine," Elya said. Was that true?

He was alive. That was better than many others. How many mothers would get a different kind of call today?

"Except for that swollen jaw," she pointed out. "Was that from the battle?"

"Actually, I, uh, tripped and fell into another pilot's fist."

"What?" Her eyebrows shot up. "What happened?"

"Hurt people hurt people. It's not her fault. It looks way worse than it actually is, trust me."

His mother gave him one of her looks. It said, *You can't fool me.* "Make sure you ice that or you'll regret it at breakfast."

"I will, Mom." He worked his jaw. "So people are talking about the battle, huh?"

"It's all over the news networks. Biggest battle with the Kryl in over a decade. Most losses we've suffered since the war ended. I think everyone's worried there's going to be another conflagration, and then what will happen to all the refugees?"

"That won't happen. Not if I can help it."

"Can you?"

He hadn't told her every detail about the relics and what he'd been through on their behalf, but he'd filled her in on the basics. Not the child kidnapping, forced mutation, and torture part. She was his mom, after all, and he didn't want her to worry. But he'd given her the highlights. "Emperor Aeris thinks so."

"*The* Emperor Aeris?"

Elya nodded. "Yup."

"Wow." She blinked and wrung her hands together. "My, how far you've come from picking bot parts out of rubbish bins..." She glanced behind her and frowned. A deep *thump thump thump* echoed through the channel.

"What's that?" asked Elya.

"Hooligans. The ansible queue is busy today. You'll never believe what I had to go through to get this room."

"Sorry."

"Don't be sorry. It's not your fault. Everything is just crazy here right now."

"Because of the battle, or something else?"

"The news isn't helping, but our particular flavor of unrest is more than that, I'm afraid. A group of Robichar refugees is causing trouble, rumors of gathering a militia and going to take their planet back."

"Really," he said, deadpan. Not really a question so much as a statement of utter disbelief. "That's a terrible idea."

"They talk a big game, but they aren't going anywhere without a ship. The Fleet just requisitioned the rest of the cruisers we had sitting in port."

Elya grunted. "That tracks. We lost a lot of ships. I bet the shipyards are busy, too."

"Running 'round the clock. And in the meantime, all those people are stuck here without an outlet for their anguish. We don't have enough housing, let alone jobs for all the new people."

"I know the mines are over-staffed, but what about the shipyards?"

She shook her head. "More people than machines to operate. We've never had this many unemployed refugees at once."

"I know. I helped evacuate them, remember? How are they eating? The ones that can't work, I mean."

"Scraping by on Imperial ration cards. But you and I both know *that's* not making a living."

He did, indeed. Their family had relied on government rations, mostly synthetic biofuel—paste in tubes that contained all your vitamins and nutrients but wasn't truly nourishing—for months after their arrival on Eskatan. It wasn't until Arn and his mother both got jobs that they had enough money to afford *real* meat and vegetables. For his mom, she never truly felt at home until she'd been able to cook again. Things had gotten better after that.

"How's Arn doing?" Elya asked. "He still leading excavation teams?"

"Even better." His mom swelled up with pride. "He's running the training program now. Training new shift managers and miners."

"Wow! Good for him."

"It's wonderful. He's home for dinner each night, he spends more time with the girls, and he doesn't get exposed to that nasty radiation like he used to."

"They wear protective suits, Mom."

"Still. You know how I feel about him being down there."

She loathed it. But it was the best paying job in the colony, even better than the shipyards due to the hazard pay, and Arn had a family to provide for.

"What about Rojer? Is he enjoying his life as a petty bureaucrat?"

"Be nice," she said with a smile. "He's got his hands full with refugee intake, and statistical analysis suits him. He likes the data side of things. Math makes more sense to him than people ever did, although it's hard to tell with your brother."

"He's never known a happiness that can't be spoiled."

She *tsked* at him, but didn't disagree. Rojer, the middle child, had always been a pain in Elya's neck. Constantly taunting and teasing him, always complaining, never happy with his station in life. He'd landed a government commission after receiving his data science certification, and now he spent his days analyzing numbers for the governor's office.

"It's better now that he's out on his own," his mom said. "He thrives on independence."

"Hopefully, the governor has enough sense to keep him behind the scenes. Put him in front of people and the jig is up!"

She smiled and then changed the subject. "Are you getting enough sleep? Remembering to eat? You skip meals when you're wrapped up in a problem."

"You know me too well," Elya said. "I admit I haven't slept much. I ate lunch." He paused. "At least I think I did."

"Elya."

"I know, I know. I'll get a bite after this, I promise. There's just so much going on right now." He gripped his temples between his thumb and middle fingers and closed his eyes. They were gritty and sore. "I'm preoccupied."

"With a new puzzle?"

"You could say that."

"I can see it weighing on you. You told me that Emperor Aeris thinks you can help. Do you see things the same way?"

"Maybe. I don't know."

"Do you want to talk it through?"

This was a famous tactic of hers from when he was a kid. Whenever Elya was feeling stuck or frustrated, she'd encourage him to talk it through. It had annoyed him when he was young, but he eventually came to realize that all she was doing was eliciting his thoughts and helping him untangle the problem. She'd helped him through more than one robotics tournament on Eskatan this way, even though that often meant long nights fixing his designs just before the competition.

Was he procrastinating with the geode the same way? Was it procrastination if you were truly stuck?

How about if you literally got yourself thrown across the room like a rag doll?

The ansible channels were as private as they could get, so Elya filled her in, doing his best to keep the story to the pertinent details. At least this time, if MOXA accessed this recording and found out he was sharing state secrets, he had the Emperor's authorization to fall back on. He hadn't *explicitly* been told not to share information on the subject.

After he'd finished telling the story, his mother asked, "What does your gut tell you?"

"I don't know how the statues work, but I'm sure there's something we're missing about the Chronicle room. Those seams in the floor mean something. I just don't know what yet."

"And what about the computer?"

"The Chronicle? I'm not sure it *is* a computer. That's how we think about it, since it's projecting a hologram of the Telos like our machines, but I swear that thing isn't a looped video. It seems more alive than that."

"AI then?"

"I'm not really sure..." He could try asking Harmony to look at it. But wouldn't the Admiral or Minister Aganaki have tried that already?

"When the student is ready, the teacher appears."

"What's that supposed to mean?" Elya asked.

"The answer will come to you when you least expect it. Take a break, get some rest, and you'll figure it out. You've always been good at solving puzzles, but sometimes you try too hard. You force it, and the Universe resists."

He took a deep breath and swallowed a sigh. His mother believed in the sentient nature of the Universe. As a follower of the Old Earth religion, she believed that the Spirit of Animus infused everything—animals, plants, entire planets. Elya had always felt these esoteric beliefs were a little far-fetched and hard to swallow. Of course, a creature was interconnected with its environment, and he could even believe that the feedback mechanism between a living creature and its environment went both ways. But was a rock alive?

His mother was deeply spiritual, whereas Elya had always considered himself more practical. Things work because he worked on them. Action, reaction; cause and effect.

But he knew better than to argue. She believed what she believed and if she thought the Universe was actively resisting his efforts, there was nothing he could do to convince her otherwise.

"Maybe you're right," he said. "And I *am* hungry."

She gave him one of those radiant smiles. "You'll figure it out. You always do."

He nodded.

"And don't let that minister push you around. If you've got the Emperor's blessing, there's nothing he can do about that."

"You're my number one fan."

"And cheerleader," she said.

That banging came through the channel again. *Thump. Thump.*

"All right, I better go before there's a riot. Other people need to use the ansible."

"All right. Love you, Mom."

"Love you too, sweetheart.

"Tell everyone I said hi."

"I will."

He broke the connection and logged off. The strip of light encircling the room dimmed, and the door popped open. He walked past the next soldier in the queue, who stepped in and locked the door.

As Elya was making his way to the cafeteria, Lieutenant Park paced across an intersection in front of him, eyes fixed on his hands as he rolled a cigarette. Elya paused for a minute as his mother's comments about the sentient Universe played back in his mind.

"Hey Naab!" he called out.

Park jumped, spilling loose tobacco and cannabis across the floor. Once he recognized Elya, the fear in his eyes faded. "Scared the bejeesus outta me, dude!"

"Sorry." Elya bent down and scooped the scattered leaves into his hand. "You doing all right?"

Park picked some dirt out of the pile and stuffed it into a new paper. He twisted the rolly up with a practiced motion, then twisted a paper filter and screwed it into the mouthpiece. "I'm fine, man."

Sure he was. Now that Yorra had pointed it out, Elya couldn't *not* see that something was bothering the guy. "I was just on my way to get some grub, you want to join me?"

Park hesitated, eyeballed the cigarette. "I'm not really hungry."

"C'mon. I could use some company. I'll take my burrito to go, and you can smoke in the shop while I finish repairing Hedgebot." They prohibited smoking in the cafeteria, so Elya knew Park wouldn't want to stay.

Park shrugged and placed the rolly behind his ear. "All right. What happened to Hedgebot?"

Elya filled him in while they stood in line for burritos. Park said he'd already eaten and wasn't hungry, but Elya insisted he take something for later, so Park stuffed a warm burrito wrapped in compostable foil into the inside pocket of his flight suit.

Back at the shop, Park lit his hand-rolled cigarette and paced while Elya re-situated Hedgebot and removed the gyroscope from the center of the bot's body. While he was in there, he saw the power core was loose, so he first adjusted its clasps and tightened the housing. With the battery snugly fitted, he took the gyroscope apart.

"You sure you can get that thing balanced again if you take it apart?" Park asked.

"I don't have much to lose," Elya said. "It's already unbalanced."

He took off a panel on either end, exposing a spherical hollow in the middle, where a round metal wheel was mounted on a metal rod and suspended by opposing magnetic forces.

At least, the forces were supposed to be opposing. The wheel had slid down and was held firmly against one strike plate.

"That's weird..."

Park strode over and exhaled. "Huh."

Elya waved the plume of smoke away and leaned down to inspect the gyro closer.

Hedgebot controlled its movements by adjusting the force of the wheel's spin and the angle of the magnets positioned around the edges. When he pumped power into one of the control wires, it would move the magnets, spin faster or slower, and allow the bot to maintain its balance and make rapid microscopic adjustments.

This clever little device was the engine powering Hedgebot's incredibly lithe movements.

But the charge of these magnets was all wrong. The wheel was pushed to the side, not in the center where it ought to be.

Had that blast from the statue altered magnetic fields through four layers of aluminite plating?

Is that how the rest of the machinery worked, too? The statues, the seams in the floor, the strange Telos shields? Was it all powered by magnets?

"Hey Naab, do you know where I could get some really powerful magnets?"

Lieutenant Park had finished smoking and was now unwrapping the burrito. *Called it,* Elya thought.

Park took a bite and chewed for a minute. "Hull repair

crew uses magnets to secure their tools while they're working outside in vac suits."

"Know anyone assigned to hull repair?"

"A drinking buddy who got moved over to the *Hyperion.* Been meaning to check on him, anyway."

"Perfect. If he has what I need, I'm wondering if you'd be able to help me with something."

"How are you going to get him to give it to you if he does?"

"Emperor's orders."

"The Emperor told you to get some magnets?"

Elya bobbed his head. "More or less."

Park gave him a wicked grin, then took another big bite. "Am I rubbing off on you, Fancypants?" Park lived for subterfuge of all kinds, whether it was cleverly winning a game of aleacc, playing practical jokes on a squadmate, or sneaking into the Archives.

Elya matched his smile, then winked. "Yorra told me you were a bad influence."

"Sounds way more fun than pacing around, beating myself up about what happened."

That was the most he'd shared about how he was feeling since they ran into each other. The dark look in Park's eyes had noticeably retreated from view, but it returned in a flash.

"All right," Elya said. "Let me just replace these magnets and align the gyro. Then, us and Hedgebot'll go ask your buddy to borrow some tools for a little experiment."

EIGHTEEN

Burnt coffee from the crew lounge churned in Casey's stomach as she paced at the exposed end of the spacecraft hangar.

Her feet carried her in a circle around a blue tarp that covered a heap of objects on the floor. Just a couple meters away, the thin blue plane of an energy shield separated the hangar's atmosphere from the frozen vacuum while allowing objects—like the starfighters parked around her—to pass freely through the plane.

Her stomach grumbled.

Casey paced.

While carting the tarp and the items it concealed across the ship, she and Yorra had scrounged a few precious slices of hydroponically grown urmelon. Just a couple bites was all she could manage. She'd been wise to keep it light. She'd never been able to eat much before a mission.

This meeting, for her, was a mission.

There'd been enough death. Too much. If she didn't rally the squad, if she was incapable of uniting them as a single team, they'd suffer worse losses on their next deployment.

Were this squabbling between her and Ruby allowed to continue, they would fall apart when it mattered most.

A squad with good leadership could survive any setback.

A squad with poor leadership was doomed even when the odds were in their favor.

This was as real to her as a dogfight against Kryl drones. If she were twisting through the asteroids currently hanging on the other side of the hangar's thin blue curtain and trying not to get tagged by an enemy missile, there would be no more risk to her life than at this very moment.

So she paced around the tarp, brooding on grief and loss, and used this last quiet moment of waiting to mentally prepare herself for the challenge ahead.

Tucked beneath the wing of a Sabre, Harmony's telltale cloud of blue-and-purple lights twinkled, distracting her. The shipmind kept quiet. Casey appreciated her ability to wait in silence. There was nothing left to say, nothing Casey could learn or change in the next few minutes.

Now, only action mattered. She had to hope her training and intuition would be enough.

Despite how some of them might feel about Casey, the Furies knew better than to be late to a muster. Ten minutes before the appointed time, 0700 GST, pilots began to trickle in. Alone, in pairs, in groups of four. With coffees in hand, bleary-eyed or wide awake, anxiously wringing hands and laughing a bit too loud at whispered jokes. Their uniforms seemed rumpled and worn. Yet each flight lead carried with them spare identi-rings, beloved threadbare t-shirts, toys, pictures, bots.

Personal items.

She felt the sorrow drag her down and purposefully straightened her spine. She stood proudly when she saw that not only the leads, but many of the pilots had brought their own contributions as well.

Word had gotten around.

Soon, nearly all the surviving Furies were present. She mingled with the men and women, greeting each person, especially those she spoke with the day before, asking after their kids and spouses, hearing stories of their calls home. Each time a pilot's eyes lit up when Casey asked a question, she felt a secret thrill. She'd worked hard to commit the details of their lives to memory, and she could tell it meant something to them.

Would it make up for their losses? No. But it would help them feel seen.

Ruby had yet to arrive, but the other pilots from Flight 4 were there. Colonel Volk had straggled in late and he lurked in the back of the crowd while he sipped from a steaming mug and busied himself on his tab. A few pilots approached the XO and asked him questions in quiet voices. The Colonel just shrugged and gestured to Casey.

Don't ask me, that gesture said. *This is Raptor's meeting.*

Where was Flight 18? Ah, there was Yorra coming now, weaving around a mechanic's cart and ducking under the wing of a starfighter as she gave a helpless shrug. Casey didn't need a translator to know what that meant: No sign of Captain Nevers or Lieutenant Park.

Earth, she swore silently. Their absence would reflect poorly upon her. Butterflies flapped in her stomach. *Butterflies.* Why think about a silly old Earth phrase, one her mother had loved to use at a time like this? She'd only seen ancient hologram videos of the beautifully patterned insects, yet no other description quite described the tickling in your gut, like delicate wings stirring open.

Her mom had loved Old Earth idioms. Though it had been years since her death, though each year that passed made it harder and harder to remember her face, Casey never forgot the love they'd shared.

That memory, rooted in loss, strengthened her resolve.

If Park and Nevers didn't show up, so be it. Everyone grieved in their own way and she would not make excuses for them. She just wished—

A clanking noise sounded behind her as magnetic boots struck and locked to the hangar floor. Another *kuh-clank* followed and as she turned Casey saw mechanics wearing vac suits and jetpacks, the kind used to inspect the hull and conduct exterior repairs, cross the thin blue plane and land inside the hangar. They carried a big metal crate full of equipment between them.

One detached his harness and swiped up the reflective visor—revealing Innovesh Park's face.

Relief washed through her body and exited her mouth with a chuckle. Casey checked her tab for the time. Two minutes to go.

Park grinned, happy as ever to be the unexpected spectacle, a joker in his element. Nevers flipped up his visor and smiled awkwardly before removing his helmet and unzipping the vac suit.

Yorra hurried out of the crowd to greet the pair. Park beamed at her, and only a sense of professionalism in front of the rest of the squad kept him from grabbing Yorra and pulling her into a kiss.

Whatever survivor's guilt he'd been suffering, knowing how many had died to bring Park home safely, he seemed to be faring well at the moment. That was a win.

It was now 0700. Captain Nevers popped the crate they'd brought in and released Hedgebot. The bot spiraled up the pilot's body and came to rest on his shoulder. Nevers walked into the middle of the crowd and stood facing her, quiet, steadfast and somber.

Their eyes met. He'd made some kind of breakthrough, though she couldn't imagine what. He wanted to share it with her… but he also knew that now wasn't the right time for it. She nodded, silently thanking him.

That exchange rippled into the crowd like a silent order. Park clicked his thrusters off and quieted. The rest of the squadron gathered in around them.

With a flourish, Casey whipped the navy tarp off the pile of floating lanterns.

Their eyes all drifted down. Each lantern was a globe about the size of the urmelon she'd had for breakfast. She lifted one and held it up, arm outstretched, in her palm.

The lantern's transparent shell was made of a thin sheet of aluminite, sand-blasted to give the yellow bulb inside a soft ambience. To the globe, an independent thruster system was mounted, much like the one attached to the backs of Park and Nevers' vac suits, except smaller. She activated it with her thumb and released it so that the glowing orb floated into the air, humming softly.

Casey scanned the squad as they gathered in closer, noting the sober presence of Tank, and the grouchy, stalwart Fuzz, whose new pilots had already changed their flight numbers by swapping out a shoulder patch. She counted the rest of her flight leads, and then considered herself lucky to have them. They were all here now, all except for Ruby.

"Thank you for coming," Casey said. "I know it's early, and I know we've all had a rough couple of days, but I couldn't let the next mission begin without taking a moment to acknowledge the friends we've lost." She paced beside the pile of lanterns as she sought the right words. "And to acknowledge the difficult thing each of us will be asked to do next: to keep moving, to keep fighting, to fly the next mission without taking the proper time to grieve."

She'd chosen this spot because it was in line of sight to the repaired corner of the hangar where an explosion had sucked their commanding officer and several others out into space during the Robichar mission, after a Kryl parasite infected a mechanic.

"We lost Lieutenant Colonel Walcott right over there, just a couple of months back. I don't know about you, but I'm still not over that. He made the Fightin' Furies who we are. He could be stern. Tough. Inscrutable. But damn, he could fly. I know a lot of you looked up to him, as I did."

Looking into their eyes, she knew it to be true.

"No one can ever replace him. We *will* remember him."

Nods all around. A few soft mutters of, "Hear, hear!"

"No one can replace the brothers and sisters we lost yesterday, either," Casey said. "We're here to honor their memories. We *will* remember them."

Eyes lowered. Hats came off. Someone sniffed.

"Scooter," Casey said. "West. Jib. Farmer."

"Quirky," someone said.

"Pelik," added another.

"Jet. Orman."

An awkward pause. Fuzz looked like he was about to burst.

"Who else, Fuzz?" Casey prompted.

"Con. Zeal. Epictetus."

"Who else, Tank?!" Casey's voice whipped across the hangar.

"Urmine! Golanz!"

"Tower!"

"Grizzly," said a woman all the way in the back of the crowd.

Ruby's deep red hair had been buzzed to her scalp. The long, thick, curly tresses were gone, revealing a puckered white scar that curved around her right ear. A scar that her hair had always hidden was now plainly visible for all to see.

The flight leader patch on Ruby's right shoulder had been replaced with Grizzly's personal patch, the head of a bear with its massive jaws closing around a Kryl drone. Many pilots had their own custom patches—this one was special. Grizzly had been an artist. He drew it himself.

The sight of it made Casey's vision swim as tears filled her eyes.

"For Grizzly," Casey said when she realized the silence was growing heavy and she'd waited too long to speak. "For all the Fightin' Furies we lost. We *will* remember them. May they be the last."

Casey bent down and picked up another lantern, which she handed to Fuzz.

"I asked several of you to help gather personal items. We'll give each pilot a proper Fleet burial or memorial when we get home, like we did for Colonel Walcott. For now, we'll do what we can, which is to acknowledge their sacrifice, salute their bravery, and set their spirits free to watch over us all during the battles to come."

Nods all around. Murmurs of agreement and the humming of the lanterns as they were activated, one by one.

"Colonel Volk," Casey said, waving their commanding officer to the front of the group.

"Captain Osprey asked me to say a few words," the gruff colonel began. He set his coffee cup down on the Sabre's lowered wing and pulled on a gold chain around his neck. The medallion at the end of his necklace depicted a blue-green planet embedded in the root structure of a broad tree with a bushy canopy. "Most of you are too young to know that when I joined the Fleet, I started as a chaplain."

"Old Earth preacher, huh?" Tank joked.

"A follower of Animus, yes. But as a Fleet chaplain, I was trained to answer the spiritual call of citizens of all worlds and religions."

The looks of surprise on their faces made the effort of keeping this secret worthwhile. Casey shared a glance with

Harmony, whose lights had collected into a smiling face for a moment before dancing apart again. The shipmind had given her the information, and although hesitant at first, Colonel Volk had been easy to persuade.

The solemn hush that gathered over the squad showed how important representation was to each of them. The spiritual practice of Old Earth from the time of the Great Migration was the primary religion among the people of the Solaran Empire, but it was not the only one. Other mono- and polytheistic practices grew on their own, from Hinduism to Zoroastrianism, especially among the colonies.

Casey kept passing out lanterns while Volk spoke. He told them how followers of Animus believed that when death came, a person's essence journeyed back out into space to join the great Spirit of Old Earth, from dust to life and from life to dust, to be remade in the future. Each soul lost was another opportunity for a new human life to be born on a new world, continuing the tradition that had been started on Old Earth and which the Empire continued today among the stars. Followers of Animus believed it was humanity's solemn duty to found new colonies. Casey had been raised the same way as Volk. The only way to ensure humanity's long-term survival was to people the universe.

It gave the pilots something to fight for. If fighting the Kryl meant ensuring humanity's survival, then the pain of loss was worth it. As for the people who were no longer with them, well, their deaths contributed to the spiritual energy—the Animus—and kept the cycle going. Volk explained how all human beings were connected, even those separated by thousands of light-years on different planets.

Many cultures, many religions... but *one* people.

Casey was grateful she'd asked Volk to speak. The XO's reputation carried weight, and all the pilots present—even the bare-headed, scarred and still-seething Ruby—held a respect for him that ran almost as deep as Lt. Colonel Walcott's had been.

In a flash of insight, Casey saw the wisdom of what Admiral Miyaru had done by placing Volk in command of the Furies. It had seemed like a temporary stopgap. There were no other officers capable of taking command of the squad in such a tumultuous time. Instead, it seemed to have been intentional. Volk was the best they had. He could be relied upon to turn the squadron around.

Soon, every pilot held a lantern. The Furies had placed their late comrades' belongings inside each one. Volk said a prayer to the Spirit of Old Earth, and then, together, the orbs were cast into the void.

One by one, each lantern was brought forward and released at speed through the shield. In space, automatic sensors activated. The lanterns drifted slowly away, avoiding objects, finding the emptiness waiting to be filled.

Being this close to the vacuum, with nothing to stop her from falling across that line except her own brains and muscle reflexes, Casey's heart pounded. She forced herself to stand at attention and put on a brave face.

It was the hardest thing Casey had ever done. She held back most of her tears, but not all of them. Twin streams escaped her eyes and coursed down her cheeks where all the other pilots could see.

Park, who had been standing by, suddenly broke rank and walked off. Yorra followed, but he pushed her away and left the hangar. Yorra mouthed, "Sorry," and went after him.

No one gave it a second thought. They all understood. Everyone grieved in their own way, and Park's life had been saved at the cost of a dozen people whose lives they remembered here today. The rest of the Furies knew how he felt, even if they didn't react in the same way he did.

Eventually, a cloud of lanterns clustered on the other side

of the thin blue barrier. Casey looked around, checking to see if there was anyone left to present their memorial offering to space.

There was only one. Ruby approached.

Prodding the levitating orb gently before her, Ruby stopped a meter from the thin blue barrier to stand between Colonel Volk and Casey. The two pilots remaining in her squad stepped up beside her, one on each side.

Ruby tore Grizzly's patch off her shoulder and placed it inside the lantern, on top of a pile that included a pint of Ariadnean whiskey and a scrap of red cloth. She placed the patch inside, and then withdrew a lock of her auburn hair from a pocket, and placed that inside as well.

With tears in her eyes, and her wing-mates at her sides, Ruby pushed Grizzly's lantern into space. She put her hands over her heart, her fingertips resting around her throat, as a brief sob escaped her lips. She quickly swallowed it.

After several minutes of silence during which no one interrupted, Ruby turned and stepped close to Casey.

She tensed.

"I don't like you, Osprey," Ruby said. "But I don't think you let Grizzly or anyone else die on purpose. You did what you had to do to get the rest of us out alive." Ruby swallowed and wiped at her eyes. "I was… hurt. Grieving, as you said. Will be for a long time. Grizzly was more than a friend. I've known him for twenty years… He was… we ran the alleys of Oltanis together." Her eyes grew distant, then refocused suddenly. "But this whole thing with the lanterns, this was a nice gesture. So thank you for that."

"We *will* remember him," Casey said.

Ruby nodded. Casey waited, her lumbar spine aching with tension. Ruby finally turned away, then thought better of it and stepped back up beside her, voice dropping to a whisper.

"And maybe you already know this, but I was wrong about Colonel Spector, whereas you saw straight through her lies. Volk didn't trust you then, yet he seems to trust you now. You must have done something right to earn that trust. So, at least for now, I'm willing to give you the benefit of the doubt. But I'll be watching you, Osprey. If you slip up, I'll be right there waiting, ready to take your spot."

Ruby turned sharply, saluted Colonel Volk, then walked off the same way Park and Yorra had gone.

For a long while, the Furies who remained watched the lanterns bob and weave into the asteroid field outside the ship. Some lanterns drifted beneath other ships, some simply diminished, slowly shrinking into pinprick specks until disappearing from sight altogether. The sensors in their thrusters would guide the lanterns away from collisions so that they drifted for a long time, until their batteries ran out, and then ran for years on momentum alone.

Eventually, each one would be sucked into a star, returning them to the furnace of life where they started.

Where they all started.

One by one, the pilots peeled off and went their own way. They didn't need to be dismissed.

Casey waited. Her stomach growled.

When they were the only two left, Colonel Volk clapped Casey on the shoulder and said, "That was very well done."

"Thank you, sir."

"Thanks to you, I think the Fightin' Furies are ready to face what's coming." He drained the last of his coffee. His eyelids were heavy, and she realized the man must have been up all night. His breath carried the faint scent of whiskey. "Let's hope the rest of the armada is, too."

NINETEEN

Kira stood rigidly in a command position before the starmap. She wanted to seem calm and collected, but felt like the galaxy hanging before her—spinning endlessly and propelled by forces beyond her control.

"What I can't get over is," Kira said, "where's the 'shrine' among all these stars? How is that a helpful clue?"

"From the poem?" Volk asked. He'd just come up from a memorial service with the Furies and was more somber and quiet than usual—which was saying something, because somber and quiet was a normal state for him. "I didn't find any of those clues to be particularly helpful, sir."

Understatement of the century.

Volk swiped from one feed to the next on his command console, reading telemetry data as they received it back from each probe. Since the star systems identified by Minister Aganaki were spread out across the galaxy, Kira had been forced to position extra starships equipped with ansibles to relay probe data back to her ship here in the Elturis system. It was a tenuous network, but necessary to prevent delays. They'd been able to recover ansibles from a few of the ships destroyed in Overmind X's attack with the photon cannon, and the Emperor had also donated his ship, which was, of course, ansible-equipped. Still, they were spread thin, and she was pushing the limits of her equipment.

As a result, half the probes relayed data in close to real-time; the other half were anywhere from thirty minutes to three hours delayed.

Armed escorts also accompanied each probe. They were small enough to evade notice, yet too small to stand against any significant Kryl force. If any one of them detected a viable relic location, Kira would deploy a larger strike force to that vicinity.

She tried to remind herself that, across interstellar distances, those response times were truly incredible. No wonder the Telos ruled the galaxy for millennia before humanity arrived. With even more advanced technology, it must have seemed like they were everywhere all at once. Such an advantage enabled them to keep the Kryl in check… until they couldn't anymore.

What in the stars had happened to that ancient race of builders?

"I just wish we had more to go on," Kira said. "Poems and orbital calculations based on old starmaps aren't enough to out-think Overmind X."

Volk frowned, swiping through the data. He paused, paged backward a few times. "Admiral, we've got movement."

"Is it the swarm?"

"No, just a few small ships, it looks like."

"From Pelaux-4?" The star systems Aganaki had identified were all remote, although, true to form, they each seemed to have at least one habitable planet in them—the Telos only built their temples on habitable planets. The systems mostly didn't have Solaran names, so for ease of reference during the operation, she'd numbered each of them and named them after the probe manufacturer, Pelaux-1 through Pelaux-4.

"Actually, sir… the movement is here in Elturis."

She blinked. "What?"

"We were calibrating some of the extra probes on the broken planet. That's where we spotted the movement. They must have come through on the far side of the planet, outside the range of our normal patrols."

She checked the telemetry data Volk was studying. Half a dozen drones and a couple gunships. They must have come in quietly, flying at sublight speeds in the halo of the local star to avoid detection. It was pure luck their probe had caught movement at all.

"Can you get any closer? I need visual confirmation so I know exactly what we're dealing with here."

Why would the Kryl go to the broken planet? There weren't any relics there. Were there?

A nagging thought tugged at the back of her mind. Maybe the repeated hit-and-run tactics used against her starfighter patrols had been a distraction. Maybe Overmind X hadn't wanted to test her defenses at all, nor get to the City, but had simply been trying to divert Kira's attention so she didn't notice extra troops moving into the broken planet.

Maybe they intended the broken planet to be some kind of staging ground.

Kira wasn't about to risk any more of her scouts or ansibles by rushing in. It could be a trap, and her armada was still conducting repairs on their ships from the last battle.

While she waited for the probe to get into position, Kira monitored the other four systems. Despite how objectively incredible interstellar communication was, she couldn't help but feel frustrated by their lack of speed. If they were too slow, Overmind X would get another relic that was even more destructive than the photon cannon. Kira proceeded the only way she knew how—with eyes wide open.

If their count was right, there were two relics remaining. In the past, it had been Minister Aganaki's discoveries about the locations of Telos ruins that had led Overmind X to the relics. Since the Kryl found a starmap in a minor relic, Overmind X had beaten them to the punch every time.

If we can't beat her, Kira thought, *let's take a tactic out of the hive's book. Let's allow Overmind X to lead us to the next relic.*

And then figure out how to eliminate her before she can use it.

"Make sure those Kryl don't know we know they're here, Volk," she said. Probably unnecessary, as he was always careful, but it was better to be clear. He nodded his agreement.

The door to the bridge cycled open, and the Emperor said, "Permission to come aboard, Admiral?"

That was actually kind of him to ask. He could have just barged in and Kira wouldn't have been able to say no. "Granted, Your Majesty."

Aeris entered, flanked by a dozen security guards. The bridge suddenly felt very crowded, but Kira pretended not to notice.

"Admiral, the probe has a visual," said Colonel Volk.

"Emperor Aeris, you may want to see this, given your previous interests."

The Emperor strode up next to Kira and crossed his arms. The golden orbs of his eyes, crawling with nanites, glistened. He was enjoying this.

"What have we here?" the emperor asked.

"Movement near the broken planet. Looks like a few Kryl ships snuck in under the radar." The image was incredibly blurry. "They don't know we've spotted them yet. Volk, can you sharpen the image? What are we looking at?"

"If we send the probe any closer, we risk being identified."

"Are we inside their radar range yet?"

"Right on the edge, sir."

She considered it, glancing over at the Emperor. Those eyes twinkled hungrily.

"Move in a little," she said. "Slow and quiet. And fly the probe at a constant velocity." It was small enough that it wouldn't register as more than space debris unless it made erratic movements.

"Copy that," said Colonel Volk, signaling for the navigation officer to make the adjustments. "Moving in."

While they waited, the Emperor bounced from foot to foot, like a little kid. He was drinking it up, every moment. Once again, she wondered why he was here.

And then she got tired of wondering.

"Why are you here?" Kira blurted. "Your Majesty," she added after a moment's hesitation.

He turned to her and grinned. "You wouldn't believe the scrutiny I get on Ariadne. Everywhere I go, cameras and millions of people watch my every move. I have no privacy."

"And you have privacy here?" she opened her hands, gesturing to the security team arrayed around the bridge. "They follow you everywhere. And I've heard you're spending more time with my soldiers than anyone thought you would."

"That's different. Security is necessary—cameras and public scrutiny are not. And I like your soldiers. They're straightforward, honest people, and I enjoy taking their money in aleacc. Regardless, thanks to military protocol and reasons of operational security, I have more freedom here than I do elsewhere."

"And that explains why you took your ship to explore the broken planet?"

"What if I'd done something similar on Ariadne, or on one of the major colonies?"

Kira snorted. "It'd be the only news story on every news network in the galaxy."

"Exactly. Plus, it's bizarre, isn't it, for a planet to be that busted up, yet somehow still hold itself together? And to be ejecting rocks with such force. It defies explanation."

She nodded. "Looks like you aren't the only one who's interested."

He smirked.

"Don't be so smug about it," she muttered under her breath.

He chuckled, and Kira couldn't help but crack a smile herself. In spite of herself, she *liked* this man. He was so very different from the image of the Emperor she'd painted in her mind.

"Plus," he added in a low voice. "Aganaki needed a little nudge."

"I don't care what your methods are if you can get me better intel out of the relics he's hoarding."

"I think your Captain Nevers is getting close. He just needed someone to open the door for him."

"Thanks for that," Kira said. "All this posturing and grandstanding about who controls the relics was getting on my nerves."

"You have a lot on your plate."

You're telling me, she answered silently. No matter how much she liked him, there was a part of her that had been long trained to keep her guard up.

As they spoke, the probe had moved closer to the broken planet. The blurry images separated into distinct shapes, and then sharpened at the edges. Now she could see it clearly—half a dozen drones, and a single gunship, hiding in a vast gap between two massive chunks of the broken planet.

Kira's whole body tensed up.

"You think your Subject Zero is with them?" asked Emperor Aeris.

"It's possible, Your Majesty. Only way to tell his drone apart is to spot the pilot in what would normally be an autonomous craft or spot him phasing. And we're not getting that close without putting this entire mission at risk. Stealth is the name of the game."

The Emperor stepped up beside her and lowered his voice. "I know how you must feel."

She flicked her head to stare at him. "What do you mean?"

"I looked it up. I know about the history between you and Captain Ruidiaz. This must be really hard for you."

Her heart thudded and ached at the same time. The pain spread down into her solar plexus and she forced herself to relax. "He's not the man I used to know."

"Still," the Emperor said. "He was, once. So it must be hard seeing him be used by Overmind X like that. I lost people in the Kryl War, too. Cousins and an uncle. But none of them got turned by the Kryl. What's happened here is a... unique situation. I'd completely understand if it was personal for you."

Is *that* why he was here? To test her fitness for duty?

She stiffened, isolating and walling off the pain and replacing it with a professional, stoic non-reactivity. "It's not an issue," she said. "Subject Zero is the enemy. Our job is to eliminate him, the sooner the better."

The Emperor studied her face. As he did, a flash on the holoscreen wiped all thoughts of Omar from her mind.

"What in the name of Animus was that?" Kira demanded. She met eyes with Colonel Volk. "You saw it?"

He nodded. "Yessir."

"Get that probe closer."

The image zoomed in yet again. They still weren't close enough to see the ridges of carapace or the bone-like wings of the drones, but something had happened that caused the hairs on the back of Kira's neck to stand on end.

The flash of light came again. It shot out of the gunship and disappeared over an invisible curved edge, like water falling off the precipice of a waterfall, a couple klicks in front of where the small contingent of Kryl starships sat.

"By the breath of Animus," Emperor Aeris said, stepping forward. "Is that what I think it is?"

"What do you think it is?" Kira snapped.

"An event horizon," he whispered softly.

A chill swept over her body. "Even if you're right and we are looking at an invisible event horizon, why are they using the photon cannon to shoot at it?"

"The photon ray won't penetrate the event horizon," Aeris said, "because light is incapable of moving across it. But they can use it to sound out its location."

The gunship rotated ninety degrees and shot again, while the drones stayed out of range.

Then again.

"If that's an event horizon," Kira said. "Why isn't the black hole sucking everything in the system into it? Why aren't those ships being destroyed?"

"Great question, Admiral. I'm not sure. But black holes have enormous gravity. Why not the same for this anomaly? Perhaps it can help explain why the largest pieces of the fractured world continue to orbit so close together after all this time."

The drones suddenly spread away from the gunship and formed up around it, a protective escort.

"Admiral, your orders?" Volk said. "Should we destroy them?"

Kira chewed on her lip. "Pull the probe back out of their radar range and monitor. I want to see what they do next."

"Have we found anything in the other four systems yet?"

"Negative, sir," reported the communications officer tracking Pelaux-1 through 4.

"Let me know if anything changes," Emperor Aeris said. Kira nodded, and he left the bridge without waiting for a response, pulling his escort along in his wake.

Kira chewed her lip and paced faster, more anxious than ever.

What else did Overmind X know that she didn't?

TWENTY

Overmind X had promised Omar a weapon.

She took the photon cannon from him, and then she'd *promised*.

Omar was still angry about it. He needed a *proper* weapon. To do… to do something important.

To destroy the humans, Overmind X growled.

Right, to destroy the humans. He needed a weapon because this phase shifter and his drone weren't cutting it anymore. That Captain Nevers was too good a pilot. Omar didn't want to admit it, but Nevers had evaded his grasp yet *again*—he'd even landed a few dangerous shots on his drone, bleeding critical arteries that demanded extra healing time in the sulfur ponds. If Omar had possessed a Telos weapon, he would have ended an irritating opponent and cost the Solarans an ace pilot.

So why hadn't she let Omar have it? He'd been nearly decapitated trying to recover the thing. He should have gotten the satisfaction of slicing through the Solaran armada and that annoying pilot as his right. Sure, the gun was heavy, unwieldy, designed for a much larger craft. And, had he mounted it on his drone, he'd barely have been able to maneuver the craft. But she could have grown him a bigger ship. She could have given him the chance.

All he wanted was a chance. A chance to…

Once again, as he grasped for specifics, the thought eluded him.

His mandibles trembled as their tips tapped an erratic beat. Omar rubbed his human hand along the back of his sweaty neck—his headaches had worsened lately, a side effect of his transformation. Overmind X had gone into his mind twice since the battle, moving with surgical precision as she cauterized his neural injuries. The headaches subsided after each operation, but they always came back with a vengeance.

Because he was a half-breed. Imperfect. Omar's body had always rejected the Kryl parts Overmind X had been forced to graft onto him to save his life. Nothing like the newer models…

Seven and Fourteen loped up beside him, hunched over and moving on four legs. Since the last temple, their elbow joints had reversed, their fingernails extending, thickening, and hardening to make claws. Glassy carapace stretched across their shoulders and backs, doubling as body armor.

Focus, said Overmind X. *You can't afford to let your mind stray, Zero. You are here on a mission.*

A mission, right.

"A mission to do what?" he asked.

To retrieve another relic.

"A weapon?"

Yes, she said after a moment's pause. *You will need it for what's to come.*

Blood sang in his veins, and his excitement momentarily extinguished his pain. "What is to come, my Queen?"

We must recover the final piece of our Inheritance.

"Final? Don't the humans still have two pieces?"

Pain flared in his mind, blacking out all thought for a moment. Omar had to bend over and clutch his head. Saliva dribbled out his malformed jaw and soaked his chest while a whimpering noise clawed out of his throat.

I will not tolerate your doubt, Overmind X said calmly. *It's nothing but a temporary inconvenience. One that we will soon have the ability to resolve.*

A sense of reassurance flooded through him, a hit of dopamine so powerful he couldn't see whatever worry had briefly clouded his mind. In the presence of such complete affirmation, his pain receded into the background.

Now go, Overmind X said. *Complete your mission.*

As her awareness retreated—still aware, still listening, but not focused on him for the time being—he found the two younglings staring at him with unblinking eyes. A half dozen flying Kryl specialists, each emitting an ambient red light, floated over their shoulders, illuminating the triangular tunnel of the Telos temple in which they stood.

"What is it?" Omar asked, unsettled.

"To wield the relic is a great responsibility," said Subject Seven.

"A burden we worry you are not prepared to bear," added Fourteen.

In the days since their last mission, the two had begun to do creepy things like finish each other's thoughts. As their physical transformation progressed, they'd become more attuned to each other mentally. It was incredibly disconcerting to Omar, who had been gathered into the Swarm much like the two of them, but without another mind to share the experience. He'd always known he was different from the rest of the Kryl. But knowing he was still too human, especially compared to the new mutants, really drove the point home.

Their close relationship also sparked a memory in him, one he couldn't readily access. It was distant and fuzzy, like a ship barely visible on the horizon, a silhouette wrapped in fog. It was a word he couldn't remember, a smell that reminded him of a place he'd lost. He knew it was about someone, a person he'd once shared a deep connection with. Though he racked his brain, he couldn't remember who the person was, or why it felt so important.

Omar shook off the memory like a wind-bitten chill. The air in the temple was thick and warm, yet the headache and pain he'd suffered left him clammy.

"You're mistaken," Omar said. "I have always been ready. I live to serve our purpose."

The swarm could hear their conversation—everything the three of them did and thought was transmitted to Overmind X's collective consciousness through the psionic link. However, with the Overmind's attention focused elsewhere, it passed without remark.

Seven and Fourteen fell silent, then turned to gaze into the darkness. Seven took two loping steps forward, then slowed and padded softly, claws clicking on stone, as the red seekers—the flying specialists—winged ahead. The creatures made irregular clicking noises as they corkscrewed through the temple, sounding against the walls and ceiling as they sought hidden openings, pathways unseen, and the infamous Telos traps.

Overmind X grew these seekers to aid in their search. They used echolocation to see and, as they moved, they shared their location and what they sensed with the Swarm, effectively mapping the temple as they went.

One memory Omar hadn't lost was a mission for the Solaran Fleet. They had used autonomous metallic drones to similar effect. Overmind X had harvested Omar's memories and used it as an inspiration for the seekers. She was constantly evolving.

They all were.

All except for Omar.

The seekers took a couple of zigzag turns and then reached an atrium, where they spread out and flew erratically. Their senses revealed five branching tunnels that spooled off from the atrium at various unusual angles.

Seven and Fourteen yipped in excitement and ran ahead.

Omar swallowed a sigh of frustration and moved after them on his own two feet. His pace was a fraction of their speed, so he had to jog to keep up.

When he emerged into the open room, it surprised him to find Seven and Fourteen halfway up the walls, and the seekers flying around in S-shaped curves as they bumped into walls and each other.

"What's happening?" he shouted into the open space.

"Don't move!" Seven shouted as she flailed in open space, sucked back and forth across fifteen meters between the mouths of two tunnels. "Gravity well!"

"Breath of Animus," Omar said. "How...?"

The atrium was shaped like a sphere—no corners, just endless curving walls. The five branching tunnels jutted off in seemingly random directions. One lay straight overhead, two more to his left and right at weird angles. Another opened directly across from him, pointing down sharply, and the final tunnel mouth was above and behind him at about sixty degrees. Fourteen hung on his left, clinging sideways to the mouth of a tunnel like she was falling off a cliff.

He took a step forward.

"No!" both Seven and Fourteen shouted at once.

Too late. He fell—headfirst up, at a weight that was twice the gravity he was used to.

Six arms extended from his back, reaching out by

instinct. Several of his claws scraped on stone and slipped off, including the weak one that Overmind X had regrown after being lopped off in the previous mission, but one caught the upper lip of the opening behind him and held.

He got another claw up and scuttled sideways. Omar looked up at a curved ceiling clinging to the opening. He got the sense that he was hanging on the edge of a great curved dam, only there was no water to contain. The wall curved below him, but with the weight now pulling on his shoulders, he knew he'd scrape half his arachnid arms off falling into the bowl of the sphere.

"My queen!" he rasped as he reached for the lip with his monstrous Kryl hand, using its superhuman strength to give himself an extra point of reliable contact with something solid. "We need your aid."

Overmind X snapped her attention to them and instantly understood the situation through their shared perception.

Let go.

He reached his human hand up and gripped tighter. One seeker slammed into the wall beside his head and broke its neck upon impact.

"What? No. Why?"

The gravity well curves left before you hit the mouth of the next tunnel. Do as I say.

He took a deep breath, swallowed, and then released his grips all at once.

Be ready to cut left.

Omar guided his body into a controlled free fall. Wind whipped through his hair as he used his arms to carve the air. Every pilot had to be ejection certified, and that meant getting comfortable in freefall and with a parachute.

Only he had no parachute this time. The tunnel mouth that had been on the ceiling was now at the very center of the sphere below him, according to the gravity he felt in his body. It quickly grew from a minuscule black dot to a gaping maw. The room was vast. He must have fallen a hundred meters when he felt a tug on the left side of his body.

Now!

He pulled his arm in and spun left, feeling himself slow as he was pulled into a separate gravity well going in the opposite direction. His eyes grew wide as the ceiling rose to meet him. He didn't think he would stop in time. Omar flailed and windmilled his arachnid limbs behind him as he turned, trying to protect his head. His claws brushed the strange, impervious Telos stone that made up the bones of these temple structures—he had reached the ceiling.

His body fell—or rather flew—across the hollow room in another direction, toward a different tunnel mouth. *Now I see,* he thought. The gravity walls were oriented from the mouths of each tunnel. As he moved, he collected a few seekers. Then—

Cut right.

He did as Overmind X bid him, shifting in the center of the sphere from one well to another. Toward the end of this free fall, Seven gripped his ankle with both hands and was whipped along behind him as he flew back across the chamber.

Overmind X had directed him expertly. They were all now flying toward Subject Fourteen, where she'd been hanging from the lip of another tunnel mouth. As Omar approached, Seven climbed up onto his back and hooked her knees under Omar's armpits. He grunted and groaned under the pressure of her movements and the shifting force of gravity.

"Hang on!" Seven said.

The image of what they were about to do flashed through Omar's mind a second before they executed it. As they came in, Fourteen and Seven locked hands and whipped all three of them *into* the mouth of the tunnel.

Omar felt something snap as his body whipped around and slammed into the stone wall just inside the tunnel. His shoulder twinged in pain and then went numb, and his arachnid limbs twitched as they were crushed behind him.

But the gravity had re-aligned to a single direction.

When Seven let go, Omar dropped to the floor and rolled onto his stomach, breathing hard, his skin prickling from being seared by the wind.

Seven and Fourteen both clambered down after him—far more gracefully than he had.

"Thank you, Zero, that fall—" Seven said.

"—was bound to be painful for one of us," Fourteen finished.

"I live," he forced out as he sat up and spat blood from a cut on his tongue, "but to serve."

"Are we even in the right tunnel?" Fourteen asked.

Only one way to find out, said Overmind X. *Tread carefully, younglings.*

Two seekers corkscrewed forward, clicking as they went, although slower and with a mite more caution. Omar was only too happy to let them go ahead this time. He lumbered to his feet and followed slowly, stretching his limbs and popping joints back into place as his body recovered from his fall. Overmind X acted swiftly, blocking some of the worst pain receptors. He'd have to get his injured limbs treated when they returned from the mission, but he'd been through worse.

It wasn't pain that stopped them, however. The hours that followed took the three of them on a labyrinthine search through the temple, full of harrowing drops, disorienting angles, and impossible turns.

Discounting the first tunnel through which they'd

entered, that left four to explore. One took them several klicks distant to a room where they had to endure the crushing weight of four times normal gravity to activate a switch at the bottom of the well. Kryl genome-detection shields guarded the switch, so Seven had to push through and activate it, as she had before. Once it was done, it wasn't apparent what effect the switch had, but they kept going.

The next tunnel they explored led to a complete dead end, a blank stone wall.

The last two tunnels took them to two rooms that turned out to be *literal* labyrinths. Designed in a manner more typical of the Telos style—gilded and carved with geometric symbols—the mazes were mirror opposites of each other. Seven and Fourteen had to walk along dizzying, impossible paths up crystal towers and across ceilings, and hit switches placed in two different rooms at the same time.

Only their ability to communicate through the psionic link enabled them to unlock the next phase of the temple.

While not immediately apparent, it soon became obvious what the switch and blocks had done. A vast archway had appeared where the dead-end tunnel had previously stopped. The doors of stone opened upon a stunning metal and crystal shrine.

A great, high-backed perch was positioned in the exact center of the room. Hanging from the ceiling like a massive stalactite the size of a building, and carved out of the impervious stone, all of a single piece with the throne—for though it hung down, a throne it surely was—loomed a massive, oversized choice specimen of the Telos.

The Enemy, Overmind X whispered to the swarm.

Its whiplike tail wrapped sinuously around the top of the throne, near its head. Muscles bulged from trunk-like arms, with two thick fists shoved into gauntlets. A robe draped over its shoulders, concealing the rest of its body—except for two long-toed feet. The feet gripped together, fingers intertwined elegantly into a stone fist a meter from the ground.

This was no normal Telos. This creature had been a legend, one who'd been elevated to a god among them. Wherever they had gone when they fled the galaxy, these creatures had been both powerful and elegant, brilliant and poised.

Rather than contempt, Overmind X radiated a great solemn respect for this creature. Even the most hated Enemy deserved respect.

At the Overmind's bidding, the three of them and the remaining seekers moved forward together into the room. The space wasn't as vast as the one in the asteroid—that had obviously been constructed much later. But it was still impressive, the way the oldest buildings and edifices on Ariadne were impressive.

As they moved closer, it became obvious that this place had once been heavily trafficked. Tiers of stone turned the area surrounding the statue into a theater of sorts, with thousands of benches and perches to rest and admire the great one from all angles. The tread of billions of feet had worn the stone down in the middle. Either this wasn't the impervious stone they'd grown accustomed to seeing in Telos structures... or it was older than he could have imagined.

They built the Temple around the shrine as a means of protection, a deterrent, said Overmind X. *This chamber was here long before the protections existed. But that is not why we're here today.*

Right. Omar glanced ahead, but Seven and Fourteen were already moving toward the back of the room. Against the far wall, a chute had been carved. They used their deceptive humanity to pass through the Telos defensive shields that kept Kryl out, and flipped into the air, falling up the chute as gravity reversed.

Omar, exhausted but determined, walked to the base of the chute and waited. He could feel the invisible shield sizzling half a meter in front of him. He reached out to test it, pulling back as his fingers tingled.

No, he wouldn't be following them. He couldn't.

The two mutants fiddled around on the ceiling for a while, then a platform lowered them—standing upside down in the reverse gravity tunnel—to his eye level.

The twin mutants regarded him darkly for a moment, looking even more alien as they hung upside down before him.

Omar held out his hand. "Give it to me."

Fourteen held a small object wrought of alien stone in her hand, gripping a handle that was too big for her child-sized hand. A curved blade extended from the handle in a half-moon shape.

It shimmered as she passed it through the plane in front of her. She swung her arm in a circle, cutting through the invisible shield.

The gravity well faltered, forcing Seven and Fourteen to flip around and land on the floor, right-side up. Their hair fell to their shoulders as the artificial gravity died.

Omar dropped his hand and cocked his head to one side. Grinning, he stepped forward—across the plane where the shield had been a moment ago.

"Just what I was looking for. Now hand it over, child."

Overmind X was silent for a long moment. Then she compelled Fourteen to hand the relic to him.

Omar took the handle in his human fist and shoved it forward into Fourteen's wrist.

She stared, slack-jawed, at the stump of her arm as her severed hand fell, spasming, to the floor.

She growled. Omar's mandibles clicked together in excitement.

Seven leaped for his throat, but Omar activated the phase shifter and she passed through his form.

All Omar got was a migraine to show the Overmind's displeasure. He could live with that. As long as the swarm still needed him, Overmind X would keep the twins from moving against him again.

And now that Omar finally had his weapon, it was his time to shine.

TWENTY-ONE

"Captain Nevers, this is Special Operations Commander, Major Invierno," said Emperor Aeris as his flowing, golden nanite eyes twinkled with mischief. "He's agreed to assist you in your… experiments."

"Thank you, Your Majesty," Elya said. Major Invierno was a stocky, clean-shaven man with ink-black hair, pale skin, a square jaw and more scars on his body than Elya could count. He was currently shirtless, as they'd interrupted his workout.

Major Invierno wiped sweat from his brow with the back of his wrist, then shook Elya's hand with a rock-solid grip. "His Majesty speaks highly of you, Captain."

"That's good to hear. I'm afraid this assignment has the potential to make me more enemies than fans."

Park was standing uncharacteristically off to the side, eyes bugged out and jaw gripped tight. Normally you couldn't get the guy to chat slower than a klick a second, yet when Elya brought him along to petition the Emperor for help, he'd clammed up and found some very interesting patterns on the tops of the hull repair equipment case they'd brought along.

"We're here to do a job, Captain," Major Invierno said, "not sell concert tickets."

Nevers grinned. A SpecOps commander *would* say something like that. "Then you're just the man I'm looking for."

Invierno's eyes scanned over Elya, Park, and the case of equipment on maglev gliders parked between them. "So, what's the plan here? We don't normally do EVAs."

Elya explained in as much detail as he could. That was part of his dilemma—he didn't know exactly what needed to be done, only that Aganaki and his scientists would definitely try to stop him.

"So you just need some muscle?" Invierno asked.

"Independent security that recognizes the bounds of MOXA's authority. And maybe a few extra hands."

The major shrugged. "All right. Getting bored sitting around here, anyway. Let me round up a team. Will eight men be enough? Two fireteams?"

"That sounds good. Sidearms only if you please, Major. We don't want to give MOXA the wrong idea."

"The boys'll be disappointed, but I'll see it done," Invierno said.

Park grunted and gave a little chuckle at his deadpan delivery. So Invierno *did* have a sense of humor. That was good.

While the major went through the Marine's tents, tapping individual operators on the shoulder and ordering them quietly to gear up, Emperor Aeris wandered off and joined three others at a folding table. He began shuffling a deck of cards and chatting amicably, like he was relaxing among friends.

Elya shook his head. If it wasn't for the emperor's supernatural youth and golden eyes, you would never know he was the ruler of the Solaran worlds. The soldiers loved him for it, though. For a man who had built a reputation as an aloof recluse, he sure was friendly. His retinue had set up camp in lavish tents nearby, far enough away so as not to appear to be mixing with the Marines, but close enough that the Emperor could drop in to socialize. This was the same position Elya had found him in when he'd approached with his hunch.

Invierno and his men were ready to go in a matter of minutes. Each fireteam took one case of equipment between them, leaving Elya and Park free to lead the way down the ramp and into the Chronicle room.

"What's this?" Minister Aganaki demanded, stepping up to block their path before they'd made it a dozen steps into the vaulted chamber. A handful of scientists watched from their desks with anxious faces. Most of them were out for lunch, intentional timing on Elya's part. "These soldiers are not authorized to be here."

"Emperor's orders," Elya said simply.

MOXA scientists fidgeted as they eyeballed the special operations team. As Elya had requested, none of the Marines brought their rifles along, only sidearms which were holstered at their thighs or under their arms. They kept their faces blank, professionally absent of emotion as they formed a protective shell around Elya and Park and pushed into the middle of the room.

"We'll just see about that." Aganaki gestured to one of his men. "Call the Emperor."

As I expected, Elya thought. He nodded to Park, who popped open the first case and began to unpack their equipment and assemble the multi-hinged arms and magnetic discs they'd chosen for this experiment. Elya tested the strength of the magnets on the floor and grinned. As with the floor of the plaza above, which they had tested before approaching the emperor, the magnetic discs snapped hard against the ferrous Telos alloy out of which this place was constructed.

Aganaki watched him with hateful, narrowed eyes. The other scientist who had been sent to fetch the Emperor came back after a few minutes, alone. "Emperor's playing cards with the Marines." He jerked his chin in Major Invierno's direction, then glanced at Elya. "Says the Major's in charge."

Aganaki took Major Invierno by the arm and led him aside, whispering fiercely in the man's ear. The major gave a helpless shrug that, though Elya couldn't hear their words, knew it meant, "Sorry, Minister, I'm just following orders."

"Fine," Aganaki finally said. He pointed at Elya. "I hope you get hurt worse than you did last time."

"I know the risk."

"Don't disturb our work," Aganaki ordered. Like it mattered. "And don't you dare damage that relic."

"Not sure the relic *can be* damaged," Elya muttered, "but don't worry, we won't bother you."

With a sigh of relief, Elya finally set to work, first clearing the detection array that had been reinstalled around the stone statue of the oversized hands, then using magnetic discs to pull on the floor tiles.

As with the other floor tiles, the magnets locked on with no problem. But though Elya had the operators use their muscle to yank on the arms attached to the discs, the tiles at the base of the statue wouldn't budge.

"Hmm," he said. "Maybe we need more force."

Aganaki muttered darkly and shook his head at them from across the room. Elya ignored him.

Park got down on his hands and knees to examine the tiles up close. "I think we just need to get the angle right. Or maybe there's some other hidden lever we haven't found yet."

Hedgebot, who had ridden Elya's shoulder down into the

Chronicle room with them, nosed around the statue, flashing shades of blue to indicate there was no danger.

He thought back to how he'd slammed the geode into place in the center of the stone hands. It had been a chaotic few minutes, his life threatened on all sides by lethal Kryl talons and phlegmy acid projectiles. He could still picture the moment vividly in his mind. The geode had activated, locking into place with a click, and being mounted had amplified its defenses, emitting a shock wave of emerald energy.

"I have an idea," Elya said. "Park, bring that magnet over this way."

Park came over to stand next to him.

"These tiles around the hand, they do something," Elya said. "I'm just not sure what yet. But the geode, when it locked into the stone hands… it *clicked* like it was being pulled down into place by a magnet."

"Right." Park said, "And after it activated, the fingers of the statue closed over top of it."

"So what we have to do is get the magnet to release the geode."

"That all?" Park asked, a jovial twinkle in his eye. "You make it sound so easy."

"You got a better idea, Naab?"

"Hey, you're the Telos relic expert. I just know how to use the levers because I worked on starships in the yards at Taj Su. Tell me what you want me to do."

"Well, last time I was down here, I tried brute force and the geode knocked me back. So let's try seeing if the magnets will lock onto the statue anywhere."

"Alright." Park grabbed one of the magnetic tools. It was a long arm with a short angle at the end, like a club foot, on which a magnetic disc was mounted. Starship mechanics used these to swing heavy metallic plates into awkward positions they couldn't reach with their hands, or mounted them as bars to pull themselves across the hull while conducting repairs in a certain spot.

Park pressed the disc against the base of the statue. It didn't attach. He tried several other areas until, finally, a knuckle joint at the base of the palm sucked the magnet into it.

Park locked eyes with Elya and grinned, then pressed a button to release the magnet. He placed another on a different joint—or rather, on the digit just above the joint, where it was flat—and again found a place to lock onto.

The rest of the Marines caught on to what he was doing. In short order, they had magnetic arms attached at several points. Each magnet attached to a joint of the oversized fingers.

Elya had seen these stone hands move on their own, once. Could they be moved manually if the team applied the right forces?

"Hope this works. If not..." He caught himself dwelling on the pain he experienced last time and tried to shove it from his mind. It hadn't been lethal, and he could take another blow if he had to.

Hopefully.

He glanced behind him to make sure the space was clear for twenty meters. It was, although that comfort was as cold and unforgiving as the Telos alloy.

"Hedgebot," he said, "climb up on the hand and be ready to scoot inside. When we pull the fingers open, you knock the geode's handle to deactivate it, and then I'll grab it and pull it out." He bent down beside the largest opening between the fingers that held the geode, between what he presumed was the thumb (with three joints), and the forefinger (which had four).

"What are you doing?" Aganaki demanded, frantically

looking up from his work and realizing what was about to happen. Though he was obviously distressed, he didn't approach. Perhaps knowing what had happened to Elya last time encouraged him to keep his distance.

The coward.

"Whatever I have to do," Elya said. "On the count of three. One..."

"You could damage a priceless stone sculpture! Stop right now."

"Two..."

"Don't!" Aganaki shouted.

"Three!"

The Marines hauled back with all their might. At first, the fingers of the statue didn't budge.

"Keep the pressure on!" Elya said. He threw his shoulder against the forefinger, which was half his height, shoving his boots against the base of the statue to gain more leverage. "Heave!"

A creaking, grinding sound filled his ears as one giant stone finger bent back—just a few centimeters. Enough for Hedgebot to slip through and throw its little body against the geode's handle.

The bot bounced off, shaking itself.

Elya reached in and grabbed the relic's handle. If the fingers retracted, his hand would be crushed. "Again!"

As the bot hit the geode's handle a second time, Elya yanked *hard* in the same direction.

The handle finally turned.

The geode's green glow extinguished itself.

The relic popped out as the magnetic lock disengaged.

As it did, the stone fingers suddenly relaxed, the pair of hands unfolding and opening like flower petals in bloom.

And the hologram of the Telos towering over them vanished.

Just blinked out. There one moment, gone the next.

The Marines and Park staggered back, some falling to the floor with the unexpected release.

Elya landed hard on his back, the geode in his lap.

"What have you done?" Aganaki shouted.

"Something you should have done weeks ago," Elya said, pushing himself to his feet and letting the geode hang from his fingers by its handle. He strode across the room toward the crystal pillar, intent on reactivating the hologram somehow.

"What if we never get this thing back on?" Aganaki snarled, angling to cut him off.

"It'll come back on."

"How do you *know*?"

"This isn't some ancient ruin that crumbles into dust when you poke it wrong, all right? Quit acting like these relics are so delicate. This is mission critical information. If we don't figure out how the relics work, the Kryl are going to get to the rest of them first and *kill us all*."

"There are processes and procedures to follow! You don't just—"

"Enough," Emperor Aeris said, striding out of the shadows with a smile on his face. "It is done."

Minister Aganaki, not one to be outmaneuvered, shoved past Elya and hurried over to the crystal relic. He slapped his hand down onto its angled face before Elya could reach it.

A faint green light, like a fine mist, swirled inside the obelisk.

Emperor Aeris seized Aganaki's wrist and broke contact with the relic's face. The light faded. "Captain Nevers and I will take it from here."

"I—but—Your Majesty! This boy knows nothing of the relics! This is not the way things are done."

"Tachi, you may be the subject matter expert here, but

your hubris and ego have jeopardized the entire endeavor. I had to fly here all the way from Ariadne to ensure that you did not fail me again. Now, step back."

Aganaki screwed his face up, gawping like a fool as he fought for the right words. "Sire, I swear, my intention was not—"

"Actions speak louder than intentions, Tachi. Now, step *back*, or I will strip you of your rank and position, confiscate your wealth, and when I'm through with you, not even the half-rate university where I found you will take you back. Not as an adjunct professor of history, not even as a janitor mopping the floors where second-rate scholars walk. Do you understand me?"

The nanites in the emperor's eyes whirled rapidly. In the absence of the green light from the geode, the Emperor's eyes cast gold discs on the minister's gaunt, frightened face.

Aganaki finally bowed his head. "Yes, sire."

Emperor Aeris turned back to Elya and jerked his chin at the Chronicle. "Ask your questions, Captain."

Shaking with nerves, half fear and half excitement, Elya stepped up to the crystal relic and laid his trembling hand along the angled face of crystal where Minister Aganaki's had been moments ago.

The light swirled amorphously. As he concentrated, it seemed to gather beneath his hand.

This went on for about a minute. Elya felt a muscle twitch in his hand. He removed his hand from the crystal and shook it out.

Aganaki scoffed and paced angrily back and forth. Only a pointed glare from Emperor Aeris stilled his feet.

"Go ahead, Captain," the Emperor said with an air of preternatural patience.

Elya blew his breath out and thought about the starmap he'd seen in Subject Zero's possession. The one relic that turned out *not* to be a prime relic. That was how Subject Zero and the Kryl got into the asteroid temple and located this room. Aganaki had shown him a similar map in the crystal relic's memory banks, had he not?

The xenoscientists had to extract that information, and then manipulate the data to turn it into something usable for the military. But Telos technology wasn't meant to work with human-made computers. The hologram of Chronicle that had hung in this room until just a few minutes ago was awfully similar to Solaran holoprojectors, but the Telos version was better in every way. While that image hung up there, he swore he could feel the thing breathing. There was no flickering light or dust visible, no interference, no sense of the source of the image, like you'd expect from a normal hologram projection. Though everyone had assumed the Telos was projected from the crystal relic, no one had found the light's source.

Telos technology was different. And the only thing he'd seen interact with the crystal obelisk so far were the hands in which it was mounted, and the geode relic he held.

Acting on a hunch, Elya lifted the geode and set it on the angled face of the crystal. The crystal shocked him by growing up toward the geode, then shaping itself into a round mounting space precisely the size of the other relic. In the span of a heartbeat, the two relics were connected like they had grown together; just like the City outside these walls, crystal and stone alloy intertwined.

"Whoa," Elya said as he removed his hand from the geode, no longer needing to keep it in place.

Nothing else happened.

Elya glanced back at the emperor and Minister Aganaki. They were staring at the paired relics, the latter with fear, the former with eager anticipation.

"Try turning the handle," the Emperor suggested.

"Oh, right, of course," Elya said.

He did. It rotated smoothly, a full 180 degrees.

Green light from the geode poured down into the crystal column. It merged with the green mist in there and darkened to a rich shade of gold. Elya extended his hands along the sides of the column and noticed that the golden light followed his fingers as he moved it along the obelisk's lateral faces.

Elya straightened and set both hands on the geode's handle. It was comfortable, with his hands resting just below the level of his heart, much like the control stick of a Sabre.

Without consciously willing it, an orb of gold light passed through the front wall of the crystal and rose into the air before him.

Starmap, Elya thought, and the orb burst apart into a thousand glowing points, spreading into the air above them.

"Are these the relics?" he asked aloud.

The stars spun into the shape of a galaxy. Seven pinpricks of light shone brighter than the rest.

Gasps and sharp inhalations filled the room as xenoscientists, Marines, and the emperor himself marveled at the sight.

Elya didn't bother to seek Aganaki's expression. He knew the annoyed shock that would be plastered on the minister's face.

One thing about this map he'd just summoned was strange. The seven pinpricks of light marking the prime relics adhered to a slightly different configuration. One of the beacons had moved to float close to another—nearly right on top of it, clearly showing that two of the prime relics were hidden in the *same* star system. He filed that information away for later and willed the map to disappear, earning grumbled complaints from the MOXA scientists.

There were other vital questions to be answered right now, and Elya was on a mission.

Chronicle, he thought.

Again, an orb of golden light flowed out of the crystal obelisk. This time, it formed a hologram in front of him.

A broad-shouldered, muscular creature wearing a purple robe. Head shadowed beneath a deep-set hood, appeared before him.

This time it stood on the ground between two of the enormous columns holding up the flat roof. The creature still towered over him, nearly eight feet tall, but it was no longer the vast, oversized image they'd been shown before.

He still didn't completely understand it, but something about the configuration of the relics, when used together in different ways, altered their function.

"State your business," said the Telos. The voice seemed to emanate from the crystal relic on which his hand was resting. His arm vibrated when the creature spoke.

"Chronicle," he said. "I'm Captain Elya Nevers of the Solaran Defense Forces, and we need your help." He glanced around him at the couple dozen people lucky enough to be in this room. Saw their wide eyes and rapt expressions, their faces cast in a mixture of fear and hope.

"I am limited in my ability to render aid," said Chronicle, "but if it is knowledge you seek, I am at your service."

Elya thought back to the words Chronicle had spoken to Aganaki when it had first been activated. "That's why you're here, isn't it?" he asked. "To acquire knowledge?"

"You wish to know my purpose?"

"Yes. What is your purpose?"

"To serve as the First People's final record of the collected knowledge and history of the Kryl."

The exact phrase it had used before. Elya couldn't forget that if he tried. Aganaki had admitted that the Chronicle hadn't spoken any more since that first day. Could Elya get it to say more than Aganaki had?

He started with the basics.

"How is it you came to speak Galactic Standard?" asked Elya.

Aganaki scoffed. The Emperor glared him into silence. Had he asked the wrong question? Elya thought it would be wise to start with an easy one.

"We learned your language when I encountered humanity in your generation ships. They programmed it into my system, along with thousands of others they had collected."

Elya blinked. "Wow, nice," he said stupidly. "And, uh, had you ever spoken to anyone else before we woke you?"

"You are the first. Although the Kryl have tried many times to enter this temple, our defenses held them at bay."

"Many times?" Elya swallowed the lump in his throat. "How many times exactly?"

"Sixteen separate occasions that I am aware of."

"How are you made aware?"

"Every time a Kryl is repelled by our defenses, it becomes part of the historical record."

"Can you show me this record?"

"It is me."

"Let me rephrase. Can you share any data about those sixteen encounters?"

"Just their stardates."

A sheet of paper-thin crystal grew out of the obelisk near Elya's right hand. He picked it up and saw, within, letters made of golden light listing a series of numbers he didn't have the skill to interpret, next to something that looked like orbital positions.

At a pleading look from Aganaki, the Emperor nodded. The minister strode forward and snatched the crystal out of Elya's hands, then hurried over to a station to analyze the data. His scientists crowded around him in a flurry of low chatter.

After a moment, Aganaki poked his head up. "The most recent attempt to access the asteroid was roughly a hundred and five years ago, Your Majesty. Before the war with the Kryl."

Elya grunted. *Let him have credit for that,* he thought. *It'll placate his bruised ego.*

Emperor Aeris paced slowly, calmly, one finger to his lips. "So the Kryl knew about the relics before we knew about the Kryl..." He mused aloud

"But not how to get past their defenses," Aganaki said.

Elya turned from the crystal and paced a few meters away. Chronicle's image remained in place, a still, quiet presence that followed him with its face. That hologram technology was so *real*. Like the giant hologram from before, this one's face remained shadowed beneath a deep, cowled hood. But the feet, like human fingers but with one too many joints, were visible beneath its robes. Elya paced as he thought through the new information, then said, "The Queen Mother knew. Not Overmind X. Overmind X hadn't been created yet."

Most of the scientists, and all the Marines, merely looked puzzled. They didn't know the backstory about how Omar Ruidiaz created Overmind X in the antimatter blast that ended the Kryl War.

Elya stepped back up to the paired relics and gripped the geode's handle. He had more questions still.

"They've changed," Elya told Chronicle. "The Kryl can fool your defenses now."

"We knew that was a possibility," said the Telos, "Which is why the last Engineer separated and hid the prime relics."

"Would that not make them difficult for us to obtain, too?"

"A necessary precaution. We gave your people their coordinates, and access to other wayfinding technology the Kryl didn't have for precisely this reason."

The poem they'd found were those hints. The ansible and hyperspace drive were those technologies. It was coming together in Elya's mind.

"Without those tools, you would have been at an extreme disadvantage," Chronicle said.

Elya wanted to laugh, but swallowed it. As if they weren't at a disadvantage with the technology they did have! "It's not enough."

Chronicle didn't respond. Elya didn't blame it. What else was there to say to that? "It's not enough" was merely a statement of fact for him. *Wait a minute...*

"You knew your defenses wouldn't last." Again, no response. "Didn't you?" he prompted.

"Nothing lasts forever," Chronicle said.

Elya's mind raced. *So many questions*! Chief among them, a burning desire to know if Overmind X's version of events—the version she'd imparted to him through a sequence of fragmented images while he had been infected with her parasite—had been true or not. An interminable war between the Telos and Kryl that raged for centuries… how the Telos patrolled her borders… the hive queen's testimony of the Telos civil war that chased the Enemy from the galaxy they once ruled…

"You say you hold the collected knowledge and history of the Kryl," Elya said, speaking carefully, one word at a time. "Tell it to me. Give me your version. You fought them for centuries, right? When did you first come into contact with the Kryl? Where did they come from?"

Aganaki, his scientists, the Emperor—even the bored-looking Marines—leaned in to listen.

"It was not first contact, but first invention," Chronicle rumbled. The Telos's voice sounded sad, a melancholy too real for simulation. "The Kryl as a species were created during an experiment run by a rogue Engineer. One of our brightest and most capable. This Engineer believed it was their calling and purpose to create the most perfect creature under the stars. One that could brave the vacuum between worlds. A creature which shared one mind *unbound* by the confines of its physical form. One which, as long as one of its aspects still breathed, would never die. In your language, you might call it... an immortal soul."

"Only it didn't work as expected," said Elya.

"On the contrary, it worked *better* than expected. The experiment ran rampant, bursting violently through the limits the Engineer imposed upon them. The creation attacked and killed its maker, triggering a failsafe that summoned the might of the entire Telos military."

Elya stood rapt, jaw falling increasingly open, as Chronicle recounted the details of those tragic events. Though the Telos rained fiery death upon the Engineer's creations, the Kryl boarded Telos starships in secret and piggybacked to Telos worlds. Once there, the Kryl worked together through their psionic link, growing in numbers underground until they were sufficiently numerous to overrun one colony after another. The Telos responded, taking emergency measures, evacuating colonies, destroying every Kryl nest they discovered. But not quickly enough.

Billions perished.

It sounded so much like the war that had been fought by humanity. The Fleet had ceded the colony of Robichar to Overmind X based on a similar logic.

As ever, history repeats itself.

Only that wasn't the end of Chronicle's story. The Telos did, eventually, get the rampaging Kryl under control, confining the Queen Mother to a single world—Aganaki and his scientists rushed to confirm that this world and Planet K were one and the same. Regardless, the decision *not* to eliminate the Kryl in one final genocidal attack tore a deep rift in the Telos sociopolitical machine. One faction believed that the species, an experiment gone wrong, should be eliminated. The other side insisted that no matter what their origin, the Kryl, as sentient beings, deserved their chance at life. For this faction, genocide was *not* an option.

"Eventually, the right to life won out. Genocide left a sour taste in the mouth of the First People. Even though the Kryl had murdered our people, destroyed our cities, and consumed worlds we'd inhabited for millennia and scraped them for their minerals and water in their mad desire to expand.... Ultimately, we did not believe they were at fault. The Kryl simply did what they were designed to do. That is all. And we created them. So, instead of destroying the Kryl, we policed their territory, making sure the Queen Mother did not expand to new worlds. This constant surveillance strained our resources and added a constant fear of failure to our societal consciousness. The task seemed endless. Looking back now, it is clear that these events mark the beginning of my civilization's decline."

Chronicle fell silent once more.

"Until, eventually, the Telos began to fight amongst themselves," Elya offered.

"Yes," rumbled Chronicle. "Until civil war broke out among our people, and we were forced to leave this galaxy behind."

TWENTY-TWO

Kira closed the tightbeam, pondering the news she'd just been given by a fractious Minister Aganaki. Two prime relics located here in *this* star system. His team's previous projections had been based on an outdated version of the starmap. The version Captain Nevers managed to dig up was newer. The alien hologram was even talking to Nevers again, if you could believe it.

Her hunch grew stronger that another prime relic was behind this spacetime anomaly the Kryl found hidden among the shards of the broken planet.

Now she knew two things: One, the Emperor must have known something was inside the planet. How he knew remained a complete mystery. Second, if this event horizon was so important, Overmind X wouldn't be far away. But so far, no one had been able to pinpoint her location.

"Any sign of the hive queen?" Kira asked one of Aganaki's xenobiologists.

"Not that I *see*," Dr. Lumago responded in a tone of barely controlled irritation. "The workers are here, but no sign of the monarch. You have to understand, Admiral, she'd be hard to spot using the best of equipment. And even if we can find her mothership, she could be hiding in any number of different xenoforms."

Kira didn't appreciate his attitude, or his fancy word for Kryl ships, but smothered her annoyance. He wasn't Fleet and she couldn't expect him to behave like it. He was a MOXA employee, basically a consultant she'd forced into her service. On the tightbeam call with Aganaki, the minister had objected and initially refused to send anyone, but the emperor overrode him.

Now, Dr. Lumago, a bespectacled man with a bushy beard, alongside several of his colleagues, squinted at lidar scans of the hundreds of Kryl creatures they'd been tracking. More had sneaked in around the backside of the broken planet than they'd initially realized, but it wasn't even close to the kinds of numbers the entire swarm could muster. The scientists had been trying to make the data tell some kind of story about Kryl operations ever since. Kira had reserved a room for them adjacent to the bridge for the effort.

Unfortunately, so far, none of the creatures appeared to be the hive queen herself. Which made finding and eliminating her problematic.

Kira couldn't cut off the monster's head if she couldn't find the right neck to chop.

"Blood on the stars!" Kira cursed. "So if she's not here, where is she hiding?"

"They're clearly building something around that anomaly," Dr. Lumago said. "That's all I can say for certain right now."

"We don't have time. Overmind X *will* come for it if another prime relic shows up."

Unless she's here already.

Dr. Lumago barely contained a roll of his eyes as he

glanced up at her, his dark cheeks above the beard pockmarked and rough.

"I know you know this," Kira said, acknowledging his unspoken annoyance. "The problem is, if I send my armada in and start shooting, even if our attack is successful, Overmind X will slip away, regrow her forces, and come back at us in the future. This needs to end here."

And, ideally, end before *they realize we're watching and turn that photon cannon on us again.*

"Like I told you, Admiral," said Dr. Lumago, "We're doing the best we can with what we've got. Pattern matching takes time." He tapped on the holoscreen, connected to Harmony's systems, to which she'd granted him access. "And this stupid tab isn't working. I've never seen it so buggy."

"No excuses," she said. "Figure it out. Work faster. I'll come back to check on you in an hour."

She turned and strode out of the room, down the hallway, and back to the bridge.

Captain Nevers' conversation with Chronicle was ongoing. She wondered what else he might discover.

She was about to check on her other probes, which had been moved to conduct surveillance in the remaining systems the starmap had identified for the last outstanding relic. None of them had found any sign of Kryl yet, but it had been thirty minutes since she'd checked. Instead, she was distracted by a bizarre sight on the main viewscreen of the bridge.

"Is that...?"

Colonel Volk nodded. "We managed to sneak a probe in closer. Best shot of the anomaly we've had yet."

Centered on the screen was the skeleton of an oblong structure, more disc than sphere. Thousands of Kryl workers, like ants from this distance, glommed onto the structure's struts and edges. The workers were flat, thin creatures featuring six claws and limbs that interlinked with others of its type, allowing them to work closely together to scale repetitive functions. Unlike the workers bred for atmosphere, these were thin and broad, with a translucent skein connecting their limbs. They had beady eyes embedded in the top of a long neck stalk.

A gigantic mass of workers had already constructed a surface, moving toward the center so that, now, only a single uneven empty oval remained in the structure's outer walls. Though she couldn't tell in this enhanced footage, she knew from experience that the workers would go back over it again, adding layer upon layer of membrane between struts, then coat it with a shiny layer to form a hull. The material would harden into carapace and create a sealed, oxygen-rich environment that they would pump full of gas until it was conducive to Kryl habitation.

Not that they all needed atmosphere to live. These worker types, for example, carried their air in big sacs on their chests. When they ran out, they would float across to a cocoon-like vessel to refuel.

Even more remarkable than what they could build was the speed at which they moved. In terms of efficiency, Solaran teams could never hope to outpace them. Was it any wonder Overmind X had grown her swarm as quickly as she had?

"Colonel Volk," Kira said. "What's the status? Any hostile movement?"

"No change, Admiral. They're building around the anomaly, but damned if I know what they plan to do with it."

"We can't let them finish it. With or without knowledge of the Overmind's location, we'll have to destroy it at some point."

He nodded. They'd already discussed several possible scenarios, and settled on one that would lure out the photon cannon and allow them to isolate it without unnecessarily endangering the rest of the armada. "I've briefed the Furies."

"You really think they're the best squad to send?"

"This is what they've been training for. Plus, given their current size, the Furies are the most agile yet experienced team available."

"What about Captain Nevers and Lieutenant Park?"

"The new mission commander, Captain Osprey, gave them a pass. They can stay on special orders."

Kira nodded. "Good." She was relieved he'd chosen a flight lead to whom he could delegate command duties, and secretly glad it was Osprey. Having Volk choose the mission commander instead of Kira obviated any future accusations of favoritism.

Meanwhile, Captain Nevers' progress with the relics was a boon, and she found herself feeling bemused but grateful for Emperor Aeris' unexpected visit to Elturis. Kira valued practical experience over almost everything else, and apparently the Emperor did, too. His instinct about Captain Nevers had been spot on. Despite being a combat pilot, Nevers had been put into a position to become her chief source of intelligence when it came to the relics.

"I hate this," Kira said in a voice pitched low enough that only Volk could hear her.

"Hate's good. Keeps you alert." Colonel Volk crossed his arms and frowned at the viewscreen. He drummed four fingers against the outside of his opposite arm. "Do you think our probes will find the other prime relic?"

"Space is vast, and our coverage is spotty. What makes you think Overmind X doesn't already have it?"

Volk growled. "It's possible, sir. I can't rule it out."

"That's why I like you, Volk. You have a healthy sense of paranoia."

Colonel Volk chuckled darkly. "It's lucky we caught their initial exploration of the anomaly on recon."

"Too lucky," Kira said. "Sometimes I think they actually *want* us to see what they're doing."

That caused Volk to press his lips together and brood silently. A long minute passed as they both contemplated trickery.

"Muster the Furies and hold them in reserve until I give the command," Kira finally said.

"Aye, sir." Volk never took his eye off the Kryl structure on the viewscreen.

It was like they were building some kind of space station. What the hell were they planning to do with it? They had to know the Solarans would destroy them once they discovered its existence.

Kira felt fatigue overcome her all at once. It came on suddenly, and she couldn't hold the line by force of will. She checked the clock—it was late in the afternoon by Galactic Standard Time. Should she drink more coffee? No, caffeine had lost its effects days ago.

"Time for some R&R?" Harmony suggested, using the voice in Kira's head to communicate.

How am I supposed to relax right now?

"You will, once you see who's waiting for you in your quarters."

A genuinely cheerful smile broke through her fatigue. The AI had been busy working with the crew on the bridge, yet Harmony still monitored movements on the ship for Kira. One of the perks of being the admiral. She always knew about visitors before anyone else.

"Besides, you've been up for 36 hours."

Kira scowled. "What about Colonel Volk?"

"He's only been up 18 hours. You sent him to rest for a while, remember?"

Oh, right. She'd forgotten about that.

Harmony had a point. Kira would be sharper after a few hours of sleep, and it didn't seem like an attack was imminent.

Kira left Volk in charge and hurried to her cabin. It felt cozier and warmer than the sparsely furnished flat she kept on Ariadne. If she was being honest with herself, the *Paladin* was the only place she'd truly felt at home since Omar's death.

When she walked through the door, the faint but pleasant scent of charred oak drifted to her nose. Her eyes quickly found the source of the smell: Eben Osprey sat on her couch with the top two buttons on his inquisitor's coat undone, lapels hanging open to reveal an alluring view of his sculpted chest. He was in his late fifties, but appeared younger and remained in top physical shape. He had one ankle resting on the opposite knee, and was gazing into a decorative hologram she kept in the corner. A glass tumbler hung from his long fingers.

He turned as she entered, taking her in with a crooked smile and swirling the deep amber-colored whiskey in the cup.

She met his eyes and kept his attention as she boldly crossed the room. Kira took the tumbler and downed the liquor in a single shot. She sighed contentedly and tilted her head back. Charred oak and… something sweet. Honey?

One of Eben's eyebrows quirked up. "Would you like me to pour you one, too?" Kira asked.

"How about two?"

"Perfect"

She crossed the room to the liquor cabinet. Like all the furniture onboard, it was bolted to the wall and floor. She lifted the bottle of whiskey and held it up to the light. "I like it. Smooth and subtle, with a hint of sweetness."

"Like you."

Kira smirked and let the compliment wash over her without taking the bait. "How many bottles of Oltanin whiskey do you have left, anyway? I know it's not cheap."

"Not many. Half a dozen. It's been, I don't know, fifteen years since I've been back. I bought a case with my signing bonus when I took my first tour as inquisitor."

"That's a nice reward for yourself."

"I never spent that kind of money on alcohol before or since." He took a sip and sighed. "Might be coming due here soon."

"Makes sense they'd give signing bonuses to inquisitors." Kira popped the cork out of the bottle. "Hard job, with few friends."

He grinned. "Honestly, who can blame them? No one enjoys being under investigation. Plus, inquisitors have all the power of military police, yet we work outside the normal chain of command. That frightens people. Especially those who are breaking the law."

"Good point." She poured the whiskey into two tumblers, added ice from a small freezer in the cart's drawer, then took them over to sit next to Eben. "Doesn't seem right to have that much power."

"Being outside the normal chain of command is the only way we can be truly objective. It means we're less likely to be influenced. We don't play the game. At least not the same one."

She thought back to her experiences on Ariadne recently. When she had to be a player of the game in order to get colonization journeys halted. "Some still say the Fleet should be allowed to police our own."

"Do you agree?"

"I don't know." She thought about it. "I'd want the chance to make things right first."

"You do. You wouldn't call an inquisitor in unless it was a problem you couldn't handle yourself, would you?"

"I didn't call you in to handle Lieutenant Colonel Spector."

"That's different. You didn't know anything untoward was happening until after I got there."

"But I didn't get the chance to make it right once I did."

"Do you think I was in the wrong?"

"Didn't say that. Merely stating the facts."

"Fair enough." He said it in a way that made it sound like he didn't agree.

"But you're different from most inquisitors," Kira said. "People *like* you. Especially now that you're retired."

"Ouch." He gave her a fake hurt look. "I hate that word. Makes me feel old."

"You don't look old," she said.

"I came out of retirement, remember?" He leaned forward and rested his hand lightly on her thigh. "I'm on special duty for the Solaran armada."

Normally, her stomach would have tingled with anticipation at a gentle touch from Eben. She was happy to see him, but… there was too much on her mind right now. She shifted her leg until his hand fell away.

He switched his tumbler to that hand and took a slow sip while watching her face.

"Speaking of your special duty, what did you discover in talking with my senior officers?"

"They're anxious. Worried. They don't like sitting on their haunches and licking their wounds."

"Hah!" The bark of laughter jumped out. "Wonderful. We're all in agreement, then."

"I wouldn't say that," he said. "Ostensibly, I boarded their ships to audit their security systems. No one likes to be inspected, but most agreed and let me do my thing. However, a few put up a fight. I made a list of those for you."

He picked up his tab and tapped the device against the base of the holoprojector in the corner. That transferred the list into Kira's tab. She jerked her chin up and located it on her heads-up display. "Mostly corvette captains under Colonel Seba's command."

"A few reporting to Admiral Quellin, too. There are others in different groups. And if there is discontent among the commanders, you can expect the same among the troops."

She studied the list for a minute, cross checking it with the post-battle analyses and pre-battle game plans Harmony had worked up for a dozen engagement scenarios. She'd studied these plans and readouts endlessly, so she knew them by heart.

"I'll make Seba reorganize the corvette groups. We have to better integrate the reinforcements the Executive Council sent, anyway, so I have a good reason. Thanks for the heads-up."

"No problem."

Eben shifted closer to her and laid his arm along the back of the couch. It made Kira's neck itch, so she got up and paced across the room. "They're scared, is all. They don't know what these relics can do, and it's been so long since we had any real defeats against the Kryl. It shook them."

"There's steel in Seba. He just needs to know it's worth the sacrifice. He doesn't want to see his corvettes, often in the front lines of any attack, thrown away for nothing."

"I'm right there with him. He knows that photon cannon damaged my ship, too."

"He doesn't see it the same way. The *Paladin of Abniss* is the flagship. You're well positioned for evasive maneuvers.

Because his corvettes are more mobile, they risk more exposure."

"He's not wrong, but that's part of the job. If he doesn't like it, maybe he doesn't have the spine to be a corvette group commander."

"Removing him now wouldn't look good. And who would you have do the job instead?"

She raised her eyebrows.

"Don't look at me," Eben said. "I'm good at criminal investigations and swordplay. Not reprimanding corvette commanders."

She went to refill her glass. Eben came and stood beside her, pressing against her shoulder. He smelled good. Like that whiskey, with an undertone of musk from the oil he put in his trim, silver beard.

"I'm sorry," she said. "I'm just distracted tonight."

"Let me help take your mind off your problems for a little while."

She was still fond of him. Of course she was. He was handsome, witty, and accomplished. He checked all the boxes. And yet... something about it didn't sit right with her. What had changed?

"I like you Eben."

When she didn't continue, he turned that wry smirk on her. She saw so much of the man in his daughter, Captain Osprey. Was that what made her uncomfortable? No, that hadn't mattered before.

"I'm not sure I can keep doing this," Kira said. "I'm not in a place where I can make a serious commitment right now."

"Serious?" Eben asked. He seemed genuinely puzzled, which surprised her. Everything he'd done made her think he wanted more. "I thought this was recreational."

"I didn't mean to break it off like this, I just—"

"Break what off, Kira? There's nothing to break off."

He set the tumbler down, and as he walked by her toward the exit, something made her grab his wrist. "Don't go," she said.

A half hour later, he was snoring beside her with his arm draped over her. It was good to be with him, but her heart hadn't been in it. It took a long time for her to fall asleep.

As she lay there next to her current lover, all she could think about was her past. About Omar and the way things ended. Or the way she *thought* they'd ended.

Nothing had been the same since she discovered he was alive. Overmind X would pay for what she'd done. Kira didn't care if she had to tear the galaxy apart to find her. Overmind X would pay.

TWENTY-THREE

"It pains me to confess, knowing that I contributed to it," Chronicle said. "Knowing my personal vendetta is tied up in our civilization's collapse."

Elya felt his eyes widen. This was the first time any primary source had shed light on the disappearance of the Telos. Humanity had long been aware of these ancient inventors... but until this very moment, no one had ever known what happened to them, where they went, or why they left.

He glanced over at the minister and saw that, for all his crowing, the implication had not escaped Aganaki's notice. Chronicle had just acknowledged his personal role in the history. Whoever or whatever this simulation was, Chronicle had once been *alive*. This crystal obelisk had been programmed, or imprinted, with the personality and memory of a living being; a Telos. Chronicle was far more than a storage program. It was a personal account.

A testimony.

Chronicle was also the closest any Solaran had come to meeting a real live Telos since the Great Migration. Maybe the closest they would ever come again. The realistic avatar sighed heavily and continued.

"The war among our people was long and terrible. Although for centuries afterward we would tell stories about the horrors of the Kryl invasions, those incidents were nothing compared to the destruction we ultimately wrought upon ourselves. I say I am responsible because... well, if I have done any good in making this record, or shepherding a precious few of my people to safety, know that it is only because of the guilt I feel for my actions. I deserve no accolades. Do not heap praise upon me. Everything I did has been a humble act of penance."

"What *did* you do?" asked Elya.

"I built the technology that tore the Telos homeworld asunder."

In the account that followed, Chronicle explained that he'd once been a leader of Hazrah—a learned order of wandering scholars who made it their mission to travel between Telos worlds spreading knowledge of terraforming, astronomy, architecture, and engineering. He said the First People revered these arts as a kind of religion, and that it was the Hazrah's job to tell stories of the achievements of the greatest among them.

In their role as wandering scholars, Chronicle told them, representatives of Hazrah were always welcome. They traveled from shrine to temple, from city to remote village. On every Telos world, Hazrah were welcomed like honored guests, showered with gifts and refreshment, offered companionship or aid in any form they desired. As a result, through the centuries, Hazrah hubs grew in size, power and influence. They used their wealth to build temples across many worlds, which Hazrah travelers could use as temporary safe houses between missions—the sacred sites where the prime relics were now stored.

Among Hazrah, all knowledge and every story they gathered was pooled and shared. It was Hazrah who first pioneered use of the ansible as a shared information system—a feat the Solarans, while versed in using the ansible as an interstellar communications device, had never managed to accomplish. Every new Telos story, every new Hazrah secret, went into a central storage system much like the crystal obelisk through which Chronicle now operated, but accessible by any Hazrah at any time.

As it became clear that the Telos' responsibility to police Kryl space was an endless punishment, and would forever remain a chain around their peoples' necks, and as tensions between the parties split by this issue increased, Hazrah elders were asked to join discussions to serve as mediators and judges.

"Hazrah was perceived as the neutral party," Chronicle said. "Because we had no world to call our own, we were often employed to arbitrate disagreements."

"What does this have to do with what you did?" Elya blurted out.

The Telos turned its attention to Elya and responded, unfazed, "It provides important context."

"Sorry." Elya blushed. "Go on."

"Eventually, Hazrah's elders became tired of being summoned around the galaxy to arbitrate increasingly hostile disagreements. I was amongst the most vocal critics of our policy of thankless compliance. For better or worse, most of the organization's leaders ended up falling on my side of the line. Over the course of a decade, I gradually assumed control of Hazrah, and then withdrew us from the negotiations.

"I was young, only thirty years Hazrah, when we took our oath of non-interference. The war started after that. It became unsafe to travel, and in addition to scholars, Hazrah were forced to become warriors merely to defend ourselves. Many of our bravest emissaries, those who continued to travel to worlds where they were most needed, were caught in attacks and killed. As our numbers dwindled, the flames of war burned hotter. The rest of the details are inconsequential. Eventually, I broke the oath rather than relinquish my seat as Hazrah's leader. I picked a side in the war. I raided our storehouses and gave the tools of annihilation to the wrong group of dissidents. This drew the last remaining forces keeping the Queen Mother at bay from their posts. For the first time in millennia, we left the Kryl unguarded."

Chronicle paused for a moment before going on. Only Hedgebot's claws clicked in the chamber's silence.

"After that, the collapse spread like a supernova, engulfing our civilization practically overnight. Billions starved. Pestilence took billions more. Compared with the long life of our civilization, our end came quick and bright and shocking, leaving nothing but stardust and our many temples behind. The remaining Hazrah gathered in council, and we devised a plan that would deliver a select group of First People from the nightmare this sector had become. We had destroyed many temples in the fighting, but not all. In those that remained, we stashed the sum of our knowledge, tools that could resist the Kryl should such a race of beings arrive or evolve after our departure. It was not much but... at that point, it was all we could think to do. Unfortunately, before we could execute our plan, a senior Hazrah of the council seized control of my technology and turned it against the rest of us. Our homeworld was destroyed. Those left alive departed shortly thereafter."

"When in all this did you first encounter humanity?" Elya asked.

"Several centuries later. I stayed behind after my kin left, extending my life with the aid of long periods of hibernation, on the off chance that another spacefaring race would enter this sector. We didn't think it likely, but our collective concern about the Kryl problem required me to render this last act of sacrifice. I was happy to volunteer. As I said, guilt was my driving force. I woke from stasis when my systems alerted me that a ship full of two-legged hominids with enlarged brains and knowledge of space travel had entered the sector."

"The Great Migration," Elya whispered in awe. "Wait, that means... *You're* the last Engineer I read about in the archives?"

"I suppose that is a fitting title, yes, but not one I use. I simply did what Hazrah do best. I traveled to meet the Solarans and told them the story of the Kryl. I guided them to a habitable planet where they would find clean air and fresh water—far from the Kryl presence. I gave your people key pieces of technology that would allow you to skip technologically ahead of the Kryl by an order of magnitude, so you'd have a better chance of surviving against them should they become hostile. And finally, I gave you the locations of the prime relics, should the Kryl move in such a way that you were forced to defend yourselves the same way that we once did."

In wry terms, Elya imagined the meeting between human leaders and the Telos during the Great Migration. "Welcome to the galaxy, skippers! You look tired. Have this nice planet. Oh, don't worry about those murderous aliens hanging out in the next neighborhood over. We've been killing them to keep them at bay for a few eons, but never you mind. Ah, and by the way, in case they come knocking, here's something you need to know..."

Elya snapped himself out of the humorous fantasy. "Maybe you're behind a bit. We don't have all the prime relics. That's why we're here. We need your help to find the last of them."

For the first time, the realistic image of Chronicle tilted its head, as if puzzled. "That makes little sense. According to my last update, I gave your people their locations and the knowledge needed to retrieve them."

Elya chewed his lip. "While that may be true, we lost such ability along the way. All we have now are vague hints."

Emperor Aeris coughed into his hands. Did he, perhaps, know something more about this history? Was he withholding information? After all, as evidenced by the nanites swimming in those enigmatic golden eyes, the royal family had access to more advanced technology than even wealthy Solaran families like the Ospreys. Or perhaps His Majesty just felt guilty because it was he who had buried the journal in the Church of Animus's archives and all mention of it wiped from the public record.

"If we don't move fast," Elya said, "the Kryl will get to them first. Will you help us?" With a thought, he brought the starmap back up. Once again, he noticed how two of the beacons were sitting side-by-side in this star system. "Start with those two markers. Why are they together?"

"After I gave the information to your people, I moved the most dangerous of the relics here and trapped one within a… what did your people call it… a wormhole."

He glanced over his shoulder, but Aganaki already had a tightbeam open and was communicating with Admiral Miyaru, whose hologram he could see in miniature.

"Okay. And what about the rest?"

With Chronicle's help, they quickly identified and removed the beacons of relics that had already been obtained. With the knowledge the Telos held, they also removed two of the four possible systems for the remaining two relics. If one was in the wormhole in Elturis, the other was almost certainly a bladed weapon, which lay "behind the shrine." Aganaki relayed the information, and Kira immediately dispatched a small force to retrieve it. In a matter of hours, a corvette captain reported finding the temple open, signs of the Kryl inside, and no relic.

"Damn. That only leaves one..." Elya trailed off. "I know we've covered this, but tell me again why you hid the relics in such difficult to find places? Why not just give them to the Solarans for safekeeping and avoid all this headache?"

"They are too powerful to simply leave undefended," Chronicle said. "And too dangerous to leave together."

That piqued Elya's interest. He'd already noted how the relics interacted. His hand had gone numb during the conversation, fingers resting on the handle of the geode, which vibrated as Chronicle's every word emanated from the crystal obelisk now holding it up.

"Are they more dangerous when used together?" he asked.

"Yes. And if the Kryl ever got all of them and could use them, your people are in danger of extinction."

A chill crawled up his spine. "What can they do in pairs?"

"It is not safe to say."

This was the first true firewall he'd encountered in Chronicle's story since the conversation began.

"Why not?"

"I cannot share such knowledge until you possess them together. I am sorry."

"What *can* you tell me?"

"The prime relics were each designed to control one of the seven primal forces. As with life, when the primal forces interact, they create life... or they destroy it."

That was odd. It had been years since he'd sat through a class on physics, but he remembered nothing about seven primal forces. "What do you mean?"

The scientists sat raptly, recording or tapping notes furiously into their tabs.

"Based on ancient principles, Hazrah teach that there are seven primal forces that make up all of creation... the so-called axioms of existence. They are the four physical laws: separation, attraction, electromagnetism, and gravity. And the three modes of being: body, mind and spirit.

"Each prime relic was designed to control and manipulate one of those primal forces. In this way, not only will the relics help you oppose the Kryl, but Hazrah's legacy would also be passed down to those who found them."

"What do you call them?" Elya asked. Ever since encountering these relics, he'd struggled to name them. Not knowing their purpose, he named them after their physical appearance: the geode or the crystal obelisk.

"In our culture," Chronicle said, "the primal forces are so important to our language and understanding that we use their names for the first seven numbers in our numerical system. Thus, the relic on which your hand currently rests is called One. Spirit."

One in a cave on a forest moon.

Elya's eyes widened. The epiphany struck him like a bell.

"And the pylon on which One is mounted. That Prime relic is called Three, or Electromagnetism."

Three to orbit a broken planet.

The dual meanings of each line from the poem lit his mind on fire. He'd been looking right at it!

"And they have unique abilities when you put them together?" He gestured to the pair in front of him.

"Yes. Spirit and electromagnetism together... My spirit, infused into the electromagnetic nodes of that pylon's molecular structure."

Aganaki's scientists leaped into action. Soon they had the relics sorted. Chronicle waited with infinite patience while the humans in the room assimilated this information and assigned relics they knew about to each force.

One: Spirit. The geode under his hand.

Two: Separation. The photon cannon Overmind X used to attack the armada.

Three: Electromagnetism. Chronicle; the crystal pylon, its memories and its holograms.

Four: Body. The phase shifter in Subject Zero's possession.

Five: Attraction. An object with the power to connect and bind life, either missing or in the Kryl's possession.

The same went for Six, Mind, and Seven, Gravity.

It was the prime relics of Attraction, Mind, and Gravity they were hunting.

Elya ran through them repeatedly until he'd committed their numbers and names to memory.

He observed that it listed the forces in a strange order, the aspects of being mixed up with the natural laws. Chronicle claimed their order implied a meaning that was simply lost in translation. When all seven were depicted together in the Telos language, they were inscribed in a circle, each aspect represented by a single glyph, with each character clearly pointing to and relating to the others with which it would most commonly interact.

Just like the seven statues of Telos hands ringing the Chronicle room around him.

Body was nothing without the law of attraction. Atoms attract each other and form objects in the physical world.

Mind was nothing without electromagnetism, which connected circuits in the brain and kept the heart pumping.

And that ancient scribe? The one who wrote the poem they'd found in the Archives? He'd not only identified the relics' locations—but also which relic was resting in which hiding place!

"Chronicle," Elya said, "We know for sure that Overmind X already has Separation and Body. We need to find Gravity, Mind, and Attraction before the Kryl do. Can you show us their locations and help us get to them before they do?"

"If they already have Body, they are likely going after Gravity next."

"Why Gravity?"

"Because only the prime relics of Body and Gravity together will open a way to the resting place of the Prime Relic of Mind. If, as you say, the Kryl have discovered a way to use the relics... Only Mind can counter their most distinct advantage—their shared mind."

Elya felt a sinking feeling in his gut. Chronicle meant Overmind X and her ability to communicate with and control her hive across vast, stellar-scale distances. "And what if they have Gravity already?"

"Pray that it is not too late."

TWENTY-FOUR

"Be cautious," Harmony warned. "I don't know how long the cloaking shield will help you avoid detection."

Casey blinked in surprise. She'd spent a lot of time in the shipmind's presence by now, and this was the first time she'd ever heard Harmony sound truly uncertain. "What do you mean you don't know? You *always* know."

Harmony rode shotgun in the cockpit, her lights spread out along the bottom lip of the canopy's seal, just out of sight like she also was trying to hide from Overmind X. Every shining mote vibrated with a frantic, barely contained energy.

Casey scoffed. "Stop that. They can't actually *see* you. Their senses are like radar, as you well know."

"I have starfighter telematics from the Kryl war, but nothing like this new... ship? station? bubble?—has ever crossed my sensors before. Besides, Captain... we don't truly know what else Overmind X is capable of. She keeps surprising us with new abilities and relics. Why not the ability to see through our stealth tech, too?"

"Doesn't matter. One sec..." Casey checked for visuals of

the other Furies—Gears on her left, Tank on her right—adjusted her lidar, and re-confirmed the count of her missile bays. "We've got our mission. I don't care if the target's the size of a card table, we're going to hit it. Then bye-bye birdies."

"Have you checked the rear couplings?" Harmony said.

"What?"

"Wait. Sorry, Captain. That message wasn't meant for you. I got my signals crossed."

"Okay..." Casey said, drawing out the word as her skepticism spiked.

"All I'm doing now is distracting you, Captain. You have this under control, and you're about to reach the edge of my transmission range. Would you excuse me?"

Without waiting for a response, Harmony's lights faded out like fireflies in the sun.

"How odd," Casey said aloud. The shipmind must be overloaded, coordinating with the rest of the ships in the armada and conducting repairs on her own destroyer. Maybe overseeing those efforts diverted power from the AI's sentient interface.

Anyway, the shipmind was right about one thing. Their mission objectives were clear.

"Destroy that bulging turkey sac and fill the canyons of the broken planet with Kryl gizzards," Colonel Volk had growled at them in the briefing, "and report back if you spot the photon cannon. That's the assignment. While you're busy, our cameras will study their defense-activation patterns. Your Sabres will be programmed to take video footage. Nothing extra you need to do, but if you get a safe chance to grab a closeup of the organism, take it. No matter what happens, after you've delivered the payload, turn and hightail it home at full burn. An escort will be waiting to cover your exit. Questions?"

The entire squad had hopped to it with a focused intent that took Casey by surprise. The Furies studied specifics of the route through the broken planet for a while, and conducted their pre-flight checks.

To avoid detection, they'd deployed alongside a squadron sent out to fly a standard perimeter patrol. The Furies flew under stealth in their wake before peeling off and angling toward the broken planet itself. Several continent-sized, sundered pieces of rock loomed massively before them as they accelerated and closed the distance.

Yawning canyons of space packed with asteroid debris separated three craggy planetoids. None of it held atmosphere, so it looked more like a planet-shaped cluster of asteroids than an actual world. According to survey data, a molten core still burned at the center of the central planetoid, but that wasn't their destination.

Had Emperor Aeris really come here voluntarily? Seeing the broken planet up close gave her the creepy-crawlies. It was unnatural. They were fortunate to have the emperor's survey data paired with additional probe surveillance that showed them where the Kryl had gathered. Their location was about ten kilometers into a large canyon, which ran between the central and left-most planetoid from her current orientation.

When a helmet-sized rock pinged off her shields, Casey's fingers twitched. Her body tensed with the urge to blast every stinking bug into vapor. She kept her fingers off her trigger, though. Now wasn't the time to get jumpy, or expose their position too early

Up ahead, she made out the Kryl construction in her sights. A greasy, purple-black smudge, roughly disc-shaped. Tiny, but growing imperceptibly larger with every passing klick.

"OK Furies, orient to drift. Engines off. Confirm by flight."

Each flight confirmed, one by one. After ten minutes, they were passing within a few hundred kilometers of straggling Kryl drones. The Furies' stealth cover kept them off the Kryl sensors. It helped that the Kryl were not yet aware they'd been detected. They were trying to stay hidden, and so their patrol perimeters lay much closer in to the broken planet's surface.

A buzz in her ear signaled a newly opened tightbeam channel.

"Captain Osprey, do you copy? *Paladin of Abniss* to Captain Osprey."

Casey blinked, confused. "Fancypants? That you?"

He blew out a breath. "Glad I got you in time. How close are you? The Admiral just filled me and Park in. We're pissed we didn't make it back in time."

She couldn't see Yorra's face, but Casey knew her friend would not be pissed, but relieved that Park had to sit this mission out. Even Captain Nevers, for all his skill as a pilot, was not well-suited to stealth.

"We're about a thousand klicks out," Casey said. "Haven't been detected yet."

Mumbling voices came through the tightbeam as Nevers conferred with someone else.

"OK," he finally said. "There's something you need to know. When used in combination, the relics have different or augmented abilities. According to Chronicle, the phase shifter Subject Zero already has—what the Telos call the Prime Relic of Body—can be used with the Gravity to open a passageway to the resting place of Mind."

Her brain struggled to grasp that. "Who's a whatsit now? Talk sense."

"Look, just... be on the lookout for Subject Zero. If

anything goes down, I guarantee he'll be at the center of it. He always carries that phase shifter on his belt. We also think this anomaly they found, this event horizon… we think that's the entry point to wherever the Prime Relic of Mind is being kept. If they're here, it must mean they already have the Gravity. That's why they're constructing a base now. They're trying to get close enough so they can use the two relics in combination to open the way."

It took her a minute to catch up. Casey's brain didn't want to accept this insanity.

But then again, intel was intel and as the Furies' leader, she had a duty to consider it. Besides, as much as Fancypants confused her sometimes, his instincts on these relics had been on target from the get-go. "A way to where?" she asked. "What am I even looking for?"

"I don't know. All we really know is that the poem speaks of a starship lost to time. Chronicle called it a 'resting place' and—"

Park groaned in the background. "Just say it, man!"

"I mean, maybe, but we don't know yet what—"

"We know!"

"Chronicle didn't say—

"Whatever. You've been spending too much time with those science nerds. Did you hear that, Rap?" Park's echoey voice shouted at the mic from a distance. "The bugs are building a space station so they can open a portal to another dimension!"

Casey thought about it for a long minute. "Affirmative," she finally said.

"That's it?" Nevers demanded. "Just 'affirmative'?"

"Does it matter? We have our orders. I assume you're there with the admiral and Colonel Volk. Have the mission parameters changed?"

"Negative, Captain," said Colonel Volk, calmly and

without hesitation.

"Then I need to focus. Stay close to that mic, Pants. Might need your help. Raptor out."

It was intel, but it didn't change the mission. Good. She had to get the Furies ready. They were rapidly approaching the location of the anomaly.

Casey flicked her comms channel to broadbeam, connecting her to the forty-one other pilots under her command—every pilot who'd been able and ready to fly was with her. About ten people had been injured enough to stay back in the sick bay on the *Paladin of Abniss*.

"Use your thrusters to stay in formation," Casey said. "Double file and less than a hundred meters between us. Remember, the plan is to pass through the outer drone patrols under stealth, then see how deep we can get until we're spotted. Got it?"

"Yes, sir!" Tank said enthusiastically.

"Copy that," said Fuzz. "Green Team is in position."

"Ditto Blue Team."

"Yellow Team good to go," Ruby reported.

"And Red Team's ready," Casey said. "I'm on point."

She may have hung back and guarded the rear in previous missions, but as the mission commander, her troops needed to see her out front now. It would give them confidence.

"First perimeter's in lidar range now," Gears reported over the broadbeam.

"Hold tight," Casey said. "Keep your fingers off your triggers and maintain radio silence starting… *now*."

Casey aimed toward the gap in the first patrol's perimeter. They'd timed it excellently. Two packs of patrolling drones had crossed and were now moving in opposite directions, giving them about a hundred klicks to thread the needle. That was one thing you could say about the Kryl—

once they established a pattern, they were extremely predictable.

The Furies passed through the outer patrols, and into hostile territory without being spotted.

Their stealth tech continued to hold. Maybe Harmony had been wrong about the possibility of detection. A sick, tangled knot formed in the pit of her stomach and sent chills through her body.

Or… the Kryl were pretending not to notice them.

Too late to do anything now. This was the part of flying that took, shall we say, intestinal fortitude.

The organism that had been built around the anomaly had grown to several hundred meters across. It was a bulging disc-shaped object with a purple-black skin, like an oversized Kryl blob, but was now taking on structure as the center lifted. It looked more like a space station than it had in their recon photos. Their briefing had shown that they were to strike it in the center from underneath to maximize damage.

"Contact!" Tank shouted over broadbeam. "Fire incoming."

Casey glanced at her lidar. The closest Kryl drone patrols were still a hundred klicks out, but they'd sent a volley of solid-state projectiles in their direction, forcing them to move or take shield damage.

"Take evasive action. Four teams, like we practiced! Red Team on me!"

Casey kicked her engine on and banked hard right. Gears, plus ten others, followed her.

Tank pointed her nose down, taking her team downwards. Fuzz banked left and nine other starfighters followed tight on his tail. Finally, Ruby hauled back and took ten fighters into a spinning vertical trajectory.

Casey's HUD lit up as projectiles pinged against her

shields. They held strong. With the Kryl's ability to communicate instantly with the entire swarm, being spotted by one meant being spotted by all of them. Her lidar lit up as every unit in the region converged on their position. She kept the cloak active because it didn't hurt and might help, and frankly, she was too busy flying to bother flipping the switch.

Sweat streamed down her forehead as she maneuvered, dodging left and right to avoid debris large and small, leading her pilots out of harm's path.

"Yellow Team clear!" Ruby said. "Reorienting."

The other team leads announced their status as well. On lidar, the swarm was gathering into a knot as it closed on them. The Furies had to move before enemy defenses became impenetrable.

"Angle through the second layer now," Casey ordered her pilots. "Be ready for contact!"

She poured on speed as the squad barreled toward a gap—a much smaller gap than the first, this one mere kilometers wide—in the second layer of patrols. The Kryl defenses comprised an overlapping, multi-layered pattern of movement, similar to an onion with a hollow center in which the Kryl structure floated.

Casey banked around enemy units, flying erratically, without taking turns too sharp that might risk slowing her down. She held the lead with Gears close by, as a new pack of drones rushed in to fill the gap. She smacked two triggers, one with each pointer finger, sending two precision missiles racing ahead. The left one nailed a drone center mass, blowing it wide open in a spray of guts and carapace.

"Eat dirt, you inbred invertebrates!" Casey said.

The right missile keyed into the heat signature of a sleek arrow-shaped skiff, which led it on a chase. That missile exploded against an asteroid.

"Raptor, there are too many!" Tank said. "It's going to be like slamming into a rock wall."

"Make a hole!" she growled, flipping her blasters to automatic fire mode and aiming at a spot in the concentrated curtain of Kryl.

The Furies spread their lines wider and fired their weapons. Red bolts of concentrated plasma melted Kryl units away by the dozen. More poured in almost as fast as they burned out, but as the wall of Kryl loomed larger, the gap widened slightly.

Casey inhaled sharply. Oxygen filled her lungs as stimchem poured into her veins through the spinal port inside her helmet. She was already speeding up when she hit the dose button, and stared ahead, unblinking, as a numerical reading in her HUD climbed up above five, then six, then seven.

Nine Earth gravities worth of force was the maximum a human body could tolerate in this direction—*without* stimchem.

She gritted her teeth as her cheeks folded back.

Eight, Nine... Ten Gs.

"You waited that long to take a hit?" Fuzz asked.

Gears just laughed while she tore the belly off a gunship with a perfectly timed missile to their rear. Casey hadn't even noticed the gunship come in, so it was lucky Yorra was watching her six.

Explosions and debris from their attack obscured her vision and made her instruments untrustworthy. "Cease fire!" she said.

They were coming within a few klicks.

"On me, Furies."

Though the four teams had drifted apart as they flew, each maneuvering to avoid fire and make use of whatever debris or cover became available, they came together now and lined up beside Casey.

They were through the second layer of patrols.

"Status?" Casey demanded.

"Ten of ten for Yellow," said Ruby. "Just scuff marks."

"Green Team's whole," said Fuzz. "Our shields are low, but we made it."

"Blue Team took a couple of hits," reported Tank. "Deej lost his left wingtip."

It was never good to lose a blaster, but that wouldn't slow them down on their way to the objective. As the second layer of patrols receded, the structure that was their target loomed ahead.

"Kryl are still closing in," Gears said. They all saw that the defensive rings, while moving much slower than the Furies themselves, were closing like the jaws of a predator who found their prey trapped. If the Kryl swarm was a massive leviathan, the Furies were the mosquitoes who'd just shot their way into the great beast's gullet.

Just as she was feeling suspicious, her HUD bleeped a loud warning noise that caused her heart to hammer double-time.

"Photon cannon spotted, ten o'clock to attack vector!" shouted Gears.

The squad split in half as a gossamer golden thread whipped through the center of their force with remarkable speed.

"Hot damn!" someone shouted into the broadbeam.

"I think I just got a haircut," said someone else.

"Mic discipline!" Casey demanded. She couldn't afford distractions right now. The structure lay within a thousand kilometers.

She spared a glance in its direction and noticed that it

seemed to pulse gently, in and out, like the beating heart of a stellar beast.

It wasn't that. Not yet. But maybe that's what it was *intended* to be, eventually.

They had to destroy it.

These thoughts all passed through her mind in an instant. Her eyes had moved on to search for the photon cannon.

"Who has eyes on the beam?" Casey said.

"It just cut through a few of our pursuers," said Ruby. "Huh. That's kind of reassuring."

"The Spirits of Old Earth are watching over this mission," said Fuzz.

Mutters of agreement all around. And the notable silence of a few skeptics.

Casey didn't rebuke anyone this time about mic discipline. The relics were designed to be used *against* Kryl, so Ruby was right. It *was* plenty reassuring that the Kryl could still make mistakes. And that the relic could harm their own as much as any Solaran ship.

Which meant…

"Max burn for the structure, now!" Casey shouted, angling her craft and pulling ahead of the rest of them as she keyed her second dose of stimchem. At three doses, her hands would begin to shake and she would lose her stomach, so this was it. This had to be the move.

"Raptor, wait!" shouted Gears.

But Casey saw it coming. She'd marked the trajectory of the photon cannon and estimated it would come from the upper third quadrant left of the structure from her position. She'd been right. The warning sensor Harmony had installed in their starfighters beeped again, and Casey hauled back on the stick, pulling into that loop maneuver Fancypants loved so much.

Never thought she'd actually have a use for it, but damn if

it didn't feel good to be forced into her seat so hard her cheeks flapped back and her neck strained against the base of her helmet.

The photon cannon's micro-thin laser cut through the space her craft had been a moment ago, then pulled away.

She came out of the loop and opened her throttle again. "Aim for this position here, Furies." She marked the top left corner of the structure from her position. That would mark the same point on all their volumetric maps. "When you get there, curl around the backside."

"The photon cannon will just rip us to shreds!" Ruby said.

"Not if you hurry!"

They complied, on a slight delay, but turning and matching her vector quickly.

Radio silence belied their confusion.

"I just put us between the photon cannon's source and the structure," Casey said. "Based on our current range..." She checked—they'd closed to within five hundred klicks now. "They won't use the photon cannon against us now because they risk damaging the structure."

"How do you know its range?"

"Harmony told me it was about three hundred to five hundred klicks."

"Animus above," Fuzz muttered, dosing up and increasing his speed.

They all did. Casey was already maxed out, but due to the angle of her flight and the loop she'd been forced to take, she was no longer in the lead. That was fine. It would give her time to set up the payload for its ultimate delivery.

The photon cannon fired twice more, shearing off a couple more wingtip blasters, but still not taking a full starfighter down. One member of Yellow Team lost their shields, though, and was ordered to move to a relatively safe position at the squad's core.

"Captain, you were right. They're not firing the photon cannon anymore," Gears reported.

"Copy that." Casey said. "About two hundred klicks back."

"You were off by a bit," Ruby snarked at her.

"Harmony was off. I did the best I could with the info I had. Focus, Furies. Ease up on throttles now."

They all needed a little breather before the last leg of their mission.

The Kryl structure loomed massively in front of them. It was the length of a destroyer, but thin, only about a hundred meters thick in the center, and as little as a meter thick at the outer edges. They came at it from the broadside, so it looked like an oblong pancake colored purple-black and covered with wet-looking scales. Its outer surface was shot through with veins like a snake egg. Up close, she could now see it was slightly translucent. She made out what looked like spiders crawling over its backside, especially near the edges where it was thinnest.

The squad breathed a collective sigh of relief to be in a fire-free deadzone... getting out alive was another story.

But they couldn't rest long. A moment later, they were forced to take evasive action because apparently they weren't too close for normal enemy projectiles. They fought off a platoon of drones, hundreds of them that broke against the Furies' lines a dozen at a time, some drones abandoning caution and flying kamikaze-like straight into one of her pilots.

"Earth's blood!" Tank shouted, spraying her blasters across a line of drones and taking out a dozen in revenge.

"May Animus keep his soul," muttered Fuzz.

It was the first fighter they had lost on this mission. Deej, who was unable to defend against the incoming craft with only one wingtip blaster. Somehow, losing just one today hurt as much as losing half her squad before, like tearing stitches from a still-raw wound.

A spark seemed to ignite within the Furies. They mopped up the rest of that attack in short order, then angled once again toward the organism, laser-focused on their mission.

"Gears, watch my six, I'm readying the payload," said Casey.

She pressed a few buttons in her cockpit, detaching her last two missiles and re-attaching the precision nuclear warhead that had been designed for this purpose. Across the entire armada, only a couple dozen of these bombs were available. The Furies had been given three.

If delivered at a point just off center of the structure—a point which was marked on her HUD as the warhead displayed a READY TO FIRE status—it would destroy the entire structure.

"Another squad of drones at three o'clock!" Gears shouted.

"I'm going in," Casey said. "Cover me."

She dove toward the organism, lining up her shot by placing a little yellow square on her HUD over top of the target area, the canyon where the anomaly was located. Her Sabre told her she was closing to within a hundred klicks. Soon, the massive structure took up her entire view, blocking out even the view of space around it.

At forty klicks, she pulled the trigger and released the warhead, then pulled her stick back to reverse her vector, barrel rolled, and took the third and final dose of stimchem her body could handle as she accelerated out of the turn.

With jittering hands, she increased her velocity to maximum burn. Ten, then twelve, then fifteen Gs of force pressed her back into her pilot's chair so hard her internal organs molded to her spine. Her Sabre rattled dangerously.

Kryl drones strafed by, headed the opposite direction.

They were nothing more than streaks of brown in her peripheral vision. She knew they were headed to try to stop the bomb, but she'd gotten close enough that it was too late. Even if they managed to blow it up before it reached the organism, the subsequent explosion would still damage it. Not annihilate it, perhaps, but cause significant destruction; enough to buy the armada the time they needed.

"Raptor, our scanners just identified a manned drone!"

The rest of the furies fell in behind her. She let off her accelerator so the rest of them had a moment to catch up. She breathed a sigh of relief as her internal organs slid back to where they were supposed to be. "That's gotta be Subject Zero," she said breathlessly.

"Roger that," Gears said. "He's headed straight for the bomb."

"Maybe he'll get vaporized for his efforts," Tank said.

She opened a tightbeam to command while she was flying erratically. "Fancypants! You seeing this?"

"We see it, Raptor. Subject Zero's angling toward the bomb now."

She checked the estimates on her HUD. It was supposed to hit in the next 30 seconds.

"Wait, he's pulling away," Captain Nevers corrected.

She tapped a few buttons in the cockpit but couldn't get a good angle on the organism. "What's happening?" she demanded.

"The photon cannon is… burning a hole in the construction."

Her stomach dropped. "WHAT?"

That was exactly what she thought the Kryl *wouldn't* do: use the photon cannon on themselves.

The last fifteen seconds on her timer went to zero. It felt like an eternity, and all the while, she had to evade getting shot. They broke through the last layer of defenses in a cloud of debris and dust from explosive rounds they set off to get through the solid wall of Kryl drones.

"The bomb just passed through the opening," Fancypants said.

There were no fireworks. No explosions to her rear.

"Did it go off?"

A shuffling as someone else came on the mic. "Captain," said Harmony. "There was a minor explosion in the probe cameras, but nothing of the magnitude we hoped for. No sign of the radiation we expected, either. It seems like the photon cannon cut through the organism to expose the event horizon, and the event horizon swallowed the payload."

"Earth damn it all!" Casey shouted.

All that for nothing.

Deej's life for *nothing*.

She forced herself to take a deep breath. If not for herself, then for the rest of the Furies. "Should we go back? Try again with the backup?"

"Negative, Captain," came the voice of Colonel Volk. "Our corvettes are coming to assist you. Return to the *Abniss*."

She swallowed an angry retort. "Copy that."

The corvettes came. The Furies' squad broadbeam remained quiet except for grunts and cursing as they fought their way out of the swarm and docked in the hangar, their mission a failure.

TWENTY-FIVE

The hiveheart pulsed with barely contained energy.

That nuclear warhead the Solarans fired at it had left behind an awful lot of radiation, even though most of the explosion's force got sucked into the event horizon. Since the Kryl evolved to use radiation to speed growth, Overmind X had altered the hiveheart to contain that heat source and absorb it, speeding repairs and then doubling the size of the structure.

Thanks to the Solarans, they had finished ahead of schedule.

This benefits us, said Overmind X.

Omar fidgeted in the cockpit of his drone.

I've prepared the way for us.

Us, she had said. So the Overmind was *here*.

Icy terror seeped into his bones. Of course, she'd be here to oversee matters personally. This was the last relic they were about to recover. The ultimate piece of her "Inheritance."

When had she arrived?

A single caressing touch from Overmind X took his fear and replaced it with a stoic calm.

You know what, it didn't matter when, he realized. Omar chuckled slightly. That was a close one. He took the briefest of secret moments to be thankful for her guidance. She'd been gentler since he acquired the knife relic, which hung sheathed from his belt next to the phase shifter.

When a breach opened on one end of the hiveheart, Omar guided his drone towards it. The passage was barely big enough for a single drone to fit through. Subject Seven and Subject Fourteen, in drones of their own, fell in behind him single file. Once they passed through, the opening resealed, closing them in comforting darkness.

Omar's ears popped as the atmosphere pressurized. The further in they went, the warmer the temperature became. And they must have been under spin because he gradually felt the weight of his body increase, settling him down against the seat.

Omar docked his drone, or rather, the creature found a soft fleshy pad to set down of its own accord. Tubes unfurled from concealed plates of carapace on its back to connect to the low ceiling. This was the drone's feeding position. Drones weren't starcraft. Not exactly. They were living creatures, and like every living creature, they needed energy to operate. While she waited, his drone would sustain herself by siphoning energy from the hiveheart, like a baby suckling from its mother's teat.

Omar used his rejuvenated spider arms to lower himself to the ground, exiting through the mouth of the drone, a disgusting process that always left him greasy and covered in bodily fluids. He fished water and a towel out of his pack and used it to wipe his face.

Seven and Fourteen squirted out of their drones behind him. They didn't seem bothered by the mucus that coated their arms and faces. They had no towels, and Omar didn't offer his. Seven licked her lips, and Fourteen only bothered to wipe mucous away from her eyes, whose ridges had thickened and grown darker on the long ride here.

In fact, both of the youngling's hides shone lustrous, and seemed to drink in the mucousy goop like a nourishing lotion. It made their backs and shoulders shine healthily.

The two stared at him for a while. He held their gazes, staring at a point between them, focused and ready for anything. Their aggression was palpable.

Enough, said Overmind X. *We are here for a reason. Come.*

All three turned as one and made their way deeper into the hiveheart.

They wove down several dark, cramped tunnels—the arteries of this creature—until they reached a vast cavernous hole that must have been its... well, stomach. Or maybe it was more accurate to call it a womb. He wasn't really quite sure. Both at once.

Regardless, the cavern was vast, its walls made of scaly flesh and shot through with thick veins. There was water or some kind of liquid pooled at the bottom of the room. It bubbled and steam rose from the pond's surface. He knew from experience being in other hives Overmind X had grown, that such a pool would be filled with larvae and other parasites. A spider scurried out of it and crossed the room, dripping, before disappearing into a seam at the corner.

Although the Kryl could grow into various shapes and configurations, adapting to various purposes as the need arose, the pattern of their biology remained the same. So he was somewhat surprised to see a sloping ramp lead out one side of the pool, extend to the wall and wrap around the chamber in a spiral until, most of the way up, it jutted out like a tongue into the center of the atrium.

A rigid membrane supported a round platform. At first, gazing up, it seemed to lead to nowhere. Why *that* spot?

But then he saw it. Felt it. A kind of mirage in the air, a warping of the vision paired with a nauseating sense of wrongness.

Up, Overmind X commanded.

His booted feet carried him forward.

"Are we ready?" Fourteen asked.

"Is it time?" Seven demanded.

It is time, chimed Overmind X. *Calm yourselves. You must be alert, and to be alert you must be calm.*

"Yes, mother," they chimed together. Seven and Fourteen were still children. Impatient. Impulsive. In the closeness of Overmind X's current link with them, he knew that was one reason she kept him around. That and... he was her first.

"Tell me what I must do," Omar said, suddenly eager. Those children didn't have what it would take. Only he did.

Perforate the anomaly using the newest relic. I will do the rest, with the help of the hiveheart.

Seven slowed her walk and placed one palm tenderly, reverently against the hiveheart's fleshy, vein-riddle wall. "Will she survive, mother?"

"She is beautiful," said Fourteen.

"We don't want her to die," they said in chorus.

We shall see, said Overmind X.

There were some things of which even *she* was uncertain. That gave Omar a kind of comfort. Something stirred deep within him. He smothered it. Overmind X didn't seem to notice.

Fourteen loped forward. Subject Seven followed with a kind of shuffling, three-legged gait. She hadn't been able to fully regrow the hand that Omar had sliced off with the moon-shaped knife relic now sheathed at his waist. It gave him a sweet satisfaction to see her hobble along on three legs.

She must have felt him staring, because she turned and hissed in his direction. He just smiled. Overmind X still needed him. He was her first, and he had the relics she needed.

Seven and Fourteen ranged ahead. Even in relatively low, spin-induced gravity, the climb caused Omar to pant heavily. The ramp was steep and walking on two feet was difficult.

The children reached the end of the spiral before he did. As he approached the end, Omar slowed. He didn't want to be winded when he got there. This high platform was a prime location for an ambush and betrayal.

His boots skated on something slick and the floor shot out from beneath his feet. His spider arms lanced backward, piercing into the floor and arresting his fall. Both his feet dangled off the edge.

Omar hauled himself back up, regaining his feet, and scowled in Fourteen's direction. Looking down, he saw they had sabotaged the ramp, cutting out a section and coating the area with fluid without him noticing.

Sensing him contemplate revenge, Overmind X threatened to forcibly seize control of his mind. He put his hands up in a posture of surrender. She was right. They needed to cooperate to succeed.

Omar kept walking. Eventually, he reached the end of the ramp, a round platform roughly ten meters across. Huge, really. It had seemed perilously small from down below, and he'd been right. Now that he was up here, his heart pounded and his hands shook. He rarely got vertigo, but he walked carefully all the same. He didn't know what would happen. The three of them kept to the edges and stared into the nest that had grown up in the middle of the platform.

Here it was. The event horizon the Telos left behind. The

air warped like he was staring into a bubble. The nest Overmind X had grown circled the anomaly and rose to cup it. As he watched, dozens of thick vine-like tendrils wriggled up to the ceiling. They found and wrapped around porous ridges of cartilage, creating a sort of cage of Kryl flesh around the anomaly, without yet touching it.

"If you screw this up," said Seven.

"I won't," said Omar.

"If you do, don't worry," said Fourteen. "We'll be here—"

"—to fix your mistake."

"And if you don't, we're still going with you."

"Mother said you have to bring us along," said Subject Seven.

"I know that," he snapped. "I hear her as clearly as you do. I know what she wants."

"Just reminding you of your duty. You seem to have trouble remembering lately."

Enough.

"Yes, enough," Omar said. He paced around the nest, looking for an opening. Overmind X guided him to where the effect was weakest, where she believed they should make the incision.

Omar reached out and put his hand close to it, thinking he would feel some heat or cold, but he felt nothing.

Shuffling sideways, he swiped one of his spider arms through the warping effect in the air. His arm distorted like he'd submerged it deep in a tank of water. It tingled slightly, but otherwise he felt no pain. No heat. Nothing else unusual.

That made some sense to him. It would have been poorly designed if it didn't allow objects to pass freely through it. The Telos wouldn't have placed such a strange phenomenon here if there was any risk of a passing asteroid or chunk of space debris knocking it out of orbit.

"Here goes nothing." He drew the moon-shaped knife and slashed through the air in front of him.

The hiveheart's tendrils quavered.

Nothing happened.

"Why isn't it working?" he asked.

You must first activate the phase shifter, she said.

He grunted. Okay. This was typical behavior, as she only let him in on information in the moment he needed to know it. But… usually she told him *before* he made a stupid mistake.

Had she not known? Or had she just wanted to see what would happen? If it killed him, she still had two backup options.

He swallowed and glanced back at Seven and Fourteen. Maybe he was more expendable than he thought.

Regardless, the swarm knew and felt all that the rest of the swarm knew and felt. Overmind X had the power to withhold information from any or all. It wouldn't do for Kryl soldiers to know they were being sent to their deaths in that moment, only that this was what Overmind X wanted. As long as the Overmind lived, the swarm lived.

Seven and Fourteen glanced toward the other relic at his belt, an oblong object with a switch on it, leering greedily.

"Over my dead body," he snarled at them.

"If you insist," they said in harmony, with one pitched high and the other low.

"Hngh," he grunted. Omar reached down with a practiced motion and flipped the switch on the phase shifter.

His body vibrated and became translucent. He stepped forward and tried to slice into the bubble again. This time, as he swung from right to left with the moon-shaped knife gripped in one hand, he encountered what seemed to be a solid object. Where the blade struck, the shimmering air parted to reveal a constellation of stars beneath it.

He gasped. Something about the sight struck fear into his heart. It wasn't right. It was *weird*. Unnatural.

He jerked his hand back, and the cut sealed itself.

Give me your fear, Overmind X insisted. *Lean into it. Once the rift becomes wide enough, it will enter this plane and I will use the hiveheart to assist.*

"How wide?"

Wide enough to give me a hold.

Omar took a minute to absorb this information. With the resistance the anomaly had been giving him, a cut a couple of meters long would take all his physical strength to make. And if he let go, it would heal itself once again. Better to do it all at once.

The phase shifter deactivated, and he had to wait through the cooling period. Once it passed, he phase shifted again. This time, holding the knife with both hands, he swung at the event horizon with all his strength.

He ripped a hole about half a meter before he stopped dead, teeth gritted and muscled quavering but nothing moving.

Keep going! Overmind X said. *Push harder*!

He leaned into the blade, straining with his shoulders, his boots sliding on the platform beneath his feet. Seven and Fourteen jumped up behind him and for a moment he was certain they would kill him, slit his throat and take the relics to finish the job.

But as ever, they were obedient to Overmind X. When the phase shifter timed out, his blade continued to cut. That's when they leaped to his aid, bracing him at his back and shoulders, adding their own enhanced strength to his elbows and wrists.

Together, they dragged the blade across the air, a meter and then two with screams of pure effort. The knife's edge glittered with a nano-thin line of golden light, just like the photon cannon. Something *ripped* and purple tendrils whipped around the top edge of the cut, pulling it wider and revealing a blanket of stars on the other side.

No, those weren't stars. At least, not any stars he'd ever seen. They streaked across a black expanse in a swirling maelstrom of dizzying motion. They were stars, as seen from inside a warped bubble of trapped space.

He strained, feeling his own joints popping, his muscles burning. More tentacles whipped up and wrapped around the lower edge of the tear, gripping firmly and growing inward, pulling heat and radiation from the air to move further into the rift.

He let go and gasped for breath. Shockingly cold air filled his lungs. The air suddenly felt thin, and he labored for breath before scrambling back. He and the children exhaled clouds for a few moments as they recovered.

There, Overmind X panted. *It is done.* She sounded breathless and exhausted, too. He'd never felt such exhaustion from her before. What she'd done must have taken an enormous amount of energy.

I must... I can hold it, but you must hurry. The nest rose from the floor, closing around the rift. Omar's limbs trembled involuntarily as Overmind X separated herself from the pile, a relatively small, soft-bodied creature with eight legs, an armored head that was mostly a mouth filled with a dozen rows of pointed teeth, and a low slung, scaly abdomen. Embedded in the center of her abdomen, a crystal object glittered. As it swirled with green light, the tendrils growing from the floor into the rift grew thicker, writhing deeper, prying the tear in the very fabric of reality wider with another shiver-inducing rip.

Take the knife, Overmind X commanded. *Get to your drones. Hurry*!

The ceiling flexed inward, down toward them. He knew

the event horizon couldn't be moved. Overmind X was manipulating the hiveheart's exterior and interior walls to expose the tear in reality they'd just made to space.

In a flash of sudden memory, he knew exactly what she was planning, and his part in it. Omar sheathed the knife at his belt and sprinted down the ramp. Seven and Fourteen bounced off the walls and ran ahead of him, circling down and leading the way back to their craft. Omar was winded by the time they reached their drones again. He clambered up through the slimy orifice, bending his spider arms into a kind of backrest in the cavity that served as his cockpit. The drone detached its fueling hoses and turned itself around. Seven's drone and then Fourteen's pushed out the opening, and he followed, feeling the thrill—yes, even now—of falling back into space and being able to maneuver on a ship's thrusters once again.

Overmind X had initially balked at the idea of a manned drone, but Omar was really comfortable here, more comfortable than he felt anywhere else among the Kryl. He was a pilot first. He was meant to fly. His mission—

A sharp stabbing pain ripped through his head. "Augh!" He cried, clutching his temples. The pain passed in an instant. He wiped tears out of his eyes. What had he just been thinking?

Focus, Overmind X said. *Focus, Subject Zero. You must enter the rift. I will hold it open as long as I can. The Solaran fleet knows we are here, so you must be quick. I'm hoping there's a way to get back once you're on the other side, but I cannot be certain. I need to ensure you return with the relic, so I will hold the rift open. I will fight the Solarans and hold them back as long as I can.*

"How long can you hold them?"

Do not doubt me, Subject Zero. They have left their beloved asteroid field undefended to come fight me. I will defeat them here and take the last temple from them. Then we'll have all we need.

Omar gave her the affirmative. Seven and Fourteen were already angling toward the rift. He couldn't let them beat him to the punch. He opened his thrusters, accelerating toward the opening, toward that wrongness in spacetime, that rift of whirling starlight.

Checking the swarm's awareness through their shared consciousness, he realized the Solaran armada was much closer than he'd expected. The squad of Sabres that had dropped the bomb must not have stayed back with the fleet for long. In fact, even while they attacked, the Solaran armada must have been moving into place. They'd zeroed in on the photon cannon. They knew what to expect from it now, and were targeting it with their best pilots.

If they took the photon cannon out, and they came with enough force, well... he'd fought enough battles to know that the odds were never greater than fifty-fifty with two forces of this size.

Unless he obtained the last relic.

Omar aimed his drone into the rift, passing out of this reality and into another.

TWENTY-SIX

After the stealth bombing, the organism had expanded like a balloon, growing at an unprecedented pace, faster than any living creature Kira had ever seen. Something happened when it swallowed that nuclear warhead, and she couldn't take any chances.

Kira ordered her forces into position and pummeled the Overmind's defensive shell. As she watched, her superior firepower broke the first Kryl line. They retreated to the second layer of defenses, reforming their blockades.

"That must be nearly all their forces," Minister Aganaki observed smugly. He and his xenoscientists had joined them on the bridge to observe the attack. "They won't be able to hold on for long."

At that moment, thousands more Kryl ships seeped out of the cracks, canyons and crevices of the broken planet.

Colonel Volk groaned. "You jinxed it." The man took out his Old Earth medallion and kissed it before placing it back in his pocket. "May Animus have mercy on their souls."

Kira added, "For we have none."

Emperor Aeris met her eyes and nodded approvingly. She didn't need his approval, but it felt good to have it.

Kira started giving orders and her crew dove to their consoles, coordinating starfighters, corvettes, cruisers, and destroyers, making sure that all their attacks synced up and that their exits were covered.

The photon cannon had gone back into hiding by flying behind one planetoid, and Overmind X continued to elude Dr. Lumago's attempts to find her. However, now that Chronicle had confirmed the last relic was definitely here in Elturis, Kira would bet good money that she was inside that organism somewhere.

Overmind X wouldn't risk letting it fall into Solaran hands. She'd be here to oversee its retrieval. And at her side, Omar.

Colonel Volk strode around the bridge, barking corrective orders, speaking to her engineers and weapons masters, and periodically, when he thought no one was looking, glancing at the door. He wanted a drink—badly. It would be good for the real fighting to start. Then he'd be too busy to think about whiskey for a while.

Volk's gaze shifted from the door to Kira. She kept her expression neutral and her posture straight as she relaxed into the command couch. She nodded at him, and he relayed her unspoken order.

"Starfighter squadrons, you're cleared for launch," Volk said.

Moments later, hundreds of starfighters jettisoned out of the hangar and split, moving into position against the Kryl swarm that had gathered. Kira felt her confidence firm up. But there was one thing that still worried her. She asked her navigations officer about it.

"No sign of the photon cannon," the woman said.

"Admiral," chimed in Seba the Knife, "Third group needs to refuel, I'm sending them back to the *Paladin of Ferro*."

"Copy that," Kira said. She nodded at Volk, who communicated with the *Ferro* to let them know the corvettes were on their way.

"Admiral?" Volk said after he was done.

"What is it, Colonel?"

"The Furies are insisting they re-deploy with the rest of the starfighter squadrons."

She grunted. "We need every gun we can get."

"Captain Nevers, too?"

"Does he want to stay back?"

Volk said something into his comms, checking. "Negative."

"This is all tied up in what he discovered," Kira said, nodding to the main viewscreen. Overmind X's defenses had hardened, shrinking inward and forming a tighter ball around the organism and the anomaly it concealed within the chasm. "Hold them until we spot the—"

"Admiral!" her navigations officer shouted, turning, her face flushed. "Photon cannon detected!"

Just as she'd hoped, the starfighter squadron which curled around the leftmost chunk of the broken planet to come at the anomaly from behind lured the weapon out of hiding. They were currently dodging the nano-thin line of golden light, which severed asteroids, Kryl, and Solarans alike as it swung about. A few Sabres reported damage, but that was a small price to pay for identifying such a dangerous foe.

"Send the Furies after that photon cannon. I want the gunship destroyed and the relic captured."

Kira stood from her command couch and paced across the bridge. Her ships were moving into position, and the Kryl remained on the defensive, but that couldn't last forever.

Emperor Aeris strolled over to join her.

"Enjoying yourself, Your Majesty?"

"It feels good to have my theory proven," he said. "An anomaly at the center of the broken planet. Likely more than one."

"More than one?"

"Don't you think? The gravity of this one anomaly does not explain the continued existence of a molten core within the central planetoid, nor does it explain the odd temperature and pressure measurements I took when I surveyed the broken planet with my ship. Even the way pieces of the planet are occasionally ejected, the orbit of the asteroid field… it doesn't add up. Unless you consider the possibility of additional anomalies."

"Respectfully, Your Majesty, we have bigger fish to fry."

"Indeed, admiral. I mean no offense. It is simply fascinating to me."

"You can continue your experiments once it's safe, and the Kryl have been eliminated."

"As you wish."

"You're not going to go rogue on me again, are you? It's not safe out there right now."

"And how would I do that when you have commandeered my starship for ansible relays?"

Kira grinned. "I needed some assurances. Parliament would have my head if anything happened to you."

"Even if it was my idea?"

"They won't see it that way."

He chuckled. "You're probably right. I'll draft a preemptive pardon just in case." Emperor Aeris winked at her with those mischievous golden eyes.

She grunted. "We better not need it," she said.

"I don't want you sticking your neck out on my behalf. This is the most fun I've had in *decades*."

"I'm glad you're enjoying yourself," she said wryly.

Kira rocked sideways as something slammed against the *Paladin's* shields.

"I'll leave you to it," the emperor said, barely staggering as he left the bridge on legs too accustomed to the unsteady movements of a ship for some cloistered, pampered emperor. She snorted. He truly was an enigma, all right.

She wished she could share his confidence in the outcome of this battle. If things went the way she hoped, she wouldn't need the royal pardon.

If they went the other way, she wouldn't be around long enough for it to matter.

TWENTY-SEVEN

The deadly beam of golden light sliced toward his canopy.

Elya shoved the stick forward, pushing the nose of his Sabre down and his helmet against the headrest. Safety straps cut into his shoulders, keeping him firmly rooted in his seat. Hedgebot slipped, shooting its feet out and clinging to seams between the dashboard and the canopy with tiny metal claws.

"Hang on, pal!" he gritted through his teeth as Elya twisted, pulling left and then right, firing his wingtip blasters and taking out a handful of drones crossing his nose as he rolled to safety.

"That damn thing is quick!" Park shouted into the broadbeam.

"Keep moving!" Captain Osprey ordered. She didn't have to tell him twice, Elya pulled out of the turn and banked hard left, coming face to face with the gunship.

His breath caught in his throat. He accelerated, pulling upward this time. Park zagged up beside him, then barrel rolled a hundred and eighty degrees overhead so that their canopies were top to top.

Seeing his wingman and reading the unspoken signal, Elya released a missile at the same time as Park did. The two projectiles shot forward. A drone veered into the path, sacrificing itself to extinguish Park's weapon, while the other projectile hit its mark, rupturing the gunship's hull and venting the ship's atmosphere, burning where it touched the engines.

"Eat vacuum, you bug-faced wretch," Park said in a quiet voice filled with grim satisfaction.

Hedgebot flared red and skittered across his dashboard to the left. "Watch out!" Elya shouted.

He followed the bot in that direction, moving out of danger—or so he thought. The golden beam of light strafed toward them, and he and Park were forced to cut away from one another, heading in opposite directions, to avoid being sliced in half.

"Shit!" Elya said, "I thought that gunship I tagged had it."

Yorra's voice came over the broadbeam. "They're sending more of the same craft in to confuse and distract us. Same model as the one carrying the relic."

Elya widened his gaze to take in the whole battlefield and immediately saw what she meant. No fewer than fifty gunships had wandered out of the third and final layer of Kryl defenses and were now crawling all over them.

Which one had the photon cannon? His eyes searched, looking for the telltale sign of the relic mounted on the belly of one ship. His eyes skipped over several of the sleek, alien vessels, but none of them seemed to carry the weapon. And while only one gunship carried the relic, that didn't make the rest of them any less deadly.

As if sensing his thoughts, the gunship nearest him unleashed a volley of standard slugs in their direction, forcing him to fly erratically to avoid getting hit. Slamming his shoulder into the walls of the cockpit as he dodged and weaved, he located Park in his sights out ahead, identifying his Sabre from the number painted on his tail and wings.

He, too, was flying erratically, but with a lack of control that made Elya's stomach churn in worry.

Ruby tagged a drone sneaking up on Park's six. Elya shouted for his friend to pull up and get out of the way of another pack of drones bearing in from his right.

The battlefield was total chaos.

Park hauled back—too fast. His Sabre's nose tilted up and then stalled. It left him coasting, moving at the same momentum at which he lost power. Moving in a predictable path in vacuum spelled certain death for a pilot.

"No!" Park said. In the chaos of battle, he'd left the squadron-wide broadbeam channel open. "No! No! No! Come on, you piece of junk!"

"I've got you!" said Lieutenant Yorra as she accelerated toward her lover while Park drifted closer to the third layer of Kryl defenses. The rest of Red Team, including Elya, engaged the gunships with blasters, forcing it to turn away from the trapped pilot. "Hang on, Naab!"

Elya checked his lidar, then switched to a tightbeam with Yorra. "You won't get there in time," he muttered.

"I've got him!" she insisted.

"I'm coming with you." Elya took his first dose of stim-chem as he surged forward, opening his throttle to full speed.

Park's engines flashed as he tried to restart them. They stayed cold, and he kept drifting, using his attitude thrusters to redirect himself away a few degrees from a direct path toward the third layer of defenses.

Yorra sent a missile at the wall of Kryl. The projectile raced out ahead of her ship, forcing the drones making up the wall to split to avoid it. The missile disappeared through their ranks, and they closed up behind it.

Elya reached Park right as Yorra did. As they got closer, Park finally sparked his engines back to life. He punched forward, inhaling sharply and sighing, the sound of an addict taking a much-needed hit.

"How much stim are you—" Elya couldn't finish the thought. Hedgebot flared bright red and kicked off the canopy, clinging to the floor. Elya punched his stick forward, throwing himself back into the seat as he reacted to the bot's timely warning.

A golden thread sheared off his right wingtip blaster, momentarily taking his shields down as he twisted away.

"Watch out!" Park said, annihilating two drones Elya hadn't even known were behind him.

"Whew!" said Elya. "Thanks! That was close. Where is the photon cannon hiding now?"

"I don't know," Park said, "But I haven't stalled my engines like that since aerial maneuvers back on Ariadne." He chuckled nervously. His words came quick and Elya knew, without having to finish the question he'd started asking before, that the stimchem pumping through Park's veins had his heart pounding and his nerves frayed.

"Stay focused and go easy on the stim," said Elya.

Park chuckled nervously. "I'm up to three already."

"I figured. Take it easy."

"What's a bit of the jitters when the alternative is sucking vacuum?"

The man had a point, but even so, it worried him.

"Besides," Park added, "I'm not gonna make you all fish me out a second time."

Like he'd almost done just a moment ago? Elya chewed his lower lip, fretting. Back in the hangar, while they'd been getting ready, Park had already been acting nervous, sweating profusely and talking too much during their walk-around checks.

"Are you all right, Naab?" Yorra asked.

"I'm chill," he insisted. "Let's focus on the mission. We have to root out that blasted photon cannon, don't we?"

They glanced around. Yellow Team was busy tying a couple of gunships into knots while Red and Green Teams took advantage of a slight reprieve to locate the gunship on their lidar readouts.

As if in answer to their unspoken question, the wall of Kryl—essentially, thousands of drones flying in the same spherical pattern, wingtip to wingtip—parted and the relic's gunship burst into sight. It had been using the defenses as cover, and probably shot straight through the wall of drones.

"Scatter!" ordered Captain Osprey.

Elya obeyed, opening his thrusters and pulling up, twisting and rolling and flying as fast as he ever had in his life. Each turn threw his whole body sideways, or lifted his butt out of his seat with the negative g-force. Hedgebot kept him on target, using its sensors to warn him of imminent danger. He relied on the bot as much as he relied on his readouts and lidar. But at the speed he was flying now, Elya barely had time to think. He maneuvered on instinct alone.

Once they were clear, they slowed, twisting around and coming back to face the defensive shell of swirling Kryl. The orifice the relic's gunship had used to exit the defenses closed slowly. While it was still open, Elya glimpsed three drones exiting a sphincter-like hole in the side of the massive, pulsing Kryl organism that had grown around the anomaly.

His heart skipped a beat.

It was *him*. Subject Zero.

It had to be. Those were the only three drones flying out of formation with the rest of the swarm. Every other enemy was organized to hold the defensive shell or engage the armada.

"Captain Osprey!" Elya said. "I've got eyes on Subject Zero."

"How can you tell?" she asked.

He started to explain what he had just seen, but stumbled over his words. He didn't have visual confirmation of the mutant soldier, not at this distance, so he couldn't say with absolute certainty. "I just know," he finally said.

"Photon cannon first!" Osprey responded.

Elya growled in the back of his throat, but couldn't argue the point. If he went after Zero now, the gunship could eliminate him while he was in pursuit. It would be reckless to leave such a powerful weapon armed and pointed at his back.

Besides, their orders had been to take out the photon cannon. Once they did, Admiral Miyaru would order the rest of the armada on the offensive. They had to complete one objective before they could take on another.

"If we keep flying like this," Elya said, "That photon cannon's eventually gonna catch us off guard."

"You think I don't know that?" Osprey asked, exasperated.

"So what's the plan, Mission Commander?" Ruby butted in.

Casey growled. "I don't know."

Tank shouted orders into the squad's broadbeam while she thought, focusing her flight's attention on a particular gunship.

They nailed it, driving two missiles into its aft port side, but not before the Kryl's railguns took out a Sabre.

"Earth's blood," Osprey cursed.

"We can't last like this, Raptor," said Elya. "The longer we play hide and seek with the relic, the more losses we're gonna take."

"I know that!"

"What are your orders?"

Selfishly, he wanted to hurry and finish the job so he could go after Zero. But he forced himself to focus. How could he expedite matters?

A chill settled over him as he realized the answer. "Use me as bait," Elya said.

"What?" asked Yorra. "You're out of your mind."

"You got a better idea?" Park said, rising to Elya's defense. "Fancypants is the best pilot here. If anyone would make good bait, it's him. Sorry, man."

"I volunteered, didn't I?"

"If you fly out ahead, we won't be able to keep up with you," Yorra said honestly.

"I'm not asking you to," said Elya. "I've got this."

"How do we get the gunship to focus on you?" Osprey asked.

"I'll take care of that. Do I have your permission?"

Osprey considered it for a moment longer—but just for a moment. "Do it," she said.

"Yorra, Park. Give me two missiles each."

That would leave them with a couple. But he needed the extra ammunition to make this work. In order to draw out the gunship he'd need to make a big racket.

Park and Yorra each ejected a couple of missiles, and then used their wingtip blasters to keep the drones at bay while he maneuvered into a loading position and utilized their guidance system to quickly take them on board.

As soon as he had the extra munitions secured, Elya accelerated toward the group of Kryl gunships.

The four dozen vessels, seeing him fly straight at them, seemed confused for a moment. This was unusual behavior, and they weren't sure what he was doing. They probably thought he had another nuclear warhead aimed in their direction. Perhaps Overmind X was wondering if she should let him pass through, to eat it like she had the other one.

That was what Elya wanted, but they wouldn't let him fly free for very long. He loosed four missiles, one at each gunship nearest him. The diversion worked. He passed quickly between the two in the front, their projectiles pinging off his diminished shield. One or two bullets made it through and pinged off his fuselage.

As the Kryl turned their fire on the incoming missiles, whatever hesitation the Kryl had shown vanished immediately. Four different gunships turned and rushed after him. He only had one wing tip blaster and a mere two missiles remaining, but he didn't need to take on the gunships directly.

He simply had to reveal the photon cannon, and give the Furies time to target it properly.

Hedgebot scurried up and to his right, flashing green. There! He took an extra couple seconds to make sure he had the right ship. The relic was attached with an arm-like appendage affixed to a tripod mounted on the gunship's belly.

It tilted to face him, no doubt fixing him in its sights. Elya's heart pounded as time slowed. He held his craft steady, moving in a straight line. As the gossamer thread appeared, he rolled hard left, barely dodging it and avoiding total annihilation.

Instead of veering away, Elya rolled back and kept pressing forward. He strafed the surface of the gunship with his blasters, flying in an erratic, inconsistent looping pattern. He rolled and dodged around the golden beam, forcing the gunship to swing wildly, hewing the tip off an asteroid and slicing toward the canyon's sheer rock wall.

With the help of Hedgebot and his Sabre's warning sensors, he avoided being sliced in half by the relic's powerful death ray. "Come on," he muttered under his breath. The beam never stayed on for long. Only ten, fifteen seconds tops.

Which could be a lifetime in close-quarters space combat like this.

He reached the gunship and peeled around its left shoulder, forcing it to swing around toward the Kryl's own forces. The beam finally cut off, whether because it reached the end of its timer or because the Kryl didn't want to slice through their own defenses, he couldn't be sure.

It didn't matter why. He'd achieved what he set out to do, identifying the craft and distracting it while the rest of the Furies closed in. Raptor announced the launch of several more missiles over the broadbeam. Elya lingered, distracting the gunship for as long as he dared before he pulled away.

Looking over his shoulder, using the Sabre's rearview cameras, he held his breath until a slow explosion bloomed in the view. A perfectly timed blaster bolt tore the tripod off, and then the gunship ruptured.

Cheers went up over the broadbeam as the Furies celebrated the target's elimination.

They'd achieved their objective, but that didn't mean they were mission complete. All at once, the third layer of Kryl drones that had tightened in like a fist around the organism surged forward. He shot into open space, trying to distance himself from the knot of drones, but hundreds of them folded around Elya's Sabre, cutting off his exit. He turned and accelerated at full burn in the opposite direction—toward the organism.

He suddenly found himself isolated behind enemy lines. He caught sight of the three drones he'd spotted earlier, hovering close to the organism with their noses pointed at it. They didn't make any move that indicated they'd noticed him. Using his HUD to zoom the view in, he noted the organism had formed a new opening. Only this one was enormous, like a mineshaft, and it was located dead-center in the mass of flesh and carapace.

Staring into the opening, Elya's mind reeled as he struggled to make sense of what he saw. At the center of the shaft, what appeared to be a heat mirage, with torn edges, blue-black and dizzying, swirled ominously. As he stared, he momentarily forgot about everything else happening behind him—about the curtain of drones, about his squadmates and the rest of the Furies, about the broken planet.

The three drones pointed at the organism activated their thrusters and flew forward into the maelstrom.

They passed through the event horizon and disappeared.

Every muscle in his body urged him to direct his Sabre toward the anomaly and follow Subject Zero, for if the Kryl were going through that thing, that meant Chronicle was right and the last relic lay waiting on the other side. There was no other reason Overmind X would send her underlings into something like that. Not while they were in the middle of a pitched battle against the Solaran fleet. The line from that ancient poem echoed in his mind.

Six on a starship lost to time.

This was the moment he'd been waiting for.

Elya accelerated towards it, but released the throttle after only a moment. He'd gone after Subject Zero without orders before, a grave error in judgment. He couldn't afford to make the same mistake twice.

The Solaran Empire—the entire galaxy—was counting on him.

"Raptor!" he said into the squad's broadbeam channel. "Subject Zero and two other drones just flew through the anomaly and disappeared. Permission to pursue?"

"Negative," she said immediately.

"But Raptor—"

"We just lost ten Sabres destroying this gunship, and you want to fly through a wormhole with Animus-knows how many enemy combatants waiting for you? It's suicide."

Elya considered this. "We don't have a choice, Raptor. If they come out with another relic, it could change the outcome of this battle."

"Hang on," she said.

Clicking noises as Osprey commandeered the communications channels and connected them with command. She quickly explained what he'd just requested.

"You're the mission commander," said Colonel Volk. "What's your judgment?"

"Too many unknowns, sir," Osprey said. "We don't know what kind of danger is waiting on the other side of that wormhole."

"The risk of not pursuing is huge," Elya insisted. When she didn't respond, he added, "What if Subject Zero comes out with another prime relic? Isn't that what we're here to prevent?"

"Captain Nevers has a point," said Admiral Miyaru, using the same mic as Colonel Volk. "We could send a squad with a greater headcount instead."

"No one knows more about the relics than me," Elya insisted. "I'm volunteering. If you want to send me through with a different escort, fine, but I'm already in position."

"Osprey, the Furies are yours to command," said Colonel Volk. "What do you advise?"

Elya waited, holding his breath. The surrounding drones had turned and begun to close in on him again.

"We go," Osprey commanded.

Thirty seconds later, Elya was forced to maneuver his Sabre out of the way as dozens of drones came flying in his direction.

But he needn't have worried. Park whooped over the

broadbeam and the Furies shouted as they fired their blasters madly into the cloud of drones and tunneled through the final Kryl perimeter to join him.

"Buckle up and follow me," Elya said.

"Stay tight!" Osprey shouted. "There's thirty-one of us left and I expect every one of you to make it out of this mission alive."

A contingent of drones flew from the backside of the organism and cut off their approach vector. They maneuvered directly into the path of the Furies, blocking access to the wormhole.

"Dammit!" Elya said. "Too slow."

As he spoke, Seba the Knife's corvettes slammed into the enemy's flank, creating a mass of confusing knots on his lidar and drawing half of the drones blocking their path away.

"We'll burn our way through the rest," Osprey said. "On you, Fancypants!"

Elya flew toward the anomaly. Using his remaining wingtip blaster, he took out two drones, then a third, and slipped past the enemy.

His Sabre slammed into the event horizon at a hundred klicks a second. It felt as if his organs were turning inside out as he felt himself pass through the rift.

TWENTY-EIGHT

Casey felt her body get wrenched in countless different directions as she passed through the rift, a sense of disorientation and nausea overtaking her. Reflexively, she gagged and barely choked down the vomit that tried to climb up her esophagus.

She re-gripped her stick and guided her Sabre away, reducing her speed and ordering the others to do so, as well, though speaking the words nearly made her want to puke a second time. It was another minute before her stomach settled.

"Is everyone okay?" she asked.

Grumbles and mutters over the broadbeam. Apart from their voices, space on this side of the wormhole was eerily still and empty. Disorienting after being caught amid a pitched space battle.

"Flight leads," Casey said, "take headcount and report."

The leads, her included, switched to their team comms and took an internal status. When they switched back to broadbeam a moment later, Casey reported first. "Red Team's all here."

"Same with Green," said Tank, "Though we lost three in the battle."

"Blue's down a man," said Fuzz. "But all spoken for."

"Yellow's all present," reported Ruby. "But where in the hell is here?"

Casey had been so focused on the well-being of her squad that she had barely looked around other than to note that they were still flying in vacuum.

Space here was vast and empty. In the distance, stars shone as fuzzy, white-and-blue blurs. There was no local sun on this side, but it wasn't exactly dark, either. Kind of like flying on a cloudy day.

Only, they weren't in atmosphere. Her HUD told her they were still in space. On second thought, rather than a cloudy day, the distance in every direction looked like those astronomical depictions of nebulas. Great, swirling patterns of blurry color painted every direction.

The Furies seemed to be situated somewhere at the region's center.

Pulling her craft around, she saw the wormhole was still present on this side. It wasn't surrounded by the Kryl organism any more, it merely appeared as a jagged tear in reality about twenty meters across and half that many high.

Blinking, she peered closer to study it. Had she just seen tentacles slithering there, gripping the bizarrely, unnaturally ripped edges, or had that been a figment of her imagination? Sparks of lightning flickered at one end of the oblong shape. Between one breath and the next, the ripped edges smoothed out imperceptibly, leaving a nearly symmetrical oval in its place.

Whatever opened that thing, she thought, it's gone now.

A sense of urgency struck her.

"What now, Fancypants?" she demanded. "This was your bright idea. I don't think we have a lot of time to kill."

"Hmm," Captain Nevers said, "I still don't see it…"

"See what, hombre?" Park asked.

"The 'starship lost to time'."

"Lost to time?" asked Yorra. "Oh, that poem. You think this is some kind of time warp?"

"Time warp?" Ruby butted in. "No one said anything about a time warp. Did we just time travel?"

"No way to know," Elya said, "I mean, I don't *think* so. From what Chronicle said, this wormhole was used to hide a prime relic from the Kryl. I don't think we moved backward through time so much as stepped out of the normal time flow into this… region of stasis."

"So," Park said, "'lost to time' was just a figure of speech, then?"

"The Telos didn't write that poem," Nevers reminded them. "That was a Solaran interpreting what the Telos had done to hide the prime relics. But it's as apt a description as any I can think of."

"And yet somehow," Yorra snorted. "Wholly inadequate."

Casey glanced around and had to agree with her friend. However, it didn't matter—pilots had standard operating procedures and it was her job to follow them. She switched from broadbeam to tightbeam to speak to command and let them know what they'd found. The three drones they chased through the rift were nowhere to be seen, and she needed to know how the admiral wished to proceed.

"Furies actual to command," she said. "Furies actual to the *Paladin of Abniss*. Do you copy?"

No response.

That wasn't good. She checked the comms system and quickly noticed that it wasn't that command had simply failed to respond. Rather, the tightbeam never connected in the first place.

Strange. She'd never known an ansible-powered comms system not to connect, no matter the distance.

Casey fought down panic as she adjusted to the stranded position she suddenly found herself, and her squad, in. After a second, she switched back to broadbeam. "We're on our own," Casey said. "There's no link with command."

"What?"

Murmurs went up around the squad. Several asked questions at once. "What's that mean?" "Should we go back?" "Those drones must be hiding somewhere nearby."

The sense of urgency she'd felt quickly escalated into panic and clawed up her throat more urgently than even the bile had before. No command comms meant they were on their own, well and *truly* isolated from the rest of the armada.

That meant one thing. Casey was now in charge. Not just the mission commander, but the only squadron commander they had.

The burden of responsibility weighed heavily upon her. She took a few deep breaths, ignoring the broadbeam chatter.

Okay, she thought. *Comms are still working between us.* That was good. The Furies could communicate with each other, they just couldn't communicate through the wormhole. She wanted to ask Harmony about it, and grew morose when she remembered that if the *Paladin of Abniss* was unreachable, so was the shipmind.

The Furies were here to do a mission, she reminded herself. As long as they were breathing, there was a chance to succeed. So, she did what she thought better and more experienced leaders would have done had they found themselves in this predicament.

She assessed the situation, took stock of the risk, and opened a separate channel with her flight leads. After a moment's thought, she added Captain Nevers in as well.

"Leads are all here. Captain Nevers, this was your idea. What do you advise?" she asked.

"We find that starship. I think I see something down there. It'll probably take us five or ten minutes under acceleration to reach it."

She checked her lidar scan and found what he was talking about—a roughly cylindrical object floated a few hundred klicks below their current position.

"Can't all go," Fuzz said. "Someone needs to guard the exit. If the Kryl leave first, they could close the anomaly and strand us here!"

"I agree," Casey responded. "How many?"

"At least half the squad," said Tank.

"Isn't that risky?" Ruby asked. "We're not at full strength."

"If the Kryl get to this Telos relic first," Casey said, playing devil's advocate, "And it happens to have some more surprising destructive power, we've put ourselves in a weak position by splitting our forces."

"There were only three of them," Nevers said, "and they won't get to it first if we move quickly."

"Hold on," Casey said.

"Less talking, more flying, Commander."

"I understand your urgency," Casey said. "but we need to have a plan. Here's an idea. What if we just left Green Team to watch the exit?"

Tank's team had already lost a couple starfighters, and she knew from the tone of her voice that she was kicking herself about it.

"I agree that the majority of our forces should be going after the objective," said Fuzz. "But what if a larger force comes through the rift?"

"It's a choke point," Ruby pointed out. "We position our Sabres behind the rift on either side and shoot so that our lines of fire cross. Anyone comes through, they'll get chewed up before they have a chance to realize what's happening. You felt how disorienting it was entering the anomaly. I bet the Kryl feel that, too. But one of us will keep watch in this direction, so we know if those three approach."

It irked her that Ruby's thinking was so sound. *This isn't the time to be jealous,* Casey berated herself silently.

"My team is down by three, and we're low on ammunition," said Fuzz.

"Yellow Team stays then," said Casey. "They're at full strength, and I think they wasted less ammo than we did. Ruby, you still have all your missiles, don't you?"

"Yes," she admitted grudgingly.

"Then Yellow Team guards the exit, and the rest of us go with Nevers to the starship."

"No Earth-damned way you're making me stay behind," Ruby growled. "I have a score to settle with those scum suckers."

"And if any drones come through the rift," Casey said, "you'll get your opportunity."

"I don't want the peons," she said. "I want the big bad."

"Zero's mine," said Captain Nevers.

"No one gets to claim enemy combatants," Casey snapped, surprising herself with the tone and speed of the rebuke. "Now quit your childish bickering and listen to your commander." She'd never pulled rank on them before. Angry silence filled the line.

"Respectfully, *Commander,*" Ruby said after a pause, "Screw you. I'm going after the objective. Somebody else can stay here."

"I'll do it," Fuzz said. "Blue Team is armed as well as Yellow Team. We only lost one in the battle. I'll split my squads, five on one side, four on the other. Crossing fire, just like you suggested. Now, stop wasting time and fly."

Casey nodded, though no one could see her face.

"Thanks, Fuzz. Yellow Team, Green Team—on me. Blue Team, take up your posts. Be sure to devise a patrol pattern so you're not sitting idle."

"Copy that, and may the Spirit of Old Earth go with you," Fuzz said.

She relayed the orders to the rest of the squad. It was a good thing she had taken her flight leads into a separate channel so the pilots didn't hear their leaders arguing.

Ruby's dissent worried Casey. Would she buck next time Casey gave an order? Would their personal conflict cause more unnecessary losses? Casey would have to set things right, eventually. Like Ruby, she wanted to put a blaster in Subject Zero's mouth and pull the trigger. But as commander, she needed to look out for the best interests of the entire squad.

She didn't have time to think more about it. Yellow Team shot ahead, and Captain Nevers went with them. Casey was forced to accelerate to keep up.

Nevers' estimates about the distance to the starship were way off. Physical space acted weird in this place. No matter how far or fast she flew, the nebulous walls—if they could be called that—of this… bubble of reality never seem to get any closer. In fact, as they flew to the object Nevers had found, which seemed to float near a swirling pattern of "clouds" below them, the backdrop seemed to recede even further back.

"This place is weird," Park said, echoing her thoughts. "Am I tripping balls?"

"No more stim for you," Yorra said sourly.

"No," Nevers piped up. "Park is right. Something about this place feels very strange."

"Did you expect it to be normal?" Ruby asked in a mocking tone. "Welcome to the time warp, where everything is copacetic, and clocks don't move backwards?"

"I'm not sure a clock would move at all in here," Nevers said, "but check it out."

As they approached the large cylinder that Nevers had taken to be the starship—and why not? It was the only object their lidar picked up on scans—her eyes grew wide.

Upon closer inspection, she saw its hull was a large geodesic structure made of interlocking triangles of that light brown Telos alloy. In the dim glow of this place, it appeared the color of bronze with blue and green highlights. It would blend in perfectly back in Elturis' asteroid field, much like the Telos asteroid concealing the City.

Once her mind stopped reeling at the massive structure, her eyes began searching for the port that would allow them access to it. If this was like the asteroid back in Elturis, then there would be some kind of porthole their ships could fly through to dock.

Nevers was two steps ahead of her, as usual, when it came to Telos-made things. He'd already curved around the narrow end of the structure.

"I found the port," Nevers said. "It's made up of smaller docks, all near each other. Three Kryl drones are docked inside."

As Casey followed Captain Nevers' path around, she saw a triangular window large enough to fit a light cruiser through. Mounted about a hundred meters below it, at the very tip of the starship's tail, were three triads of enormous engines.

The clue in that poem had been right after all. This *was* a starship.

Looking through her canopy, she saw what Nevers had pointed out. Three drones parked on a small hexagonal pad. There were other pads arranged around a broad room, at various altitudes and levels. They wouldn't be able to park next to the drones, but they could land on another pad nearby and follow a path deeper into the ship.

"Okay, let's—"

A shout from Fuzz cut her next order off. "Osprey we have Contact!" Then a *womp-whoomph,* the sound of blasters being fired, came through the comms.

"Target that gunship!" Fuzz said

Screams and cries came over the broadbeam as intense fighting sounded. Casey's breath caught, her hands freezing on her stick.

"Raptor, we need reinforcements!" Fuzz called. "There's just too many."

Casey glanced between the Telos starship and the position of the wormhole, back the way they'd come. It would take her precious minutes, even at full burn and full of stimchem, to get back to provide support.

"Raptor, we've got to go into the ship after Subject Zero," said Nevers. "This is exactly what they want. If we go back to help Fuzz, we're giving up any chance at recovering the relic."

Casey hesitated, her eyes darting back and forth. What could she do? What would Colonel Volk and Admiral Miyaru *want* her to do?

Nevers was right. They had to stop Subject Zero from getting the prime relic, or she might risk not only the lives of her own squad, but the lives of every person in the armada. As painful as it was to lose friends, their purpose here was greater than just the Furies.

They were all Fleet pilots on a mission. They knew the risks.

On the other hand, if she didn't go back and help Fuzz, she might lose another nine starfighter pilots *right now.*

She was torn between the immediate need of going to her comrades' aid, and the higher cause of the overall mission objective: put an end to Overmind X's rampage once and for all.

A calm settled over her as she decided. Instinct took over. Casey targeted the three static drones in her crosshairs and fired. Bolts from her wingtip blasters tore into the Kryl fighters, blowing them to pieces on the platform where they sat. "You go," Casey said. "Yorra, Park, Nevers, stop Subject Zero and get that relic. Ruby, pick your best two shooters and go with them for support. There were three drones, which means there are at least three enemies inside that ship, so I want at least two-to-one odds in our favor. The rest of you, with me."

Without waiting for a response, she activated her thrusters and accelerated back toward the wormhole, taking a dose of stimchem as she went so she didn't have to worry about blacking out as she rocketed back the way they'd come.

Two minutes had never felt so long. She watched in her rearview as Park, Nevers, Yorra, Ruby and two other starfighters entered the hangar and docked inside the Telos starship. Once they were in the craft, the dots representing their ships disappeared from her lidar. At the same time, dozens more dots representing enemy combatants poured out of the rift ahead of her.

She checked her missile load and the energy levels on her wingtip blasters. Her body vibrated as she was forced back into the seat. She gripped the stick, keeping her Sabre on vector, and hoped fervently that she'd make it back in time to hold the wormhole.

TWENTY-NINE

With every step Omar took, the pounding in his head grew worse.

With every step, he moved deeper into the Telos starship.

The pain had begun the moment they entered the rift. When they emerged on the other side, the strength of Overmind X's commanding mental presence quickly faded. Seven and Fourteen reported feeling nauseated and squeamish when they crossed, but for him, a blinding pain had left him incapacitated for several minutes.

By the time he recovered enough to take stock of his surroundings, their drones had docked inside the Enemy's dead starship, and Overmind X's voice had vanished completely.

In all his time with her, that had *never* happened.

The silence was deafening.

And then it filled with a *thrum thrum thrum* pounding at the back of his eyes, warping the edge of his vision.

Had the rift caused this? It was unlikely, since he'd asked the younglings and he seemed to be the only one affected. More likely, Overmind X had been doing more than he'd realized to suppress the nerve pains and suffering that were a side effect of his haphazard transformation.

She'd literally been holding him together, mentally and physically.

Seven and Fourteen ranged ahead of him now as Omar fought to control his breathing and keep pace. Their loping strides ate up the vast geometric hallways of the Telos ship. They bounced off the walls, trying to reach high panels, shelves and compartments set into the uppermost corners—supposedly controls, access ports, and pathways to ductwork and other plumbing built for the crew that once inhabited this empty vessel—but even with their physical prowess, the sheer, inclined walls proved difficult to scale.

Thrum thrum thrum.

His mandibles twitched. The many joints of the extra Kryl arms folded into Omar's back ached in unison.

The pain got so bad that he had to pause and rest his head in his human hand. The dreadful hammer continued to slam against the inside of his skull.

"Hurry, Zero," hissed Seven.

"The humans aren't far behind us," added Fourteen.

"Humans?" he asked, confused, as he stared at the two children.

Why were they talking about humans? The people of the Solaran Empire never referred to themselves as *humans*. They called themselves Solaran or, more commonly, the name of their colony of origin.

I'm Ariadnean, he thought.

A sudden memory appeared in his mind's eye: a squat blue cottage with a peaked roof and a single orange door. He'd painted the door himself. Though he couldn't see it from this angle, he knew there was a modest hydroponic prefab unit in the back.

Home.

Omar's eyes shot open. *Where had* that *come from?* he wondered.

Seven and Fourteen cocked their heads, like dogs listening for a sound he couldn't hear. His fear forced his substantial headache away as the parameters of his mission came into sudden focus once more. He pushed off a wall he hadn't realized he'd been sagging against and stepped forward.

"Right," he said. *Thrum thrum thrum*. "We have to keep moving. Find the last relic."

He strode past them, trying to ignore the way his head pounded and his joints ached. Seven and Fourteen followed and then overtook him, running forward again. They occasionally glanced back, obviously suspicious of his behavior. He pretended he didn't see their looks.

Where in the universe had that memory been dredged up? Why his childhood home?

Because I miss it, he thought. *I pine for the peace of those days.*

His body tensed up, expecting at any moment for something to seize hold and neutralize his traitorous thoughts. But then he realized the presence that had watched over him, working to keep his pain at bay and his mind focused on his mission, was no longer there to correct him. Overmind X had been cut off. He was finally in command of his own mind again.

She must have been blocking his pain receptors along with his memories, so that he could continue to operate on her behalf without interference. He didn't know how long or how well he'd be able to continue in this condition without her, but he felt like he was seeing clearly for the first time in many years.

He needed a plan.

First of all, he couldn't let Seven or Fourteen catch on to

what had happened. As soon as they knew he was recovering his memories, they would kill him.

He inhaled sharply. Of course! Now that his mind was clear, it was so obvious. Overmind X had ordered the mutant twins to murder him if he stepped out of line. The moment he was no longer useful, they'd eliminate him.

He knew they didn't trust him, didn't like him. But it was so obvious now that their suspicion came as direct orders from Overmind X. She'd never wanted him to think for himself. If he ever did, she had contingency plans in place to ensure his swift removal.

His mind raced on. The pain of his headache didn't disappear, but somehow it became less important. Animus, what he'd do for some Fleet-quality painkillers right now. Or stimchem; most pilots didn't realize it, but they put painkillers in the stim when your fighter's systems detected any sign of injury.

Why was he here? Why would Overmind X send him on a mission like this if she knew he'd recover his memories?

Because he was disposable. And maybe she didn't realize what he'd remember once he was free of her influence, if she had even guessed that would happen.

What *did* he remember? An idea that stood out only for its apparent importance nagged at the back of his mind. Not the fact that he was Ariadnean. Not anything about his childhood home. Something else. It was on the tip of his tongue…

He racked his brain as they stalked through the halls of the vast, dead starship. The walls glowed with an ambient light, like it was running on backup power. They found several panels that might be lights, but they remained off. He couldn't put his finger on the idea that bothered him. The pain in his head continued to ebb and flow. When it got bad, it became difficult to do anything but breathe and walk. For the second time, it got so bad he was forced to pause for a second, doubling over in pain and leaning against a wall for support.

Seven and Fourteen paused and came back to watch him. When the pain subsided again, they were peering strangely at him and exchanging meaningful glances. The looks in their eyes were predatory. One of them smiled.

"What are you staring at?" he growled, drawing the blade relic and bearing it before him. "Do you want me to take another hand?"

Seven flinched away from the weapon and made a guttural noise in her throat as she cradled the stump of her wrist.

"Are you well enough to proceed?" asked Fourteen.

Omar sheathed the knife back at his side and nodded. "Of course I am."

"If not, you must give us the relics so that we can complete the mission. Mother's orders."

"I'm good," he said. "We're wasting time"

"Let's hurry then," said Seven. "The humans are exploring the landing area now."

Omar inhaled sharply. She must still be able to communicate with the drones. Without Overmind X's presence, he had lost that ability. But not them. Not the newer models.

But they don't seem to be recovering their memories, he thought. That was just happening to *him*. Perhaps it was a product of the method of his transformation versus theirs. He shuddered, recalling his own awful experience. The way his skin had burned, the way she'd rearranged his internal organs and grafted Kryl creatures onto his body. In fact, the memory made the pain of his headache seem mild in comparison. He took a deep breath, flexed his mandibles, and stood up straight again. He could do this. One step at a time.

"The Solarans are disembarking now." Seven said. "They've destroyed our ships."

"Mother will send more," Fourteen said. "What next?"

"We move forward," said Omar, using the most confident voice he could muster.

Fourteen turned and gestured to the door at the end of the hall. It was perfectly round and made of Telos alloy. The door itself was beautifully decorated: etched with carvings and runes in their language, plus geometric designs, lines, spirals and other symbols. It spoke of advanced mathematics far beyond his understanding. He thought he saw some kind of orbital diagram, but couldn't make sense of it.

He still didn't completely understand Telos technology, but Overmind X had guided him through enough of their temples to know what to look for.

Searching, he located the keyhole. Centered horizontally and slightly down from the middle, he reactivated the atomic knife and slid it into the slot.

Turning left, a hidden bolt clicked and the stone door parted in the middle, each side rolling smoothly into the wall and revealing a path that led deeper into the ship.

Seven and Fourteen scrambled forward, only to yelp and jump backward as spiral designs on the floor turned red hot the moment they put weight on them.

Omar activated his phase shifter and moved past the spiral markings on the floor. While he was phased out, they didn't react to his presence. These kinds of automated defenses were the hallmark of Telos tech. And while this wasn't one of their labyrinthine temples, it stood to reason there would still be some protections.

Something else itched at his mind. This starship reminded him of so many other starships. He recalled glimpses of them in the ruined house of his mind as more memories returned.

Bridges, hangars, berths, and the tiny closets that served as toilets. Solaran ships. Yes, of course, his mind had stored many images of Solaran ships—cruisers, destroyers, corvettes. Omar had been a Fleet pilot. He spent a lot of time on ships.

Doubt crept in, but once again he couldn't put his finger on the reason for the anxiety Overmind X had spent so much time suppressing. Yet the uneasiness remained, growing with each step, causing his throat to close up and his hands to tremble on the bladed relic at his belt—and on the grip of his old Fleet-issued sidearm.

He reached the other side of the heat defenses and found the switch to deactivate them, driving a knife into the control panel to make *Off* more permanent. Once that was done, Seven and Fourteen walked cautiously through the hallway and met him at the intersection.

"Which way next?" asked Seven.

Fourteen was watching him. "Are you okay to proceed?" she asked Omar again.

"Stop asking me that!"

"This mission is paramount. If you cannot complete it, we must—"

"I'm fine. My head just hurts. It's a side effect of not being able to speak to Mother."

Subject Fourteen and Subject Seven made non-committal sounds in their throats like they didn't believe him.

"Go ahead and try to take these from me," he said, pulling the knife out once again and poising his other hand on the phase shifter, which should be recharged in about thirty seconds. "I dare you."

"She will not be pleased."

"She'll be even less pleased if both of you bleed out on the floor here."

"This mission," said Seven, "is critical," finished Fourteen.

With their words, another new memory slammed into him.

A critical mission.

The fate of the Solaran Empire hinging on its outcome.

A single pilot. Him. A corvette that brought him into the nameless system where the homeworld of the Kryl, Planet K, orbited a red gas giant.

His descent, under stealth, to the planet. And his ultimate target: the Queen Mother, the Kryl Overmind from which Overmind X had been born.

Fourteen cocked her head at him again, but Omar strode forward before they could get a good look at his face, taking a right-hand branch at random.

"I'll look this way. You two check the other paths." He didn't want to be around them for a moment in case his body language gave away what he just realized.

Which was that Omar should be dead. He'd undertaken another mission, long ago, that required the ultimate sacrifice. Fortunately, those memories had come crashing back so fast, and Seven and Fourteen were so eager to proceed, that they'd hurried down the other two pathways without additional questions. So they didn't see him pause and rest his throbbing head against the cold metal of the angled wall as he reeled, the recovered memories unbalancing his mind.

Thrum thrum thrum. His vision darkened.

"I shouldn't be here," he muttered. "I died."

This mission, these relics… None of this should have happened.

Why had it?

Because he'd failed humanity. He'd let the Solaran Empire down.

He found nothing down the hallway he'd chosen except for what appeared to be crew quarters. Once again, everything a Solaran would want was stored in compartments, on shelves, and behind panels high on the walls. The floor, as always, was left bare. Poles of crystal, cut to look like thin, reedy trees with broad leaves—though no trees he'd ever seen before—filled the space. All the berths were high near the ceiling.

This wasn't what they were looking for, and he couldn't afford to loiter. He turned and went back the other way, his mind grasping for a plan. Seven and Fourteen were waiting for him at the intersection. "This way," they said, and loped off down a hallway.

He followed them to another engraved alloy door. He used the atomic knife as a key to open this one as well. It slid aside and revealed a large room with ribs running up to the ceiling along each of the four walls. Like everything else in the ship and in the Telos temples, the important objects in the room were mounted high on the walls. Unlike those other places, the walls of this one were strapped along the ribs with a hundred different objects of various surprising shapes. His eyes picked out curved blades of metal, gauntlets, helms, pieces of armor that were twice the size of even the largest human frame, and some in shapes he didn't recognize, for a body no human had ever seen.

As they entered, new designs on the floor—hash marks and horizontal pairs of lines—flashed in warning. With a rumble of metal on metal, four large spheres roughly a meter across separated from the corners of the room. They crossed and came to rest in the center in a diamond shape.

Little portals spun open—so much like the doors through which they'd passed—revealing the business end of rifle barrels.

"Cover!" Omar shouted.

Seven and Fourteen dove in opposite directions. Omar backpedaled to the door, ducking around its curved frame and putting the wall between him and the sentries.

Blaster bolts sizzled as their opening shots ricocheted off the walls and sizzled out against the floor and ceiling. He activated the phase shifter relic as he stepped back into the room, the atomic knife in his Kryl hand, while he drew his blaster in his human hand. The next three shots fired by the sentry orbs passed straight through him. The moment the phase shifter deactivated and his body rejoined the solid state again, he landed two quick blaster bolts of his own on the shell of the closest orb.

The automated sentry ate his shots with nothing more than glowing red spots on its shell to show for his efforts.

Spinning the atomic knife around in his hand, he grabbed it in a reverse grip, the blade pointing downward, and sank it to the hilt into the sentry's metal shell. The alloy screeched as he wrenched the blade toward himself, opening a jagged gash. He saw crystal plates, thin silver wires, and other circuitry beneath.

He pulled the knife out and sank it in again, ripping the gash wider this time and twisting the blade through some of the crystal plates.

Whatever had been powering the sentry gave out, and the orb rolled limply to one side, seesawing back and forth, evidently dead.

He took a blaster bolt in the arm from another sentry for his efforts and screamed in pain. He scrabbled back against the closed door at the far end of the room, using the dead sentry orb to shield himself from more incoming fire.

Meanwhile, the two mutants were avoiding blaster bolts by bouncing off the walls and performing acrobatic maneuvers he couldn't do even if he tried. Seven bounced up high and tore one of those heavy alloy swords off the wall. It was too heavy for her, but she dropped it at the right angle to slice a quarter-moon chunk out of one sentry.

It kept rolling, however, less steady but still shooting deadly bolts at them.

Suddenly, the three spherical sentry robots swiveled toward the doorway through which they'd entered.

Six Solaran pilots stood in the round doorway, jaws hanging open, surveying the scene. They each bore sidearm blasters of their own—Fleet-issued, like Omar's, but newer models. A couple of them held rifles. They still wore their flight suits, but their helmets were gone, and he recognized one of them. It was the young pilot he'd faced off against on Robichar, and then again in the Telos asteroid habitat. The same skilled pilot who'd been chasing him through the asteroid field.

Omar stood, stepping out from behind his makeshift shield. Seeing the young man was surreal. It reminded him of a younger version of himself—he was just a few years younger than Omar had been when he died.

Had he not stood just so, facing off against the Kryl, on that fateful suicide mission so many years ago?

He stared at the boy—at the reflection of himself—for a frozen moment.

"Kill them!" Seven hissed.

Glancing down, Omar realized he was holding his blaster in his injured arm. The barrel was pointed at the ground.

Omar didn't want to shoot the young man. He wanted to talk to him.

But he never got the chance. The room erupted in a hail of blaster bolts as the Telos sentries sensed an additional threat and opened fire on the Solarans.

THIRTY

Subject Zero spread his vicious mouth and leered at Elya. *Earth, is that a smile*? He shuddered.

The mutant pilot had slavering mandibles where his lower jaw should be. They widened and his mangled teeth glistened wetly. It was more disgusting than he remembered. Bloodshot eyes fixated on Elya in the moment he saw the mutant's face. Zero stood partially shielded behind a sphere made of that alloy the Telos were so fond of.

Three more spheres pivoted toward him. They were scattered throughout the room, arrayed against two more Kryl he'd never seen before.

A shock of horror rippled through him as he realized he *had* seen the Kryl before. Or rather, he'd seen others like them, school-aged children during an identical unpleasant transformation.

But apparently he hadn't saved all those kids. In a flash, he took in the state of these two. Scaly hide and elongated claws. Eyes enlarged and faceted with huge pupils. One was small and lean. The other was slightly more muscular and more… feral-looking.

Both alien. Both far too gone to save.

They belonged to Overmind X now.

That was his last thought before Hedgebot flashed red and scrambled backward. Elya dove in the bot's direction as three sentry orbs simultaneously opened fire in their direction.

Yorra and Park, and one man from Yellow Team, the squat brick of a soldier they called Hairpin, jumped for cover to the left and the right, behind the round doorframe.

Leaning around, Hairpin fired his sidearm randomly into the room. This gave Ruby and the other pilot she'd brought with her, the tall rangy weapons officer named Sticks, the opportunity to push themselves off their stomachs and scramble into cover with them. Ruby tripped over her rifle strap when it slipped from her shoulder, but the others caught her before she took a dive.

Elya scrambled up with them, though he was too stunned to shoot his sidearm. He'd drawn it and flicked the safety to OFF like the rest when they first heard the noise of fighting and came to find it, here in this room full of Telos artifacts—most of which seemed to be melee weapons. He had a moment to think this room might make a good sparring gym, and perhaps it had been that once, but then he flinched and ducked down as a plasma bolt sizzled off the doorframe near his ear. He made as small a target of himself as possible, pressing back against Yorra or whoever was behind him. Hedgebot spun and crouched between his feet as bolts of sizzling plasma struck the floor where his boot had been a moment ago.

Movement from the mutants in the room drew fire away from the pilots for a beat. Sticks leaned out and added his blaster bolts to the fray. Elya stepped back to get a better angle on the room and saw the mutant children taking cover behind a smoking sphere, which lay still. The spherical robot was missing a chunk of alloy in its upper half, revealing an overlapping stack of rainbow hued transparent crystal sheets. Like a circuit board made of clear quartz.

He yelped when someone grabbed his collar and yanked him to the side. A red-orange bolt of pure plasma sizzled by his head close enough to singe his cheek. He fell into Park's lap.

"You idiot!" the man growled angrily.

"Those are the children she turned," Elya said. "We didn't save them all." Saying the words made his chest ache.

Park shoved him off, then tried to jump to his feet, only to slip forward and slam his head against the wall. Elya helped his wingman to his feet while the others covered the door with alternating blaster fire. Park's hands trembled violently on his shoulder as the man steadied himself.

"You mean those groundlings on steroids?" said Yorra, raking concerned eyes over Park, who had his eyes closed, catching his breath.

Her eyes widened as she made the connection. She glanced around the curved doorframe for a moment, nearly getting a haircut in the process as two more blaster bolts sizzled down the hall past them. "Animus give me courage," she whispered, resting her back against the wall, then bringing the stock of her blaster rifle up beside her temple before turning and firing several shots in rapid succession.

Park pulled her back. "Stop trying to get yourself killed!"

"Shut up, all of you," Ruby hissed from the opposite side of the door. "They'll be coming after us when they finish those."

Elya peeked around and saw two of the sentries ripped open, crystal innards exposed to the air.

"We should move while they're distracted," said Yorra.

Sticks tapped Ruby on the shoulder and gave her a look.

She nodded, motioning for Park, Yorra and himself to step back.

Elya's blood pumped through his veins, but he did as he was told. Ruby raised the sights on her rifle and fired into the room at a forty-five degree angle.

Sticks looked both ways, then darted forward, coming to a low crouch behind the dead metal sphere closest to their position, roughly halfway into the room. The rangy man crouched and compressed his body behind the robot to hide himself from view.

While Sticks ran and Ruby provided a distraction, Hairpin rushed his blocky body across the doorway to take up a position opposite Ruby, shouldering Yorra out of the way. When Ruby had emptied a full charge pack into the room, shooting toward the far corner, the stocky man pivoted and opened fire with his blaster on the opposite side.

Elya tensed up as an explosion rocked the room. His ears rang and smoke roiled toward them. Elya took cover while the sentries fired again, and then one sphere rolled through the doorway, forcing them to scatter into the room as the robot opened fire where they'd been hiding just a moment before.

Someone jostled him and Elya stumbled through the doorframe into a thicker cloud of smoke. He dove left as something leaped at him through the haze, claws extended.

His chest flared with pain as he landed, stretched out, on the floor. Hedgebot flared red as the bot skittered by his head.

Dead spheres, chunks of crystal, bladed weapons, and pieces of other unknown black objects littered the floor. A still robot sentry had a jagged black gash torn in its shell, the thick bronze metal twisted and ruined. The alloy around it was covered in soot, and smoking from the heat.

So that material *could* be damaged. By Telos-made blades and... explosives, apparently. Good to know.

The smoke cleared, revealing an open circular doorway at the opposite end of the room.

Two of the three mutants slipped through it.

The last paused by the door. This smaller mutant didn't appear to be a misshapen horror show like Subject Zero, but neither was she human any more. Not with those enlarged pupils, elongated femurs and reversed knee joints. Her skin had morphed into a pseudo carapace-armor. Her entire form radiated danger. One of her arms ended at the wrist.

She slipped through the door and was gone.

The single remaining sentry swiveled and wobbled, emitting a slight whirring noise as it tried to calibrate on the six Solarans who remained. It stood between them and the door, and it was still armed.

"Be still!" Elya froze.

The six of them were arranged around the room, trying to use the pieces of neutralized robot spheres to shield themselves as they studied the final sentry.

"Anyone got any bright ideas?" Yorra whispered.

The bot swiveled from Ruby to Sticks to Park, the barrel of its single center-mounted gun shimmering as it emanated residual heat.

"Uhhh," he said eloquently.

Did I see a Telos-made blade somewhere? Elya's eyes darted around the room.

Hedgebot flashed a soft orange light where it hid behind the explosive-damaged orb in front of him. Not a dangerous red, but a subtle orange. A hint. He finally spotted a sword with a curved handle. Its arm-length blade was stuck under the damaged bot. Elya bent slowly down, grabbed the handle, and tilted the blade up.

The dead sentry bot rolled forward and drew the attention of the remaining active sentry bot, which lay in front of him about five meters.

Charging across the gap, Elya leaped up as the first plasma bolt flew beneath him, kicked off the wall, and swung the sword vertically toward the sentry. Its round shell split open. It swiveled toward him, trying to defend itself, but he danced away, narrowly avoiding eating two blaster bolts that fizzled out against the wall behind him. Elya hacked down again, and this time the blade buried itself in the bot's metal shell, getting stuck. Shouting angrily, Park fired his blaster into the robot's exposed crystal innards. Repeatedly. Elya staggered back, shielding his face, as Park kept firing and firing. Eventually, the violent robot slowed to a halt. Park continued to squeeze the trigger long after it lay still.

"Hold your fire, Innovesh!" Yorra shouted.

The man finally stopped pulling the trigger. The robot didn't move. Yorra reached for Naab's wrist, then gently pried the gun from his fingers. He wheezed as he leaned against her.

"He's had too much stim," Sticks observed.

"Shut up," Yorra spat.

"Cool it," Ruby said. "Is anyone hurt?"

"We need to go after Zero," said Elya.

"Cool your jets, Fancypants," Ruby said. "They're on the run. Chasing them now isn't a winning strategy. We almost bought it just now."

Yorra rotated one wrist and winced, but stubbornly held her silence while Park leaned against her. A blaster bolt had grazed Hairpin's thigh, but as was typically the case with blaster fire, hits that didn't penetrate merely burned several layers of skin along a straight path, so he could still move on it. Elya himself was shaky and the scratches on his chest stung, but they were shallow and only bleeding a little. Four red lines ran below his left clavicle, the thick vac suit material around it torn open.

"We have to get moving or they're going to get to the relic first," Elya said. "Hedgebot'll sense danger before any of us do. He can scout ahead."

Hedgebot glowed a soft blue from the doorway.

"Look, he's saying it's clear," Elya said. The corridor they entered was about half the size of the one through which they'd come. It went about twenty meters before curving to the right and upward. He had no idea where he was going, and unless the mutants did, they'd eventually have to come back out the same way they went in.

"Why don't we wait for them to come back?" Ruby said. "Set a trap here. Sticks, you still have munitions?"

"A few."

"We rig the door. They have to come back through here to leave."

"Unless there's another route to the hangar we missed," said Yorra.

"Which is likely," Nevers added. "Regardless, that's not the mission."

Ruby glared at him.

"You're welcome to call Captain Osprey and confirm if you want to," Elya said evenly.

Ruby chewed on that. "Negative."

Elya dropped the sword he was still holding. He would be more comfortable with the blaster, and that blade was remarkably heavy. MOXA would undoubtedly claim it, once this was all over, anyway. "We still outnumber them two to one. And those little ones? The ones who looked like children?" He hadn't discussed the mutants with Ruby, Sticks or Hairpin, not like he had with his friends. Yorra and Park understood the situation because they had been there in the

City. Flight 4 hadn't been. "Don't be fooled. They're Kryl, not human. Don't hesitate."

Ruby and both her lieutenants nodded slowly.

They hurried down the corridor after the mutants with Hedgebot speeding before them. Nevers changed Hedgebot's LED light settings so the bot's signals were dialed to the minimum, so as not to give away their position. He also extended its sensors as far out as they would go and used Hedgebot primarily to scout around corners and into new rooms.

There was no biodegradable material, but they found countless bladed weapons and projectile weapons, scientific equipment that looked like scales, and what seemed to be laboratories. Many of the rooms were built for exceedingly tall creatures, and he had time to marvel at how the Telos must have been both much larger than he imagined—in which case even they'd feel cramped on this ship—and built to climb.

It also got him thinking back about the Telos temples and structures he'd been in. Like all of their temples, no two were the same. Xenoanthropologists theorized this was according to some religious principle, or maybe variety was the spice of life to the Telos. The cave on Robichar was on the simple end of the spectrum, while the City in the asteroid was far more complex.

What kind of reason would there be for that difference? As he'd learned talking to Chronicle, their temples were safe houses, but also held religious significance. Was this ship built for the same purpose? It was a good theory. He wished he could bring Chronicle here so he could ask about it.

Hedgebot skidded back into view suddenly, sliding around a corner before careening to a stop by Elya's ankles. He flashed a dim red.

"Quiet," Elya whispered, putting a finger across his lips. "Hedgebot found something."

He crouched and padded around the corner, letting Hedgebot lead him. The small bot paused at a large doorway that opened into a vast circular chamber that rose as far as his eye could see—hundreds, maybe even a thousand meters, straight up.

In the center of the room was the trunk of a great crystalline structure. A tree as thick as a small starship. Made of that transparent crystal, but growing branches of many earthen colors, and flowered with an overgrown, tangled abundance of colorful leaves and bushes.

All six of them stopped and stared upward. Elya had the sense that they'd come to the very heart of the starship.

He'd been on many starships before, but had seen nothing quite like this. As he studied it, he realized the tree doubled as a nexus. It connected the trunk to various other levels extended upward through the outer layer of the cylindrical starship.

Branches were large and sufficiently plentiful that climbing up would be tiresome, but simple. What looked like a kind of main path led from the floor up in a spiral. The enormous chamber was lit by the ambient glow of the alloy walls, but the crystal material making up the tree itself *also* glowed from within, mixing soft green and gold-tinted light. Similar to the halls through which they'd passed, the light was soft, like the starship lived in its own eternal twilight.

This was the first true confirmation for Elya that whoever built this starship had also been responsible for constructing the City hidden in the asteroid. Same materials, different designs. But based on everything he'd seen in this place, as well as in the City, it was clearly Telos in origin.

And now he knew, without a shred of doubt, that the

Telos had been climbers. Perhaps they'd designed this starship after their home environment.

Not a starship lost to time, then. A *tree*ship.

"I'll bet they're up at the top of the treeship somewhere," Elya said. "Hedgebot must have heard movement or he wouldn't have rushed back to find us. You ready?"

His friends nodded, hefting their weapons. Hedgebot scurried directly up the trunk before dashing outward on a thick branch. Elya clambered up onto the footpath and climbed into the foliage.

THIRTY-ONE

After the Furies punched through the final defensive shell and went dark on comms, the Kryl changed tactics.

The core of the swarm formed a tight barrier around the organism, while the rest divided into two factions and alternated attacks against Admiral Kira Miyaru's forces.

She reacted at once, pulling the Knife's corvettes out of their advanced striking maneuver, and putting her heavy cruisers and destroyers into elongated defensive firing positions so that the armada formed a spearhead that allowed them to engage the Kryl on both sides. Using a combination of the broadside cannons on the destroyers, the railguns on the cruisers, and liberal deployment of warheads from the corvettes, she prevented the Solaran forces from getting surrounded.

As was typical when the Fleet fought any Kryl force, the Solaran ships were greatly outnumbered. For every Kryl annihilated, another six flew forward to take its place. Though the Kryl preferred a mass of smaller ships to the destroyer-sized vessels, the xenos were like the mythical hydra... they reared a thousand hidden heads from hiding places in the broken planet.

And Overmind X continued to evade detection.

The Kryl attacks had their intended effect. Kira couldn't advance any farther as long as she was forced into a defensive position by wave after wave of Kryl attacks. And they couldn't win the war unless they eliminated Overmind X.

"Harmony!" Kira ordered. "Find me a path in there to bust that shell open! They're just using their overwhelming numbers to buy time."

"Y-yes, Admiral," stuttered Harmony. "C-calculating."

Kira's eyebrows knit together as the *Paladin of Abniss* rocked to the side, sending those not buckled in—like Kira—staggering and reaching for support. Several officers on the bridge shouted in surprise or fear as Kira struggled to stay standing.

"What the devil was that?" Colonel Volk demanded. "Report!"

"A gunship just destroyed itself by flying into our shields at full speed, Colonel," Harmony announced to the bridge. Her swirling lights tried to form her androgynous personage and ended up with a flickering purple-and-blue hunchback form instead.

"We've lost our portside forward cannon," reported the weapons officer.

"Why didn't the shields work?" Kira asked.

"They went down a moment after Harmony began running her route calculations," said Volk.

"You seem to be correct," Harmony confirmed, without a hint of remorse.

Harmony, what the hell is going on? Kira thought at the shipmind, taking the conversation private so as not to worry the crew. Though Volk shot her an anxious glance.

"Sorry, Admiral," Harmony said. "I seem to be experiencing some technical difficulties."

Belay my previous order, Kira said, not wanting to continue a process that had caused such an issue. *Run self-diagnostic.*

"As you wish, sir."

Kira called Volk over.

"We have engineers shoring up the hull," he said. "They hit us in the same spot the photon cannon struck before."

Kira cursed. Overmind X knew how to pick her flagship out of the armada, and now she was resorting to kamikaze attacks in weak areas. Kira couldn't afford to have her flagship lamed in the middle of the battle.

"Send engineers to reinforce the shields. Focus their efforts in areas around the defensive laser array and missile launchers."

Volk nodded and turned to his engineering officer to relay the orders.

Kira opened a new tightbeam. "Seba, are you in position?"

"Almost, sir," the Knife said.

While her heavies drew into a defensive position, she'd ordered a portion of the Corvette group to pull back, then jump out and around to flank the Kryl—and give Overmind X a taste of her own medicine. It had taken an hour because they had to jump way out to avoid being detected, then jump back in behind the Kryl and maneuver at sublight speeds to come around behind them, using the angle of Elturis's star to conceal their approach as much as possible. Overmind X would realize the ruse eventually, seeing as how she'd done the same to bring her forces to the broken planet, but by that point she'd be forced to pull her attacking forces back to defend her rear line.

"Autodiagnosis complete," Harmony said. "The previous attacks by the photon cannon seem to have damaged my processing systems. To solve it, I've limited myself to a smaller number of concurrent tasks."

"How did you not catch this before?" Kira demanded.

"Scans showed the damage did not pose a high enough threat risk, and our engineers had limited time. I asked them to prioritize repairs to the crew's atmosphere and artificial gravity, while de-prioritizing my own needs."

"Lot of good that does me now," Kira growled. "Have you reduced your background operations already?"

"Yes, admiral, I have three workstreams free at the moment."

"Double check the corvette group's approach vector," Kira said. She didn't doubt Seba's ability to navigate his ships. She just wanted to test Harmony on something with relatively little risk before she trusted her with the lives of her crew again.

The battle raged on. In another test for Harmony, Kira ordered the AI to run a munitions burndown chart and had her weapons officer double-check it manually.

"It seems accurate, sir," the weapons officer reported.

"Volk, I need you to communicate this to the rest of the armada. They're to hold the line until the corvettes get into position, then attack all at once. Tell them to use their shipminds to dole out the ammunition carefully and make it last as long as possible. I don't want them to run out of ammo or fuel before the Furies return with that relic."

Kira anxiously checked the broadbeam for any sign of a report from Captain Osprey and was disappointed to find nothing.

Had they perished after going into that rift? Had they found Subject Zero, or the so-called 'starship lost to time' they presumed would be there?

She'd never know what happened until they dislodged the Kryl from around the anomaly and sent a scout through. It wasn't unusual for the Kryl to jam their comms. Something about their psionic communication was like ansible communication, and if they broadcast enough noise, it could sometimes be hard to use their systems. But she'd never seen it happen like this, where comms cut out completely. Normally, they'd just be drowned in static.

"I don't believe the Kryl are using their psionic ability to jam our signal," Harmony said, reading her thoughts. The AI had reformed her androgynous hologram. It wasn't deformed anymore.

"Are you sure?" Kira asked, still suspicious.

"I don't detect any noise from the Overmind except what they're using to communicate with each other."

"Admiral," Seba called through a tightbeam. "We're in position. Three minutes to contact."

"Relay those orders, Colonel Volk."

"Yessir!"

Seba and several dozen corvettes cut down and accelerated toward the knot of Kryl still holding tight around the rift, blocking Kira's view of the anomaly.

She called the xenoscientists on her comms and made sure that they had their eyes fixed on the view.

Rather than risk firing a nuclear warhead again, the corvettes were ordered to use their lasers to burn through the Kryl forces, and then rely on their superior speed to draw their defenses out.

It didn't work as Kira expected. To her surprise, before the corvettes even reached them, the organism split itself into a dozen spherical sections, and darted out under drone escort in as many directions, staying close to the surface of the broken planet, but no longer trying to defend the event horizon, which was held open by a much smaller Kryl organism that had glommed onto it somehow.

"Where is Overmind X?" Kira demanded of the xenoscientists.

"We can't tell, admiral," Dr. Lumago responded. "She must be in one of those… satellites."

Kira punched a fist into the palm of the other hand, glaring at the dozen spheres on her lidar readout. So she wanted to play a shell game, huh?

"Harmony, your best guess?"

"No prediction available, Admiral."

A squadron of Kryl drones flew toward the rift and disappeared through it, something she could see now since Kryl defenses were no longer blocking her camera views. Her blood went cold. Colonel Volk looked up, and she locked eyes with him.

"We need to contact the Furies and get a timeline," Kira said.

"Aye, sir. I'll assemble a small recon force," he said. He began speaking over the broadbeam, pulling seven flights of starfighters away from positions that could spare them. It would take them a while to reach the rift, for each time they approached, the Kryl forces attacked them vigorously.

"Target those organism fragments," Kira told her weapons officer. "Harmony, move us into position."

She flipped her comms to speak to the xenoscientists again. "I need to know which one she's hiding in!"

"We don't know, Admiral. There's no way the equipment we have can detect her. If we had some kind of x-ray, maybe, but even then it's a longshot."

Frickin' Kryl, Kira thought. Overmind X was in one of those organism satellites. She just knew it. But now she had to play hide-and-seek while also fighting the rest of the battle *and* trying to get the Furies out of that rift alive.

This was exactly what made the Kryl so dangerous in

space battles: their ability to wage war on multiple fronts simultaneously, controlled from a single mind that had the use of millions of different eyeballs. Instantaneous psionic communication made even the most rapid ansible relay move at a snail's pace. For all their coordination and training, the Solaran Fleet was made of individuals, whereas the Kryl were a single organism working without delay between thought and action.

That was the main reason the shipminds had been put to use piloting Fleet vessels. Faster computation and reaction times made a massive difference in these engagements.

There's only one thing left to do, Kira thought.

She checked the munitions burndown chart to ensure the armada had enough firepower left for what she planned to do next. The chart said they had about three more hours at the anticipated rate of use. She hoped to Animus they wouldn't need it all. The Kryl didn't really care if they ran out of ammunition. They would just start slamming their ships into Solaran vessels. Kryl never questioned those orders because they came from a single mind—and Overmind X had enough units to spare. If the armada ran out of weapons, they'd never be able to withstand the onslaught. It would be like a billion killer ants swarming over the carcass of a lame wolf. One, two, even five attacks, her larger ships could withstand. But if the winner was determined by the last-ship-standing, sheer numbers would overwhelm the Solarans.

Kira performed one more check with engineering before she gave the order.

"The damage isn't critical," the sergeant in charge reported. "It's a mess down here, but Harmony sealed the area, so it should be safe to jump if we need to."

Can you fly? Kira asked Harmony.

"Yes, Admiral."

Don't let me down, old friend, she thought. "Volk, I want you on manual backup." Kira pointed to the command couch.

Any of the crew could pilot the destroyer if they had to. It was slower and more cumbersome, but always possible to override the shipmind's control.

"Aye, sir," he said, sinking into the thick cushion and cinching the straps tight around his lap and shoulders.

Kira opened the broadbeam to the entire armada and gave the order. Harmony and the other destroyers, piloted by shipminds of their own, advanced. The heavy cruisers rotated out and met the Kryl head on.

She lost two heavy cruisers, a destroyer, six light cruisers, and five corvettes over the course of the next half hour as the armada pushed forward to gain access to the only strategic asset in this battle—the rift. Maneuvering so close to the broken planet was risky, but they avoided getting struck by any planetoids.

She took several more devastating losses before she got close enough to make her next move. Kira hardened her heart and focused on the job.

With a prayer to Animus and her fingers crossed, Kira deployed a single tiny probe toward the anomaly. That craft was small and harmless, and as a result it was expected to slip through the Kryl's remaining, scattered defenses with ease.

The entire crew held their breath as the probe approached.

As soon as it passed through the rift, the camera feed cut to black.

"Now we know for sure it wasn't Overmind X interfering with our comms. It's the wormhole."

It's programmed to fly back through and report, right? Kira asked Harmony.

"That is correct," the shipmind said. "Although I'm not

clear if it will be able to. Its sensors weren't built to detect event horizon anomalies like this one, and we don't know what it looks like from the other side."

Earth's last lights, Kira thought darkly. She hoped her gambit would pay off.

THIRTY-TWO

Casey was halfway back to the rift with sixteen fighters trailing behind her when her HUD beeped in warning. She swerved to dodge shrapnel.

"Watch out!" she said reflexively, though it probably wasn't necessary. Every pilot's automated warning systems would be screeching at them like hers was.

Bobbing and weaving by instinct, she avoided the worst of the debris. "Sixty seconds out, Fuzz," she said as she barrel-rolled to port to avoid a tumbling drone wing, then pulled up to let a severed fuselage pass by. It was still steaming and venting liquid that froze immediately upon contact with the empty vacuum.

The shrapnel was the first sign that Blue Team's trap had worked. As drones emerged from the rift, they were picked apart by blaster fire. The shards left after they'd flown through the gauntlet went tumbling toward Casey and the rest of the Furies, who were hurrying back to aid with the defense.

Unfortunately, the smaller shrapnel they couldn't avoid drained her shields unnecessarily. She ordered the Sabres tailing her to split off and go around the bulk of it on a vector away from their target. This would save their shields, but take them a few seconds longer—a few seconds that may be the difference between life and death for Blue Team's starfighters.

"Fifty-five seconds," Casey sounded off, reading the number from her HUD.

"Our position's getting too hot," said Fuzz. "We've got to take evasive action."

"Lead them around the back of the rift away from us."

"Copy that," Fuzz said.

It was then that, instead of shrapnel and pieces of Kryl ships, the first full drone appeared, a straggler who had somehow gotten through Fuzz's team's crossfire and noticed her group.

It seemed to fly erratically, too. It targeted first Casey, and then another Sabre off her left wing before coming back to her, like it couldn't decide who to shoot at first.

"You see that?" Casey asked. Two Green Team skippers with sharp eyes confirmed.

Kryl never hesitated or showed any sign of indecision—unless they coordinated it. She easily locked her targets on this drone, released a missile, and veered around the explosion of guts and shell.

"Too easy," she muttered, immediately suspicious. Casey flew on, putting the drone's erratic behavior to the side and focusing once again on helping her people. "Thirty-five seconds."

"We've lost two so far. I've got drones hot on my six!" Fuzz said, "Whew. Thanks," he said to another pilot, who must have helped him get clear of the drones. "Raptor, I think I just saw a probe come through the rift in my rearview."

"Where?" Casey asked. But one hand was already flying

across the controls on her dashboard, quickly picking out the probe.

Ident signals confirmed the probe was Solaran. Pelaux-2, to be precise. That meant that Admiral Miyaru must be trying to reach them. But without working comms, if she wanted to contact the armada, she'd have to go through the rift.

She didn't look upon the prospect with pleasure, but accepted it as her duty. Going through the first time had been nauseating and weird, but the Admiral needed to know what was going on.

She designated command of Red Team to the next highest ranking pilot, thankful now that she'd learned everyone's names and flight records more intimately. Something she used to agonize over had become second nature.

Since the same indecision marked the drones who came through the rift now as the one they'd destroyed before, her starfighters easily drew several more apart, dodging their attacks and delivering killing blows as they came down the line of advancing Sabres.

She told Fuzz what she was planning and changed her course.

"Copy that," he said. "Now that we have reinforcements, I think we can hold them. Furies, on me!"

Casey landed shots on four more drones herself before aiming her Sabre toward the wormhole and punching it. She came out the other side with a mouthful of bile. She tried to orient her Sabre. It was complete chaos on this side. The Kryl structure was nowhere to be found, which surprised her. However, a dozen smaller organisms of the same material now orbited the anomaly like it was a tiny sun.

She signaled the *Paladin of Abniss.*

"Captain Osprey," came the Admiral's voice. "Finally. Were you able to get your comms fixed?"

"They never broke, sir," Casey said. "They just can't transmit through the rift. I came back to report."

"That confirms our theory. Was the probe destroyed?"

"No, sir. Is it going to record and take measurements inside the wormhole? MOXA will definitely want to see what's on the other side, and I don't know how long that thing will stay open."

"My robotics officers aren't confident in its ability to navigate back through the event horizon. We may need your help leading it."

While the admiral spoke, Casey had to dodge several projectiles, more debris—which she was really getting tired of—and put distance between herself and a few different gunships floating nearby.

She examined her HUD, then danced away from a group of corvettes that were engaging the Kryl equivalent of heavy cruisers—larger than gunships, with side-mounted cannons that shot large pellets of uranium at them, like a railgun but radioactive and somewhat slower. Those shots would eat through shields if they were traveling at the right velocity, and hers were already dangerously low on power.

"Were you able to locate the relic?" asked Admiral Miyaru.

"Not yet, sir," Casey said. "We found the Telos starship, though. Fancypants is pursuing the mutants, and he took five other pilots with him to board the ship. The rest of us were called back to defend the rift when more drones started pouring through."

"Then what the Earth are you doing back here without your squad, captain?"

"Requesting reinforcements, sir! The Kryl have units to lose, and we don't have enough firepower to keep them at bay forever."

"We're getting closer. My destroyer should be in a position to cut off passage through the wormhole soon."

"How soon?"

"Hopefully within the hour. Can you hold the rift until then?"

Casey swallowed a groan.

"I've got several flights coming to assist you," the admiral went on. "The Kryl are making it difficult for us to maneuver. And we still haven't figured out which organism fragment Overmind X is hiding in."

Ah, Casey thought. *So that must be what those little spheres orbiting the anomaly were.* Overmind X was playing a risky game of find-the-pea-in-the-shell with the remnants of her dismantled space base.

Casey took aim and shot at one. With the help of her targeting system, one of her blaster bolts hit a worker crawling across the outer surface as the object hurtled through space on a curving vector. But as soon as one fell off, another rose to take its place. They weren't nearly as good as energy shields, in Casey's humble opinion, but living armor that could detach itself if damaged could defend against Solaran attacks for quite some time.

"I see the problem, sir," Casey said. "What are your orders?"

"Make sure that the Furies get that relic before the mutants do! And if they don't, you make damn sure the relic doesn't come back through in enemy hands."

"Solid copy."

Her HUD pinged.

"I just sent you the location of the reinforcement flights that Volk deployed to help you out. Guide them through the rift and—stand by, Captain, I've got incoming."

The admiral closed the line without waiting for a response.

Casey didn't have time to be annoyed. Her HUD screeched at her, and she was forced to dodge a knot of hurtling uranium rounds.

She picked out the Sabres Admiral Miyaru had pinpointed. They were stuck on the other side of a mass of Kryl swirling in the distance to her nine o'clock. It looked like a group of gunships had engaged them. Casey couldn't get to them without significant risk to her personal safety, however—risk that would take her farther away from her squadron and the pilots relying on her.

She cursed as another group of six drones slipped past her and hurtled into the wormhole.

None of these drones showed any sign of the hesitancy they had on the other side. Was it because the Kryl had as much difficulty communicating through the rift as the Solarans did?

If that was true, maybe she had a chance. All she had to do was survive long enough for reinforcements to arrive.

Turning her nose around and dodging one of those Kryl satellites, she held her breath, accelerated and passed through the rift once again.

THIRTY-THREE

"This better be important, Aganaki," Kira growled into her mic as she braced against a console. Uranium shells were pummeling her destroyer, and though the shields still held, their energy augmented and reinforced by her engineering teams, the massive flagship shuddered with each impact.

"First you commandeer my people, then you strand me here!" Minister Aganaki sounded like a vein in his neck was about to pop. "You'll pay for this."

She grinned maliciously. "There are several ships in the region. I couldn't possibly leave the City unprotected with the Kryl so close."

"No ships I can access! And your Marines won't even let me leave."

Something caught her eye on the lidar feed. She glanced at Volk and gestured at a pocket of space, a gap between the Kryl line and theirs. He nodded and ordered the light cruiser group to turn fifteen degrees starboard and close the gap.

Animus, but that man needed his own command. She didn't show her appreciation for him often enough. He was the best tactician she'd ever known. Why had he stuck around as her executive officer for so long? If she'd put him in charge of the cruisers, she wouldn't have had to give that order to move up in the first place. He'd already have done it.

But, of course, she knew why. Her presence was a stalwart reminder to Volk to keep tight reins on his drinking problem. And he had. Volk never feared the Kryl. He never feared command. The only thing he feared was finding himself at the bottom of a bottle. He hadn't lost his lover in the war like she had, but he had lost his family in a nasty divorce of his own making.

Had Kira contributed to his stagnation by keeping him here? Had she enabled him? She vowed that if they made it out of this alive, she would see that he was given a command of his own. Kira caught her mind as it wandered too far into potential futures.

She forced her attention back to the conversation at hand. "You'd have figured this out hours ago, Aganaki," she growled. "Why are you calling me now?"

"I learned something new from Chronicle."

"See?" Kira said. "I didn't strand you there. I've just learned a thing or two about how to motivate a man like you."

After a moment, he asked, "What kind of man is that?"

"A servant of necessity."

She knew he would retaliate later, but by then, it wouldn't matter. "No doubt you asked Chronicle about how best to protect your interests. Either escaping the City, or protecting yourself somehow. So tell me, what did you learn?"

"Fine. Not because you deserve the information, but because my interests and the good of *all* of Solaran civilization are firmly aligned, I will tell you."

Yeah, whatever, you conniving serpent, Kira thought.

"Chronicle's crystal pylon," Minister Aganaki went on, "is

passive. It's primarily a storage mechanism and vehicle for information. But not all the relics work that way. As you know, the Prime Relic of Spirit—"

"Which one's that again?"

"The one currently attached to the crystal pylon," he said acidly. "The one we've been calling the geode. This one has defensive properties that are designed to protect its wielder from the Kryl by forcing them away. According to Chronicle, it functions by targeting the psionic wavelength on which the Kryl communicate, broadcasting a 'noise', so to speak, on that same wavelength that causes them physical pain."

"We already know that."

"We knew what it did, not how it worked," he complained.

"Talk faster. I'm fighting a war here."

"The photon cannon that the Kryl possess has offensive properties. That makes three types—offensive, defensive, and passive. According to Chronicle, one of the missing relics—the Prime Relic of Mind, which we believe may be located in this rift—is also defensive. It apparently causes a different effect. Instead of broadcasting on the psionic wavelength, it *blocks* transmission on the same wavelength, preventing the Kryl from being able to communicate with each other."

"Earth, but that would be useful," she muttered. She gestured to Volk. He put on a pair of headphones to listen in on the conversation. "That must be why Overmind X wants it so badly."

"Exactly. She needs to keep it out of our hands. Some of the relics she can use, but this one won't do anything but harm her. She wants to find it so she can destroy it, is my guess."

"Reasonable guess. Not that it makes much difference to our strategy."

"What, that's not enough *motivation* for you?" he sneered. "I thought you were trying to protect the Solaran people."

"Don't be a sore loser."

"I don't like being manipulated," he spat back.

"I know the feeling well." The way Aganaki had tricked Kira into a bad deal with the Colonization Board back on Ariadne still stung. *Jerk.*

He chuckled dryly.

"Do you have anything else, or can I be done with you yet?" Kira asked.

"Indeed, I do. And this is the really interesting part. The prime relics can be put together in different combinations to *augment* their effects. Assuming you can get the Prime Relic of Mind, for example, when used in combination with the Prime Relic of Spirit, the range of the two defensive relics greatly increases. I can't get exact numbers out of Chronicle, but he says their effects are increased a hundred times when used in combination."

Volk whistled, and he glanced over with a wolfish look in his eye. She knew what his tactician's mind was thinking. An effect with that kind of range could make a massive difference in this battle.

She asked several more questions about the relics and was relieved to learn that he believed the other offensive relic wasn't a ranged weapon like the photon cannon. Chronicle claimed it was a melee weapon with a supernaturally sharp blade. In that case, they could afford to be a little more aggressive.

"And you thought me stranding you there was a bad idea," Kira said.

"We still don't have all the relics. If Overmind X gets them first..."

"Let me worry about that."

Kira caught Volk's eyes. Once again, he read her thoughts.

They'd been together long enough. "You're one of the best leaders I know, Volk. Make the Fleet proud."

"Sir?"

"Your bridge, Colonel." Then Kira strode out of the room.

She sent a light cruiser to retrieve the geode from the City. On her way to meet him in the hangar, Kira tried and failed to reach Captain Osprey several times. The Furies—Captain Nevers in particular—had been frustrated when she'd held the geode relic back. It likely would have come in handy pursuing Subject Zero. But since the mutant had at least some immunity to it, it was too risky to send the relic into battle. Let alone put it on a Sabre. As they'd proven with the photon cannon, small craft were always among the highest casualties of a fight against the Kryl, and she wanted the relic kept safe until she was certain of the most strategically sound way to employ it.

Thanks to Aganaki, her patience had paid off. She knew now what to do with it, and precisely how it could help them.

She tried Captain Osprey again and failed to reach her on the ship's tightbeam.

Where the hell is that woman? Kira demanded.

"She'll be there," Harmony said.

You have that much faith in your coaching abilities?

"I am but a Fleet AI with damaged processing systems, Admiral. My confidence is in Captain Osprey."

And the rest of the Furies?

"Animus be with them," said Harmony.

It was the first time in all their years together that Harmony had ever expressed anything like faith. But she had to echo the sentiment.

May the Spirit of Old Earth be with us all.

THIRTY-FOUR

Hedgebot had no difficulties scampering up through the massive tree's branches, but the rest of them struggled to climb. Rough crystal handrails and other holds were plentiful, but overall the structure was not designed to be scaled by the human form. Rather, it seemed to be outfitted for creatures much larger, much stronger, and much more accustomed to climbing.

Still, the Solaran pilots were fit—the Fleet had made sure of that, and Elya pulled himself and shoved the others up a dozen floors in artificial gravity that was at least equivalent to Ariadne normal. As they neared the crown of the tree structure, which led off in several branches around and above them, Hedgebot spun and stood, pointing its body up to the final floor. He flashed a low, angry red—the color of danger.

Elya fumbled for his tab and quickly put the bot on no-glow stealth mode again.

He needn't have worried. Something flared brightly in the room above them. They watched shadows clash and move apart through a ceiling of hazy, translucent crystal. When the flash faded, the light dimmed considerably. A savage snarl preceded shouting and was punctuated by a yip of pain and a thunderous crash. Then blaster fire—one shot, and done—cut the noise to sudden silence.

The Furies stared at each other for a moment, shocked that something had incited the mutants above to violence against each other.

This is our chance, Elya thought. Hedgebot was already scampering up a curving ladder of oversized handholds. There was a hundred and eighty degree opening around the hollow they currently were hiding in.

"Wait—" Ruby hissed, but before she could get another word in, Park scrambled up the ladder after Hedgebot, with Yorra chasing and cussing behind him, while Elya ran across the room to the opposite side and ascended rapidly.

Six or eight pullups later, with his arms burning, he shoved himself into a frightening scene.

The one-handed mutant child held an old Fleet blaster pistol in her only hand. Her chest heaved as she pointed the barrel at Subject Zero's head.

The former pilot-turned-Kryl was standing across the room, holding himself upright by leaning against a round doorframe. A massive gash in his gut seeped blood. He gripped the wound shut with his hand, his fingers ruby-colored, wet and glistening.

The third mutant lay on her back just a few feet in front of Subject Zero. This one had both her hands, and she bore in them a knife of Telos alloy with a blade that was so thin it seemed to vanish into the air. When the blade twisted so it was precisely perpendicular to him, Elya caught a golden glimmer that reminded him of the photon cannon's razor-fine line.

Time slowed down. Elya's eyes bounced around, trying to figure out which one of the weapons was the Prime Relic of

Mind. He breathed in. Elya heard the rest of the Furies re-grip their blasters and take a half-step forward. Two against one odds and, this time, no blaster-wielding sentries to interfere.

Zero twitched. The skin around his eyes screwed up in pain and, perhaps, sorrow before he glanced down at the device in his free hand.

A geode made of the metallic Telos alloy.

In the drawn-out space of that frozen moment, Elya noted differences from the relic he'd retrieved on Robichar. The base of this one was not round, but octagonal. It didn't have a stone handle either. Zero was forced to grip it by its base. At first, Elya mistook the sharp crystal for a knife, like the one the mutant on the floor held. He quickly realized it wasn't a blade—it was a thin pyramid of crystal. Contained within the crystal was a long, thin needle.

Not a needle, he thought. Zero held the device upside down.

An antenna.

With a grimace, Subject Zero released the wound in his stomach, took the relic in both hands and twisted, activating it and emitting a bright green light.

Elya breathed out and squeezed his trigger.

Blaster fire filled the room. His first bolt slammed into the mutant's Kryl shoulder, knocking the relic from his blood-soaked hands.

A dozen more shots erupted at once, deafening Elya and throwing angles of red light across his vision. The one-handed mutant went down, the Furies flaying her with bolts from their rifles and blasters until she was nothing more than a burnt, smoking carcass.

Meanwhile, the two-handed mutant jumped to her feet and lunged after Zero, bearing her Telos blade and screaming. The mutant pilot staggered back, brushing his fingers across an object on his belt. His form shimmered as he phase-shifted, passing through the door against which he'd been leaning.

Gone.

The knife-wielding mutant ran into the solid alloy of the door and staggered back. She spun, snarling.

Elya had already started moving toward the geode on the floor. This had to be it. There was a small obelisk in the middle of the room where it could have been lying before they arrived. He dove forward, scooping up the geode before scrambling back.

She didn't attack. The knife-wielding mutant shook her head in confusion. Elya caught a brief look of panic on her face. Having used the other geode on Kryl, he was surprised she wasn't scrambling away in impossible pain from the green rays it emitted. But then he remembered that Overmind X had transformed human children into mutants precisely *because* they wouldn't be as affected by the Telos technology's targeting mechanism.

Yet, this new prime relic seemed to have some effect on the mutant child. Just not one that caused physical torment.

So it surprised him when she stepped forward with the knife.

Except then the mutant noticed her dead, smoking companion, skin bloody and blackened from taking so many blaster bolts at close range. Turning from Elya, she screamed and charged at the pilot standing between her and her dead companion.

Lieutenant Olara Yorra.

Elya gasped. He fumbled with the relic in one hand, his blaster pistol in the other.

But Park didn't hesitate. Hopped up on stim as he was, he probably didn't even think. He just reacted.

Lieutenant Innovesh Park stepped in front of Yorra at the

last second. That terrible knife with the unnaturally thin blade rammed into his solar plexus and sliced through his ribcage near his heart.

The mutant sliced Park a second time in the other direction before Elya's blaster bolt took her in the face, blowing off her lower jaw. Ruby fired next, a bolt which slammed into the mutant's hip. A second shot took her in the head, blowing her brains out the back of her skull.

Lieutenant Park didn't suffer for long. With his lap covered in blood and gore from the X-shaped wound in his abdomen, he fought for breath for only a few moments. Yorra gathered him in her arms and began to weep.

"I love you," Park mouthed, though no sound came out. He coughed, choking on his own blood, before exhaling one final time and going still.

"I love you, too," Yorra said. "Please, don't! Stay with me. Innovesh! Innovesh, I love you too."

The room was quiet for a long minute except for the sound of Yorra's heaving sobs.

With a roar, Elya hurled the Prime Relic of Mind at the door Subject Zero had disappeared through. It bounced off, then rolled on the floor, unaffected.

He stood with his eyes closed for a moment before retrieving the relic his friend had died for, feeling ridiculous. Then he picked up the knife and tried to cut through the door. But the Telos alloy repelled even the Prime Relic of … stupid atomic blades.

Subject Zero didn't come back out. And though he searched for ten minutes, Elya couldn't find a switch to open the door. Both relics seemed to be useless for that.

He held them up and regarded the objects. The octagonal alloy base out of which a crystal antenna rose, and the curved Telos knife.

They'd better be worth the cost.

THIRTY-FIVE

Casey closed the tightbeam line to Captain Nevers and closed her eyes. Twin tears tracked down her cheeks and her breathing was shallow.

Naab, dead? How could it be?

She didn't want to believe it, but Nevers and Yorra wouldn't lie. Not about something like this. Fancypants had contacted her as soon as she came back through the rift, but she couldn't answer until she fought her way to a safe space. Now, she was glad she'd waited, because the sorrow that overtook her was too much to fly with. She disengaged her thrusters for a moment and let herself drift.

This wasn't just another pilot lost under her command. This wasn't just another Fury whose life had burned up in the atmosphere of this Kryl engagement.

Park was her *friend*. And that hurt worse than any loss so far. She hadn't experienced this kind of bone-deep sorrow since her mother died. To lose someone close to you was like losing a part of yourself.

And then the anger arrived. Rage, like a great sizzling blaster bolt of the soul. Casey should have been there with them. Knowing she'd made the right call as squadron commander didn't help one Earth-damned bit.

She kicked her thrusters back on and shoved the throttle forward, navigating back into the rift to get the reinforcements Admiral Miyaru had promised.

If they were going to lose this many outstanding pilots, those Kryl would *pay*.

"There you are!" Admiral Miyaru said the moment she pinged back in. "Change of plans. Get your ass to the flagship's hangar right now. I'll give you further instructions upon arrival."

"Sir? What about the reinforcements?"

"Just fly!"

Harmony swirled inside her cockpit as she raced toward the *Paladin of Abniss*.

"Harmony, what's going on?"

"The admiral is adjusting to new information."

"What new information? I didn't even get to tell her what the Furies found."

"What did you find?" Harmony asked. "I can relay it to her."

"We found the prime relic they were looking for. Two of the mutants are dead, and Subject Zero is fatally wounded, a deep slash to the gut that will surely kill him, though the pilots can't reach him now." Her throat constricted, and she choked on the next words. "We lost Naab. He's gone." She got control of herself with an effort of will. "They're bringing his body back for a proper burial."

"I am sorry, Captain, but I have to ask. There's more than one mutant?"

"Apparently we didn't rescue all the children."

"Oh, dear," Harmony said. "Bad news, indeed. One more thing, Captain. When you go back through the wormhole, make sure someone helps that probe find its way back. It seems to have gotten lost."

"Time seems to travel slightly faster on this side of the rift." Casey had seen how much the armada had moved in the time she'd gone through. "Maybe it's just a weird temporal delay due to the nature of the rift."

"Perhaps. I will examine it. You're coming up on the *Abniss* now, I'll see you inside."

"Got it."

"And Captain?"

"Yeah?"

"I can tell by your biorhythms that you don't feel good about what's happened, and that's understandable. But you found the relic and commanded a squadron with no backup. That deserves a moment's recognition."

"Mission's not over yet," she said.

"No, it is not. I just wanted you to hear it from me. May Animus speed you and the rest of the Furies to safe harbor."

The shipmind vanished before she could respond. It left her shaken and hollowed out. She didn't deserve any congratulations.

Whatever weird glitches Harmony had experienced before seemed to be resolved and that, at least, was positive. Casey soon set her Sabre down inside the *Paladin of Abniss'* hangar, which was abuzz with activity. Hundreds of Sabres and corvettes were landing to refuel, while hundreds more exited through the hangar's thin atmospheric barrier. To the untrained eye, it was chaos. To her, it was at least rushed and frantic. The armada had established itself in a defensible region of space near the rift, and every starfighter nearby, whether they were stationed on this destroyer or not, was rotating back for re-outfitting.

Casey popped her canopy and climbed out. When her boots hit the floor, she was surprised to find Admiral Miyaru already approaching. Her cadre of crimson-armored guards, who normally accompanied her any time she was out of her quarters or off the bridge, were nowhere to be seen; they must have been redeployed to other more desperate regions of the battle. Instead, a handful of MOXA xenoscientists in white coats hurried along at her heels like obedient pups.

Admiral Miyaru shoved a small object into her hand.

It was a Telos relic. The geode.

The xenoscientists had waved down some mechanics nearby. They immediately began welding a metal ring to the underside of her Sabre's fuselage, near the nose.

"Why are you giving me this?" Casey asked.

"Harmony told me Captain Nevers obtained another prime relic. The two work together. I need you to take it to him."

"Send someone else." Casey hung her head.

"What for?"

"Lieutenant Park is dead. At least two others, probably more by now. I failed them. Send someone else."

Admiral Miyaru gripped Casey's shoulders in her powerful hands. They squeezed and braced her as she bent against turbulent emotional headwinds. "This is war. I'm sorry about your friend, but you can't give up now. If you give up, Lieutenant Park's death is for nothing."

Casey straightened the rest of the way on her own and gazed up at the Admiral's face, blinking away the shameful water in her eyes.

A wave of grief swept through Casey again, making her stomach twist and her fingers tingle. "Yessir," she said, fighting to match the admiral's tone, her determination and strength. "Sorry. You're right."

"Nothing to be sorry for. Now, listen closely. If the relic Captain Nevers found is the one we think, it will pair with this one. Connect them together and activate them *both*.

Once combined, their effects will co-mingle and their range will be greatly expanded."

Casey's mind churned, and the admiral gave her a moment to process. Finally, she asked, "How far?"

"Unclear, but even back when the Telos faced them, the Kryl were a spacefaring species. So it seems these weapons—these prime relics, as we've been calling them—were designed to be used both planetside and spaceside in a battle. Given that the Telos have forgotten more about space travel than we may ever know, I am hoping we'll be able to use them to our advantage. To end this once and for all."

Casey felt her eyes widen and her jaw clench. A fresh wave of energy swept through her, washing away the grief—at least for the moment. "To make the Kryl *pay*."

The admiral nodded sharply, ignoring the way Casey, caught up in the moment, forgot to add "sir."

"Exactly." Admiral Miyaru glanced at the mechanics. They'd finished welding the ring and were now attaching a clear aluminite bubble, then sprayed in a liquid foam insulation from a can. "When you've got the relics, activate them and throw them in there, then lead your squadron back through the rift."

"How do we put the relics together?"

"Don't know. We couldn't test it. Captain Nevers will figure that out."

"Got it. Thank you, Admiral." Casey climbed back up into her Sabre.

"Captain!"

"Yes, sir?"

"Give 'em hell."

THIRTY-SIX

Omar phased through the closed door and sagged to the floor, the impact of his knees causing blood to gush as his human hand slipped from the wound in his stomach.

A knot of white worms spilled out. He gathered up his intestines and carefully stuffed them back into his gut with shaking hands. Air wheezed through laboring lungs. His vision blackened at the edges, but he held on and maintained consciousness through sheer spite.

The pain of his wounds, and the headache that continued to slam repeatedly into the back of his forehead, didn't matter anymore. Neither did the new relic he'd lost, nor the mutant twins he'd abandoned in the fight.

Only his memories remained.

He could see Kira's face now, her short hair golden as dawning daylight. Soft brown eyes and full lips.

He knew the sacrifice he'd made to save her. To save all of Solaran civilization from the Kryl.

And he knew how his mission had gone wrong.

As a last resort, Omar had flown into Kryl space alone.

The plan was for him to land on Planet K and sneak an antimatter bomb into the Queen Mother's lair, using the Prime Relic of Attraction—though no one knew that's what it was at the time—to disguise the weapon so he could get close enough to strike the killing blow. He'd set the bomb on a timer, planning to detonate it once he exited the atmosphere.

The Queen Mother tricked him, trapping him on the planet, and Omar had no choice but to set off the bomb. She retreated deep underground to shield herself from the blast, but there was no way for Omar to escape in time. However, due to the relic's ability to absorb energy and modify matter —in other words, to grow and change through rapid genetic modification—the blast splintered the Kryl hive queen in twain and gave birth to Overmind X.

Overmind X was the first and only Overmind to ever splinter from the Queen Mother and create her own swarm, free from the Queen Mother's influence or control.

Overmind X had then sewn Omar back together, using the relic to rebuild his arm and jaw. It had been horrible for him, but mostly he didn't remember the details. Only the pain. It had taken *years* to recover, and years more for Overmind X to raise her own brood. After that, their hunt for the rest of the prime relics began.

He didn't want to remember any more of that, so as he fought to stay awake, his mind wandered back to something else—or rather, some*one*.

Kira Miyaru. Her muscular legs wrapped around his waist. Her smiling, sun-kissed face. She had once been his squadmate, his lover, and his best friend.

She was the reason he'd felt a spark of recognition when they encountered each other in the hidden Telos City in Elturis. Why he'd hesitated instead of attacking her, as Overmind X wanted. He hadn't understood at the time, not while Overmind X had been suppressing his memories.

Yet his love for her had caused him to hesitate. He was sure of it. Thinking of her now made his vision blur. Tears ran down his cheeks and into his horribly disfigured mouth.

After a time—Minutes? Hours?—his memory of Kira gave him enough strength to stagger to his feet. Omar nearly fell again, his knees quaking, but with a sudden desperation, he stayed upright.

Although he'd failed in his last mission as a starfighter pilot, and though he'd been used as a pawn by Overmind X to gain Telos relics and create shameful abominations out of children—*Animus forgive me, children!*—he wasn't dead yet.

And as long as there was some fight left in him, there was a chance to make things right. But how?

Omar looked around the room in which he found himself, searching for some way to atone for his sins.

His heart fell. There was nothing in this room. No weapons, no visible control panels, no additional treasures. Nothing he could use to make a difference, to attack Overmind X or disrupt the battle raging beyond the rift. Nothing even to kill himself with, since his blaster was on the other side of a door he dare not open. He laughed suddenly. Nevermind. All he had to do was wait and his wounds would kill him. The only satisfaction in that prospect was that dying here would certainly deprive Overmind X of the relic on his person.

But he didn't want to die. It wasn't enough. He wanted to finish his original mission. To save Kira, and by doing so, save the rest of the Solaran people.

The room he stood in was oddly shaped. Not round, but full of curving nooks and crannies. The ceiling was carved as if it capped the crown of a bushy tree. Thick, winding ridges rose along the wall and twisted overhead.

He noticed all lines led to a central point. Or rather, to a kind of rotunda, though it hung upside down from his view.

He walked over, still holding his stomach wound with one hand, and examined it from below, craning his neck to see better. The ridges were more pronounced here, extending down and creating a kind of sling. In the center of the sling hung a crystal obelisk, like the one they'd found in the Telos asteroid, only set into the ceiling.

"That's odd," he croaked, "I wonder..."

Holding his stomach with one hand, Omar hopped up and grabbed a small ridge with his powerful Kryl hand, which had twice the muscle mass and perhaps five times the strength of any human limb. Extending spider legs from his back, he rotated his body and used the extra limbs to pull himself into the oversized sling. He exhaled sharply, resting into it, the crystal pylon hanging down by his face within arm's reach.

From this perspective, the room made more sense. The ceiling sloped down from this central point to a half dozen other nooks with handholds and crystal obelisks of varying shapes and sizes. Stylized as inverted boughs of a branch, the nooks must have been cubicles for officers on a starship's bridge.

He reached for the angled face of the crystal obelisk and hesitated. Most of the Telos relics he'd tried to use had been booby trapped. Would this one finish the job of killing him as soon as he touched it?

He looked around the room again and failed to see what he had left to lose.

He activated the phase shifter and passed his hands through the relic a few times. Nothing happened. When the phase shifter reset, he used his free hand to feel around the edge of the crystal. It didn't shock him or throw him across the room with kinetic force. If it was booby trapped, he would have expected to set it off by now. This room had been closed off, with the prime relic hiding out in the lobby beyond. So, no booby trap.

Probably.

Still, it didn't seem to have any buttons to turn it on, and touching it with his Kryl hand hadn't made anything happen.

Wait a minute.

With a groan of pain, he switched which hand was holding his gut wound closed. Omar was then free to lay his blood-coated human hand across the angled face of quartz.

Despite his injury, he felt nothing but sheer excitement as the pylon activated, a soft green light glowing from within. He was rewarded with a soft humming sound.

How do I work this thing?

The walls of the room immediately softened to transparent, showing him a view of space beyond. His mandibles clicked together in excitement. The view scrolled left and right as the control room swiveled, showing him the nebulous background of the rift space.

Then he realized that it was shifting with his thoughts. In his pilot's mind, he inadvertently imagined himself in the cockpit of a ship, and the Telos vehicle responded.

This was even better than he dared hope. Not only had he found the bridge, but he could fly the ship, too.

After a few experiments, he felt like he'd gotten the hang of it. It took focus—he was in so much pain that it was difficult to concentrate—but as long as he imagined himself in the cockpit of a starfighter and pictured himself moving the stick around, it moved more or less where he pointed.

Omar pointed the ship in the direction of the wormhole, and accelerated.

THIRTY-SEVEN

Elya's legs were screaming at him by the time they made it back to the hangar of the treeship, where their Sabres were parked.

"Set him down here," Yorra said.

Elya helped Hairpin and Sticks set Lieutenant Park's body down. Ruby hobbled up beside them, limping heavily. Elya squatted on his haunches, his leg muscles burning, and caught his breath.

Their Sabres were all still present. A good sign. The busted remains of three Kryl drones still sat on the other landing pad, which meant that Subject Zero was effectively stranded. The wound in his gut had been severe, and while Elya wasn't a doctor, he'd learned enough about field medicine in his training to know that it would likely be fatal for the mutant.

It was only a matter of time.

So he put Subject Zero out of his mind and focused on his friend.

"I'll take him in my Sabre," Yorra said.

Elya nodded. He'd expected that, given how close she and

Park had been. "You got it, Gears."

Elya motioned to Hairpin and Sticks, then took Park's ankles in both hands. The man's head lolled loosely as they took up positions at his shoulders and ankles. On the count of three, they heaved him up and wrangled him into the second seat of Yorra's Sabre.

Park didn't need a helmet, but Yorra stepped up and put it on her dead lover, anyway. Out of respect, he supposed. And also, if anything happened to her in the battle and she was forced to eject, if he wasn't wearing a suit, his body would be mutilated. Better safe than sorry.

Hedgebot chirped, drawing Elya to his own Sabre. He located a repair kit and patched his own vac suit where it had been torn, careful not to get any of the powerful sealant on his skin.

"Raptor to Fancypants, do you copy?"

Elya climbed up and made sure the two extra relics in his pack were safe before answering. "What's up, Captain?"

"Are you still in that starship?"

"Affirmative. We're getting situated and about to leave."

"Hang tight. I've got a gift from the admiral for you."

That piqued his interest. He motioned to the others, who quickly ran through their pre-flight checklists so they'd be ready to move at a moment's notice.

It didn't take her long. Osprey curled into the hangar and set down beside Nevers, popping her canopy and hopping out with something cradled in the crook of her arm.

Elya recognized it immediately. It was the geode. He met her on the landing pad with the new geode in his hand and Hedgebot chirping at his heels. The bot made a figure eight between Osprey's legs. It was happy to see her. He shared its evident relief.

"Glad to see your face," he said.

"Likewise." She gave him a pained smile.

"How is Blue Team's fight going?"

She grimaced. "They have more casualties than I'd like, but the admiral sent reinforcements and we secured the rift. That the new relic you got there?"

He held up the octagonal geode, careful to avoid poking himself with the long crystal antenna. It was about the same size as the one in Osprey's hands, but without a convenient handle. "It seems to have some effect on the Kryl, as that one does, but... different somehow. Less useful. I'm not really sure what it does."

"I'm glad you got it. Didn't Subject Zero have another relic? Did you get that one too?"

"We have another—a knife with a crazy sharp edge. He took the phase shifter with him. We'll... MOXA will have to work on recovering it later."

She nodded. "Just glad you kept hold of this one. Admiral Miyaru told me that these two relics would pair together. I can see what she means now. They seem to be of a similar model, don't you think?"

He nodded. The same way a danger detector bot of a different model might have similarities with Hedgebot. His astrobot cocked its head up at Elya and Captain Osprey, watching them curiously.

"So," Osprey said. "How do we make them work together?"

"I'm not sure... here, set it down for me?"

She did, and he set the other relic next to it. The antenna of the new one rose about the same height as the handle of the original geode. Their round and octagonal bases were roughly the same diameter. "If they're supposed to connect, I don't see any ports or mounts or anything like that."

He tried pushing them next to each other, turning one and then the other over in his hands and examining them for anything he might have missed.

Hedgebot flashed blue and nudged his foot, chirruping.

"What is it?" he asked.

Hedgebot bumped into his foot again.

He backed up a bit, leaving the geode he'd been examining on its side on the floor for Hedgebot to examine.

"What's the bot doing?"

Elya shrugged. "I don't have a clue."

Hedgebot backed up a foot, then without warning charged forward and knocked the other geode onto its side, shoving it until it was pressed up against the bottom of the other one.

"Ohhh," Elya said, smacking the heel of his hand into his forehead. "I should have figured."

"What?" Osprey said.

Elya knelt beside the original geode from Robichar and twisted its handle. The bottoms of the two relics snapped together like strong magnets.

"This is how the geode locked into the Telos hand statue back in the City. We found that out the hard way, when the magnets in Hedgebot's gyroscope switched polarities."

Elya pitched forward and slapped his hands onto the platform to steady himself. A great rolling motion had destabilized him. *What the...?*

"What was that!?" Osprey demanded.

The other pilots sprinted for their Sabres.

"Earth-damned thing is moving!" Ruby shouted as she struggled up the wing of her starfighter.

Elya cursed. "Subject Zero must have found the control room and managed to turn the engines on somehow."

"Put the paired relics in there!" Osprey ordered, pointing to a cage welded to the belly of her starfighter that Elya hadn't noticed until now.

He did as he was told. Raptor came behind him and quickly welded the cage shut.

Then he jumped into his Sabre, made sure Hedgebot was inside with him, and fired his own engines.

They exited the treeship inside of twenty seconds.

The treeship—which looked like nothing more than an oblong asteroid from the outside—was, indeed, moving. Slowly, but under its own power. The triad of round ports that were obviously its engines now shone white-hot. A few remained dark, seemingly at random. Perhaps those engines no longer worked.

He'd expect a few of them to malfunction after the Spirit knows how many eons in this wormhole.

Yorra's voice came over the Furies' broadbeam channel. "Looks like it's headed for the rift."

"It won't fit," Osprey said. "That starship is way too big."

"We can't let it damage the rift, though." Elya had a moment to wonder how the heck they'd gotten it in here in the first place, then shook the thought from his head. "What do you think will happen when it hits?"

"I don't know, but I really don't want to find out," Osprey said. "There's still a ring of Kryl gunk attached to the wormhole on the Elturis side. We should fly ahead and take the rest of our ships through before it gets there."

"Subject Zero has one of the relics! If he does destroy the rift, it'll be trapped here with him."

Silence.

"Tough luck," Osprey said. "Better to trap one relic here than trap us."

"What if the admiral wants them? I know MOXA does. The Emperor, too, probably."

"Chalk it up to acceptable losses," Yorra said. "Not worth the risk." Her hard tone said everything: *We've already taken enough losses. Someone needs to tell Park's family their son is gone.*

Nevers chewed the inside of his cheek. He didn't know why, exactly, but they needed all seven of the prime relics.

"We can't lose that relic. There's got to be another way. What if we shove the ship off course?"

"How?"

"Brute force?" he suggested. "That alloy is indestructible."

"If we fire missiles on the Telos ship and accidentally destroy it, the relic's as good as gone anyway, Fancypants."

"Take out the engines, then?"

Osprey thought about that for a minute. "Try it."

Elya sped up and targeted the nearest engine port at an oblique angle, so he didn't get caught in its burn path. He fired a dozen blaster bolts, which had absolutely no effect. Then he homed in with a missile and let loose. The heat given off by the engine caused it to explode before it even reached the engine nacelle.

"Well, that's not gonna work."

They brainstormed for a few more minutes, but Yorra quickly pointed out that the treeship was speeding up. After trying a few more missiles, Osprey ordered him to stop wasting ammunition.

"I've got an idea," she said. "Nevers, can you match speeds with the starship and dock on its nose?"

"I suppose… oh. I see. We don't need to destroy it, just keep it from hitting the rift."

He brought his Sabre in close, matching speeds and extending his adaptive landing gear. He docked on it and used his maneuvering thrusters to press his starfighter down against the hull.

"Now, fire your main thrusters while you push your nose down." Osprey said. "Harder!"

He did as he was told. The starfighter's chassis groaned with the force and Elya gasped as the stick tried to shove him off.

"Anything?" he asked, panting.

"Still on the same vector," Yorra said. "We're gonna need a *lot* more power."

"All hands on deck," Osprey said. She called in a dozen more starfighters on this side of the rift. Nevers stayed put while Sabre after Sabre landed beside him like ants on the side of a massive tree trunk.

"A hundred klicks out," Yorra counted. "Activate all thrusters starting… Now!"

Elya's wrists and arms ached, holding his stick forward with both hands, but he didn't dare back off. That was their only exit and if the treeship hit it, they might be stuck here forever.

"It's working!" Yorra shouted. "Push! Push!"

Slowly, the treeship's angle changed as they shoved its nose off course. Elya craned his neck back as the rift passed overhead, and the treeship drifted into space beyond.

The treeship made no attempt to turn back. It continued on at the angle they'd left it. Perhaps the gut wound had finally overtaken Subject Zero. Or maybe he just didn't know how to get it to change course.

Mission accomplished.

"Now, everyone back through the rift!" Osprey ordered. "Let's move."

Elya looped back, veering through the wormhole with a sigh of relief.

He felt a twist of nauseating inertia. Elya came out in the middle of a full-scale battle, blaster bolts and missiles crossing every which way around, above, and below him.

"Whoa!" he shouted, swerving to avoid a rapidly spinning, apparently disabled Kryl drone.

In fact, as he watched, every Kryl drone and gunship flew off kilter. Every creature within visible range, Kryl who normally flew in harmonic unison like they were following some unheard choreographed dance of the void, suddenly veered off course and crashed into canyon walls and jutting mountain ranges rising off the nearest fractured planetoid's surface.

Two drones flew into each other and exploded.

A gunship shot bullets at random, aiming at no target in particular, until a corvette's railguns ripped it in half.

"I think it's working!" Osprey cackled gleefully as she laid into her wingtip blasters. "I can't believe it!"

Elya watched on his lidar as the Kryl lines nearest them rapidly dissolved. The Furies mowed them down, separating the drones into cohorts and annihilating them.

Elya joined the fray, and within moments his blood sang. He flew by instinct, taking out dozens of Kryl drones in the first ten minutes, then more until he lost track of his count completely.

The kill count didn't matter anymore. This was no longer a competition. Everywhere the Furies went, every place the paired relics came within range, communication between the Kryl was immediately disrupted, and the Solaran forces picked their lines apart with barely an effort.

It was a slaughter.

The battle of Elturis would later be recorded as the fastest rout of a Kryl force in the history of the war.

Omar groaned weakly as the rift sailed by the starboard window of the ancient ship's bridge.

He tried to use his elbow to push himself upright so he could turn for another pass, but he slipped in blood that had pooled beneath him in the sling. His hand fell away from the crystal face of the control panel.

He repositioned himself and once again touched the crystal. Try though he might, he couldn't muster the willpower to focus again. What was once a vivid image of a cockpit and stick fell apart in his mind. He'd lost access to the starship's controls.

He let his hand drop and breathed in silence for a while. With a detached sense of awareness, he noticed blood no longer leaked from his wound so quickly. His life was fading, his wounds taking their final toll.

He closed his eyes. A grayness was setting in.

His memories now freed, Omar saw faces from the past, heard their voices.

Kira's ringing laughter, so full of joy.

Her screams, so full of sorrow and loss.

Others came and went. His parents. His childhood best friends. Other officers from the Fleet, the enlisted men and women he'd served alongside. He said his final goodbyes.

And then one voice, stronger and more terrible than any of them, forced its way to the front of his consciousness.

THIRTY-EIGHT

It was remarkable to witness.

Everywhere the Furies flew, the Kryl lines fell to pieces.

With the paired relics disrupting their psionic communications within a radius of about five hundred kilometers, the enemy lost their ability to hold against the Solaran armada.

Kira wasn't sure what was more shocking. The paired relics' remarkable effect, or that Minister Aganaki had been right about them.

Regardless, victory was theirs. It was just a matter of time.

It took hours to dismantle the remaining Kryl forces. In matters of space warfare, a five hundred kilometer radius was rather small, so the Furies were ordered hither and yon over a volume hundreds of thousands of klicks in every direction around the wormhole, seeking bugs hiding in crevasses of the broken planet. Corvettes and heavy cruisers followed, and as the Furies tore each group apart, the rest of Kira's ships swept behind them, cleaning up.

The *Paladin of Abniss* systematically annihilated the

remaining half dozen spheres of organic material orbiting near the wormhole, where she suspected Overmind X had been hiding. They had destroyed roughly sixty percent of the Kryl force when one sphere popped, and the last semblance of structure in the Kryl lines collapsed all at once. Kira sighed heavily. Finally, the sign she'd been waiting for.

Overmind X had been destroyed.

"We're not taking any chances," Kira said after an hour of watching her ships obliterate helpless clusters of Kryl. They put up a fight, but without Overmind X's active control, their tactics were utterly scattered and hopeless.

"No, sir, of course not," Volk responded.

"I want every last ship blasted into space dust. Do you hear me?"

Volk gave her a lopsided grin. "Loud and clear, sir. It would be my pleasure."

Kira plucked two glasses from behind the command couch and pulled out a flask she'd procured from her room on the way back from handing the geode off to Captain Osprey. She poured two fingers of whiskey into one, and water into the other. She handed the water to Volk. "Well done, Colonel. You've been indispensable to this mission, and I can't thank you enough for your discipline and reliability."

Volk eyed the glass in her hands as if it were a snake with its fangs bared. "Ah… Thank you, Admiral," he said. "Very wise."

"You can have a proper drink when you're off duty. Never on the bridge. And don't get any ideas. I'm taking this flask with me."

"No," he sighed, "you're right to be worried. But with the battle at hand, I've been sober for a couple of days now. I think it's wise to continue the effort."

She blinked. That surprised her. He'd never expressed an

interest in drying out before. "Good for you. I respect that. A toast!" She raised her glass. "To a clean start."

"To your victory."

They tossed back their respective drinks, and Kira returned the glassware to the service cabinet. Volk watched her carefully until the flask disappeared into her coat pocket.

"*Our* victory. You're in command now, Volk. I'm going to make some rounds and check on a few things."

Kira left the bridge, more confident than ever that he would do her proud.

"Harmony," she said as she strode through the halls, "draft a letter of recommendation to the Executive Council of Admirals. Volk should be promoted to Rear Admiral. I'm sure he'll make a great Fleet commander, and he is now easily the most experienced battle tactician on the *Paladin of Abniss*."

"Excepting yourself, of course, Admiral."

"That's assuming I stick around. And I don't plan to."

"You don't, sir?"

"Aren't you an advanced AI? Can't your learning algorithms predict my retirement?"

"To be honest, Admiral, I thought you'd retire years ago, but it has never come to pass. Your consistency has always surprised me."

"Hah! Well, I think it's high time I start surprising people in different ways."

Kira visited engineering to make sure that repairs to Harmony's processing unit and core systems had been completed. The lead engineer took her on a walkthrough and showed her where the photon cannon had sliced through one of her memory banks, and how Harmony had hidden it from them by telling an engineer to weld a patch over the cabinet.

That was awfully sneaky of you, Kira said to the shipmind.

"It seemed like a good idea at the time. We had bigger problems."

You almost caused an utter disaster.

"With respect, Admiral, I took what I deemed to be a necessary risk."

You still should have run it by me first.

"I probably would have if my processing units were intact and functioning at full capacity."

Kira grunted, thanked the engineer—without informing her of the silent conversation with the invisible AI—and went on her way.

She spent the next several hours in the hangar of the *Paladin of Abniss*, at first just enjoying watching the flow of traffic as hundreds of Sabres and corvettes flew in and out for refueling and re-arming pit stops. The ebb and flow of this many starcraft had a calming effect on her, the way some people claimed they felt watching ocean waves lap against a beach. She didn't know what that was like. It had been three decades since she'd seen an ocean. Ariadne didn't have any large bodies of water and she spent most of her time on the destroyer. Kira would have to fix that.

When she saw a mechanic stagger under the weight of a spare box of railgun rounds—after carrying a dozen such loads across the hangar in front of her—Kira ran to his aid, catching the box and helping him load it into a corvette's undercarriage. Walking back to her seat between two parked Sabres, she spotted Eben's salt-and-pepper beard, and smiled.

He'd entered the hangar beside a loadmaster pushing a maglev cart piled high with fuel canisters and extra equipment. Unlike her, he didn't have a proper duty assignment on the *Paladin of Abniss*. Yet he'd done his best to make himself useful anyway, even if it was only moving freight.

Eben looked up, caught her eyes, and returned her smile

with a grin, recognizing her amusement at seeing an Imperial inquisitor of such renown doing grunt work… and showing no shame whatsoever.

Kira really hadn't been fair to him. He'd been nothing but kind to her, nothing but loving. She'd rebuffed him, acting cold and distant. She resolved to make it up to him. Now that she'd made her decision, they would have a lot more time to spend together.

Kira allowed herself to imagine a new future with him. Outside the Fleet, where she might actually be happy. She could imagine worse fates than spending time at his side. He always seemed to know what to do, how to make her smile or laugh, or even just sit in silence when that's what she needed. For the first time in a decade, she finally began to picture a better life.

Eben's jaw fell open and his eyes widened, interrupting her train of thought. He let go of the maglev cart, leaving it to drift forward on its own momentum, and sprinted in her direction. He shouted from across the hangar, but she couldn't hear him over the noise of spacecraft coming and going.

What had gotten him so worked up? Something behind her?

As Kira turned, a foot-long talon slashed down at her clavicle. She barely got a hand up to block it in time. Instead of cleaving her in half, the razor-sharp bone sliced into the muscle fibers of her shoulder, and a monster's maw snarled into her face, snapping.

Subject Zero.

The malformed creature brought the talon up to slash at her again, and Kira threw herself backward to avoid a fatal cut to her chest. The talon lopped off the hand of a starfighter mechanic who'd leapt to her defense. His severed hand went flying, spraying blood as if in slow motion, and painting the fuselage of a nearby Sabre. The canopy was open, and she realized the mutant must have sneaked onto the ship somehow.

And, of course, being who he was, Omar knew exactly how to fly one.

The mutant Kryl fell on her with a savage snarl. Mandibles snapped at her throat. Kira craned her head sideways to avoid taking twin rows of razor-sharp teeth in the jugular.

That nearly distracted her long enough to get a claw through the face again. The talon came down once more, so Kira threw her wrists up, crossed, catching his Kryl hand. The talon stopped inches from her left eye, and she saw that the bone extended through the torn flesh of his monstrous claw.

She struggled, groaning, and straining her muscles for all they were worth. Kira was as fit as she'd ever been, and she'd never been so glad to have trained so hard her whole life. It all came down to this. Subject Zero angled his cold, scaly Kryl arm between them and tried to break her grip, but with adrenaline-fueled strength, she held fast. He slammed a fist and sank it into her jaw, splashing stars through her vision and causing her grip to loosen. She gasped for breath, tasting blood, as the talon came down again.

Eben slammed his body into Subject Zero at full speed, rolling the mutant onto his side with Eben on top. This gave Kira a chance to use gravity to her advantage. Though the mutant was inhumanly strong, Kira pushed the talon and his scaly Kryl appendage out to arm's length.

Eben added his strength to hers and together they bent Subject Zero's wrist backward until the talon pointed at his own face. Kira saw a second set of eyes and six more rows of teeth inside his open mouth. The horrifying sight sent a shiver up her spine, but she couldn't afford to let go now.

Kira used the power of her legs to muscle up on top of Omar. Spider legs squirmed beneath him, scrabbling at the metal floor of the hangar. Eben slammed his knees and boots down on the invertebrate limbs, making cracking sounds each time the carapace splintered.

She met Subject Zero's eyes. There was no hint of recognition there, just a monstrous fury. Tiny parasites streamed from his eye ducts and into his nose and mouth. Mandibles snapped hungrily. Each time the mouth opened, she caught glimpses of that extra pair of eyes at the back of his throat.

Overmind X! she realized with a flash of insight.

Her muscles screamed, but a reserve of strength she didn't know she had surged through her. With Eben's strength added to her own—and that of several other mechanics and soldiers nearby who had seen the struggle and dog-piled onto them—they pushed the talon down to point at Subject Zero's gaping mouth.

Omar's eyes suddenly focused on hers, and they widened. She saw in those very human eyes a hint of recognition. They flashed in defiant anger so unlike the inhuman fury from before, and his resistant muscles suddenly slackened.

Kira's weight drove the talon into his throat, piercing the head of the creature inside and severing its spine.

Omar's body bucked several times, and expelled a spray of yellowish blood and gore before going limp.

THIRTY-NINE

As the blade sank through his neck and pinned him to the deck of the hangar, Omar felt satisfied.

He'd finally resisted Overmind X's control. Not for long —just the bare moment it took to relax his muscles and allow Kira to deal the finishing blow. Her righteous anger was followed by recognition, and then shock. Her eyes filled with tears, and Omar knew in that moment that she'd never stopped loving him.

That was all he needed.

Overmind X screamed through their psionic link, shouting her rage at having her brood destroyed, at having her own talons shoved into her brain.

And then nothing.

True silence, for the first time in a decade.

Though Omar had railed against her when Overmind X found him aboard the Telos starship and climbed into his body, sealing his gut wound from the inside; though he'd despaired when she made him pilot the Sabre the Solarans left behind; and though he'd been filled with horror when he landed in the hangar of the *Paladin of Abniss*…

He'd finally accomplished what he'd been trying to do all those years ago—to die for the cause.

At last, he knew peace.

Kira let Eben pull her off Subject Zero. She'd watched the light and the fight go out of his eyes. She watched her once-lover's soul extinguish. This time, by her own hand.

Trembling, she pulled out of Eben's grasp and called over several mechanics to help her. Using pocketknives and box cutters, Kira bent to the bloody work, taking care so as not to cut herself. Slowly, carefully, they carved the Kryl creature out of Omar's body.

The Overmind was nothing like she'd imagined. It looked like a thin spider with a soft torso roughly the size of a small child. The creature's lean, segmented legs were buried deep in the man's torn flesh. Smaller tendrils had grown out from the arachnid abdomen to fill the hole in Omar's gut, clotting up the horrific wound.

Overmind X had been using Omar like a meat puppet.

Kira gagged as her knife slid and slashed, but she was determined. With some effort, she finally pulled the creature free.

Free. Omar was finally free.

Kira took a deep breath and exhaled shakily.

She set the body of Overmind X on the floor. Someone handed her a rag and a bottle of water, and she used it to wash the blood and xeno guts from her hands.

"Harmony," Kira said, not caring if anyone saw her talking aloud to the AI right now, "Please get in touch with Minister Aganaki and let him know we have Overmind X's body in the hangar. If they wish to study it, they should come quickly, before I burn the rotten thing."

"Right away, Admiral. Colonel Volk is calling you. Shall I put him through?"

"Go ahead."

"The last of the Kryl forces are retreating now. Even those outside of the range of the paired relics. It's like they all lost the will to live at once."

"Overmind X tried to kill me in the hangar. She sneaked aboard the ship in one of our Sabres. It really is over now."

He swore, then demanded to know if she was injured or hurt. She said she didn't think so, other than a cut to her shoulder, then promised to let the medics who had just arrived at the scene bandage her up.

As she closed the call, fatigue overtook her. Eben stood by her side, silently waiting.

She leaned against him, thankful for his solid, steady presence.

"Thank you for the warning," Kira said.

"I'm just glad you're okay."

For the first time in Earth knew how long, she pined for her bed, for rest. "Can we get out of here?"

"Say no more." Eben whisked her away.

FORTY

Casey had never felt a thrill like being the spearhead of the armada. Everywhere she flew, the Kryl fell to pieces. Unable to communicate psionically, they were no match for the searing blaze of her starfighters.

The Furies took their vengeance on the xenos. The whole Fleet did. It took thirty-six hours to track down and mop up the rest of the fleeing creatures. They took no prisoners. They left no survivors. Harmony thought that a few Kryl escaped and headed back toward Robichar, but only their largest ships were hyperspace capable. Most of those that escaped the blasters and railguns of the Solaran armada would starve and die on the journey home. The rest of the Kryl still inhabiting Robichar would be razed to the ground by a Solaran force that had already deployed from Ariadne, specially outfitted for the job.

All that mattered to Casey was that the sacrifices they'd made had been worth it. Her brothers and sisters had paid for this victory with their lives.

In the end, she flew back to the *Paladin of Abniss* exhausted but satisfied, calm yet full of a deep sorrow. She couldn't change what had happened. However, knowing that she could contact the spouses, parents, and children of the pilots she'd lost with her chin up, look them in the eye, and let them know that their deaths had brought peace back to the Solaran Empire—that the galaxy was once again safe and secure—that was what mattered.

She parked her Sabre and climbed down on shaky legs. Lieutenant Yorra and Captain Nevers met her on the hangar floor, helmets in their hands, sweat-soaked hair plastered to their heads. They both wore sad smiles.

"We did it," Nevers said.

Yorra said nothing at first. She'd flown to battle with them after dropping Lieutenant Park's body off on the *Abniss*, and had only exchanged necessary words since. Yet she'd flown like an avenging angel, eliminating more Kryl than most. Casey put her arm around her friend's shoulder.

"It's finally over," Yorra said at last. "I need to call Park's mother."

"There will be time for that later. I'll be there to support you when you do. For now, I think Naab would want us to celebrate the victory."

"If he were here, he'd be lighting up a spliff right now," Nevers said with a sad smile.

"And cracking inappropriate jokes," Osprey added.

Yorra buried her head in Casey's chest and sobbed, unable to say anything more. Casey pulled her into a hug and let her cry. Nevers wrapped his arms around both of them.

"He was one of a kind," said Captain Nevers. "And my best friend. I already miss him like hell."

"We'll give him a proper sendoff," Osprey said. "Come on, Olara, let's get you to your room."

"I want to see Innovesh first."

"After you shower and eat something. Then we'll all go with you to see him."

Yorra eventually relented. They were all completely wiped out. Osprey led her back to their cabin, while Captain Nevers agreed to stay behind and make sure the relics welded into that cage beneath Casey's Sabre were properly secured. Such valuable weapons couldn't be left lying around.

After Casey cleaned up, while waiting for Yorra to get ready, Ruby appeared in the doorway. She paused, glaring hatefully at Osprey.

Here we go again, she thought. But she did as she had learned to do in the presence of insubordinate behavior. She nodded at the woman, showing as much respect as she could muster.

Ruby didn't salute her. Instead, she screwed up her face like she was about to cuss Casey out again. Or maybe she just had one of those faces. So it shocked her when Ruby said, "I owe you an apology."

She somehow kept a straight face. "Oh?"

"I judged you unfairly, Raptor. I was hurting, and I blamed it on you."

"It's okay. No hard feelings."

The other pilot studied her warily as she ran her hand over her shaved scalp along the scar by her ear. "We're good?"

"We're good. You're an excellent pilot and a great flight lead, and I know you have my back in a fight. We don't have to play cards or hang out or anything like that if you don't want to."

"I'll kick your ass in a game of aleacc. Bet?"

Casey grinned. "Bet."

"See you 'round, Raptor."

Ruby spun on her heel and left. Yorra ducked into the room a moment later, head wrapped in a towel with a clean uniform on. "That was big of her."

"It was, yeah." Casey fell silent for a moment, thoughtful. Then, "Are you ready?"

"Just a minute."

On their way past the sick bay to the place where they kept the bodies of the fallen, Casey was surprised to run into her father. He walked beside Admiral Miyaru, who was covered in bruises and had several cuts that had been recently bandaged.

"Dad? What are you doing here? I thought you went back to Ariadne."

He exchanged a half-smile with Admiral Miyaru. He'd been a widower for years, limiting himself to casual relationships, all of which he kept very private. Seeing him with the admiral in public opened a dam in her heart, and she felt happy tears spring to her eyes.

She cleared her throat and tried to get her emotions under control. There would be plenty of time to talk to him about that, and she forgot it quickly as Eben told them about the attempt on Admiral Miyaru's life. Yorra and Casey were both shocked to hear that Subject Zero had commandeered Park's Sabre—left behind on the Telos starship, since they hadn't had an extra pilot to fly it back—then sneaked aboard the *Abniss* to attack the admiral.

"It's not your fault," Admiral Miyaru said. "In a weird way, I'm glad it happened. I got to free Omar from the Overmind's control. He'd been suffering far too long. But all that's over now." She turned to look at Yorra. "And I'm terribly sorry to hear about Lieutenant Park, by the way. I know you were close with him."

Yorra blushed, but managed to squeak out a, "Thank you, sir."

"Take all the time you need to grieve—both of you. I'll approve as much bereavement leave as you require, regulations be damned."

"Thank you, Admiral."

"And you," the admiral said. "I owe you a debt of gratitude, Captain Osprey. You did fine work delivering that relic. We owe our victory to you."

"Respectfully, we owe our victory to you, Admiral Miyaru. I was just following orders."

"The best soldiers usually do. That doesn't make their actions any less courageous. Go see Colonel Volk when you're done here. I have it on good authority that your work will be rewarded, Squadron Commander."

"Sir?" Casey said, stunned. Her father's eyes glistened. She'd never seen him look so proud, and felt her face flush to what she felt certain was a deep red color. "I'm sorry, did you just say Squadron Commander?

"Major Osprey has a nice ring to it," Eben said, "don't you think, kid?"

Yorra's eyes went wide as saucers. She clapped Casey on the shoulder. "You'll be the youngest officer to lead a squadron since the Kryl war!" she said excitedly—the first sign of life coming back into her voice and eyes since Park died. "Wow, Casey, that's incredible. Congrats!"

"And," Eben added, "one of only two women who have ever commanded a squadron of starfighter pilots as a major during the Kryl war."

Yorra whistled.

"Who was the other, sir?" Casey asked.

"Me." Admiral Miyaru reached out and intertwined her fingers with Eben's. "We should be going. I'll see you around, hmm?"

"Congrats again, Casey," her dad said. "I'm proud of you."

Her chest swelled. As they walked away, Harmony's lights flickered to life beside them. Though she didn't take a form, the lights danced through the halls between Yorra and

Osprey then faded as they made their way to say goodbye to their fallen comrade.

"Retire?" Eben asked. "Are you sure?"

"The refugee problem is a boiling kettle, our victory the whistle. Chairman Card and the Colonization Board will start clearing voyager launches as soon as the news reaches them. Count on it." Kira winced as she sat down on the edge of her bed. Her everything hurt. She wanted to sleep for days. Eben sat beside her and she leaned against him, his presence solid and supportive. He wrapped his arm around her and squeezed. "Once that happens, my armada disbands and I'm back to merchant escort and colonial security posts. I'd rather stand in front of a firing squad."

"Surely, they'll find something more interesting for their war hero to do. Have you considered an appointment on the Executive Council?" He paused. "Or, perhaps, training to be an inquisitor?"

She blew air out her nose and shook her head ruefully. "Haven't I given enough to the Solaran Empire? I've done my duty. It's time for someone else to take up the mantle."

"You know, I used to idolize the idea of retirement. Thought I'd live a glorious civil life, attending parties and theater performances, competing in foil competitions. Then I got there and realized I didn't have a plan or a goal. It got really boring, really fast. There was nothing important for me to do."

"Well, I won't have *nothing* to do." She elbowed him in the side and gave him a sly smile.

He grinned. "True enough. I'm only on a temporary contract."

"It'll take me a few months to finish my business here. I've got to deliver my final report and make sure the command transition goes smoothly."

"And after that?"

"Vacation," she said. "A nice, long holiday. On a beach somewhere. Do you like the ocean?"

"Love it. The smell of salt and tequila. Oltanis has some really beautiful, peaceful islands. We could spend an entire season there, if you want to."

"Mmmm," she said, stretching out her aching body and lying back on the bed. Eben pulled his arm away and lay on his side next to her, speaking softly.

She never heard the words. Kira was sound asleep in an instant. Her dreams came slowly, lapping at the shores of her consciousness, echoing with the sound of ocean waves.

FORTY-ONE

"Ah, Captain Nevers." Emperor Aeris' golden eyes glittered. "Welcome back."

"Your Majesty," Elya said, bending over in what he was certain was an awkward bow. He wasn't accustomed to scraping for royalty and still felt weird about the whole thing, although if the emperor noticed, he gave no sign. Hedgebot pressed its metal body into the floor and dimmed its blue light. He'd taught it that move in the several days he spent on light duty before being invited back to the Chronicle room.

"How can I be of service, sir?" Elya asked.

Instead of answering, the emperor took Elya by the arm, causing him to straighten, and hauled him deeper into the vaulted chamber beneath the City.

They stopped in the center of the room before a long table, standing opposite Minister Aganaki, two MOXA scientists in white coats, Admiral Miyaru, and Colonel Volk. A half dozen of the Emperor's security guards loitered off to one side, their weapons hanging from shoulder slings, looking bored.

Elya was anything but. His gaze fell to the seven objects laid out on the table, and his eyes grew wide. "Are these...?"

"The seven prime relics," Minister Aganaki said, looking down his nose at the pilot. "Yes."

"But... how?"

Admiral Miyaru answered. "We took the phase shifter off the body of Subject Zero after he attacked me in the hangar." Her voice was stiff, formal, belying the powerful emotion he knew must lie beneath the surface. Elya had heard about the attempted assassination like everyone else, and they both knew about the admiral's history with the man once known as Captain Omar Ruidiaz.

The attack had surprised him, but he supposed Overmind X had always been a vengeful creature. It was her driving force—and her weakness.

"This one—" Admiral Miyaru gestured to a small, seamless cube whose surface was covered with tiny, intricate carvings of Telos runes. "MOXA found *this* hidden inside the body of Overmind X when they performed their autopsy."

"How—I—what?" he stuttered, stunned.

"Our theory is that this relic is what Overmind X used to separate her consciousness from the Queen Mother," said Minister Aganaki, "as well as to keep Subject Zero alive. And likely to turn the children into mutants, too."

"How's it work, exactly?" Elya asked.

"It's a sort of gene editor with the ability to accelerate growth, according to Chronicle." Minister Aganaki gestured to the crystal pylon, which had been removed from its spot in the stone hands and laid out alongside the others. "The Prime Relic of Attraction."

"I see the geode here, and the psionic disruptor as well," Elya said, pointing to the Prime Relic of Spirit and Mind, respectively. The two geodes had been separated and deactivated. "There's the knife—the Prime Relic of Gravity, right?" He'd puzzled that out over the last couple of days.

Minster Aganaki nodded in agreement.

"What about that one?" Elya pointed to a long, thin tube with an opening at one end.

"That's the photon cannon," rumbled Colonel Volk.

"Prime Relic of Separation," Aganaki added.

"Whatever," Volk continued. "You sent it spinning into space during the battle, when your starfighters destroyed the Kryl gunship on which it was mounted. Took a few days of searching, but once Harmony's processing unit was fully restored, the shipmind helped us locate and retrieve it."

That was all of them, then. The prime relics of Mind, Body and Spirit; Gravity and Electromagnetism; Separation and Attraction. Weapons crafted to take advantage of all seven primal forces of the universe and arm their wielders against the Kryl.

Elya wondered... If the Telos had known these weapons were at such high risk of falling into the possession of the Kryl, would they have made them in the first place? Would they have been more careful in storing them?

And what are we supposed to do with them now?

He finally looked up and found everyone staring at him, so he voiced his thoughts. "We need to make sure these don't fall into the wrong hands again."

"Very wise," Emperor Aeris said cheerfully. "And what would you propose, Captain?"

"Well... I'm not sure, Your Majesty. Oh!" he said as it hit him. "That's what this room is for, isn't it? The stone hands lock the relics in place for a reason. We could keep them here."

"That's one option," said Minister Aganaki. "But if this is the safest place to keep them, why would the Telos go through the trouble of scattering the relics across the galaxy?"

Elya narrowed his eyes and stared at the minister, who tucked his long fingers into the sleeves of his robes. "I assume that means you have a better theory?"

"I thought you'd never ask," said the Emperor, grinning. "Since you're the one who figured out how to lock the relics into the stone sculptures to begin with. Would you like to help us do the honors?"

That was a strange reason to bring Elya—a fighter pilot who, while interested in the relics, had no other credentials—all the way down here. But the idea had piqued his curiosity. "Of course, Sir."

He picked up the geode and took it over to the pair of stone hands he'd first locked it into. Setting it down and turning the handle, the relic snapped into place. He snatched his hands back as the fingers of stone threaded together over top of it, closing in a fist. A soft green light glowed in the gaps between the stone fingers.

Admiral Miyaru placed the knife into another pair of hands. Colonel Volk set the phase shifter in next. Emperor Aeris placed the psionic disruptor, and Minister Aganaki placed the crystal pylon of Chronicle back where it had been before. The other two MOXA scientists set into place the last two relics, the photon cannon and gene editor.

When the crystal locked in, the image of the robed Telos appeared between the columns. When all seven relics were present, a great grinding noise rumbled through the chamber as the columns around the room began sinking into the floor.

They aren't sinking, Elya realized. The floor was rising toward the ceiling.

Tiles around the base of the statues folded back one by one with the soft clicking sound of stone on alloy. The stone statues shifted outward to a secondary position. The emperor's guards murmured and put their hands on their weapons as they edged toward the center of the room, away from the moving, transforming stone and metal pieces. Emperor Aeris grinned crazily, while Minister Aganaki took in the sight with greedy eyes.

Elya had a moment to panic as they approached the ceiling. Then the hexagonal tiles folded rapidly away from each other, and he sighed in relief. A giddy feeling bubbled up from his belly and he laughed aloud.

The floor rose until it met the ground level of the open plaza. Elya thought it would stop there. But no! *It continued to rise.*

Hedgebot flashed red and scurried a figure eight between Elya's boots. With the bot running close at his heels, he hurried to the edge of the round platform, now ringed only by statues of closed Telos fists, until he could see the crystal buildings of the City growing smaller beneath them. Soon, they looked like a child's tiny playthings far below.

His heart pounded. Gazing up again, he saw a surface fold open overhead. The platform on which they stood rose, at last, into a hidden chamber at what seemed to be the very apex of the asteroid.

They found themselves in a chamber nearly identical to the one below. Only here, the ceiling was a geodesic dome made of transparent crystal. Empty space surrounded them on all sides.

Elya deduced the crystal material must be like one-way glass, because while he'd seen the asteroid from the outside, and extensive surveys had been conducted by MOXA, as far as Elya knew, no one had discovered this room until now.

"By the Spirit of Old Earth," said Emperor Aeris. "It's more beautiful than I ever imagined."

It was also the first time he'd ever seen the man visibly surprised. His nanite-filled eyes rounded in wonder.

"Huh," said Admiral Miyaru. "Maybe your theory has legs, Your Majesty."

Emperor Aeris turned to the Minister of Xeno Affairs. "Tachi, if you would do the honors?"

Minister Aganaki frowned, approaching the Chronicle relic. He laid his hand along the face of the crystal.

Elya waited for a minute, but when nothing happened, he could no longer contain his curiosity. "Your Majesty, if I may ask, what is this theory of yours?"

The emperor pointed out through the transparent dome of crystal. On the other side, asteroids orbited; beyond them, enormous slabs of the broken planet surrounded the wormhole. "No one knows how that planet was destroyed," Aeris said. "I conducted a thorough survey when I arrived, and determined that the anomaly we discovered is precisely aligned between this asteroid's peak and Elturis." He pointed beyond, to the star at the center of this solar system.

"But… how did you know?" The memory of a journal with missing pages came to the forefront of his memory. "*A Treatise On Ancient Alien Technology & Its Primary Applications*. You were the one who tore out those missing pages, weren't you?"

"Well, not me personally. My ancestors, yes. The author didn't know exactly what would happen, hence my surprise at seeing this room. But they had a few ideas. One thing they didn't know was why or how the Telos homeworld was destroyed." He gestured to the broken planet. "Only that the Telos did it to themselves. Chronicle has given us a little more information about his involvement, but he remains vague about the mechanism. Could this, perhaps, be the mechanism?"

"You think this room is some kind of weapon? Like all the

prime relics in combination create a planet buster, or something?" There were scientific theories about bombs powerful enough to shatter worlds, but thankfully, no one had ever tried to use one before.

"We're about to find out."

The view above shifted, but then it stopped. Minister Aganaki pulled his hand away with a frustrated huff. "Nothing's happening, Your Majesty. I'm going to need to spend some time with this."

"Perhaps we let someone who is a more instinctive pilot try it, hmm?" said the emperor, glancing pointedly at Elya.

"Me?"

Aganaki glared hatefully at him, but even the stubborn minister knew when to acknowledge defeat. His bitter expression gave way to resignation. "As you wish, Your Majesty."

"Go on, son," said the Emperor. "Show us what this thing can do. Don't worry, you can't damage the planet any more than it has already been damaged."

"Aren't people working in there?" He jerked his chin at the wormhole, knowing scouts had been sent inside after the battle to explore it further.

"They've all returned to base. We also retrieved the probe from the singularity. Not the treeship, though, I'm afraid. It's too big. I'm optimistic we'll be able to puzzle that out some day, but this is more important. Go on, now."

The words of encouragement urged him forward. Elya stepped up to the crystal obelisk and laid his hand upon it. The image of the Telos avatar fixed its gaze upon him, as if in recognition.

It said nothing, but he felt a sense of openness flood through him. Other people could operate the tech, but it seemed to come easier for Elya. *Just like flying,* he thought.

Once he had a feel for the throttle, he stopped thinking about the starfighter and operated by instinct.

At first, nothing happened. Elya remembered he had to guide it with his intention. But what did he want? He gave it some thought. In the end, there was only one mystery that stood out in his mind. One mystery puzzle Solaran scientists had never been able to solve.

Show me where the Telos went.

The view before him shifted until it was pointed directly through the asteroid field at the broken planet. Something glimmered in the distance—the anomaly, highlighted in the crystal somehow? Certainly it was too far away to make out with the naked eye, but the glimmer was unmistakable.

As he watched, the planetoid slabs spread apart and began to spin, the stones of the asteroid field clearing and rotating, whirling faster and faster around a central point.

Around that glimmer, like a growing star marking the distant event horizon.

Simultaneously, around the room, the various relics came alive, shining in different colors. Green light from the geode mixed with gold from the photon cannon, and more hues from the other relics, some of them glowing in colors he'd never seen them emit before, each with a unique resonance of light and sound.

He felt them through his connection with Chronicle. As the humming noise reached its peak, the stones of the broken planet aligned and fused together, forming a vast, unbroken ring.

The glimmer within grew brighter until, finally, the space within the ring shimmered, undulating like a vast mirage, and flashed blindingly bright.

Elya squeezed his eyes shut against the flare. When he opened them again, the painful brightness was gone, and he gazed upon a shimmering violet aperture. He let his hand drop from the crystal face. The ring remained in place, its center undulating with a wavering amaranthine veneer that was hard to look upon.

Emperor Aeris stepped up beside him, grinning. "Well done, Captain. I believe you've found the portal the Telos used to leave the galaxy."

Admiral Miyaru and Colonel Volk stared with mouths hanging open, expressions of wonder mixed with equal parts fear and shock.

"Where do you think it goes?" Elya wondered aloud. Hedgebot chirruped sheepishly and stood on its hind legs, the astrobot's way of expressing curiosity—feelings Elya found he shared.

"Only one way to find out," said Emperor Aeris. "Are you ready for your next adventure, Captain?"

Starfighter Origins

Want to know more about the circumstances and hardships that forged Elya, Casey and Kira into incredible leaders and pilots?

Want to know the full story about how Omar was captured by the Kryl?

Read *Starfighter Origins*, a series of prequel novellas in the *Relics of the Ancients* space opera adventure universe.

Get them now:

Elya's origin story: *Spare Parts*

Casey's origins story: *Raptor*

Kira and Omar's origin story: *Coming soon!*

THANK YOU

A note from the author

Five years ago, I dreamed up a series of space opera novels.

As if in a fugue state, I outlined the whole story in a single weekend.

I was a madman, a genius… and a fool.

That outline didn't survive. It evolved, though. The seed germinated in my mind, and two years later a little novella sprang out of an anthology call for space opera stories.

My old ideas came together to form a new vision.

Spart Parts is what I called that first book. It's about a danger detection bot who saves a frightened refugee boy from bullies, and the starfighter pilot that boy would one day become.

After that first story was finished, I couldn't get it off my mind. I finished up a couple other pieces of work and turned my full attention to the project. I wrote *Starfighter Down* during a roadtrip through Colorado, and four more books after that.

Although *Rogue Swarm* is the final novel to complete my original vision, it barely resembles the original outline.

It's way better.

This universe is so much bigger than I initially imagined. While this won't be the last *Relics* story, it is the culmination of the first story arc.

A milestone, of sorts.

Seeing this project through to the end was a challenge.

Juggling a full-time job, our first *and* second foster placements, the death of my Nana—whom I loved—and other life rolls, gave me a lot of perspective. I learned lessons in patience, grit, and stick-to-it-iveness along the way.

Trying to write a series this complex through all those challenges was one of the hardest things I've ever done.

And, the most rewarding.

I never once thought of giving up.

I had a deadline to hit.

I had readers waiting.

I had backers to whom I'd made a promise.

Thanks to all of you for the inspiration. Truly, there is no motivating force like the power of accountability.

Of course, a book is never truly a solo endeavor.

Thanks to Kickstarter backers, for supporting this project from the beginning.

Thanks to my concept artist, Elias Stern, for bringing the Sabre to life and for the beautiful artwork.

Thanks to my family for their enduring support.

Thanks to my wife for her everlasting love and encouragement. Shelly, you are a gift to everyone around you. Especially to me.

Thanks to my editor, Steve Statham, for his keen insight and contribution to the story.

Thanks to my beta readers for their eagle eyes. Jenny Avery, Maureen Henn, James Green, and Tim Birmingham were instrumental in blowing off the dust and polishing this book to a shine.

And thanks, most of all, to you, dear reader. I hope you found this space opera adventure a welcome escape from your normal life. I hope you enjoyed spending time in the Solaran Fleet, that you think of that time fondly, and that you go on to read more of my stories.

I may be a fool for dreaming so big, but if so, I'm the luckiest fool alive.

—M.G. Herron
Austin, TX
February, 2023

A Special Thanks to Kickstarter Heroes

This series was first launched on Kickstarter! The campaign raised $12,879 in 4 weeks, and it wouldn't have been possible without the support of 271 backers.

A special shoutout to these heroes, who backed the original campaign at the highest levels:

Tim Hebel, Jennifer Whitesell, Jacob Moyer, Gregory Clawson, Jerry Leake, James Herron, Tim Cross, Leigh, Lawrence Tate, Sebastián, Tyler Prince, Adam Knuth, MJ Caan, Jacen Spector, Jerome, Chad Anthony Randell, Linda Schattauer, Peyton, Marouane Jerraf, Mette Lundsgaard, Destin Floyd, Pierino Gattei, Rhett and Kathy Leonard, Dietrich Thompson, Becky Herron, Missy Burrows, Cindy Lorion, Chris Wooster, Lauren Appa, Nikhil Daftary, and Joe Bunting.

ALSO BY M.G. HERRON

Relics of the Ancients

Starfighter Down

Hidden Relics

Rogue Swarm

Starfighter Origins

Spare Parts

Raptor

Translocator Trilogy

The Auriga Project

The Alien Element

The Ares Initiative

The Translocator (Books 1-3)

The Gunn Files

Culture Shock

Overdose

Quantum Flare

The Gunn Files (Books 1-3)

Other Books

The Republic

Boys & Their Monsters

Get science fiction and fantasy reading recommendations from MG Herron delivered straight to your inbox. Join here: mgherron.com/bookclub

ABOUT THE AUTHOR

M.G. Herron writes science fiction and fantasy for adrenaline junkies.

His books explore new worlds, futuristic technologies, ancient mysteries, various apocalypses, and the vagaries of the human experience.

His characters have a sense of humor (except for the ones who don't). They stand up to strange alien monsters from other worlds... unless they slept through their alarm again.

Like ordinary people, Herron's heroes sometimes make mistakes, but they're always trying to make the universe a better place.

Find all his books and news about upcoming releases at mgherron.com.

CPSIA information can be obtained
at www.ICGtesting.com
Printed in the USA
JSHW030922030423
39825JS00003B/13